BLOOD
OF THE
DELPHI

Harmatia Cycle:

BLOOD
OF THE
DELPHI

M.E. VAUGHAN

MAG MELL
PUBLISHING

Published 2017 by Mag Mell Publishing
Winchester, Hampshire
Great Britain
www.magmellpublishing.com

Copyright © M.E. Vaughan, 2017
Cover Art by Stef Tastan

ISBN 978-0-9956149-1-8

To find out more about The Harmatia Cycle world, visit:
www.harmatiacycle.com

Printed and bound in Great Britain by Clays Ltd, St Ives plc

To Jonathan,

I'm sorry I killed you in the last book.

No hard feelings?

x

The GODS of MAG MELL

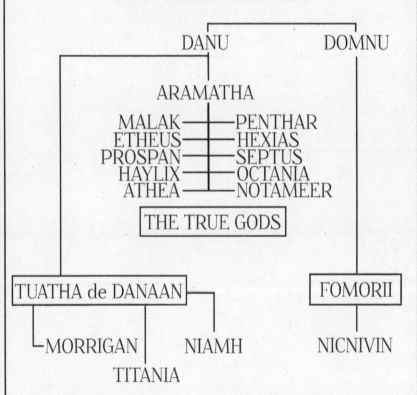

DANU   DOMNU

ARAMATHA

MALAK	PENTHAR
ETHEUS	HEXIAS
PROSPAN	SEPTUS
HAYLIX	OCTANIA
ATHEA	NOTAMEER

THE TRUE GODS

TUATHA de DANAAN   FOMORII

MORRIGAN   NIAMH   NICNIVIN

TITANIA

THE TRUE GODS	TUATHA de DANAAN	FOMORII
Worshoped by humans in Harmatia Bethean, Kathra and West Réne	Worshiped by Sidhe, Faeries of the Seelie Court and humans in Bethean	Worshoped by Faeries of the Unseelie Court

PROLOGUE

"And so the crow cries, and summons us to war."

It was a lifeless night. The clouds suffocated the stars in a hushed embrace, thin trickles of moonlight seeping out from small tears in the blanket of the sky.

Fretting hands, calmed by what was now a familiar craft, traced a knife across the shaft of what would be an arrow. Although he moved in precise, sweeping motions, the Magi's clear blue eyes weren't set on their task, but roamed the muffled dome above.

"Stray a thought on moonless night, Fomorii dance in cruel delight," his song broke out, barely a whisper, almost toneless it was so soft. "For silent wish in faeries' grasp, are like a weapon they can clasp."

He rested back against the tree, his hands moving deftly, eyes still trained on the small shard of sky that could be seen through a rip in the clouds.

"They'll steal your shield with a pretty switch, grant you favour and make you rich."

The knife was stowed away, and in its place agile fingers ran along the wood in inspection.

"But when the time comes to pay the price, your hands are bound within a vice."

A sharp snap cut through the stillness of the night and the Magi's eyes hardened. His gaze dropped from the sky to the little village that sat, nestled below him, cradled by the hills.

Figures shifted through the darkness around him, creeping like shadows as he slowly hunched his shoulders, leaning further back into the tree.

"So run, run, thou fool of a man," he continued breathily, his fingers tightening around the arrow as he heard a figure move around the tree behind him. "For death shall follow, sword in hand."

With a sharp twist, he spun around the trunk and embedded the arrow deep into the approaching alchemist's collar.

With a gurgled scream the Kathrak stumbled back, choking as two hands found their way to his stomach and with the force of a pressurised gale, propelled him back into the undergrowth.

The Magi dropped his hands and slipped back into the darkness, away from the surprised cries of his attackers.

Leaping down a dry bank, he slid through the foliage from one clearing into the next, ducking behind trees as voices tore after him. He half-expected to hear the barks of hunting hounds, but it seemed his pursuers had learnt their lesson after the last time.

Running through the trees, he met another alchemist who immediately raised his hands, preparing to attack.

Too slow, the Magi thought to himself, and threw out his own attack before the alchemist had time to concentrate his magic. The earth beneath the Kathrak reared up into spines, piercing him from all angles through the stomach and chest. The alchemist spluttered in death, flecks of blood hitting the Magi's cheek as he sprinted past. He couldn't afford to mourn his enemy.

All around voices were rising up as the alchemists tried to coordinate their attack. They'd thought to take the Magi by surprise but the forest had long become his element.

Skidding down into a ditch, he hid, fingers curled over the

12

edge of the dirt wall as he glanced over the gnarled roots. If it had been day, he might have been able to make those roots rise up around him and camouflage him completely from sight, but it was too late to draw on the power of Notameer or Haylix—the two water stars—and so he hunched in silence and waited wearily for an opportunity to flee.

"Rufus Merle, I know you're there." A familiar voice drawled out between the trees. Rufus sank lower to the ground, his heart racing. "We both know how this ends. Surrender, and I'll return you to Harmatia, on my honour."

"Honour…" Rufus muttered into the dirt.

"I'll count to five. Come out peacefully, and we can end this without any fuss. No need for anyone to get hurt."

Rufus thought about the two men he'd already killed. He wiped the blood from his cheek with a grimace.

"One," the Kathrak began, and Rufus shifted further back, still and quiet. The count was a ploy, a given time-frame set to make him panic and rush an escape. The alchemists had formed a net around him—one hasty move, and they would capture him in minutes. Rufus trampled his nervous instincts and forced himself to stay still and calm.

"Two, three—be reasonable, Rufus. These games are really starting to bore me."

"You may forfeit at any time," Rufus said, almost too loudly. His fear escalated into a pulsing terror, his neck, face and hands palpitating as he held his breath, worried he'd betrayed himself. The count, thankfully, continued.

"Four…" The Kathrak left a tantalising pause, and then with a tangible glee finished. "Five. Find him."

"Papa," a lilting voice said from beside him. Rufus jolted in surprise and twisted around, exhaling in relief. A set of blue eyes, glowing faintly, stared up at him, and Rufus opened his arms and drew his little brother in carefully. "Kathraks?"

"Yes. I told you not to come up here, Joshua," Rufus berated, but despite his worry, he felt strangely relieved to have the boy close. It made his racing mind calm.

"I saw flashes," Joshua said, and Rufus pressed his mouth to his brother's curly hair, listening . He could hear them moving through the forest, sweeping it for signs of him.

"You need to return to the village," Rufus told the boy, when he was sure that the Kathraks had passed. "Can you find your way?"

"I think so." Joshua didn't sound confident.

"I'll take you to the path—then you run. I'll draw the Kathraks away. Go straight to the Hirondelle's house. Tell them our friends caught up to us sooner than I anticipated."

The boy nodded and Rufus gripped his hand, listening intently before, with a deep breath, they climbed out of the ditch and darted out through the trees, their footsteps silent from years of practise.

Moving through the forest, the emptiness that met them was eerie. Rufus didn't trust it, wary of the silence. His fear was justified. With a sudden crash a figure dropped from the branches above and landed behind them, giving a cry of victory. The sound was short-lived, as Rufus, who had a nervous disposition at the best of times, yelped and released an instinctive burst of flames from his hands. The fire burnt bright and hot, and left little of its victim. Rufus swallowed thickly and ran. He'd just set off a beacon for his enemies.

Sprinting through the darkness, the Harmatians dove for cover as silhouettes stalked behind them. Below, the light of the village became visible again and Rufus turned to Joshua. "Go," he said. "Go!"

The boy gave him a lingering look, face pinched with worry, then ducked into the darkness and tore away, as light-footed as a Sidhe. Rufus watched anxiously after Joshua, his throat tight, then threw himself back into the encroaching attackers.

Skidding through the maze of trees, the grappling roots

14

snatched at his feet, almost tripping him. A few years ago, he would have fallen ten-times over, but Rufus was used to negotiating the perilous forest floor now. The enemy swamped closer around him.

Reaching a small dip ahead, Rufus scrabbled down the dirt path and began to sprint, his mind racing as he tried to orientate himself. He could see his enemies from the corner of his eyes, and his heart clenched as he realised how many of them there were. They'd doubled their hunt since the last time he'd seen them. He'd been too lax, allowing them to catch up to him like this. If they caught him—

No, it didn't bear thinking about.

With a hard lurch he threw his weight back, skidding in panic as he emerged into an unexpected clearing. Not two strides from the last tree, he saw the ground cut off into a cliff-edge that jutted outward into the night. The harsh darkness made it impossible to see how deep the ravine below was, but Rufus could hear the muted roar of running water far away.

Glancing back, Rufus swallowed as they emerged from the trees all around him. They'd herded him here on purpose. He took a few tentative steps back toward the edge, heart racing.

There were at least sixty of them, forming a human fence around him, blocking him off from the forest. Rufus took another step back, his gut clenching as he drew nearer and nearer to the edge. They'd all raised their mental shields at once, pooling the power together. If Rufus attacked now, with their combined strength protecting them, he would stand little chance. His mouth grew dry as he stepped back again. His heels met the air behind him, and he stood, balanced on the edge by toe-point.

"Quite the fox, aren't you?" a voice rose from the gaggle, the same that had called out to him earlier, and Rufus's stomach burned with fear and anger.

His enemy stepped out brazenly and strode forward.

"A good chase—not the best, mind, but..." the Kathrak

smiled. "This one, I think, will be the last."

"Don't be so sure, DuGilles," Rufus spat, and the dark-haired Kathrak tipped his head, his bold features twisting in the muffled moonlight.

"Of course—you have a choice. Me, or death. If it's death you prefer, I won't stop you—I'll even help. But Rufus," he said the name like an old friend, and it made Rufus shudder, "is this really how you want it to end? Alone, in the dirt? You don't belong here. Come home. Come with me. Let me make it all better."

The sick feeling in Rufus's gut rose, a serpent writhing within him. Had it come to this? Death or DuGilles? Were those really his only choices?

Looking around him, Rufus knew he couldn't fight his way out—not as he was. He could feel Athea's power burning through him, waiting to be releasing, but he forced it down.

"You're right," Rufus murmured.

DuGilles was stunned. He blinked several times, looking around to his comrades, as if to make sure they'd heard the same thing as him. "I don't believe it," he said. "Has the stubborn Rufus Merle finally come to his senses?"

Rufus nodded.

"Well praise the day!"

Rufus didn't reply. His mind was on his little brother, waiting for him back in the village. Trusting him to return safely.

"An honourable surrender then?" DuGilles motioned for his men to move forward.

Rufus drew in a long deep breath. "Yes," he said serenely, and stepped back over the edge of the cliff. The darkness swallowed him.

CHAPTER 1

Rumours were dangerous. Always the first tool in swaying public opinion, some rumours, if left unchecked, had a bad habit of growing wild lives of their own. This, in itself, wasn't entirely detrimental to a civilised society, just so long as there remained those with enough common-sense to identify the falsehoods. But when even learned men started to embrace lies, unrest and corruption were sure to grow. And with them, hysteria. Yes, rumours were dangerous and Arlen Zachary knew this.

It pained him sometimes that he now stood among the few in Harmatia who recognised truth from propaganda. Once again a new generation of Magi were about to be apprenticed, having suckled on a decade of lies, and there was nothing he could do about it.

Zachary exhaled, lengthening his stride irritably. At his side, Emeric raised an eyebrow as he and Marcel matched Zachary's pace. The three of them had been summoned to help Belphegore address a class of 'freshlings', students from the academy who were applying to take the Warriors' Assessment in the hope of being apprenticed.

Of course, Zachary had his own suspicions about his summons

to this address. For the last year, Belphegore had been pushing him to take an apprentice of his own. Zachary had seen several students eyeing him keenly with that in mind. Likewise, Emeric was of an age to do the same, and Marcel—who'd apprenticed Emeric almost sixteen years ago—was another popular choice for potential new master. Zachary, who had no inclination of taking charge of any of the brats, doubted that Marcel would either. Emeric, in contrast, seemed more enthusiastic about the prospect, though he was yet to be taken by any one applicant.

Zachary sniffed. It was a cold, bright morning, much too early for productive thought. He would rather have been abed, tangled naked in his sheets then attending the address.

"Are you unwell?" Emeric asked as Zachary sighed again. Marcel's apprentice had grown bolder in his years, but his soft brown eyes and dimpled smile still radiated thegentle kindness that came so naturally to him. Zachary wasn't fooled by it. For all Emeric's sweet-tempered looks, his timidity could be as easily banished as it was given.

"He is thinking about Merle," Marcel, uncharacteristically, spoke. Zachary growled and quickened his pace. It didn't deter either of his friends, who kept easy stride with him, though he was the tallest of the three.

"I heard the King funded a new hunt." Emeric's face was unreadable.

Zachary had heard the same, but that wasn't why his thoughts were on Rufus. Like Zachary, Belphegore had been pressed by higher powers to take a new apprentice, and like Zachary, Belphegore hadn't been tempted by the proposition. There would be no easy replacement for Rufus, and despite suggestion, Belphegore had no intention of raising another warrior either. Apparently, Zachary had been exhausting enough.

"Let's get this over with," Zachary grunted as they stepped into the assembly room. If they finished quick enough, he could return to bed for another hour before his next duty began.

As they came into the room, a few of the students caught sight of them and offered the respect due, standing and bowing deeply. Most of the others continued their chatter and Zachary stood, appalled, at the front of the class. Ten years ago, every single one of them would have stood in respect, but the times had changed. These weren't warriors born in an age of terror, the age of the curfew and the Night Patrol. No, these were rich boys with good training, whose hearts were filled with noble ambition, and their heads with hot air. Zachary studied them and decided that, for the few who would inevitably be apprenticed, he saw none with the potential to be among his own ranks. He was almost disappointed.

"He isn't."

"I swear, he is! He is a faerie!"

"No, he's not!"

Two students at the front of the class were arguing and Zachary slumped. The topic of conversation was increasingly familiar to him, and he'd heard enough of it.

"He has to be! Who else in their right mind would abandon their title and station to go and live in a faerie wood! He *has* to be a changeling or a half-faerie at least!"

"He *hid* in a faerie wood, and that was after they caught his trail in Corhlam! Do you really think that Lord Odin would have apprenticed a *faerie*? He's just a traitor—a Betheanian! And he can die like any other man!"

Zachary followed Marcel's lead and slunk to the back of the room, hiding in the shadows, arms folded. Marcel lit his pipe, and Emeric and Zachary echoed his example, taking out and filling their own. The three stood together smoking, huddled beneath the billowing fumes like dejected old men.

"On the last hunt, only a handful of the alchemists came back—they said that he ate the men he killed," a third boy chimed in. There was a spatter of muttered agreement and nodding. Zachary choked on his smoke and snorted.

"That still doesn't make him a faerie—just barbaric."

"Not all of them are born faeries—you can turn into one, you know," another said conspiratorially. "My father says he's renounced the True Gods and given his allegiance to the *Dark*. It's the Fomorii who grant him power now."

Several of the boys hissed, licking their thumbs and drawing a quick line across their foreheads in the Mark of Notameer. Zachary struggled to stifle his laughter.

Renounce the True Gods? Preposterous. A Magi didn't renounce the True Gods. They couldn't—they were born of them, a living part of them. To renounce the Gods was to renounce life.

"Does he really? Does he worship them now?"

"He pays monthly tribute in human sacrifice and in return they teach him dark magic. He gains his power by bathing in his victim's blood. One month no one came after him. To appease the gods for his lack of sacrifice, he had to hack away at his own body instead—that's why he's only got one leg."

Zachary's laughter burst out of him in short, sharp pants as Emeric pulled a face of mock-horror. Marcel lifted his own leg and shook it, as if it were hurting him.

"Is it true he can control the weather? Make storms and torrents of rain by doing some sort of faerie dance?"

"Of course—why do you think the crops were destroyed by floods last year? It was him."

More and more of the students began to join in the conversation.

"They say he gave his eye to the Queen of the Unseelie Court for that power."

Zachary collapsed against the wall behind him, his body in spasm as he imagined it—a legless, bloodied, one-eyed man dancing a storm in to ruin a few crops. It was farcical at best. Emeric gave Zachary a consoling pat on the back as Zachary sucked in a huge lungful of air, trying to calm himself.

"It doesn't matter what power he has—when I am a Magi I

shall join the hunt and bring him down myself in the name of the King!" the first boy announced grandly.

"Don't be ridiculous, you're no match for him."

"My father *knew* him," the first boy insisted. "Said he was nothing but a theorist, strange and bookish with no great powers of combat."

"That's not true," his companion snorted. "Otherwise how could he have done what he did?"

"What do you mean?"

"When he *turned.*" The second boy rolled his eyes. "Or don't you remember? That he attacked a woman and child, and battled through over thirty Magi?"

"*Thirty?*" Zachary's voice exploded and the boys all jumped, noticing him for the first time. "*Thirty!*" Zachary repeated. "Oh for the love of Malak's jade-tipped nipples, this has got to stop! You *hear* that, Fold? Hathely? Thirty, they said—*thirty!*"

"I heard sixty the other day." Emeric shrugged. "And that he summoned an army of the dead."

"He performed necromancy?" Marcel muttered, blowing a few strands of his long blond hair out of his eyes. "I must have dropped off."

"Thirty?" Zachary groaned. "Sons of the gods, the author of these stories ought to be proud."

"Correct them, if it pains you." Marcel took a long drag of his pipe only to realise his tobacco was spent. He narrowed his pale, golden eyes, glaring at the pipe as if it were the one at fault.

"You know we can't…That's one unwritten rule that might as well be law," Zachary snarled. He gave the boys who watched him a feral grin. "He eats rodents live, you know, my former brother. He likes the way they feel wriggling in his teeth."

"Zachary…" Emeric's voice was half-hearted.

"But it isn't just rodents—hah! You think he waits until his victims are dead? No boys, he's got venom on his tongue strong enough to paralyse a horse. He'll rip into you alive, and let you

21

live long to watch him feasting."

"Zachary, *really*," Emeric said with more conviction this time.

"Oh what's the matter?" Zachary barked, his temper flaring. "Their mouths are already foaming with the shit—what's one more lie going to do? Thirty—*thirty* they say! A half-crazed, one-legged necromancer with a single eye and a renounced religion battling through *thirty* Magi? I am disgusted by the lack of common sense in this room."

He saw several of the students draw back, their faces pinched in indignation at these insults. Zachary didn't care.

"In fairness, they were only claiming the necromancer part to be true of the time," Emeric defended lightly.

"Oh, that's right. He was only controlling the dead that day— he still had both of his legs. My mistake," Zachary snapped and Marcel raised his eyebrows.

"Correct them, if it pains you," he repeated monotonously.

"Were that it was so easy," Zachary lamented and Emeric rolled his eyes.

"Oh Hexias give me strength." Emeric turned to the students, who'd now all been drawn into the spectacle, whispering. "There were never thirty Magi. There were only three. They were not protecting anyone, but were sent to stop Prince Jionathan from crossing into Avalon. In doing so, they started a fight with the Prince's Sidhe companion. Rufus Merle interceded at great risk to himself, before anyone got hurt. Because of him, nobody died that day. That's the truth."

A stunned silence filled the room and Emeric turned back to his friends. Zachary was wide-eyed, and Marcel had dropped his pipe from his mouth in veiled surprise.

"That was *excruciating*," Emeric said sarcastically and Zachary barked a laugh, smacking him across the arm.

"Madman," he whispered. "Never mind a new apprentice— you need to keep your fair cousin on a tighter leash, Hathely. He's growing bold."

"Bold and rebellious—just as my sister warned me." Marcel's face twisted in an unusual display of horror and Emeric and Zachary roared with laughter.

"By Notameer's Light." A voice interrupted them as from the head of the room. Tall and upright, with bright white hair, the familiar figure of Belphegore Odin appeared at the door. "I cannot think what has put you three in such high-spirits at this gloomy hour of the morning."

The men and students alike rose to their feet and bowed respectfully as the leader of the Magi swept into the room.

"Come, share the joke then," Belphegore said, "unless you deem it to be too inappropriate for my sensitive constitution?"

"They were talking about Rufus Merle, Lord Odin," one of the students blurted, and all of the good humour was immediately gone from Belphegore's face. For Zachary, the rumours of Rufus were a mere agitation, but for Belphegore, to hear his favourite being so carelessly slandered, was an infinite torture. Even in that second, Belphegore seemed to wither and age under a heavy fatigue.

"Rufus...?" he glanced up at Zachary, and there was almost a look of betrayal in his pale blue eyes. "I see. Yes, a new hunt was sent after him. I forget how swiftly dead conversations can be revived."

"They said," the student continued, eyeing Emeric dubiously, "they said that he only attacked three Magi when he turned. That he didn't kill anybody."

The students looked between each other, confused. No one had ever corrected the speculation before—nobody dared portray Rufus as a victim, not when he was a traitor. "Is it true?"

"Are you accusing me of lying?" Emeric asked sternly. Zachary knew that, in his own way, Emeric was giving Belphegore a chance to dispel his gloom and take control of the situation.

"No...that's not..." the student stuttered.

"My apprentice—" Belphegore started, and then corrected

himself, "my *former* apprentice was never a violent man. That he is a traitor now is a sad reality, but during his time serving this kingdom, he never hurt anyone."

"That's open for debate," Zachary muttered. His voice carried further than he intended, and Belphegore narrowed his eyes. Zachary quickly expanded. "With an intellect like that, he moderated the pride of quite few established Magi—present company included. That's the danger of associating with a genius, I suppose."

"So, he really wasn't a faerie?" The students' voices had dropped to a whisper.

"No," Zachary dismissed. "Just a tenacious little shit."

"Arlen," Belphegore said sharply.

"Oh what?" Zachary pushed back. "You're as tired of this as I am. Make no mistake, I have no lingering affection for the man, but the truth is, compared to the rest of us, Merle's as guiltless as a child and should be left to his misery. And yet these," he gestured angrily to the students, "these mindless, gaudy puppets are raised on the idea that it would actually be an honour to drive a sword through his heart. As if Merle would know which end of a sword to hold," Zachary scoffed. "What an honourable ambition. You'll excuse me Master, but I fear I made a mistake coming to this address." He strode toward the door.

"Arlen…" Belphegore tried to reason as Zachary passed him.

"Do you see your new apprentice amongst them?" Zachary said, shaking his head. "Because if their greatest ambition is to kill a head-sick man then I wonder at what hope there is for our kingdom."

Belphegore bowed his head. "You are excused," he said, and Zachary stalked from the room, leaving Marcel and Emeric to fend for themselves against the fools.

CHAPTER
2

By the time Rufus pulled himself out of the river, he was three miles down the valley. He lay on the bank, exhausted and gasping, and then hid as the Kathraks came looking. They scoured the area for half an hour or so, then moved on, allowing Rufus to begin the long trek back.

As he walked, Rufus prayed that the Kathraks would keep following the river south. Most, from the little chatter he'd heard when they passed, believed him dead, or at least too badly injured to keep fleeing. DuGilles wasn't satisfied with their speculation, persisting with the search.

"He's a Magi—he has more tricks up his sleeve than you've got thoughts in your head. So keep looking! He's not dead until I've seen his body."

In this assessment, DuGilles had been correct. Long ago, Rufus had theorised a technique which could be used if a Magi found himself falling from a great height. The purpose of creating the technique had been for his own peace of mind, as a long sufferer of what the Réneians called 'l'appel du vide', an almost instinctual desire to leap from the top of high-places. Paranoid that he may one day fall in with this internal craving, Rufus had theorised a way to survive if he did, and had then tested it by jumping from the top of one of the Magi towers.

The technique itself involved emitting a highly pressurised ball of air below you just before you struck the ground, thereby cushioning the impact of your fall. Usually the theory relied on having at least a basic understanding of the terrain, but Rufus had been falling blind, and it was only because of his quick estimations and instinct that he'd survived hitting the water.

Near dawn, exhausted by the river and the chase, Rufus stopped in a glade to rest. When he next opened his eyes, it was to the fullness of the morning.

Sitting up from where he was slouched against a tree, he groaned, his body stiff and cold. "Oh no, no…" He flumped back. His ribs and back hurt from the fall, and he still felt light-headed and water-logged, though he was mercifully dry.

"Are you hurt?" a voice asked and Rufus sat bolt upright.

"Athea—damn it!" he cried, turning furiously on the boy at his side. "Joshua, don't do that!"

"Sorry."

"You scared me witless!"

"Sorry," the boy repeated and the Magi fell back with a grumble, rubbing his chest.

Joshua scooted closer, peering at Rufus worriedly. "*Are* you hurt?" he asked again.

"No," Rufus said. "Only a little battered." He leaned across and ruffled the boy's hair. Joshua slapped his hand away playfully, his expression breaking into a wide smile, which Rufus returned. At twelve and a half years, Joshua looked so astonishingly like Jionat, that were it not for his bright blue eyes, to a faded memory, they might have been the same person. Rufus didn't bother asking Joshua how he'd found him in the dense wood— the boy had inherited the Delphi skill for finding blood kin, and whilst it wasn't as strong as Rufus's ability, Rufus knew he could never stay lost from his little brother for long.

"What are you doing out here, Joshua? I told you to stay in the house."

Joshua huffed grumpily. "It's morning and you've been gone for hours. I thought...I thought they might've caught you again."

Rufus caught a flash of fear in his brother's eyes, and his heart squeezed. He forced a laugh. "No, no—never got close. I jumped into the river and led them away."

"I know."

"What?"

"I *saw*." Joshua didn't seem amused. His eyes flashed knowingly. "You jumped thirty-three strides down into the river."

"Well, yes—"

"With no guarantee you'd survive."

"There's no guarantee I'll survive breakfast every time I take it, but that doesn't stop me eating. The jump was a risk, but it was calculated," Rufus said firmly. "I'm sorry it took me so long to walk back."

Rufus watched as Joshua sorted through this information, his anger and concern melding into a reluctant relief. He sighed.

"You've got to be more careful, Rufus."

Rufus sat up, despite his aching body and pulled the boy into a tight embrace. Joshua relaxed against him.

"The Kathraks?" Rufus asked faintly.

"Passed through the village, but they're gone now." Joshua stood and helped Rufus to his feet, snickering as Rufus gave a long groan, bent forward like an old man.

"Gods, but I'm sore." He arched back, trying to loosen his spine. It cracked loudly and he gritted his teeth, massaging the base of his neck. "I wasn't meant for this life."

"And yet it chose you—be honoured," Joshua quipped, but there was a reservation in his voice. When Rufus turned back, he found his brother deep in thought, face pinched in an expression beyond his years. "How did they find us so quickly? It used to take them months." His voice was small and uneasy. Rufus slumped, running a hand up through his hair.

"I don't know," he said. "But we need to be more on guard."

Joshua nodded and gave a stifled cough, covering his mouth. Rufus frowned.

"Are you coughing again?"

"No." Joshua put his hands behind his back.

"You are. You're coughing." Rufus knelt down beside him. Joshua, despite his natural athleticism was still slight for his age, and on his knees Rufus was only a little shorter than the boy. He peered anxiously into his brother's face. "Let me see."

Carefully, he touched one hand to Joshua's throat, and rested the other over his forehead, running a small current of magic through him. Long ago, Lord Edwin, leader of the Healing sect, had taken both Rufus and Zachary to the side and taught them this technique of diagnosis. It allowed Rufus to feel an echo of his brother's pain, and though he possessed no great mastery with healing, with this technique, Rufus could at least catch the illness in its infancy.

Instantly he could feel the slight tightness of his brother's lungs and throat. Rufus's stomach sank in worry, but he masked his expression, forcing a smile. "Come on." He dropped his hands. "Let's go."

Trudging slowly through the forest, they made their way back to the village. It would have been a pleasant walk, but Rufus was unsettled by even the slightest shift in noise, his mind wary.

"Are we leaving again?" Joshua asked.

"We have to," Rufus said. "The townspeople will know who I am now. Loose tongues are too easy to buy. I'm not sure how the alchemists caught my trail but I'd rather they lose it."

"But Sir Hirondelle said he'd teach me to fight with a sword," Joshua whined. His curls gleamed in the sunlight as the pair approached the village.

"Fine, you can stay here then," Rufus said. "I'll go ahead on my own."

Joshua hesitated at this exclamation, his brow lowered, "Really?"

Rufus coughed. "Don't be ridiculous. We're not separating."

"But we could—"

"No, Joshua."

"Rufus—"

"No! We're leaving and that's final!"

"Don't command me," Joshua bit, angered by Rufus's tone. "*You're* supposed to follow *my* orders, remember? I'm the Prince of Harmatia."

"You are," Rufus agreed. "And as far as Harmatia's concerned you've been dead twelve years. Which means that until you've got a beard and a dainty little crown on your head you're under *my* charge. So don't get bratty with me, young man."

"You're my brother, not my father."

"*You're* the one who calls me Papa."

Joshua growled and marched ahead. Rufus, regretting his tone, reached for Joshua's hand and pulled the boy back to his side. He remembered those hands from infancy, so small in his palm.

"I'm sorry, I shouldn't have gotten angry with you," he said, his brother still refusing to look him in the eye. "I'll tell you what," Rufus consoled, "when you're King and we've taken back Harmatia, and I've become an acerbic, old fool, I promise I'll do whatever you ask of me."

Joshua paused and glanced at him from the corner of his eye. Rufus knew that his brother, however angry, couldn't refuse such an offer of peace. The boy spoke cautiously, as if he still weren't sure whether to forgive Rufus. "Anything I want?"

"Anything," Rufus said. "You may use me as your personal footstool and I'll call it an honour."

Joshua's giggle was like running water and Rufus knew he'd redeemed himself.

"I'm sorry," he repeated. "I know you wanted to stay a while, but it isn't safe for us here."

"Papa—" Joshua began.

"I wish I could change things, but I can't."

"*Papa*, look." Joshua tugged him back and pointed urgently to a tree just at the mouth of the village. On it, pictures and notices had been nailed for the attention of all those moving in or out of the town.

"Oh no…" Rufus tore down a likeness of himself which had been nailed up. Beneath the picture, the text boasted an extortionate reward for anyone who could deliver Rufus's head to King Sverrin's court.

Joshua touched the page. "It's a good likeness. They drew your scar on the wrong side though."

Rufus's own fingers automatically reached up to the scar that ran along the side of his left eye, from the eyebrow to the top of his cheekbone. A gift from his first encounter with DuGilles.

"I don't think it'll make a difference." Rufus's voice shook. It had been over twelve years since he abandoned his duties in Harmatia, becoming a traitor. But until today, the object of the chase had been to capture Rufus and bring him to trial. Now, DuGilles had changed everything. It wouldn't only be emissaries from Harmatia coming for Rufus, but every hungry, greedy or law–abiding citizen who saw his face. His blood ran cold.

"We have to go. Now. Quick."

Without a word of argument, Joshua followed Rufus as they sprinted past the village, up to the Hirondelle's house.

Even before they reached the back door, it had been opened and a set of anxious arms had pulled them inside. "We've prepared your horses and packed your bags—you must go immediately, before they find you here." Samual Hirondelle was a stout but powerful man, with thick arms and a red moustache that quivered whenever he spoke. Rufus and Joshua had been a guest of his for only a few weeks, but already they were being run to their next safe-haven. "Little Prince, you frightened my husband and I near to death when we found you missing from your bed this morning," he said. "And you Rufus—when the Kathraks passed through, we feared the worst. They've made a sport of you—you must get to Beshuwa to the Moineau family."

"Which way did the Kathraks go?" Rufus asked.

"I cannot be sure, but I think they are following the river down to Lemra on the coast. They will probably recuperate there." Samual hurried them along.

"Do you know how they found us so quickly?" Rufus pushed Joshua ahead of him as they moved into the stables at the back.

"No, we have been trying to find their source, but there have been delays in all our communications. I have heard nothing from the Alouettes in weeks. I fear they have abandoned their post."

Rufus swallowed. The Alouettes had given him and Joshua shelter a few months before, and had been incredibly welcoming to bone-weary travellers. Rufus didn't want to consider the possibility that something evil might have befallen them on account of that kindness.

"They won't have been hurt, will they?" Joshua asked fearfully. "We left nothing to incriminate them."

"No, they've probably gone to Brexiam—we have a force gathered there now. It's safer for the existing Knight families, but it means we have lost another correspondent in our chain. Information comes slow."

"Just as long as they're safe, delays don't matter."

They stepped into the stable where two horses had already been saddled, ready for departure. Rufus clasped Samual's hand. "Money should be sent through for me soon—when it comes, take what is owed for your hospitality."

"I may not have seen him in many years, but your father is a true friend of mine." Samuel shook his head. "What is mine is yours."

Rufus insisted, "Please, don't be generous—you've given

enough already. Joshua and I are indebted to you and your family."

"Nonsense." The first smile broke over Samual's face, his cheeks glowing red like his moustache. "The world is indebted to you, my boy." Samual knelt before Joshua, bowing his head. "Your Highness, I regret that I could not teach you the skills I wished to. But know that I am forever your faithful servant and will honour and serve you as long as I live."

"Rise," Joshua invited, and suddenly he had all the presence of the Prince he was, his tone mild, but regal. "We're indebted to you. I promise, when I'm King, your loyalty won't be forgotten. Until then, my thanks is all I can offer you."

Rufus watched Joshua with a swelling pride as Samual rose to his feet and bowed deeply to the Prince. "It is all I need, Your Highness," Samuel said solemnly. "You have raised him well," he congratulated Rufus, who shook his head. Joshua's grace and geniality were natural to him—he was truly his father's son. "You must go." Samual broke Rufus from his thoughts. "Ride swiftly, my friend."

Again, Rufus clasped Samual's hand in thanks and, following his brother's lead, he clambered up onto a horse. Samual opened the stable door and with a final salute the Prince and Magi charged out of the stable, up toward the woodland path, leaving the house far behind. Just as with the Kathraks he'd killed, Rufus didn't look back. He couldn't afford to look back.

CHAPTER 3

To Aeron Faucon the backward streets of Lemra were a place of infinite possibility. Here men could walk in the shadows like they were shifting between reality itself and no law stood above nature's first rule—that the strong ate the weak. Aptly named 'The Pit of Bethean', Lemra had long since forged a reputation of being a nest of thieves, pirates and cut-throats. It was certainly not a place for the fainthearted, which suited Aeron well—his city bred survivors, anything less was unwelcome.

Leaning back against the dusty wall of an old building, Aeron watched the sun setting over the water, keeping half an eye on the shifting forms of mice-like children who ran bare-foot and soundless through the gutters.

Up along the road, two figures appeared and Aeron watched them leisurely as they approached. They were Kathrak, bold in feature and strong-faced. One was tall, shaped like a boulder, with rounded shoulders and hunch. The other was smaller with a long nose and hairy chin. Aeron spat in the street as they reached him. "Milords?" he said, his accent thick, voice deep and gravelly.

"You are the one they call the Black Falcon?"

Aeron sucked his front teeth loudly. "Point out which feckless fuck called me that stupid name, and I'll forgive you for repeatin' it."

The Kathraks considered him. Without warning, the smaller one threw a hard punch toward Aeron's kidney. Despite his lazy demeanour, Aeron anticipated the attack. With a swift shift of his body, he avoided the strike. The Kathrak's knuckle cracked painfully against the wall. He yelped and swore loudly.

"You damn—" he began but before he could say any more, Aeron had drawn his knife in one slick movement and pushed it against the Kathrak's throat. The assassin tutted softly.

"Now that's no way to charm a favour from a man, is it?" Aeron let his accent drawl, watching the Kathrak's cheek twitch as the knife rose higher up his neck. "Or is this some sugar-coated Kathrak greet I don't know about?"

The larger man moved in to help his comrade, but Aeron warned him back.

"Ah-ah! One step closer and your mate gets a new singin' hole," he warned.

"You will take us to the Faucon brotherhood," the Kathrak under Aeron's knife demanded. Aeron tittered, a strange sound coming from such a formidable man.

"And here, I thought the man with the knife to his throat *took* the orders."

The second Kathrak drew his own blade and held it up to Aeron side. "You are outnumbered, Betheanian shit. You will do as we ask."

Aeron grinned, skull-like. "You think because I stand unhidden, that I'm out here by my whoopsie-savvy self? Hm?" He licked his lips and then removed the blade, settling back against the wall. "But let's not make enemies of out of money-lenders, as the old proverb goes. You fine folk look in need of business, so put that slinky blade away from where it's accusin' me kidneys, cross my palm with silver, and I'll see what I can suck."

"I don't think you understand how this is going to work," the larger of the Kathraks barked, the point of his blade still pushing lightly into Aeron's side.

"And I don't think you've fully brained who you're talkin' to," Aeron replied easily, and something in his tone must have unnerved the two Kathraks, because with another nod the blade was withdrawn and the pair pulled back. "Obliged," Aeron said, making himself comfortable back against the wall. "Now, give me a minute. I have to count the merits of not stickin' you both—and fairs warnin' to you, you're trippin' a little short of the chord." He tapped his chin thoughtfully, running his fingers through his dark beard. Finally he gave an exaggerated sigh. "Well, you fine boys just about thumb the test," he said. "You look glinted enough. But I'm sorry to say I'm sodded if I can assist. There's no Faucon Brotherhood here."

"Listen here, vagrant—we do not have any patience for your games. Take us to them, or die where you stand."

"I wonder how that'd be...death?" Aeron hummed, spinning into a lazy tangent as he turned back toward the sea. "Must be brain-numbin'ly dull."

"We can solve that mystery for you." The larger Kathrak still had his hands on his blade.

"Aw, that's sweeter than a honey-apple in swine," Aeron cooed, "but I'm not sure how you'd tap back to me when you'd found out."

"For the last time, take us to the Faucon Brotherhood! We have been sent to find a man by the name of Cethin!" The Kathrak's knuckles were white around his sword. Aeron sobered immediately at the name.

"Cethin's no name, it's a title like King," he corrected sternly. "And he's no man nether—he's the master of death. The head of the Faucon."

The Kathraks smiled to each other. "You know of him? Take us then. We wish to hire his strongest assassin."

"Sorry, but Cethin's a hundred thousand miles north-west of here, on a Shinny throne in Isnydea," Aeron growled. He started down the street. "If you want a Faucon assassin, come with me. But I'll warn you now, don't point the finger when your double-dealin's on Betheanian soil bury you in your own festerin' shit."

Quietly he led them down a narrow path away from the sea, debating with himself whether or not to simply kill them. The tension between Kathra and Bethean had only grown in recent years. These Kathraks had no place here in Lemra.

Reaching an opening in the wall, Aeron cast his thoughts away and decided to put his mind to the business at hand, rather than grand politics. He was an assassin at his core—a weapon. Though a weapon rarely got the chance to turn on its wielder, whereas Aeron still delighted in the thought of killing both Kathraks and hanging them up as a warm welcome to any other Northerners who might be passing into the assassin's street.

Pulling back the heavy beige curtain that served as a door, he moved into his abode, nodding to the few comrades of his who were already there. 'Early risers' in the nocturnal sense, they sat and waited for the next job, squandering their time gambling, reading and having sex. Aeron was the eldest amongst them, already in his early fifties, and yet as nimble and adept as all of them combined.

Walking toward a ragged desk, Aeron sat behind it, putting his feet up. He motioned for the two Kathraks to approach. "So, what'll it be milords?"

The men eyed the room and its occupants warily before speaking. "My name is Bendth Gregos, and this Ivenn DuRien," the smaller said. "We were sent on behalf of Lord Brandt DuGilles to alert the strongest assassin in Lemra of this bounty." They pushed a piece of paper across the table toward Aeron. The assassin took it, but didn't look, his brown eyes never leaving the two men before him.

"We work by commission," he said. "Not bounty."

36

"If the Faucon Assassins are as capable as your reputation states, you will have no trouble killing this man. The bounty far outweighs any commission price."

Aeron sucked his teeth in false consideration, and then took the bait. "Alright then, let's talk straight, golden business—where is the sucker? What is he? And how d'you want him dead?"

"Our information dictates that his next port of call is here in the East, to a family by the name of Moineau, though we are unsure yet of their location."

Aeron snorted to himself, but the Kathraks ignored him and continued.

"He is an outlaw—a rogue Magi, but no trained fighter. A quick death is all we require, any second he is tortured is another he breathes, and he is unpredictable when provoked. Better to slit his throat while he slumbers."

"Aye." Aeron nodded slowly. "Quick death is cheaper, but a Magi... You'll be double coined, fair warnin'."

"The price is set and grand, provided you can bring his head." Bendth bristled, maintaining an arrogant air despite his surroundings. The other assassins present would gladly snap his neck at a single click of Aeron's fingers.

"Sweetness, have you no faith in us?" Aeron asked sweetly.

"You Betheanians have a reputation for having soft stomachs."

"Not met many Betheanians, have you?" Aeron leant back again, his eyes on the huddled figures behind the Kathraks who continued their game, tossing the dice in turns as they played. He exhaled. "You see them behind you, milords? Them humans bundled in black. Well we've known each other for a thousand beats, all of us—we're family of sorts. We've shared our meals, our weapons, our sweat and blood." He paused again as both Kathraks turned to look at the figures, shrouded in their cloaks. Aeron considered his comrades for a long moment, putting his head in his hands. "Seven," he called softly, "kill."

Almost instantly, the assassin on the right side of the gambling table flicked a knife into her hand from where it was concealed in her sleeve, and slashed it across her partner's throat, catching the dice as they tumbled from the other's hands. The man fell silently backward from his stool into a heavy pile and Aeron applauded.

"Now that's a good kill—clean. Psht, psht. Throw that organ-sack in the back," he ordered two other figures, indicating to another room behind him, also curtained off. The cloak-clad assassins did as they were told, dragging the body without complaint as Aeron turned back to the Kathraks, who watched, faces mixed with horror and a gross fascination.

"You refer to each other in numbers?" Ivenn finally dared to ask.

"Course—givin' your name in a place like this would be foolish as fuck," Aeron said pointedly, grinning again. The Kathraks looked between each other, trying to disguise their dismay as they realised their mistake. Aeron continued. "So I kill your man...What guarantees me I'll get paid?"

"We are honourable men—"

"Honourable men don't send a cut-throat to kill a man in his sleep." He bared his teeth wickedly. "But fair's fair. I have all I need—tell your commandin' officer that I'll be slicin' stern words with him if I find my pockets picked after a hard day's work. And that's after I've *picked* the lot of you. Accord?"

Both Kathraks maintained their composure, but their faces were pale as they left the abode. Aeron laughed after them. "Now let's see..." He took up the page they'd left him. It was a bounty with a man's likeness, and a heavy reward printed on it. Below the drawing were fine details of the rogue's appearance and habits, but Aeron didn't need to look past the name. "Hah. And just when I thought everythin' had drugged down to a pretty stupor, they hand me this? What a whip to wake me up." Aeron stood, throwing the paper down and moving into the back room, where his comrade's 'corpse' sat up, touching a hand to his throat.

"She nicked me," the 'corpse' complained, staring accusingly up at Aeron with reproachful green eyes.

"Go weep a weddin' dress—she didn't reap you Cal, seal your barrel."

"I couldn't complain if she had," was the sharp retort. "But honest—we'd lose more cut-throats then jobs gained if we killed each other for every customer. How's it people are still fallin' for this ploy?"

"So far as they can savvy our numbers are limitless, and I don't care to wisen 'em up." Aeron pulled a pair of daggers down from where they hung along an iron hook. Below him, the younger man continued to grumble into his hands, massaging the faint cut.

"I've been reaped three times since the moon's turn. Next time, I kill her."

"But Cal, you're so *good* at it." Aeron kicked him, none-too-gently in the side. He pulled back. "Clean up the mess in here, you bone-rapist. I've got to speak to Cethin."

"Why?" Cal asked tightly, saying nothing of Aeron's abuse and wisely so. Last time he'd tried to complain, Aeron had pinched his face between his fingers and cut both of his cheeks open. "Who's the mark?"

"Why, none other than Harmatia's famous run-away—Rufus Merle," Aeron rolled the name across his tongue as he strapped his daggers to his side. "Ah," he sang, "I smell a blood-bath."

CHAPTER
4

"And then she leapt down from the fountain top and dove head-first into the bandits!" Rufus exclaimed dramatically, leaping around the fire in imitation as he spun haphazardly. "She was like an acrobat, twisting and turning. Not one of those murderous thieves could rise to meet her skill, and when it seemed she might be overwhelmed, she moved faster and faster until she was almost a ghost, shifting gracefully through the air like—ah!" he stumbled on his own long legs and collapsed into a heap at Joshua's side. The boy laughed as Rufus propped himself up onto his elbow with a huff. "Well, not like that obviously."

Joshua laughed even harder and it turned into a long cough. Rufus shifted, his expression pinched with concern.

"Right," his tone became brisk, "I've upheld my end of the bargain, now drink the brew." He pointed to the foul, paste-like drink that Joshua held in his hand. Rufus had mixed it earlier.

"You haven't finished the story yet," Joshua complained, taking a tentative sip.

"What more is there to tell?" Rufus sighed, lying back. "You've heard it a thousand times. Fae fought her way through the bandits, delaying them enough for my uncle to prepare his men.

And when they captured her, Jionathan sprung from hiding and saved her."

"By threatening to cut out his own eyes!" Joshua exclaimed.

"Yes. And he'd have done it, too."

"And then you freed Fae, and Luca saved you from Bruatar."

"I don't know why I bother—you know the story better than I do," Rufus huffed, looking up at the shimmering foliage above. In recent years the Myrithian forest had become a sort of home to them, a sanctuary away from people. Of course, Rufus wasn't foolish enough to forget the dangers that lurked in the dark— he was still rightfully afraid of those—but it seemed to him that the forest welcomed them, even protected them. In return, he and Joshua had shared their fire with many creatures of the Myrithian.

Joshua coughed, interrupting Rufus's thoughts. The boy had always been prone to sickness of the lungs and throat, despite being in good form. The cold often aggravated the tightness in his chest, but then so did heavy pollen, and fear. In recent years, Joshua's ailment had calmed and become less frequent. But exposed to the elements as they were, and with the added pressure of the looming Kathraks, Rufus was worried that his brother might fall prey to his old sickness.

"Do you think I'll ever meet Fae?" Joshua asked wistfully.

Rufus sat up, extending his hands into the fire which rose up to meet him. "Someday, yes, I'm sure," he said. "She was too fond of Jionat to miss meeting his brother."

"*And* yours," Joshua reminded him.

"And mine," Rufus smiled, "though we hardly look alike, so no one would know."

"We look a little alike," Joshua insisted. "Otherwise nobody would believe I was your son."

"Hm." Rufus cupped a flame in his hand and watched it dance. When Joshua was young, they'd dyed his hair black to match Rufus's. Certainly at that time, they'd made a convincing father and son, but the dye had been one of the things that agitated Joshua's lungs, so they'd stopped using it. "We have the same eyes, and maybe a similar smile," Rufus conceded, "but you've always looked more like your father, and I like mine."

Rufus watched fondly as Joshua's face creased, small, thoughtful lines appearing between his brows.

"What was he like? My father?" Joshua finally said. He'd asked many times before, but never seemed to tire of the question.

"Wise, strong, authoritative—a man of great foresight." Rufus threw some more wood on the fire, reaching in to adjust it carefully. The flames licked harmlessly across his fingers.

"Not great enough."

"Joshua, no one could have foreseen what the Queen would do."

"Jionat did."

"Jionat had the gift of Sight and even that didn't save him," Rufus said. Joshua loved to talk about Jionat but even after all this time, it still made Rufus's heart ache. Joshua too seemed to dampen at the conversation, looking miserably into the fire. Rufus knew he missed the parents and brother he hadn't known.

Eager to dispel Joshua's gloom, Rufus rolled away and, reaching into a bag, opened a hard leather case which was strapped carefully among his meagre clothes. Inside lay a fiddle. Rufus pulled it out, twirling the bow in his hands. At the sight of the instrument, Joshua sat up. Rufus carefully tuned the fiddle before standing.

"And for His Highness's pleasure tonight, this talentless minstrel will perform an assortment of music he's heard all before."

Joshua sat forward, eager. It didn't matter to him that Rufus's repertoire was limited to a few choice favourites—the music always seemed to brighten the Prince's complexion. Joshua laughed as Rufus gave an exaggerated bow, tossing his fringe to the side as he placed his chin against the violin. "To begin then," Rufus allowed his voice to grow pompous, "a soft melody composed by Galamorth Forthright in the last century, written to soothe the troubled mind and calm the spirit." He started up a lively Betheanian jig. Joshua clapped his hands as Rufus raked the strings for a minute before stopping, his nose up-turned. "Hmm...I recalled it somewhat mellower." He continued in the act, Joshua giggling. "No matter. The next is a tragic lament, written to commemorate the death of Lady Ariad, commissioned by her husband."

He replaced the bow against the strings and almost immediately the jig returned, doubling in speed as Rufus added trills, the exultant sound pouring into the woodland. He ceased again, exhaling dramatically. "I...I do apologise, I do not know what has come over me," he stammered, bowing to Joshua. "Forgive me, my Prince. This one will be of a more appropriate nature, I assure you. The Lover's Lament from the Kathrak Opera *The Death of Sensibility*."

Once more the bow was replaced across the strings and once more, the jig returned, Rufus's eyes widening in false panic. "No, that's not it! No! The fiddle! It's controlling me! It's turning my mind to sordid things!" He gave a cry of distress, pretending to struggle against the violin. "No, No! I am possessed—I cannot stop!" He blinked rapidly as if his mind were being taken over, and then abruptly grinned, leering like some villain in a play as Joshua whooped.

He performed a set of rowdy Lemra'n and Killian port songs, which were always popular in the taverns they passed, not least for the vulgar lyrics that no twelve-year-old should have been subjected to.

Rufus played them anyway, Joshua singing merrily along until, at last, Rufus finished with a flourish and bowed deeply. His brother applauded him, and he wasn't the only one.

From beside the Prince came the sound of titters and cheers. Rufus realised that they'd attracted a small audience of a dozen feeorin. Rufus bowed to them in turn and they chittered excitedly to one another. Of all the characters Rufus and Joshua had met in the forest, the feeorin were their most common companions. Slight, miniscule figures, they had large leafy-yellow eyes and greenish skin. Flowers, mushrooms and grass grew wherever they trod. Supposedly some of the shiest of all the faerie, Rufus had come to learn that the sound of music never failed to draw them out, and that to share a fire with them was to have a blessing from the forest itself. Rufus was always sure to be kind to them—they were generous hosts, after all.

"Another," Joshua demanded, and the feeorin chittered in agreement, their tiny dragonfly wings quivering in pleasure. Rufus complied, though his fingers were already starting to ache. Luca would beat him if she knew how little he practised.

As Rufus played, the faeries danced below him. Joshua dropped down onto his chin so that he was at eye level with them. Some clambered into his hair and hung from his ears.

Finally, when his fingers felt like they might bleed, Rufus stopped, sitting down heavily with a gasp. "Enough, no more—my hands will fall off," he heaved, his chest rising and falling. Joshua moaned, pleading with him, but he shook his head. "No—you can't buy me with those begging eyes! I shan't!" Rufus insisted playfully, only to see that the tiny feeorin were similarly prostrated, large, slanted eyes wide in longing. Rufus groaned. "One more," he finally allowed and his audience cheered. "Only one, mind! What would you like?"

"Swallows," Joshua ordered without hesitation and Rufus paused.

"Swallows…" he said a little doubtfully. "Isn't that a little sad? Surely something more upbeat?"

"Please, Rufus?" That look again, Joshua's blue eyes bright. During Joshua's youth, Rufus had become very aware that the boy possessed a talent for manipulation, a talent that went deeper than his sweet face and disposition. Much like Jionat with his visions, and Rufus with his talent for finding his brothers, Joshua possessed an ability that allowed him to read and influence the mood of those around him. As of yet, Rufus didn't think the boy capable of suggesting new thoughts, but he was quickly becoming more adept at bringing buried ones to the surface.

For Rufus, who'd been the target of such mental abuse in Joshua's younger, more demanding years, the technique no longer worked so well, but tonight the Prince needn't have bothered at all. Rufus couldn't deny him.

"As you wish. I'll play it."

"And sing."

"My throat is run raw—I've no voice for this."

"Please?"

One word and Rufus had the fiddle to his shoulder again and was retuning the strings. He placed the bow gently onto them and slowly drew the horse-hair across. To the soft melody, he sang.

"Sweetness, don't you fret now,
I'm right beside you dear.
No need to think what's coming next,
no reason left to fear.
You'll wake again, I promise love,
in a better place,
You'll have yourself a new life,
yourself a new face.

And swallows dance at windowsills,
they dance, they dance for you.
The Nightingale does sing his song,
lamenting his heart too.
The Blackbird cries, the Falcon bows,
The Lark does sing his due,
And Swallows dance at window sills,
they dance, they dance for you.

Now hush my dear, no need to cry,
the heavens love you so.
Your body's weak, but mind is strong,
you're pure and that they know.
And if you fear, just hold my hand,
I'll stay throughout the night.
And when the dreams do lull you there,
I'll pray with all my might.

And Swallows dance at windows sill,
they dance, they dance for you.
The Blue-tit nestles in his home,
quiet and subdued.
The Hawk won't hunt, nor Sparrow fly,
The Dove cannot construe,
And Swallows dance at windowsills,
they dance, they dance for you.

So quiet now, your breath is dead,
but still I won't let go
The birds have gone, the Swallows flown,
left in their place a crow.
Your sweet face shows your peace of mind,
I'll weep 'til dawn will break.
A solemn pyre of wild flowers,
for you, love, I will make

And Swallows danced at window sills,
they danced, they danced for you.
The Nightingale has sung his song,
lamented his heart too,
The Blackbird cried, the Falcon bowed,
The Lark has sung his due,
And Swallows danced at window sills,
they danced, they danced for you."

Slowly, Rufus opened his eyes, allowing the bow to drop.
Across from him the faeries had gathered in a semi-circle and
were watching him solemnly, eyes brimming with tears. One by

one they stood and bowed to him, as if he'd bestowed on them a great gift, and then trailed off back into the forest.

Joshua had settled back against the saddle-bags and drifted asleep mid-song. Rufus had sung it as a lullaby when his brother was a baby, and it had had a sedative effect ever since. The Magi replaced his instrument. Fetching a blanket, he covered the Prince and placed a gentle kiss on his brow. Joshua stirred and, with a quiet murmur, buried himself deeper beneath the blanket. Rufus threw some more wood onto the fire. Alone now with his thoughts, he gave a worried sigh, tugging at his fringe.

Athea, he hoped the alchemists had lost their trail.

CHAPTER 5

⤜⊰⊱⤛

"We have received a report regarding the latest hunt for the traitor, Rufus Merle." Sverrin was to the point. He'd always been a blunt child and age hadn't changed this quality about him.

None of the Magi dared say a word as Sverrin went on. They kept their gazes down, fearful of catching the eyes of their peers. The only two men who might have spoken kept their peace—Zachary because he was too weary to care, and Belphegore because he was too diplomatic to stir trouble. Especially when Sverrin already knew he was speaking to a room full of men who'd once known and respected Rufus.

"The report states," Sverrin continued, "that my alchemists were able to locate Merle in the woods. Despite their best efforts to calm and placate him however, he chose to leap from a cliff rather than surrender himself. The fall was long and the local authorities believe Merle to be dead."

Zachary felt his master stiffen at his side. His own jaw tightened. They kept their tongues locked.

"A body has yet to be recovered." Sverrin glanced down the parchment. Zachary doubted he was reading from it. The King would have already studied the report at great length. "Until such time as it is, the search will continue under the assumption he lives. A reward has been set for anyone who can bring back his head. It has been made clear to all Harmatian and Betheanian authorities that he is too dangerous for custody and is to be killed on sight."

"Killed on sight?" The news was too much for Belphegore. Zachary kept his gaze on the King's feet. He didn't have the courage to meet Sverrin's eyes as Belphegore spoke. "Your Majesty, I must protest."

"And it is your right to do so," Sverrin said lightly. "My decision, however, is final. It has been twelve years. Merle has had ample time to overcome his grief and return to us peacefully."

"There was no peace. He's been hunted like a dog." The words left Zachary's mouth before he knew it. From behind he felt Emeric's fingers snag the back of his robe and give a tug of warning. Sverrin kept his attention locked challengingly on Belphegore.

"I made it clear to him he would be welcomed back if he returned. Even so, he has continued to run," Sverrin said patiently, almost kindly. "Now he has killed too many of my men. His power is too great and he is a liability to our whole kingdom. I know how fondly you thought of him but let me assure you, Lord Odin...*Belphegore*," his voice dripped with sincerity, "there is nothing left of the man you knew. His grief transformed him. He is an enemy of Harmatia and an enemy of Bethean."

Belphegore's expression was unreadable. He nodded stiffly and Sverrin gave a chaste smile. On his right, the King's mother sat forward in her throne. Regent for two years, Reine had relinquished much of her power to her son but remained an imposing political figure even now.

"As you all know, your duty as Magi is the highest honour in our court." She clasped her hands together daintily. "You are the pillars of the kingdom and we rely on you all to keep it strong. Rufus Merle was once your brother, but he is a rogue now. When he turned his back on Harmatia, he turned his back on you. I advise you then, not to be saddened by this news but to rejoice that soon justice will be seen. The good he did can be honoured without this taint." The firelight bathed her face, flickering hungrily over her. Her vicious mouth curled in each corner in a red-lipped smile as Sverrin leant across to her.

"Wise words, Mother," he congratulated, before addressing the Magi. "I wished only to keep you informed of this development. Thank you for your time. The banquet will be served in the hall for those who have the appetite to join us."

"Your Majesty." The Magi all bowed in unison and, led by Belphegore, made their way from the room. Sverrin rose from his seat and went to the fire, deep in thought. As Zachary made for the door, Sverrin called out for him.

"Lord Zachary, Lord Fold, if you could stay—I wish to speak to you in private."

A cold feeling enveloped Zachary's stomach and he stopped a few strides from the door, giving it a masked look of longing. Emeric too had gone white. Tentatively, the pair navigated their way back through the tide of Magi, all of whom quickened their step, unwilling to linger. From the corner of his eye, Zachary saw that Marcel had stepped out of the flow of people and was making his way back into the room. Zachary wondered vaguely if, had his master heard the request, Belphegore would have stayed too.

As the room emptied, Zachary put himself half-between Sverrin and Emeric. The King turned back to them and feigned surprise.

"Lord Hathely," he eyed Marcel, "you seem to have misunderstood the words 'in private'. Allow me to reiterate that it means 'alone'."

Marcel remained unmoved. "Lord Fold is my apprentice. Any fault of his lies with me. I take full responsibility."

"Marcel," Emeric hissed, his eyes flashing fearfully up to Sverrin.

Sverrin chuckled, a rich and pleasant sound but for the thin streak of malice that weaved through it. "You are quick to assume I've found fault in him. Perhaps I meant to praise him?"

"In private?" Marcel cocked a golden eyebrow. Sverrin and his mother both laughed, though the air was heavy and hot with discomfort.

"You are a loyal and dutiful lover, Lord Hathely," Reine said, scorn on her lips. "One that any woman would be proud to call husband."

Sverrin joined the jibe. "Or 'Master', in Lord Fold's case."

Anger filled Zachary at the spiteful nature of these words. There had been no laws in Harmatia against 'sodomy' for near a century, but with Kathra's growing influence in Sverrin's court, there were quiet considerations to reverse this. Subtle as the pair were in their relationship, people knew both Marcel and Emeric had been dedicated to each other for years. Sverrin's unspoken blackmail was enough to shake Zachary's apprehension. He strode forward, blocking his men from the King's view. He knew what this was really about—he'd been waiting for the reprimand.

"Stop," he said. "Stop it. It was my fault. I was the one who caused the ruckus with those students last week." Zachary caught Sverrin's arm as he attempted to turn. "Sverrin!" He lowered his voice. "It was *me*."

Sverrin met his gaze patiently and, for a dreadful minute, Zachary felt his resolve waver. There was something dark brewing beneath the King's gaze as he smiled again. "Lord Hathely, Lord Fold," he said, "kindly accompany my mother to the banquet— we will be along shortly."

Reine stood and walked gracefully by, stopping only to squeeze her son's hand, as a mother might when reminding her child to play nicely. Reluctantly, Emeric and Marcel followed the King's mother from the room. The door shut behind them.

Sverrin waited until their distant footfalls ceased to echo in the corridor outside, then returned to his seat, settling back into the wooden throne. He filled it as well as his father had, a muscular figure, powerful and strong. When he spoke however, his voice was gentle. "Zachary." He lost all formality, beckoning his friend over. "Did I ever tell you what it was like?"

"What?" Zachary joined him, standing at his feet.

"The two years I spent dead."

Zachary cleared his throat. He didn't like to think about those years, when obsession had made him devoid of anything good or pure. Sverrin watched him steadily.

"Did I ever tell you what it was like?"

"You said it was like being suffocated," Zachary said. "Crushed in darkness."

"Yes." Sverrin nodded sombrely. "You did not burn my soul free, so I remained, unable to pass into the next life or return to the old until you saved me. It was like being buried alive. But you, above anyone, can understand that terror."

Zachary shifted with discomfort and Sverrin sighed.

"But even from death, you faithfully returned me. I've always been able to trust you, Zachary. You have been a great friend and teacher to me for over twenty years. Which is why it pains me to see you turning from me now."

"Sverrin?" Zachary's stomach constricted as Sverrin lunged forward in his throne and seized Zachary's jaw between harsh fingers. His eyes burned like wild-fire and Zachary could see a sudden madness strumming through his King's blood. One look into Sverrin's face and Zachary's knees grew weak, nausea rising into his stomach.

"What is Rufus Merle to you?" Sverrin's grip didn't loosen, his voice terse.

"Nothing."

"Don't lie to me."

"I wouldn't," Zachary insisted.

Sverrin released him, pushing him back. The King's expression was torn between betrayal and anger. "You tried to kill him once for my sake," Sverrin reminded. "Why do you defend him now? He is a traitor."

"I defend the truth, no more," Zachary said.

"Rufus Merle is a dangerous man."

"And I would be too, if I were hunted! But I would be a man none the less." Alone as they were, Zachary allowed his voice to rise. "Athea—he's not a demon! He's not…not a monster. Sons of the gods," he cursed, "those Kathraks have turned him into a living nightmare!"

Something in those words seemed to stir Sverrin's interest. "*Those* Kathraks?" he said softly. Zachary didn't reply. "Not this again, Zachary." Sverrin rolled his eyes.

Zachary hesitated, glancing at the door pensively. "I am not alone in this. There's unrest, Sverrin. Kathra is our ally, but they're starting to take liberties. There are alchemists roaming our libraries, trying to get into the archives! They're learning techniques which are forbidden to all but the Magi. We are sworn to serve the kingdom, but these alchemists have no similar binding. Each day, they learn more and more of our secrets and Kathra grows in power."

Sverrin appeared puzzled. "But Zachary, did you not defy the stars to put a Kathrak King on this throne?"

"No, Sverrin." Zachary shook his head. "I defied the stars to put *you* on the throne. And the blood that makes you King is Harmatian."

Sverrin seemed to concede this, nodding thoughtfully. "Blood right is a funny thing in this city," he finally said. "I learnt that the day I shed mine at the hands of that Delphi assassin. The assassin you failed to stop."

The words struck hard, burrowing deeply into Zachary's gut like an arrow shaft. In an instant he felt defeated. Sverrin considered him, pleased by Zachary's beaten expression.

"Kathra is our fathering nation. The Magi have been greedy with their knowledge and stunted the growth of our neighbouring kingdoms. Having Magi Ambassadors is all very well but by sharing in this knowledge we have earned a favour far greater. You see, there is a crop in Kathra superior to ours. Do you know what it is?"

Zachary shook his head. He felt numb.

"Men," Sverrin said. "Soldiers, farmers, workers…cheap labour. The coffers of the castle have never been more full nor the bellies of my people."

Zachary didn't reply. He'd seen the cheap labour of which Sverrin spoke—men who were almost slaves, taken from their homes and put to work. As for those who reaped the benefit of a full coffer…It was a much more particular number than Sverrin liked to boast. Zachary kept his thoughts to himself. Sverrin seemed satisfied and quickly steered the conversation back to its original purpose.

"We have long underestimated the enemy. My father did and it led to my death. No more—I will rule with an iron fist and see that everyone knows Harmatia is not forgiving to those who betray her. So next time word comes up of Rufus Merle, word which has been warped to install a rightful sense of fear…Zachary, I would ask that you do not *defend* him. Am I understood?" There were unspoken words in this question, a threat, a warning, and maybe even a cruel invitation.

Zachary bowed low. "Yes, Your Majesty."

"Good." Sverrin clapped his hands, the sound loud in the hush of the room. "That will be all."

Again Zachary bowed, stepping back and walking out of the room. In the darkened corridor, Zachary composed himself. To the far right he could hear the large gathering in the hall, preparing for the banquet. Turning on his heel he set off to the left, up a flight of stairs. Zachary could hardly show himself in the great hall now, shaking as he was.

"There, see—Beshwa." Rufus lowered the map and pointed, with some satisfaction, down toward the village. Cushioned between the forest and the hills, it was a small industrial town, with a constant stream of smoke rising from the forger's chimneys, and water-mills that tirelessly worked the river. "I told you we weren't lost," Rufus said smugly.

Joshua scoffed. "We're three hours late. It would've been quicker to go through that passing rather than around it." Joshua broke off to clear his throat.

"The forest was too dense and there could've been a swamp. I had no desire for a repeat performance of our last venture. I'm never trusting the will-o'-the-wisps again."

Joshua gave a small snigger and urged his horse on toward the town. Rufus followed, pulling his dust mask up over his nose.

As they entered the town Rufus was struck by how different it was to their previous posting. Here, he could see poverty in the ill-keep of the houses and the beggars in the street.

Glancing around the street, Rufus pulled up and tried to get his bearings. He didn't know the Moineau family, nor were they expecting him, so there was no indication where they lived.

Spotting a common stable in the corner, Rufus waved to a rather bleary looking stable boy, who blinked stupidly. "Yes, you." Rufus beckoned again as the stable boy pointed up to himself, unsure. "Have you got room for two more?" Rufus held up a couple of coin.

The stable boy glanced back into the stable behind him, and then signalled Rufus to wait, as he went in to check.

Rufus grumbled, rubbing his eyes. They were tired already from the dust which hung in the air. Turning back, he found Joshua was engaged in conversation with a rather haphazardly dressed woman. She had a good figure, rolling hips and buxom breasts which bulged over her frail, openly cut chemise, her waist bundled into a sensuous purple corset.

Wonderful. Rufus gritted his teeth. *My brother is being accosted by the local whore.*

"He's lovely," she said, stroking Joshua's horse, her fingers tickling its velvet nose. "I've never ridden a fine breed like this. Bet his stride's smooth as satin."

"You can have a go if you like, I don't mind," Joshua offered and Rufus shuffled his own horse across, intervening with a warning cough.

"Bless you, sweetness," the whore cooed, "but I'm not sure your companion would approve. Good day to you, sir." She caught Rufus's eyes mischievously.

"Good day," he said tersely, tipping his head.

"Your page's offerin' me a turn on his horse."

"He's my son, and so I hear." Rufus frowned across to Joshua, who ignored him, trying to flatten his hair which was wild from the wind. Glancing back to the stable, Rufus searched hopefully for the stable boy. He'd yet to emerge.

"Your son?" the whore continued. "Beggin' your pardon sir, I see it now—you've the same eyes. Wager he takes after the lady then?"

Rufus didn't reply, still looking desperately for the stable boy. The whore remained undaunted. "Will she be joinin' you in Beshwa? Or are you free for the night?"

"We're free," Joshua answered in Rufus's stead. "My mother died a long time ago."

"My blessed boy—I'm so sorry! And my condolences sir, what a heartache you must've borne."

"Yes. I certainly bore it," Rufus said between his teeth, glad of his mask. He didn't feel comfortable out in the street, exposed.

"I can help with that." The whore moved across to him, unabashed by his dismissive tone. She studied him carefully, her eyes a pale grey.

"With what?" he asked, almost aggressively.

"Your grief. Your anger. I know just the way to ease your troubles right out from under you. Especially after so long."

"I'm sure you do," Rufus's said snidely. "Harlot."

"Papa!" Joshua gasped, and the whore smiled, putting her hands on her hips as if the name pleased her. "I'm sorry, he's tired from the journey," Joshua said, eyeing Rufus who turned away sulkily.

"No, no—I understand." The whore seemed amused. "Harmatian men can't always stomach the open way of the Betheanian women."

Rufus grunted in disagreement, his thoughts on Luca with her hitched skirt and shoulder-less dresses, and how she would candidly strip naked to swim, never ashamed of what nature had given her, nor embarrassed of how others might react to her sweet body. Rufus missed her sorely in that moment.

"Apologise," Joshua commanded him.

"No."

"*Rufus,*" his brother said in a warning tone and Rufus turned angrily back.

"I only called her what she was," he snapped and was surprised to find the whore laughing. She beckoned him down toward her, as if she meant to tell him a secret. Despite himself, he leant across. She reached her hand up and pulled down his mask.

"Rufus Merle?" she asked and his heart seized. She released the mask and stepped back. "Easy." She saw him tighten his grip around the reins. "The Moineau said you'd come. They gave me the key to their house to deliver to you…Though you're six months early."

Rufus couldn't believe his ears.

"It can't be. You mean to say—you're a Delphi Knight?"

She squawked, tossing back her head, her hand on her hip.

"The man who bedded my mother was, so I suppose there's a lingerin' attachment. No need to sound so horrified."

"Apologies," Rufus said sheepishly.

"Forgiven—but only because you're handsome." She winked, fluttering her eye lashes.

"Where have the Moineau gone?" Rufus pressed. She gave a languid roll of her shoulders.

"How should I know? Way I see it, they fled to sanctuary."

"Why?" Joshua leant in, worriedly.

"Your guess is as good as mine. Bethean's growin' dangerous, don't you know? Kathraks are walkin' these roads now, askin' questions, lookin' for the Knights. Sometimes they even catch one. I'd flee too, if I had a neck worth gold. Here." She pulled up her skirts and stripped away a heavy set of keys, which had been sewed into her undergarments. She passed them up to Rufus. "It's the third house on the far right of the square. I'll come and deliver food, and any messages that get past on, and maybe you'll let me stay for a night, if you're feelin' generous?"

"I won't be," Rufus assured.

"Hard one to tempt." She didn't seem put out by the challenge and caught a coin expertly as Rufus flicked it down to her. She examined it, giving him a grin worthy of a Korrigan. Rufus shuddered. "I'll be gone then. Don't fret, pretty—my legs are always open but my mouth remains sealed."

And with that she sauntered off, just as the stable boy arrived to take Rufus and Joshua's horses.

CHAPTER 6

<P>erhaps the most unforgiving part of court life was that privacy was a rare luxury. In a castle teeming with servants, Magi and the rest of the gentry, Zachary had learnt from a young age that no place in Harmatia was truly safe. People saw and people listened.

He was eight years old when he first came to the capital. Unimpressive, scrawny and tight-lipped, he was four years younger than the rest of his class and had learnt very quickly where he stood in the hierarchy of the academy. It took him years of steady investment to build up the loyalty of his peers and, at the height of his career, Zachary had enjoyed the sanctuary he'd built in his new home. Harmatia became his city, a place where he was respected and even loved—a faithful wife for whom he would gladly lay down his life.

But the times changed, as they were prone to, and where once the streets had offered him a modicum of power and security, they reverted now to their conspiratorial and watchful state. Fortunately for Zachary, his childhood status as an outcast had provided him with an intimate acquaintance of the castle grounds. He'd come to know well the dark nooks and corners where secrets might dwell unnoticed a while. For the most part, he was much too big now to fit comfortably into many of them but there was one that had become a frequent haunt in the growing months—a small, secluded perch on the roof between the Great Library and the castle.

It was here Zachary stood now, smoking between two squatting gargoyles. These days it seemed one of the only places he could think clearly, away from the pressures of endless court politics. Zachary needed a space where he didn't have to train his expression according to who was watching. Up here, he could be as playful or as gloomy as he liked.

Blowing out forcefully, Zachary watched as the smoke dispelled into the crisp air above him, his fingers tight around his pipe. He felt wretched. An uneasy energy had been waging siege on him for some time, battling against a muscular lethargy that refused to let him expel it. He'd tried a number of things to rid himself of the heavy feeling—daily rides, extra training, long walks at night—but more and more he'd begun to grow wearily accustomed to it. He would stay abed hours longer than he ought to, and would sigh and heave at the thought of doing things which had once brought him pleasure. He'd grown still in a speeding world. When he wasn't submitting to this fatigue, he would feel flushed and nervous instead. Paranoia ruled him and Zachary knew why.

At first, the joy of Sverrin's revival had blinded Zachary to the truth. Sverrin was just as he'd been—strong, decisive and ambitious. He laughed loud and hard, drank and duelled with Zachary, raced him around the city on horseback. But as the years had ripened, a dark ache of uncertainty began to form like a stone in Zachary's gut. It had been small things at first—the hollow way Sverrin sometimes looked at people, how he could stand so still like death was upon him again, the strange hunger that sometimes appeared on his face when he thought no one was looking...

Over time, there were little occurrences—irregularities in behaviour, so small one might not have noticed them. Sverrin forgot simple things or replaced certain truths with others, as if they were facts. He would fabricate tiny events that Zachary knew hadn't happened and seemed uncertain about his own memories. The first time the changes had really struck Zachary however, was the incident with the dog.

One of Sverrin's hounds obtained an injury during a hunt, after being kicked by a dying buck. The poor dog was old, slower than it used to be. They'd discovered it keening and moaning in pain beside the dead deer. Sverrin had frowned, tutted and then, without any occasion, shot the dog through the head and turned homeward with their game. Zachary had been horrified. The dog may not have been capable of hunting again but it could have certainly lived another few years, retired and warm by the fire. It had been such a loyal and loving pet, Zachary couldn't believe Sverrin had been capable of putting it down solely on the loss of its usefulness.

Up until then, Sverrin's peculiarities were easily ignored, but from that moment their presence grew on Zachary until they were all he could see. Soon the truth was stifling him, like a foul and potent poison in his veins. Each year, Sverrin seemed to be less of himself and more of something else.

Loyalty became a formality, an empty shell. Even Sverrin had sensed Zachary's unease. And like that, the sparks of a once roaring friendship died, withering away like an aging man. For Zachary, who'd loved Sverrin, the frustration of it all could have brought him to tears, did it not simultaneously rob him of the ability to indulge in such a relief.

Zachary brought the pipe back up to his mouth. He sucked it and expelled a huge cloud of smoke, allowing it to billow over him. He felt truly hopeless.

"Arlen?"

A hand touched his shoulder. Zachary's heart bolted and he

pushed off from the wall, spinning on the spot. On the narrow ledge, he stumbled slightly and an arm shot from the darkness and held him in place as he regained his balance, poised on the edge. Belphegore exhaled in relief and pulled Zachary back safely against the wall.

"By Notameer's Light, you gave me a scare there," Belphegore said. Zachary slumped into a crouch, his arm clutched against his chest as his heart thundered.

"Oh, I am intimate with the feeling myself, Master," he said. "How did you get up here?"

"The same way I presume you did, Arlen—there was a window, rather conveniently propped open, on the top floor corridor."

Zachary felt himself smile. At over a hundred and seventy years, Belphegore was as agile as a man a quarter of his age. Even so, it didn't cast away the rather amusing image of his master hoisting himself up through the window and shinning up the ledge onto the flat of the roof.

"How did you know I was here?"

"I heard renewed rumours that the gargoyles were coming to life." Belphegore came and sat beside Zachary, settling himself at his apprentice's side. "It took no great stretch of the imagination to guess you might be responsible."

Zachary cackled. It was true that on several occasions he'd transformed into his Night Patrol form up here and been spotted by walkers in the courtyard below. Rather than call him for what he was however, they'd mistaken him for living stone, and tales of Harmatia's cursed gargoyles quickly spread among the students. Zachary was so delighted by the rebirth of the stories that, on occasion, he would even swap the heavy gargoyles at night just to give the tale more gravity. It was one of the few treats he allowed himself and one of the few things that could draw him from his drained stupor.

His laughter died down and he felt immediately drained

again. He sat and stretched out his legs, sticking them over the ledge.

"How do you do it, Master?" he sighed deeply.

Belphegore considered his question a long while.

"That's a rather ambiguous question, Arlen. But I suppose I can tell you that, for the best performance, the key lies in the correct rotation of the wrist."

Again Zachary sniggered.

"I have no idea what you're referring to, Master, and I am perfectly sure I don't wish to."

"No?" Belphegore asked innocently. "I speak of sword play."

"Of course you do."

"I am not sure I like what you're implying, Arlen." Belphegore scowled but there was relief in his voice as Zachary chuckled again. "It's good to hear you laugh," Belphegore said and Zachary sobered, hunching a little. He felt like a boy who'd been freshly apprenticed again, and he pressed his face into his hands. They were cold from the stone.

"If I may ask a more pertinent question, what are *you* doing up here?" Belphegore asked, and Zachary grunted, shaking his head. "Speak to me, Arlen, please. I am worried."

For a minute Zachary struggled to find the words.

"I feel so tired," was all he could summon. He saw Belphegore frown. His master shifted closer so their shoulders touched lightly.

"You are a quarter my age, Arlen, and less than a fifth of the way through your potential life. You should not be tired."

"But I am." Zachary pressed a fist into his chest, almost desperately. "In here, I am tired. I feel lifeless, listless."

"Arlen…"

"Am I sick, Master?" Zachary asked, almost hopefully.

Belphegore pursed his lips, his eyes cast over the city before them.

"Perhaps," he eventually whispered and Zachary exhaled,

shutting his eyes. "You argued with the King, did you not?"

Zachary huffed.

"Argued implies there was a fair exchange of words. I was scolded for speaking out of turn."

"Is that so bad?"

Zachary couldn't explain that threats, which would have been laughable coming from anyone else, held a more sincere gravity from Sverrin's lips. His King knew almost all the horrors about Zachary, had seen his scars and known a truth that very few were privy to. A truth that made Zachary vulnerable. For those he loved, he was a slave.

"I would rather he had me whipped."

"Do not say that so lightly."

"I say it with the greatest consideration," Zachary grumbled, bringing his legs up against the cold. A great portion of the Magi believed he had some advantageous ailment whereby he couldn't feel pain at all. It wasn't true—Zachary felt everything very keenly, but he knew how to prioritise pain and when to bite his tongue.

Belphegore made a sound of discomfort.

"You and I have had our differences Arlen," he almost seemed to apologise, "but I do not want to see you hurt." He turned to his apprentice. "And I do not like to see you in this state either."

"Apologies." Zachary bowed dutifully.

"None are required—least of all to me. But I think that Lord Fold and Lord Hathely would not be pleased to see you out here alone like this. Indeed, I believe they would be very frightened."

"Frightened? For what reason?" Zachary couldn't mask his surprise, and the lines on Belphegore's brow deepened.

"As any friend would be," Belphegore said, "when another looks down with despondence to the courtyard hundreds of strides below—and considers it."

Zachary's whole body clenched sharply. He refused to meet Belphegore's eye as the older man stood and began to make his way back toward the corner.

"Master," Zachary called, before Belphegore could leave. "Do you think he's dead? Merle, that is?"

Belphegore contemplated the darkness before speaking. When he did, his voice was firm and almost angry.

"Rufus—an apprentice of mine—die in such a way? Never," he said confidently. "Absolutely not."

"Oh, the ever unwavering faith in the favourite," Zachary replied snidely but there was no real malice in his words.

"Jealous, Arlen?" Belphegore didn't deny the accusation. Zachary grinned.

"Jealous? Of Rufus Merle? The man who will be hunted now for the rest of his life? No, there's pity owed to the poor bastard."

⁓⁓

"The point is to watch the sunset." Jionat's elbow met his ribs and Rufus squirmed. He cracked an eye open, almost suspiciously. Jionat stared at him pointedly.

"I've seen a hundred sunsets from this spot," Rufus said, looking out over Sarrin town which lay below them. "It was the peace I was enjoying. Until you spoke, of course, and spoiled it."

Jionat grumbled but didn't reply. The pair sat and admired the golden, autumnal hue that blazed over the town. Jionat began to hum softly to the tune of 'Swallows', kicking his legs. Further along the wall, a nightingale hopped along the stones, singing in short, sweet verse.

She wasn't alone either. A shadow passed over them, a large falcon circling overhead, dropping steadily in height. The nightingale didn't seem deterred by his presence and sang her chorus louder.

"This is a dream," Rufus realised.

"How do you know?"

"I just thought of how much Joshua would like it here…"

"Then imagine him up. He can enjoy himself while we talk."

"You're not real," Rufus said softly. Jionat laughed.

"I'm as real as you are."

"No," Rufus murmured. "This is a fantasy—a fiction. You're not Jionat."

"I never said I was."

Rufus frowned. An uneasy darkness spread from the corner of his peripheral, almost like he was waking up slowly. The nightingale disappeared into the shadow, her cries shrill, but the falcon swooped lower, steady in his circles. Jionat continued to laugh—he sounded nothing like he was supposed to.

"Honestly," he said, "you summon me here to collect your thoughts and then waste your time arguing with me, when all I am is you answering yourself."

Rufus's mind stirred with the confusing words. This was a nightmare—he needed to wake up. Rufus turned sharply, but he couldn't escape Jionat. The rest of the world blurred into a dark streak of intelligible colours. They swirled nauseatingly.

"You can't run from me, I'm as trapped here as you are. You conjured me for a reason."

"You're not real!" Rufus felt himself grow tight with agitation, trying to cast away the unwanted phantom.

"Then neither are you."

Rufus growled, throwing his hands in the air. "If you're truly a manifestation of mine," he said, "and I'm arguing with myself, than why in Athea's name would you appear as Jionat?"

"We both know the answer to that." Jionat raised his eyebrows, as if Rufus had said something stupid. "You're obsessed by your loss. Do you recall another man like that?"

"Stop it." Rufus pressed his hands to his ears, but couldn't drown out the voice.

"Obsession drains a man of life by giving him a reason to live," Jionat said. "Frankly, if I could change faces, I would. But it's not up to me."

"Leave me alone."

"Alone, you die. I'm your instincts—ignore me at your peril."

"I don't want you here."

"It's not about want anymore, it's need. I'm here because you need me. So you'd better start paying attention to what I tell you."

"You haven't told me anything."

"Now that's simply not true." Jionat tsked as the shadows finally reached him and swallowed him up, the world turning black. "Pay attention, Rufus."

CHAPTER
7

⁓

He woke to the sound of someone being silent. Rufus had always been a light sleeper by nature but his recent circumstances had accentuated that to the point where even the lightest shift in the room could wake him. Nothing seemed to move at all in the dark. The room was paralysed. Rufus knew he'd already betrayed himself. It was impossible to pretend to still be asleep. His heart was racing, and the natural state of slumber had left his muscles.

"Ah, sensitive as always. Figured I'd let you sloth some more, but now you're goin' to piss your pot."

The voice was thickly accented, and gravelly from sea-air. Betheanian—port town, probably Lemra'n. Rufus shuddered and then rolled from the bed. He dove to the other side of the room, his back against the wall as he faced his enemy. In the dim light, the figure that greeted him wasn't a reassuring one.

The man wasn't as tall as Rufus but nearly twice his width with firm muscles and a heavy build. He was bearded, supporting a thick mane of full brown hair, and similar coloured eyes. His features were unremarkable but there was a terrifying sense of dexterity about him. If he hunched his shoulders and pulled a cloak over his toned arms, he could fade into a crowd. Rufus shook, edging along the wall as the man took another step toward him, eyes never leaving Rufus's face.

"Who are you?" Rufus's voice came out horribly weak. "How did you get in here?"

"Don't snivel now—I'm not some second-rate slit-throat. I'm from the Faucon. You can relax."

"Oh, you're a *professional* assassin. That's infinitely better." The snide retort didn't cover the tremor in his voice. "What do you want?"

"What any man wants—not to be pocketless. But only beggars choose which purses they cut. I've been landed with you. Still—and you can mark me on this—havin' to be a trained ejaculator for those Kathrak bastards really buggers me up sideways. It's the sweet talk, you know? It rots the mouth." He bared his teeth proudly. They were strangely sharp and gleaming white. "Still, I'm here for now. Lesser of two evils, if you will. What Cethin says goes, so no point questionin'."

"I understood about a quarter of that," Rufus admitted, despite his fear.

"You've clearly never been to Lemra," the assassin almost purred. "I'm here to resolve that. So be a good 'ti kitten and get in the bag."

Rufus remained where he was and the assassin gave a dramatic sigh.

"Or I can la'man you like the high-pitcher you are, if that'll take your fancy somewhat more. And if you're unplucked, all the sweeter for me, accord?"

Rufus tried to translate the words. He had a feeling that whatever the assassin was proposing, Rufus wouldn't enjoy it. Alternatively, he was almost certain that when kittens were put into a bag, the general design was to drown them. He edged along the wall slowly.

"And if I were to refuse both kind offers?"

The assassin seemed surprised.

"Now that never crossed my mind," he admitted. "Didn't brain you'd be so difficult...Bollocks on ice—now you've put me in the corner." He paused, deep in thought. "Alternatively, I might remind you that you don't have a choice."

"Ah." Rufus's hands touched wood behind him as he found the door.

"I don't like to use force in these situations," the assassin said with a careless shrug, "unless it's part of the routine. I'm no shine-grabber per say—wouldn't be glazed-eyed about nobody else's job. But in cases like this I'd prefer it if I could just play it fast and calm-like. I can be a real thumb-screw if I want, so don't be a fire-eater about it—"

He didn't get the chance to finish. Rufus threw his back against the door raised his hands and summoned a ball of flames large enough to suck the very air from his lungs. He launched it at the assassin, throwing himself back out of the room.

Rufus hit the floor as the assassin bellowed in surprise. Rufus scrabbled back and found his feet. Beyond the wall of fire the assassin was still standing, his arms raised up around his head. The fire had not touched him.

Rufus's stomach plummeted. A magical shield had appeared around assassin—he could use elemental magic then, and was a level four at least. Rufus didn't wait, diving backward through the corridor toward Joshua's room. As he did, he threw his own mental shield back toward the assassin. As long as the Lemra'n used a mental shield to protect himself from the flames, he couldn't cross Rufus's.

Throwing Joshua's door open, Rufus came face to face with the sharp point of a drawn arrow. He threw his hands in the air in immediate surrender. His little brother drew away, letting the bowstring back as he lowered his weapon. Rufus didn't need to say anything. One look at his face, bathed in the dying light of the fire, and Joshua turned and gathered his things, throwing a cloak over his shoulders. Rufus praised their luck that they'd been too exhausted to unpack their saddlebags properly.

Together, the pair hurried down the stairs. Rufus snatched his shoes from the doorway in passing. He didn't bother to put them on, running bare-foot and half-naked into the streets. It was cold and raining, a light mist hanging in the air. In the back of his mind, Rufus felt the assassin's shield drop. Either it had failed or the Lemra'n had found another means of escape. Rufus immediately let his own fall, dispelling the flames he'd summoned before they caught in the house and spread to the surrounding buildings. Rufus wouldn't be responsible for burning the entire town to the ground.

The brothers broke into the stable. The stable boy jumped up in surprise from where he'd been slumbering in the corner. Without the time to explain their predicament, Rufus grabbed him and threw him into one of the unoccupied stalls, bolting the stall door shut after.

"Rufus!" Joshua cried in horror, but Rufus pushed his brother on. He spotted their two horses stalled in the far corner. They didn't have the time to tack the pair, and neither would take the weight of them both. Without hesitation, Rufus found the strongest, healthiest horse he could see and began to tack him instead. Joshua objected but Rufus ignored him, throwing his bags over the horse's back. He dumped everything but the bare essentials.

Hoisting Joshua onto the horse, Rufus climbed up behind, his body quaking as his bare feet met the cold metal of the stirrups. He urged the horse on, one hand gripping the reins whilst the other held his boots pinned against the saddle. His legs caught painfully on the stirrup straps through the soft cotton of his night clothes, but he ignored them.

From in-front of him, Joshua shifted uncomfortably.

"This might be someone's only livelihood, Rufus," Joshua whispered. Rufus felt the words rather then heard them.

With the cold biting his skin and his heart hammering, he

snarled, "I don't care."

They came out of the stable, the horses' hooves loud on the cobbles. The hair on the back of Rufus's neck rose and his senses prickled in warning.

Before he had time to think, Rufus pushed Joshua down against the horse's neck just as a blast of air came flying out from the gloom and struck them. Rufus didn't have time to raise his shield properly and was sent tumbling down onto the hard, icy cobbles below. He landed directly in a puddle.

"Papa!" The horse reared in panic as Joshua screamed. The Prince had managed to stay on. Rufus gasped, pain searing down his body—something had cracked in his ribcage.

"Go!" Rufus dragged himself to his feet, cotton trousers clinging to his legs. Already his teeth had begun to chatter from the cold. "*Go!*" he choked again and struck the horse along the hindquarters, sending it galloping off toward the forest.

Rufus staggered, trying to find his boots which he'd dropped in the fall. Fat, heavy droplets of rain blurred the hazy outline of the houses as Rufus squinted, raising a weak shield around himself. It was hard to breath, and the pain made his magic waver.

Another attack came from his left. Although the shield dispelled most of the force, Rufus still found himself flat on his back. His body cried out at this mistreatment but Rufus didn't have the time to indulge it. Wheezing, he struggled to his feet again, trying to spot his attacker. The rain made it difficult to summon anything but a substantial flame, and that ran the risk of getting out of control. In an environment where he couldn't see well and was surrounded by houses, the risks were too high for Rufus to blithely throw about his chosen element.

Fortunately for Rufus, his assassin was a confident man.

He emerged through a curtain of rain like death itself, hair dripping and face twisted in disturbed amusement. "Now that was unnecessary—fire-ballin' me in the face like that. I might've died."

"That was the general idea."

"Bastard," the assassin chuckled. "But you took my surprise, I'll give you that. Wasn't very professional of me. I'm no gold-licker per say but if anyone found out you nearly cooked my balls, I'd be sure to lose some grain. Lucky then that you and I are the only whoopsies who'll ever know."

"You talk in a distressingly odd way," Rufus replied. He needed to buy Joshua as much time as he could to flee. "Is it all Lemra'n slang or do you put an extra effort into it?"

"You know what?" The Lemra'n grinned. "I've decided I like you, Rufus Torinson Merle."

Rufus winced. His full name was hardly a secret but Rufus didn't appreciate hearing it rolling off this stranger's tongue.

"Who sent you?"

"Hah—who didn't?" the assassin laughed. "Honest to Notameer, everyone wants to suckle from your teat. What d'you do?"

"You know my name, you know what I am. I've killed dozens of men." Rufus circled slowly, putting himself between the assassin and the path Joshua had taken.

"Rah, you're a murderer, but then I'm a murderer and n'one's huntin' me...'least not very well." He gave a playful look over his shoulder and Rufus quickly assessed his situation. He was at a heavy disadvantage. The assassin's shield was sound and protected him completely, whilst Rufus's own was wavering and weak. Pain was robbing him of crucial concentration. What was more, his magic was limited by the proximity of the buildings around him and his own exhaustion. If the fight escalated, he risked drawing attention to himself and alerting the local authorities to his presence. The alchemists who hunted him were one thing, but Rufus had no desire to hurt the innocent town guards who would be obliged, by law, to arrest him on sight. The assassin, armed as he was and with no similar restraints, had the advantage.

The Magi gritted his teeth. His only choice was to run. Half-naked, barefoot and exhausted, the odds against him in combat were too great. His odds of escaping, unfortunately, were no greater.

"Are you going to kill me?"

"You ask some real brainless questions."

"I try."

"Rah, but if you've quite finished dawdlin' the point so your little younglin' can fly, then perhaps we can cut to the business and I can get after him whilst you dry off in the Pit? Lest he loses himself in the wood and meets somethin' worse than I."

All the hairs rose on Rufus's body. He dropped his forced stance into a defensive. The assassin was after Joshua as well.

"I won't let you!" he snarled.

"Eh?"

"You won't touch a hair on his head. I'll kill you before you do!"

"Woah—easy now, snake eyes! I'm not some pleasure-seeker scoutin' the nursery—don't be pointin' your sharp at me." The assassin, for the first time, seemed offended.

"I'll make you regret ever taking this contract, assassin!" Rufus's anger drove his hopelessness away and his shield strengthened with his resolve. Orbs of flames appeared in both hands, burning brightly despite the rain.

The assassin whistled between his teeth, eyeing the fire that licked harmlessly over Rufus's skin. He raised his hands, as if to negotiate.

"I really don't think you're seein' the order of things here. You're not supposed to sun-kiss me. Seems like you're hoppin' a little too far along the steppin' stones. Take a minute now, breathe and consider your cards—I'm the least of your troubles."

"At this time, you hold prime position." The flames around Rufus's hands grew white hot, the rain around him dissolving into steam. Their positions were shifting, Rufus into an offensive

74

and the assassin into a wary defensive.

"You're makin' this difficult for me," the assassin said, his tone dropping. Rufus didn't reply, the fire extending up his wrists to his elbows. The Lemra'n sighed. "What's a man to do? Everyone's a-gone a hibernatin' and left me with a quarter-wit. I'll have some words to pick and chew when this is done, mark me. Put those suns down, Merle, and clear your trap of smoke. Look at me. Now look around you. You've nowhere to run, so stop bein' a muscle about it. Stubborn's good and an' all, but you've got no rock to cling to."

When Rufus gave no obvious sign of surrender, the assassin threw his hands irritably into the air.

"Just *give in*, you high-mined tommy boy. Don't make me cut you."

"Come at me, if you dare," Rufus snarled.

The assassin's face twisted into an impatient scowl, as he slowly began to circle around looking for an opening.

"You're startin' to try me."

"And you're starting to speak coherently."

"You know what, I said I savvy'd you—I take it back."

"The feeling is mutual," Rufus replied, his shield growing as his mind focused. The assassin gave a defeated shrug and from his back retrieved a short bow, which he began to string.

"Right, that's it—you're losin' a leg," he declared, as if it were a reasonable exchange. Rufus confidence withered a little. He wasn't certain of the speed of his reflexes. It was possible he could burn the arrow before it hit him, but that might not stop the arrow head itself from reaching him. If he were in the woods, he might have been able to make the earth rise around him in a protective wall but the cobbles below him were more difficult. He'd never been an expert on the manipulation of pure stone.

His only chance was to knock the projectile off course by using a burst of air. But the assassin had been clever with his timing. It was nearing the eleventh hour and Etheus's power was waning as the Air God's star set. Rufus might be able to divert the first arrow, but the one that followed would be up to chance. He set his teeth hard into his lip, worry weakening his shield again.

An arrow shot over his shoulder, clattering between the cobbles at the assassin's feet. The assassin grunted and stepped back, startled. Rufus looked around, his heart in his mouth. For a terrible moment, he thought his brother had returned to save him. Instead he found the whore from that afternoon. She stood on a balcony above them, reloading a crossbow, which she trained on the assassin again, her eyes ablaze as she shook out her mane of dark hair.

"You stay where you are," she said, and Rufus sagged with relief. The assassin cocked his head and slowly put his hands in the air.

"Piss-pox and plagues, is this a joke?" the assassin laughed in disbelief. The whore smiled, her crossbow never leaving its mark.

"'fraid not, slit-throat. Lay your bow or I'll pin you good."

"Put it down, woman," the assassin said darkly. "This has nothin' to do with you—go back to your mirror!"

"Nothin' personal, lover, just been paid to see him through." She glanced to Rufus. "Go—your son can't have gotten far. I'll hold him off."

"Thank you," Rufus said.

"I'll be sorry to see you go, pretty one," she tittered, her eyes trained back on her target. "Was looking forward to spendin' more time with you. Never mind. If you're ever in need of some company, my name is Emerald Colombe. I'll come, if you call—for the right coin, of course."

"Thank you, Emerald." Rufus bowed his head, then with a quick look back at the assassin, Rufus seized his boots and dove after his brother into the night.

CHAPTER 8

"Don't you ever, ever, *ever* do that again, Rufus!"

Joshua was bowed over the saddle, his entire body raking with sobs. Rufus reached for him, but Joshua turned sharply away, face hidden in the crook of his elbow. From beneath his arm, Rufus could see the Prince's mouth twisting, his arm jerking in time with the deep, uprooting sobs.

Tying the horse to a branch, Rufus dragged Joshua down from the saddle and held him fiercely, pressing his face into Joshua's wet hair. The pair shivered violently.

"I'm sorry," Rufus croaked. "But this is the way it's always been. I face the enemy, and you hide."

"No, it's not the same!" Joshua cried. "You don't *face* them— you don't *fight* them! We've always run from them!"

Rufus flinched, but it was true. It was one thing to overpower men in the spur of the moment, as he dodged between the trees and ambushed them, but Rufus was no warrior. He'd only ever faced one person in open combat and Arlen Zachary hadn't really been trying to kill him, of that Rufus was sure.

"It's different now." Joshua was furious amidst his fear. "The Kathraks wanted to capture you before, now they're trying to *kill* you! I can break you out of a cell, but I can't bring you back from the dead! You should've let me help! I could've *helped!*"

"I'm sorry, I wanted to protect you. I'm sorry. I won't do it again."

"You can't promise that," Joshua hiccupped, his voice strained and high.

Rufus's resolve sank and he fought back his own sobs at his brother's misery.

"You're right—I can't," he admitted. "I won't even promise to try…" his voice lilted up and broke off.

"Don't leave me behind!" Joshua wailed. "Don't die and leave me alone!"

"You wouldn't be alone, Joshua. There are people who care for you, people who would—"

"No!" Joshua pulled violently away and his voice pierced Rufus to the core, eyes burning blue and glowing with magic. "You're the only thing I have! Don't leave me. Don't leave me, Papa. Please don't leave me. Please…" His voice broke off as Rufus pulled him urgently back in, heart thundering.

"I won't," he said. "I promise, I promise I won't leave you. I won't. Never. Please don't cry. I'll never leave you. As long as you need me. Please don't cry Joshua. Please," he sobbed, collapsing to his knees in the mud. "We'll find a safe place…"

Joshua nodded jerkily and reluctantly released Rufus, allowing him to stand. Rufus went to their saddle bags and pulled on a long tunic and his cloak, the fabric sticking to his wet skin. Dressed, he helped Joshua back onto the horse and, climbing up after him, he untied the reins and pushed it on into a trot. They needed to find shelter and, when they did, Rufus would build the biggest fire he could.

~~~

As the night fell into its full glory, Harmatia settled into sleep. The castle lay still as its occupants floated through the privacy of their dreams. But for some, who'd been trained to keep vigil over the night, the habit wasn't so easily shaken.

Having removed himself from his perch, Zachary descended into the castle and went to the chapel. It was an ornate, round room with ten alcoves carved into the stone and a painted, domed roof. Each alcove housed an altar, each with a statue of one of the ten True Gods: Malak, Etheus, Prospan, Haylix, Penthar, Hexias, Septus, Octania, Athea and Notameer. Directly opposite the door, and against the far wall, was a large statue of Aramathea, the mother of the True Gods, depicted as she often was, with a blindfold, pearly tears seeping out from underneath. She held a sword up in one hand, and in the other, a baby.

The walls were decorated exquisitely with the depictions and silent stories of the gods. Above Penthar's altar, a great battle was being fought between the Warrior God with his six swords, and the Wild Hunt—the Fomorii forces of darkness. In contrast above Haylix, the goddess of children and youth, there was a depiction of a young woman, lounging in a field of white flowers, weaving them into a garland.

Athea and Notameer, stood either side of Aramathea, were decorated with contrary but echoing images. Above each, a shapeless, human figure stood emblazoned with light. For Athea, it was a sunset, casting a fiery red hue around the silhouette, whilst for Notameer it was a sunrise, bright and golden. It was a depiction of the Children of Aramathea: those born at precisely six o'clock at night, or six o'clock in the morning.

It was said that the Children of Aramathea were the living vessels of the gods themselves, walking the earthly plain. Those born at sunset were Athea reincarnated—passionate, emotional, with fire raging in their blood. Whilst those born at sunrise were Notameer—just, thoughtful and patiently calculating.

Zachary had known one of each. It was strange to think that his bookish brother Rufus, so fond of knowledge and so pacifistic, had been the vessel of Athea all along, whilst

Belphegore, leader of the Magi, warrior and founder of the Night Patrol, was the incarnation of Notameer. It spoke in abundance on the complexity of the gods, so easily misunderstood by the humans who tried to interpret them simply.

But Zachary hadn't come to the chapel to think about that. Instead he sat before the more modest statue of Septus, the God of Healing. Zachary knew that his master had been down before him, because a customary red candle had been lit on Septus's altar. Red candles were to commemorate the dead.

It hadn't been long now since Morgo Edwin, previous leader of the healing sect, had passed away. In his careful attendance to others, he'd contracted a dreadful illness of his own. His final hours were a confusion of fever and pain, where he gabbled and talked in incessant panic. The sickness itself, which had come on suddenly, hadn't spread to any of the other Magi. Zachary had heard whispers of poison, though the physicians who'd attended Edwin—his own apprentices—had denied anything of the sort.

Zachary and Belphegore were with Edwin in his final moments. Edwin had been the greatest and truest friend to Belphegore, whilst to Zachary he'd been an uncle and protector throughout his youth. His loss weighed heavily on the pair of them. Zachary could only imagine what it had been like for his master to outlive a friend he'd served so diligently with for decades. It would be akin to Zachary losing Marcel—a thought which he couldn't abide.

"Edwin," Zachary huffed softly. He sometimes liked to come and speak with the man, though he held no true belief that his former guardian could hear him. "Harmatia still misses you, old friend. I wouldn't mind your council. To be frank, I don't like or trust your apprentices." He snorted to himself. "Yes, yes, I know—I am being stubborn. Alas, men are not so easily trusted these days."

He studied the red candle intently, willing it to give him some sort of reply. Unbidden, Edwin's final minutes came back to

Zachary. They'd not been happy ones, and though great cares had been seen to diminish Edwin's suffering, no one had been able to quail his confused panic.

"*It was wrong. We should have never done it. It was wrong,*" Edwin had gabbled and Belphegore had cast everyone else from the room, lest they hear this confession.

"*Belphegore, my ambition clouded me. It's all clouded. And now I will be punished. The gods will punish me.*"

They'd tried to assure him, to put him at ease—a man such as Edwin, who'd dedicated so much of himself to the care of others could never be condemned to anything but the highest paradise. And yet, none of their words had brought him peace, only more agitation. He'd gripped at them desperately.

"*We should have never brought him back. That thing—it's not human! It's not our King. We should have let him lie. My friend, I was so obsessed with my need to revive the lost, I negated the consequences…and now I will suffer for it. As we all will suffer. My friends, heed me! There is darkness. There is madness in his eye. He will raise us to the ground—his only commitment is to the dead now. We should not have brought him back. We should never have brought him back!*"

Zachary dispelled the uneasy memory with a sharp shake of his head and clenched his hands tightly together. He almost wanted to shush the silent room, as if Edwin's dying words might still betray him.

A sound from the corridor alerted Zachary to someone's approach. He rose to his feet and silent as a ghost, darted between the pillars, hiding from view. As he shrouded himself in the darkness, Zachary wondered why this had been his first instinct. He hadn't been doing anything wrong…

Spying back into the chapel, Zachary relaxed as Emeric appeared in the doorway, peering into the dark room curiously. Zachary almost stepped out to greet him but was immediately overcome with by a desperate childishness that rooted him to the spot. He watched Emeric come into the room, looking suspiciously around.

Emeric—ever superstitious, Zachary thought to himself, as Emeric eyed the caskets of ashes lining the walls above them. In Kathra, it was considered bad luck to keep the remains of the dead on the same level as the living, as these were the tethers of spirits. Best to bury them or scatter the ashes, else phantoms may be attracted back.

Emeric sniffed dismissively and turned to leave.

Zachary grinned and whispered after him. "Emeric."

In the domed room the sound circled eerily, becoming a loose line of syllables. Emeric froze, his shoulders set. "Who's there?" he demanded.

Zachary let silence settle uneasily over the room. Emeric breathed out slowly and gave his eyes a cursory rub, shaking his head with a soft mutter.

Zachary allowed a pause, and then recommenced his spooky chatter. "Emeric. *Em-er-ic.*"

Emeric's entire body grew rigid as he spun around, trying to find the source of the sound. The reverberation made it difficult to pin, and Emeric twisted, his hands slowly raised in defence. Seeing his chance, Zachary quietly removed his shoe and, taking careful aim, threw it at him. It struck Emeric in the base of the spine.

"Etheus blind me!" Emeric cried, scrabbling back against the wall and Zachary exploded with laughter.

Emeric recovered from the shock and pushed himself straight with a growl as Zachary emerged from his hiding place.

"Your face!" Zachary chortled.

"That wasn't funny," Emeric said, massaging his chest.

"You thought I was a ghost."

"I should have known," Emeric replied sharply and Zachary cackled, dropping back onto a bench. There were tears in his eyes. "This is what I get for worrying about you."

"Sorry." Zachary wasn't in the least. Emeric scowled and came to join him at the bench, kicking over his shoe. Zachary put it back on.

"Where have you been all night?" Emeric asked, with an accusatory air.

"Oh, here and there. I went home a while."

"No you didn't. Marcel and I crossed paths with your housekeeper—she was asking after you. Seemed to think you might be 'up to mischief', as she put it."

"A totally groundless assumption," Zachary sniffed. "How did you find me then?"

"We chanced upon Lord Odin," Emeric said. "You know, I don't think that man sleeps at all—he was in the middle of work. He said he'd seen you and suggested you'd either be here, or in the library swapping the scrolls around again."

Zachary sniggered to himself. "Oh, he knows me so well."

"It's late, Zachary."

"It is, yet here you are."

Emeric gave a wry smile, shaking his head. "Old habits," he admitted. "I can't seem to sleep any more until dawn. It might, however," he continued, surly, "also have to do with the fact that at three o'clock, instead of being in bed, Marcel and I are out looking for you." Emeric turned to the altar of Septus. "Were you here for Lord Edwin?"

"None of your business," Zachary growled, his good humour draining away. He didn't like to talk about Edwin—it left a bitter taste in his mouth.

Emeric wasn't deterred.

"You can't scare me away," he said softly. "Not by playing ghost or monster."

"And I used to be so frightening." Zachary sighed.

"You still are," Emeric said, patting him lightly on the knee. "Why, I don't know a single apprentice who isn't a little intimidated by you."

"Small blessings," Zachary grunted. "I am not yet a dog without teeth."

"Give it time." Emeric patted his arm consolingly. "Zachary, about this evening—"

"Oh please Fold, don't be dull."

"No, I simply…Thank you." Emeric sat straighter. "Thank you, Zachary. And *please*—try not to get yourself executed."

"*Me*? You were the one who corrected those students."

"And yet you so hastily took the fall."

Zachary grinned. "It's as you said—some habits are not so easily shaken. Come," he rose, "let's go and find Hathely, and—"

Zachary cut himself off and abruptly pulled Emeric to his feet, dragging him behind the pillars, out of sight. Emeric made to object but Zachary shushed him.

From outside the holy chamber, the sound of footsteps grew and Emeric went quiet. Both of them recognised the footfall. Beyond the doorway, Sverrin appeared, striding with a purposeful gait. He came into the room, passed all the altars, and moved toward the far side. There, he laid his hands upon the detailed mosaic that decorated the wall, and pressing his fingers into two of the pieces, released a mechanism that revealed a hidden door. Zachary, who'd already known about the door, looked on, but Emeric's mouth dropped.

The door slid back and from beyond it a staircase appeared, leading into the bowels of the castle crypts. Sverrin descended and Zachary and Emeric stepped out from their hiding place.

"Where does it lead?" Emeric asked faintly.

Zachary frowned.

"To where the Delphi is laid," he replied and made to follow his King.

"What are you doing?" Emeric hissed, grabbing at him. "Zachary, leave it! You're already out of his favour."

Zachary shook Emeric's hand off and started down the stairs. He felt like he was being drawn after Sverrin. He heard a small grunt of anger and glanced back to see that Emeric had followed him.

"Oh, are you joining me?" he whispered.

"You're going to get us killed."

"I would never get you killed—Hathely would curse my soul to damnation."

Emeric scowled. "If you get me killed, *I* will curse your soul to damnation." He wrung his hands in frustration. "Never mind Hathely."

"I shall hold you to that."

They continued in silence, creeping slowly down. Below them, a strange blue light crept up from the end of the tunnel. As they reached the bottom, they both stopped, peering cautiously out. Sverrin, far ahead, hadn't noticed them and was walking steadily toward the source of the light, bathed in the blue glow. Zachary and Emeric darted behind one of the pillars in the chamber and watched.

Sverrin came to the centre of the room, where an altar was carved from the rock. A figure lay upon it, hands clasped together like a corpse. Jionathan of the Delphi breathed still, his chest-fall so slight he might have been sleeping. His face was peaceful, light flickering over it from the blue faerie-lantern that glowed high above him, the strange blue hue shifting like rippling water, trapped in a crystalline cage. Zachary wasn't sure as to its exact purpose, but the Korrigans had presented it as part of their spell, insisting that Jionathan remain beneath its glow. Zachary didn't like it—it was far too pretty, just like the Korrigans themselves—forever concealing something beneath their ethereal faces.

Sverrin went and stood beside his brother, stepping boldly over the Korrigans' intricate array which was carved into the floor all around the altar. It wasn't uncommon for Sverrin to come down here but something was different today. The King's usually powerful demeanour seemed strangely disturbed, his expression twisted. He looked anxious.

"Brother," Sverrin whispered. "Brother, I don't understand." He circled the altar, forcing Emeric and Zachary to retreat around the pillar before they were spotted. "You're the source of my life, and yet I live yours. Eat, drink, sleep, feel—everything that it is to be alive, I do in your stead." He grew still and Zachary peeked out just in time to see the King swoop down and clutch his brother's face. "But the dreams!" Sverrin whispered intensely. "They're yours, I know they are. What do they mean? What are you trying to tell me, Jionathan? This image of a dragon you haunt me with, this *Hunter*—are they fantasies? Or are they truth—a vision, like a migraine in my head? I can't *bear* them." Sverrin stared intently into his brother's face, as if willing the Prince to answer.

Silence rang out, and something in Sverrin's posture grew taut. He gently released his brother and stepped back. Zachary retreated behind the pillar again, heart in his mouth. He knew the set of those shoulders—Sverrin had sensed he was being watched.

"Show yourself." The King's voice chilled Zachary to the bone, cold and commanding. When neither Magi stepped out in surrender, Sverrin spoke louder, the sound ricocheting across the room. "I said, show yourself, *Athea damn you!*"

Zachary and Emeric pressed their backs into the pillar, trying to squeeze themselves further into the dark. Footsteps clattered toward them as Sverrin advanced in their direction. Zachary could scarcely hear for the sound of his own heartbeat. His stomach twisted, his knees growing weak. In an instant, he wished desperately that he hadn't been so curious—so utterly foolish. But gods—let it be any other man and Zachary's mouth wouldn't have tasted like bile. Any other man and he would have stepped out instantly and presented himself. The Magi clamped his eyes closed and prayed to Athea that he was having a nightmare.

A doorway from across the room slammed shut. Zachary jumped and heard Sverrin whirl around and start quickly toward it. As the King's footsteps retreated, a hand clamped hard over

Zachary's mouth and dragged him back. Zachary panicked. He lashed out at his attacker, only to be met by the disgruntled sight of Marcel. The blond Magi pulled Zachary and Emeric into a little alcove, out of sight. Zachary fell on his back against the stairs. Emeric dropped beside him.

Alone and safe, Marcel finally spoke.

"Enjoying yourselves?"

"Oh gods. Oh gods, thank you." Emeric's voice quivered.

Zachary sat up slowly. He felt dizzy, his head reeling. He hadn't realised he'd been holding his breath. It came back to him now in heaves and he fought to control it.

"You used magic to slam the door on the other side," Zachary said, his arm clamped against his chest.

Marcel grunted an affirmative.

"Why didn't I think of that?"

Marcel didn't respond. Leaning across he pulled Zachary to his feet, before the pair of them gently manoeuvred Emeric to his own.

"He will come this way next," Marcel said. "We must go." He nodded toward a tunnel to the left, which Zachary knew led up and outside the castle. It was narrow and cramped, and Zachary's stomach tightened at the prospect of it. But Marcel was right, the King *would* return this way, and if he found them in the main tunnel or near the chapel, they would be in trouble.

Swallowing his apprehension, Zachary moved toward the tunnel. He stopped briefly at its mouth, his stomach churning as he looked up into its narrow depths. A fresh sheen of sweat appeared on his brow and his courage wavered. He felt Marcel close to his back and, reminding himself that there was no time, pushed himself in.

The entrance, whilst narrow, opened up a few strides in, allowing Zachary to pace forward. The rock either side was cold, but he felt hot and flushed and moved as quickly as he dared. He realised he was holding his breath again. He forced himself to breathe long and deeply. The weight of the castle high above didn't comfort him but he knew it was ridiculous to think on it. With each step they moved closer to the surface.

Neither Marcel nor Emeric spoke as they climbed and Zachary was glad. He couldn't afford the concentration or distraction of their words. Despite his regulated breathing, he felt starved of air, the heat rising around them in an uncomfortable wave.

Seeing the end of the tunnel ahead, it took all his control not to break into a run, his head pounding. The walls grew tight again, forcing them all to edge along on their sides, their heads stooped.

And then Zachary was free, breaking out into the open and almost falling into the stable courtyard in his haste. He stopped short, teetering on his heels as the cold air struck him. It was an instant bliss. With a breathless gasp he sagged against the wall, unable to support his weight. For a terrible moment he thought he was going to be sick, but the heady feeling passed.

"Zachary?" Emeric approached worriedly. Zachary shook his head, gulping in deep lungfuls of air and exhaling slowly. He pushed himself from the wall and straightened, pressing a cold hand to his now clammy face. He knew he'd gone grey but he tried to keep his expression neutral. "Are you alright?" Emeric asked.

"That is not an experience I care to repeat," was all he said.

"Then perhaps next time you'll listen when I tell you to leave well enough alone?" Emeric chuckled queasily.

"Oh, don't get smart with me."

Marcel came over and stood between them. Zachary eyed him and saw his second in command give him a subtle once-over in turn.

"I am sorry the pair of you wasted so long in search of me only to be put through that," Zachary said solemnly. "The hour is late and your beds are yet empty—you ought to return to them."

"Your *own* bed-chamber misses you, too," Emeric chided.

Zachary moved away from the wall of the stable, looking up and around to the looming castle.

"Yes, as yours must surely miss Hathely."

Marcel coughed and Emeric hummed in soft agreement. Zachary gave them both a curt smile.

"Be assured, Fold," he continued, "I have every intention of returning to my faithful pillows tonight. This adventure has drained me."

"You look pale."

"Then what a sickly pallor the moon lends us all," Zachary said, and bidding them both a brief goodnight, he left as quickly as he could, eager to be out from under Marcel's watchful eye.

CHAPTER 9

Joshua was wheezing in his sleep. Rufus paced backward and forward to the sound, his body strumming with a nervous energy that forbade his exhausted body sleep. He'd made the biggest fire he dared and wrapped his little brother in all the blankets they had. And yet still Joshua shivered violently, his breathing erratic. The noise was terrible.

Rufus dropped down by his side and stroked his fingers through his brother's hair, trying to comfort him. There was nothing else he could do—in his own state he didn't dare try to use magic to ease his brother's suffering. The body was far too delicate an instrument to meddle with carelessly. What if Rufus aggravated the condition? Caused the breathing to worsen? Filled Joshua's lungs with blood? Rufus began to fret, what if by doing nothing he was putting his brother at worse risk? What if the coughing only grew worse anyway? What if—

"Pull yourself together!" Rufus hissed to himself, rolling onto his back and staring up into the leafy roof. Between the branches, the star of Aramathea, the mother goddess, was visible. "Please," Rufus whispered to her, "if you know mercy, show it to me now. *Please.*"

Joshua stirred and Rufus turned to him in time to see the boy's eyes open. They glowed in the half-light. "Papa…"

"I'm here."

"Do we need to leave?" Joshua's voice was a husky whisper, almost lost to the still air.

"No."

"Why aren't you sleeping?"

"Adults don't sleep," Rufus joked gently and Joshua raised his eyebrows in sleepy doubt before allowing his eyes to fall closed. His breathing softened once more and Rufus stroked his hair soothingly, as he'd done when Joshua was a baby.

From the outer circle of their camp there was a soft crackle, so quiet it might have been a crow landing among the leaves. All the same, Rufus rolled into a crouch, his eyes wide. He'd learnt to be suspicious of even the most innocent of sounds.

A shadow moved through the line of trees and Rufus watched it warily, summoning Athea's power to him in preparation. Faerie, assassin, bandit or Kathrak—Rufus weighed up which would be worse.

The shadow stopped moving and stood, hidden just beyond the ring of light. A pair of eyes glowed ominously as they peered in. Faerie then. Rufus wasn't sure whether to be comforted, or frightened. He raised his hand, preparing to attack. "Identify yourself!" he ordered. The faerie didn't speak, but Rufus saw its eyes flick quickly to Joshua. He stood protectively over his brother.

"Mo chuisle, mo chroí," the faerie said in Betheanian, her voice deep and luxurious. Rufus faltered as her words settled over him. *My pulse, my heart?* It was an intimate endearment for someone he didn't know.

"I said—identify yourself or be gone!" he repeated.

"Peace," she raised her hand. "I mean neither you, nor your ward harm this night."

Rufus was wary. "Say it thrice and the deed will be done,"

he ordered. His extended time in the forest had warranted him to learn more about the faeries and the Sidhe. He knew that full-blooded Sidhe couldn't lie but, above that, any faerie who repeated a promise three times was forever bound to it by honour. An honour they couldn't defile.

The figure beyond the trees inclined her head. "I mean neither you, nor your ward any harm this night," she promised.

"Again." Rufus didn't relax. "Say it three times!"

"I mean neither you, nor your ward any harm this night," she repeated dutifully and stepped into the circle, moving cautiously toward him, mindful of his nervousness. Rufus watched her warily. She was cloaked and hooded, so he couldn't see much of her face, but her hands were long and almost white. And she was very tall, at least his height, if not more. Power radiated off her—a Sidhe, he sensed.

"I am here," she said, "to help you."

"I don't need any help," Rufus said. Offers from the faerie-folk were often a double edged sword.

She smiled at his cautiousness. "Not a minute ago, you begged Aramathea for mercy."

Rufus was surprised. "You speak the goddess's name like you know it."

"You think that only humans know about the True Gods?"

"The Sidhe have their own," Rufus said.

She exhaled. "Yes—the Tuatha de Danaan, the Sidhe forefathers, gods of the earth. Whilst yours are the faceless gods of the sky. It is a rich pantheon, is it not? But Bethean may have a King and still recognise Harmatia's. I can acknowledge both powers for what they are, because each comes from the same source—the one uniting power Danu. You should not be so surprised. Was it not, after all, the Delphi who taught the humans of the True Gods in the first place? And were they not descendants of Niamh?"

Rufus's head spun. He was sapped of energy and it was difficult to both reflect on her words and maintain his distrust at the same time. Finally, he lowered his arms. If she'd meant to attack him, she would have done so already. She inclined her head.

"Why are you here?" he asked.

She ignored his question. "An bhfuil Betheania agat?" she asked instead, and it took him a moment to realise she'd changed language back to Betheanian, and was asking him if he could do the same.

"Tá, beagán," he replied. Betheanian was his mother's tongue, one he'd tried nurture. It was an ancient language and in the faerie forest it held power. He could understand why a Sidhe would want to speak it above the Common Tongue, which was so new in comparison.

"Tá me sásta a bheith anseo in éineacht leat," she said. "Magicus," she added, and his heart skipped a beat. Magicus—the old word for Magi.

"How do you know what I am?" he converted to the Common Tongue, his guard raised once more. He wouldn't give her the power of language if she was his enemy. She reached up and placed a soothing finger against his lips, quietening him.

"I know a great deal about you, mo chuisle."

My pulse she called him again, like they were old lovers or friends.

"Who are you?" Rufus demanded.

"You know me." She moved her hand to gently cup his cheek. "Look deep, I am your destiny." She tipped her head back so that her hood rose and he caught sight of part of her face. His heart leapt into his throat. She moved in toward him invitingly, and he reached forward and removed the hood.

Outside the shadow, he saw first her lips—berry-coloured and soft as rose petals, sweet with dew. Her eyes were the colour of aquamarine, shimmering between green and blue like shallow water on a sunny day. And her hair...A curtain of fiery red ringlets, so vibrant everything else seemed dulled around it.

As the hood dropped, she pulled the waterfall of curls free, allowing them to cascade around her neck, framing her face. Rufus swallowed, his hands automatically moving up to bury themselves in the fine silken strands. They were cold, even though they should have been burning hot. Desire, like a beast stirred from sleep, rose up in his stomach and he pulled himself free of her, searching for a reason to distract himself.

"I have never met you before," he said, trying to put conviction into the words.

"No—but do you deny the feeling of kinship?" She guided his hands back up toward her and rested them against her face.

"No," he whispered. "Somehow…somehow I know you."

"Yes, you do," she said. "I have waited a long time to meet you, Rufus."

His name on her lips sounded sweet and melancholic. He wasn't surprised she knew it. He moved into her, like she was an open hearth.

"Why are you here?"

"I have come for you," she said. "But before I can offer you help, I must give you some truths. Truths you will not like, but are a sign of my good will tonight. Sit with me, mo chuisle. And let me say all I must before you cast your judgement." She beckoned and like a love-struck lamb he followed her to the floor, inching forward, enticed by her scent.

She settled herself down, her arms open and he moved against her. She clasped him protectively and he rested his head to her chest. In an instant he felt a companionship so natural it was like returning home.

"Will you hear me?"

"Yes," he said dreamily, so calm now he could have almost slept. He reached a hand back to her face, captivated by her beauty. He could just fall into it.

"I am divine," she whispered, her hands moving down his chest.

Yes, he agreed silently. *You most certainly are.*

"I am a divine Sidhe," she continued, her lips pressed to his head. Rufus stilled as the words sunk in. She wasn't just any Sidhe—she was one of the Tuatha de Danaan, an original, immortal daughter of Danu. She was one of the faerie gods of whom Rufus had just so casually spoken. One of a set of beings so powerful, so ancient that many Harmatians didn't even believe they existed.

And yet here Rufus sat, entangled in her arms, as she moved her hands down his body. She felt real enough, though Rufus's mind was so clouded, it was difficult to think straight. What little he knew of the Tuatha de Danaan he'd treated as barely tangible truth. Of course he remembered the tales of how these ancient Sidhe forefathers had come to Mag Mell—his mother had told it to him as a child. But he'd never given any of it much credence.

The story went that the Tuatha de Danaan descended from the heavenly plane many years ago and lived, for a time, in the land beneath the sea, which they conquered from the Fomorii. Over the years, however, new invaders had arrived and pushed the Tuatha de Danaan out, until they fled back through the water to the shores of Mag Mell.

Here they conquered again, taking the land of Avalon for their descendants, before retiring to live in splendour on the hidden Sidhe Islands of Tír na nÓg.

Though Rufus had known the Tuatha de Danaan to take lovers, and produce descendants, such as the Delphi, it had never occurred to him that the earthly gods would leave their islands. He'd always felt that, like the Harmatian True Gods, they lived in their own plain of existence, disconnected from the real world. He'd certainly never expected to meet one. Never expected them to be so tangible—almost human.

And yet she was so warm, warm where the world was cold, and Rufus was caught between his desire and his fear. As her lips touched his skin again, peppering him with gentle kisses, his desire won over.

"W-who?" Rufus managed to stutter. "Which…?"

"Which of the Tuatha de Danaan am I?" Her hands drew still. "You know that already. Say my name, Rufus."

"I don't—"

"Yes, you do. Do not think—*feel*. Who am I?"

Rufus's mind was clouded.

"I…I really don't—"

"Rufus," she almost pleaded, her hands entangled with his. "Clear your mind. What does your heart say?"

All at once, the muffled warnings that had been tolling through Rufus stilled as a name came to the forefront of his mind. He found enough strength to push himself up and away, stumbling back.

"Morrigan."

She nodded, remaining where she was.

"You're the patron of the Korrigans!" Rufus felt his faculties return to him, his mind growing clearer, free of the friendly haze.

"Yes," Morrigan said. "I am. I understand that you have an unfortunate history with my priestesses."

"They tortured me." Rufus breath quickened. The memories of the Korrigans, however distant, always brought him out in a cold sweat. "They created the spell that *killed* Jionat! You—*you*—"

"I do not answer for all of the actions of my followers," Morrigan spoke over him. "What they do in my name is not always a reflection of my will. Calm yourself, mo chuisle. I had no ill-will to your Prince, just as I have no ill-will to you now."

"Why should I believe you?"

"You know I cannot lie," Morrigan reminded him, and Rufus's knees grew weak.

He sat back, facing Morrigan now, still closer than he should have been. His exhaustion caught up with him, and he glanced at Joshua to make sure the boy was alright. Morrigan followed his eyes.

"How can I express my good intention?" she asked, leaning over and hovering a hand over the Prince.

Rufus threw himself up, snatching the goddess's wrist before she could touch Joshua.

Morrigan didn't seem to mind his steely grip.

"I have already promised that I mean you no harm," she said and, with fingers impossibly strong, she pried his hand away from her arm, gently resting her palm on Joshua's forehead.

Rufus watched tensely and then relaxed a little as he saw his brother do the same. Under Morrigan's gentle hand, the sickly boy's laboured breathing eased.

"Before anything, the Korrigans were people of healing, an art in which I am familiar. It is a cold night for a child to be out," Morrigan murmured. "He needs a bed. As do you." She retracted her hand. "You are wary of me," she noted. "That is wise. But take comfort—I can help you."

"Why would you do that?" Rufus whispered.

"I know much of the sadness you suffer." Morrigan rose up, reaching over to him and coaxed him closer, as if he were a trusting puppy. "Ask me anything. I will answer you. See my true intentions."

Rufus edged a little nearer. He couldn't be away from her for long—she was as a fire to him.

"When the Korrigans took me, they stole my blood. Was it for…was it…?" Rufus didn't dare finish the question, his throat tight.

"For the spell that revived Sverrin DuBlanche? Yes. They required the blood of Death itself—a child of Athea, in order to defy her. You are mortal—death is your promise at birth, but in your body is a drop of the divine."

Rufus could have wept. He'd always suspected that his blood had played a part in killing Jionat but to hear it confirmed was like a blow to the chest. Morrigan made a sympathetic noise and Rufus pulled himself from his grief.

"The Korrigans took me on your behest," he accused. "They told me they kept me alive for their master—you."

"Yes," Morrigan said, almost with difficulty. "It is true. I have been waiting for you for a long time, Rufus. I felt your birth stir the heavens, felt the gods sigh. I saw what they intended for you…and I could not abide by it."

"What do you mean?"

"You know the fate that lies on children like you—the hatred for those born of Athea, ever the villains of your own tales. Blessed but forced down a path of woe. You are cursed with the God's Luck. Do you know what that is?"

Rufus couldn't stop his eyes straying down her body, following her hands as they stroked from neck to chest, then down to the naval and the crib of her legs. "The God's Luck," he repeated moronically, trying to draw on his usually reliable memory. "An unbelievable luck that comes at the cost of those around you."

"For instance." Morrigan's hand skimmed down her leg across to his, her fingers light as she reached for his hand. "A man who survives despite the odds, yet loses both future wife and friend."

It was like great scoops were being taken from his chest. "Don't," Rufus begged, reliving each awful moment.

"And I think there has been more. More loss?" she read in his face. "Another lover?"

"Leave me be." The memories came, unbidden, not as distant as he would have liked. Memories of a healing heart, the feel of a body next to his when he woke, tender kisses that were more than instigations. And laughter—laughter, above all—like loving arms. Yes, in the years between Harmatia and now, it hadn't only been him and Joshua. There had been a time of companionship too. One of happiness. A lover with whom Rufus might have been content.

"Unleash your grief, mo chuisle. I am here only for you," Morrigan said. "Who were they?"

Rufus shook his head, a lump in his throat. "A man." He

swallowed. "Howell."

"A Delphi Knight?"

Rufus said nothing, his eyes squeezed closed. Morrigan pressed her hand to his chest. The pressure was strangely comforting.

"Did he die?" Morrigan asked. Rufus shook his head. "Then what has separated you?"

"I couldn't...We...The Kathraks...I changed."

"You have not changed since the day you were born."

"You mistake me for another." Rufus's hand found hers and gripped it fiercely. "You mistake me for Athea."

"You *are* Athea."

"I'm *Rufus.*"

"Yes, but mo chuisle," she knelt before him, tipping his head against hers, her free hand clenched so lovingly into his hair as she manipulated his body, as malleable as clay, "that is exactly the problem. That is why I am here. For Rufus you may be but that is but one drop of Athea. Her true nature burns within you as a temptation you cannot deny. You are a brick, a central piece of a grand plan on which you have no voice. Already you can feel it, can you not? This divide within you—Athea herself has worn your body. And that part of you is one you can no longer ignore. One that keeps you alive."

"I feel him," Rufus admitted, his mouth close to hers. Her autumnal scent was so rich he could taste it on his lips. "When I'm scared, I feel him. DuGilles brought him to the surface and now he won't be silenced. The darkness. The killer."

"He is not your enemy." Morrigan's lashes tickled his forehead as she kissed the scar around his eye. "All your life, you have been made to conform to an ideal, because the latter is perceived to be mindless. It is not—*you* are not—and I am here to prove that. I can show you how to master your power, this other half you perceive as a stranger, a killer. I will show you how to use it to your will, so that you may never again lose that which the gods would take from you."

Rufus groaned as he felt her full weight on him, her legs parting so that she could sit over his thighs, his arms entwined around her, as inseparable as the rooted embrace of the trees. "I don't understand."

"You are both a Delphi and Child of Aramathea. The product of both the Sidhe and human gods. You were not born of coincidence but of necessity—to rebalance power. And yet, you would be muted through fear. You understand. What you are…it is not worth being ashamed of, not worth hiding. You should not fear your enemies, they should fear you."

Rufus couldn't contain himself, the tantalising movements of her hips made him sick with lust. He gripped her thighs and pulled her tighter over him. She took his invitation and pressed her mouth aggressively to his. She tasted of wild berries and he kissed her greedily. In the back of his mind he could sense his brother close by and a sensible part of him recoiled at the thought of committing such acts here and now.

"The True Gods, who rule from their heavenly plain, cannot directly interfere, unless through you. That is why you are here— you are their flesh on earth. But you are a power unto yourself. As a daughter of Danu, I am a god of my own and so might you be, Rufus Merle…By my side." She spoke into his lips, sweet temptations, and he rolled and pushed her beneath him. She slid her hand under his shirt. Her touch brought his skin to life, his flesh humming beneath her fingers.

"I don't want to be a god." He leant down to her exposed collarbone and ran his mouth along it. She arched up into him and his mind grew white-hot, thoughts disintegrating.

"But you want me," she said. "So be it, as long as I may have all of you in return."

Rufus growled wantonly. It turned into a long moan as her hands reached down to his belt, unbuckling it with quick fingered ease. He suddenly understood just what she was. She was a manifestation of emotion, of uncontrolled lust for all things, dangerous and beautiful. She was the weakness in every person, their deepest darkest desire brought to life, and for all her sweet-laced intentions, Rufus saw with a clarity that, as with all clever traps, she was enticing him with exactly what he wanted.

He tried to pull away, but his body disobeyed him. He wanted to submit to her, though beyond the hot flush of flesh, he felt sickly and cold, as if drugged.

"No." He tore his mouth from hers. "I won't. Stop this."

She grew stiller but didn't cease her gentle caresses entirely, her hips swirling succulently until Rufus was seeing white. He tried to maintain himself, to look through the fog of this glamour-like lust.

"What I offer you is limitless power. No more running, or hiding. I could give you an army to take back Harmatia. And all I want in return—all I ask—is you be mine and never stray from my side."

Stop! Rufus desperately tried to order himself, but his body was no longer his own. The intoxication reached a breaking point as she kissed him, passion running like life-blood through his veins as her scent overwhelmed him. She excited him in a way that was unfathomable, and his hands found their way up beneath her skirt to her hot thighs. He could feel the wetness between her legs and ached to be inside her.

Please, stop, he begged. He didn't want this, he didn't want any of it, but he'd lost the will to fight the sweet tide. He could feel power strumming beneath her skin, and it was so well known to him, he might have been holding her all his life. She wrapped her legs around him and he kissed her again, savagely.

Beneath his lips, he felt Morrigan smile and at last the cold clarity broke through his heavy limbs. Morrigan was beautiful, her voice luscious, and her promises even more so. But freedom couldn't be bought in this way—Morrigan offered a lesser imprisonment. What would it be, to be hers? She made it seem so sweet, and yet Rufus could feel that there were truths beneath those berry-red lips that Morrigan had chosen to keep. Fighting the confusing cloud of lust, he was able to break his will through it and recapture control over his body.

"No." He pushed himself up from her, prying her legs from his waist. "No!" He repeated, louder.

She gave him a playful, tantalising smile. "Why?"

"Because it's not up to others to tell me who I am, nor will I be the price of another's dictation." He managed to get loose of their tangled legs and stood. "If the gods truly have an agenda—and gave me this power to fulfil it—then *you* are an unnecessary medium."

She looked at him calmly, and then tossed back her head with a feral laugh.

"Silly pup." In the next second she was gone from beneath him.

He jumped, startled, and found her immaculately dressed once more, towering over him as he scrabbled away.

"If that is your will, so be it—say it thrice and the deed will be done. I will return twice more. Perhaps next time, you will see more sense, mo chuisle."

～⁂～

Rufus sat bolt upright, hands clasped to his chest as his heart thundered. He stared wildly around the glade, which was filled with the early bright light of a cold spring morning. The fire smoked lazily, down to its last embers, and Joshua shifted in sleep. Rufus held his breath and then released it slowly, lying back down and throwing his arm over his eyes.

"Say it thrice and the deed will be done…"

He wasn't sure if he could cope with two more encounters from Morrigan, be they dream or reality.

CHAPTER
10

The monastery was filled with worshippers. Rufus and Joshua blended in easily amongst the crowd. The Prince sat on Rufus's knees, sunken into his chest, his feverish forehead tucked beneath the Magi's chin.

The monastery service was as familiar to Rufus as walking, and yet the responses and hymns felt foreign to his tongue. Rufus partook all the same, anxious not to be herded back out into the rain by tutting priests. He muttered the prayers over and over, bobbing his head like a madman, drunk on sorrow.

From where he was swaddled against Rufus's chest, Joshua murmured, face buried in the soft fabric of Rufus's shirt. Rufus kissed him on the brow, rocking him.

Beside him, his neighbours had noticed and were glancing across, their eyes sweeping up Rufus's long, grim form, from his tattered cloak to his unkempt beard. Rufus paid them no mind, his stomach growling with hunger. He hadn't eaten properly in days but he'd been on longer stints of such self-abuse and could forgo food a while more. The fact of the matter was they had no money. In their haste to escape the assassin, Rufus had left most of his belongings in Beshuwa, including his fiddle.

Unfortunately, where they might find shelter in the forest, the nights were getting cold. As Morrigan advised, Joshua needed a warm bed.

The congregation began to sing again. Rufus tipped on his heels, almost falling as he struggled to maintain his balance. It had been several days since Morrigan had come to him and Joshua's condition had steadily worsened. Rufus hadn't slept for worry and, at last, unable to risk the bad weather, they'd returned to civilisation. He didn't know where they were but the monastery was inviting and warm.

Joshua's hand curled around Rufus's arm. "Rufus..." he wheezed. "Too hot, I'm going to be sick."

Rufus nodded and slipped out into the aisle. He ignored the disapproving frowns and tuts as he carried his brother clear.

Joshua was sick the moment Rufus put him down outside. The Magi knelt beside him and rubbed his back. Joshua quivered like a leaf. There had been little in his stomach already, so the retching was hard and painful. Rufus cleaned his brother's face and mouth with a handkerchief and carried him back to their horse. They couldn't return to the monastery now without attracting attention, so Rufus placed Joshua in the saddle and led the horse on through the town. The streets were blissfully empty, an old rickety inn-sign rocked eerily in the wet wind. They couldn't afford to go in. Even if Rufus had enough coin, inns were hardly centres of discretion. Rufus pulled his hood down lower and continued on until they came upon a whore-house. Rufus stopped, considered it, then lifted Joshua down to his side and strode forward. He knocked on the door.

A Gancanagh responded.

Or, what Rufus presumed to be at least a halfling, for though he felt the familiar amorous tug as he took in the tall, muscular man, his pale skin didn't have that strangely bluish undertone, and he'd aged beyond a point that most Gancanagh did. The halfling eyed Rufus keenly, until he spotted Joshua bundled at his side. Instantly his face fell.

"We don't do rooms," he said. "The inn's three doors down."

"Please." Rufus snapped out his hand, holding the door. "I have no money for the inn, but if you have a fiddle to spare, I could entertain your guests instead…"

"Not interested," the halfling dismissed.

"Please," Rufus pressed. "My son could die."

The halfling batted Rufus's fingers away. "That's not my problem. If you want money for a bed, go sell your horse."

"We need the horse."

"More than your life?" The halfling reached across and yanked Rufus's hood down with a sharp tug. "That's what I thought. I know your face—you're a wanted man."

Rufus stepped back, hugging Joshua close to him. He hadn't expected to be so easily recognised.

Kill him. The instinct jumped to his fingers, which twitched, ready to summon a flame. He pushed it down. The halfling hadn't called him by name and wasn't shrinking back either. He clearly only knew Rufus for a criminal—not a Magi.

"It's a misunderstanding," he said.

"Is it now?" the halfling cocked an eyebrow. "Well, even so, you've put me in a sticky spot. I'm law-bound to report sightin's of renegades and crooks—I should be callin' for the town-guard right now."

Kill him! The thought felt more like an order. Rufus shuddered, grinding his teeth. He wasn't a savage—he could negotiate. He could find another way. "Please," he said tightly. "Please don't. Please."

"Now why should I be doin' favours for a man on the run?" the halfling picked at his nails, leaning on the door frame. There was an invitation there—an opening.

If you don't want to kill him, then what are you willing to offer instead? The question throbbed in his mind.

He looked down at Joshua. The boy was barely conscious,

slumped against Rufus's side, his face milky white. Rufus already had his answer. Anything—he would do anything.

"Well?" the halfling waved his hand.

Rufus swallowed, bending his head submissively. "I'll do whatever you want," he said in a low voice.

The halfling's eyes grew heavy and dark. "Hm…" He pretended to deliberate, tapping his lips. "I'll tell you what then," he offered, his gaze travelling down Rufus's body, "you're skinny and sickly lookin', but you've a pretty enough face, so I'll give your boy a room…so long as I get to keep you in *mine*."

Rufus felt his stomach twist, but he kept his voice steady. "Yes, sir."

It was threatening snow. A cold wind had harrowed the city all morning, clouds gathered forebodingly in the sky. The forum was deserted, and anyone who did brave the streets hurried about their jobs as quickly as possible, eager to return to the warmth of their homes. Zachary sat at the top of the stairs above the main entrance in the Magi academy, his head rested in his hands, elbows on his knees. The hallway was silent and dark, but he didn't mind. It had been announced there was to be a council meeting with the King in the next hour, and the solitude gave Zachary time to compose himself.

The door below him opened and three haggard looking students bustled in with the first flurry of snowflakes. They hugged books close to their chests and shook off the snow which clung to their hair and boots. They were older, no doubt waiting to be apprenticed. Zachary watched them lazily as they went by, each glancing briefly at him and bowing their heads in respect. He responded with a cheerless nod, waiting for them to be gone before, with a quick look in either direction, he reached into his pocket and produced a stone.

As boys, he and the other students had played a game upon

these stairs, and without anything better to do, Zachary had gathered a number of stones and come to test his skill. Holding the stone up, he dropped it on the top step and watched as it bounced down, counting how many of the ledges it struck before stopping. Eighteen—he could do better. Zachary tried again and watched the second stone bounce eagerly past the first to the twenty-fifth step.

His sense of triumph was short-lived. Zachary stared glumly up at the doors below him. It was here that he'd first seen Rufus Merle. That day Zachary had caught sight of the boy sneaking through, disguised among the other students, as he went into the library. He'd stuck out to Zachary because he'd been carrying a stack of books far too complex for a boy his age. Zachary remembered thinking him to be a foolish student, overambitious and trying to impress his tutors. Little had he known that Rufus was actually carrying the books to conceal the even more complicated, forbidden scrolls within, which he was stealing away to read. Never had Zachary known a man so effortlessly able to understand magic and mathematics, and recall the finest details of anything he read so easily. In many ways, that was what frustrated Zachary the most—Rufus was an innovator, and in ten years should have brought Harmatia into a new age...Instead, he'd fallen head-sick and deserted them for the wilds.

Zachary lobbed another pebble onto the stairs. It bounced all the way down and skidded across the floor to the feet of Marcel Hathely who stepped into the building, his shoulders peppered with snow. Marcel stopped short, staring at the stone. Slowly he panned his pale, golden eyes up to Zachary who raised his hands innocently, another pebble already clenched in his fingers.

"Go and sulk somewhere else," Marcel said.

"I am not sulking."

"You are throwing stones at me—you are a sulking."

"Well I am *now*," Zachary said, tossing the last one down sullenly, "but only because you said it."

Marcel gave a listless sneer and started up the stairs. Zachary edged over and Marcel sat heavily down beside him.

"Are you here to scold me?" Zachary asked, and Marcel pulled out his pipe. He filled it carefully and lit it in silence. Zachary rolled his eyes. "Oh, I see," he muttered. "You're above it all."

"You are not a child." Marcel breathed out heavily. "Throw stones if you wish."

"Oh, you know what I mean." Zachary leant over and stole Marcel's pipe, putting it between his own lips for a drag. Something dangerously predatory appeared in Marcel's face. Zachary returned the pipe quickly and Marcel took it, and tucked it into the other corner of his mouth. Zachary watched him, tapping his foot impatiently, waiting for the reprimand. It didn't come.

"You're angry with me," he prompted, impatient to get it over with.

Marcel exhaled, his brow furrowing. "You have not earned my anger, however much you want it."

Zachary shivered. "I almost got Fold killed the other night."

Marcel again took some time to respond. He never spoke without thought. "Emeric went of his own volition," he finally said.

"Oh, horse-shit—we both know Fold wouldn't have done anything of the sort were it not for me."

"I did not state otherwise." Marcel blew out a ring of smoke and watched it float out across the stairs. Zachary pinched the bridge of his nose.

"You haven't spoken to me for days."

"You chose to avoid me."

Zachary winced at the truth of it. He'd gone through pains to avoid both his friends the last week, though he hadn't been entirely conscious of his efforts. He messaged his temples.

"Hexias give me strength," he cursed. "Can't you just be angry with me and have done with it? This is like bleeding a rock!"

"Your own anger is punishment enough."

"Sons of the gods—what is wrong with me?" Zachary hid his face with a moan.

"You dwell too much."

"But it was so *stupid*. Notameer be my witness—the King is not a man I wish to cross…And yet my own foolish curiosity drove me to pursue him, when I should have left well enough alone." Zachary closed his eyes tightly. "And when he discovered he'd been followed, *I* should have caused the distraction to escape, not you. But I couldn't conjure a coherent thought. I was reduced to a snivelling child."

"You are yet young," Marcel said and Zachary choked.

"I am thirty-nine years old."

"Hm," Marcel hummed in agreement, and then shrugged. "They say our minds age slower."

Zachary had heard the same thing. Everyone knew that the more magic you used, the longer you were prone to live. In-fact, it was often possible to assess the level of a Magi's strength by how young he looked comparative to his age.

New theories, however, suggested it didn't end with looks alone. Analysis in the last four decades had shown that the delayed aging process wasn't only external, but affected faculties of the mind as well. It made sense—young Magi were notoriously regarded as immature when they were first apprenticed, and often behaved closer to adolescents than men. If the theory was correct, then developmentally Zachary was barely in his twenties.

He wondered if that really excused his behaviour.

"The tunnels afterwards…?" Marcel suddenly said.

Zachary went cold. Marcel watched him.

"Would you like to talk about that?"

So his hesitation and tense shoulders hadn't gone unnoticed as they were fleeing Sverrin. Zachary had known they wouldn't, even so, he'd rather hoped no one would remark on it.

"Not particularly," he said. Marcel gave him an expectant look and Zachary threw his hands in the air. "You can't have *all* my secrets, Hathely!" he joked. "You'd be too powerful."

Marcel harrumphed and then conceded with a nod. Zachary was glad he didn't push the issue. A peaceful quiet grew between them.

"Perhaps," Marcel eventually said, and Zachary was surprised to hear him break the silence again, "you should take some time away?"

"Away from Harmatia?" Zachary asked. "To where? Certainly not to Corhlam."

"Kathra."

"Sigel'eg would be no better."

"La'Kalciar."

Zachary thought on this.

"Thornton lives there," he recalled. During his time at the academy, Zachary had made many enemies, especially in his youth when he'd been a favourite to pick on and bully. One boy in particular had been his rival—Isaac Thornton, a rather soft-faced lad with brown hair, fair skin and dark grey eyes which betrayed a certain sadness Zachary recognised. Even then, he'd understood that Isaac's disdain for him had been more out of self-preservation than malice. The pair shared a common trait in tragic childhoods. Isaac had known that so long as the teasing was focused on Zachary, he himself would be spared from it.

Of course, the brusque attitude they'd had for each other had changed as they grew, and though they never exchanged pleasant words, Zachary had always delighted in fighting Isaac, who was as dedicated to the sword as he was. They'd duelled often, and in that a companionship had been formed—a companionship which became friendship during the Warriors' Assessment.

"He owes you," Marcel remarked and Zachary shook his head. "No he doesn't."

"You saved his life."

"And he defended mine." Zachary thought back on the day.

The path to being a Magi required that each student catch the eye of a current Magi and be apprenticed to him. Whichever sector you wished to enter would mark how you showcased your ability. Theorists would write papers, architects produced designs, and warriors would go through the Warriors' Assessment. It was the only assessment with a history of fatalities, and students entered it prepared for the risk.

Each year the mode of assessment would vary and often attracted a crowd who would come to view it as a sport. It would begin with meagre tasks— duels, shows of strength, speed and skill, then there would be the final exam. Some years were bloodier than others, but for Zachary's a dangerous course had been constructed, and the students had been split into two groups. Zachary had led one, and Isaac was in the other. The purpose of the assessment was to traverse the course, collecting items, and make it together to the other side as quickly as possible. Magic, to everyone's surprise and horror, had been forbidden.

"We are to be Magi! And yet they will not assess us on what we aspire to do!"

Zachary recalled the complaints and laughed at people's simplicity. Magic was a tool—the mark of a Magi wasn't his ability to use it, but the qualities he possessed that defined how he would.

Both teams had traversed the course, and Zachary took great pains to see his through safely and without injury. The other team had used Isaac's natural wit and quick feet to their advantage, and sent him ahead to clear a path.

The course had been partially constructed around a lake just outside the capital. The winter had been particularly harsh that year, so the lake was frozen over. The competitors had all been careful to avoid it, unwilling to test the strength of the ice.

So cautious had some of them been about the lake, however, they hadn't watched their feet properly, and one of the boys accidentally set off a hidden trap buried in the snow. Isaac took the brunt of it and was struck by a sling so hard he was knocked onto the ice. The force of the fall had been enough to shatter the top layer, and Isaac, barely conscious, was swallowed into the water.

Zachary had watched from where his team was already ahead, dismayed to see that rather than lose time in fetching him out, the opposing group—all Isaac's childhood friends—decided to leave him for dead and continue. Zachary had only had a few seconds to make his decision. He relegated his position as captain to another member of his team, barked instructions for them to finish the course, then turned back for Isaac. He negotiated his way through the perilous traps back to the lake and, with a burst of magic, split the ice and dove in. Zachary could still remember the suspended moment of cold panic as he hit the water, his mind growing numb. For a few dreadful seconds, he'd forgotten what he was trying to do. Then he'd spotted Isaac in the gloom, and with great difficulty had seized the boy around the waist and dragged him out of the water. And just in time too, for Isaac was near drowned, and spluttered out a lungful of water as Zachary pounded him on the back.

Of course, regardless of the deed, Zachary's use of magic disqualified him from the assessment. This, he'd been happy to accept, but nothing could prepare him for the mocking taunts of the opposing team who, for their decision to leave Isaac, had all been able to finish the course. They'd laughed and jeered, and Zachary had been gobsmacked.

"*You fucking animals—you're boasting? You left your friend to die! You should be ashamed!*" he'd cried, but his words had only elicited more mockery. Shame was the last thing on their minds.

Before he knew what he was doing, Zachary had launched himself at the leader, bellowing profanities. He bloodied the boy's nose, wiping the ill-deserved glee off his face, and it had taken three Magi to haul Zachary off.

Zachary had been sent straight before Belphegore to answer

for this 'violent attack'. Many Magi had been present, including several professors who thought very little of him.

Fear had gripped Zachary then. His professors threw their accusations with pleasure, denoting him as savage, calling him uncontrollable—though he'd seen other boys do worse without reprimand. Their allegations grew as the father of the boy he'd struck came and put gravity on the situation. Zachary had stood, small in the middle of this web of hatred, defended only by Isaac, who'd stormed into the room, still wrapped in a blanket, lips blue from the cold.

"This man owed me nothing and risked everything to save me. If this is the kindness Arlen Zachary extends to a mere bully, then there's no man I would sooner call brother."

The words had given Zachary strength enough to keep his back straight. The professors squabbled amongst each other and decreed that there was no way he could be welcomed back into the academy.

Fortunately for Zachary, Belphegore had agreed, but for an entirely different reason. He'd been looking over Zachary's reports throughout the commotion, and having confirmed his success and notable grades in class and in battle, Belphegore decided that Zachary was indeed no longer fit to be a student, and would thus have to become his apprentice as a Magi. When asked, with horror, by the father how Belphegore could come to such a conclusion, Belphegore had calmly stated:

"Perhaps, were my choice dictated by politics, it might have been your son I chose. Fortunately for me, I may choose my apprentice as I see fit. And for that, I am very glad, because I could never apprentice a man so swiftly capable of putting gold, glory or success before the lives of those he leads."

Zachary celebrated those words every time he donned his Magi robes.

Isaac too, for the firm friend he'd become to Zachary, was apprenticed by Lord Farthing, and went on to become an ambassador in Kathra, in the province of La'Kalciar. He and Zachary exchanged letters still, though they'd not seen each other in many years now. The idea of visiting him was certainly tempting, but...

"I can't leave Harmatia," Zachary finally decided. "Not now."

"You think it needs you?"

"I think I would struggle to come back." He rose to his feet. "We'd best go," he said, Marcel rising too. "It's almost time for the council meeting—Sverrin has never been a patient man."

CHAPTER
11

Rufus lay still on the bed, curled around himself. His lips and body were tired and his mind sluggish. The halfling hadn't bothered to undress him properly—his trousers were around his ankles, his decency covered only by his chemise which he huddled beneath, cold and shivering.

"You did good." The halfling lounged in a decedent chair opposite, smoking. "I pride myself in sellin' the finest the market can offer. You'd fit nicely in my ranks. Your father must've been a Gancanagh, like mine."

Rufus shook his head, and the halfling snorted.

"Then your mother must've bedded one and kept it to herself," he insisted. "You've got a fine taste on you…A real pleasure." He sucked deeply on his pipe and let the smoke out through his teeth. Rufus grimaced.

Never before had he allowed himself to be used in such a way. Never had he given himself to another's lust out of necessity instead of love. And yet twice now, in the last few days, he'd been taken advantage of—first by Morrigan with the toxic lust which she'd left smeared on his body, and now the halfling. The whole affair left Rufus with a sour taste in his mouth as he'd tried both to please the halfling and keep himself from gagging.

Now that it was finished, Rufus felt empty and altogether heavy, as if he were floating above the bed, but couldn't move any of his limbs. He was conscious of pain—the halfling had made no attempt to be gentle, and Rufus hadn't dared to complain, conscious of Joshua sleeping in the room opposite. The boy could never know what Rufus had done to secure him that bed. Rufus wouldn't let his brother bear that burden.

"It's a shame about the…" The halfling went on, gesturing to Rufus's semi-clothed body. The Magi curled around himself tighter, ashamed. "Still, keep your clothes and I suppose most people won't mind." The half-ling sniffed thoughtfully. "Might even be that some folks like it. Tell me, would you let yourself be whipped? There's a market for that."

Rufus didn't speak. The halfling's words were muffled to his ears and he didn't have the energy to concentrate on them. Faint and distant memories of Howell floated into his mind. Rufus forced them down. He didn't want those sacred memories to be tainted by his encounter with the halfling. He didn't want there to be any association.

"Pity." The halfling took the silence in his own way. "If you were mine, I'd fatten you up a bit, too—bit bony for my usual taste. But the performance made up for it. Don't look so ashen, outlaw—it's a compliment."

Rufus's skin crawled. He cast his eyes to the window close by. Through the curtains, he could see it was dark. Joshua would probably be fast asleep by now. Rufus wanted him to remain so as long as he could.

"Would you like to go again?" he asked, pushing himself up, a weak smile on his face. The halfling's eyes flashed.

"I would." He stood. "But we don't have time."

Rufus's breath hitched. "Why not?"

"The magistrate'll be here soon, I reckon." The halfling turned toward the door instead, and Rufus rose from the bed, stumbling under his own weight. He pulled his trousers up, his fingers trembling.

"What?"

"I sent for the town guard. Knew it'd take the oafs almost an hour to get here. Thought I'd amuse myself in the meantime."

Rufus almost lost his stomach.

"You," he gasped, "you promised—"

"To give your boy a room," the halfling tutted. "Never said anythin' about keepin' your secret, outlaw. And why would I? I may not remember your name or your crime, but have you *seen* the bounty on your head? I wasn't likely to forget that." He gave Rufus a pitying once-over. "Don't worry. They'll be here soon enough. So long as you don't fight, it'll be painless. I won't tell them about your son—he can stay here. If he has anythin' of his father's blood in him, then he may turn out to be very profitable."

Rufus trembled from head to foot, his vision turning white.

"Don't you go anywhere near him." He advanced, but his legs wouldn't function properly and he almost tumbled into the wall, head spinning. His skin burned like it might catch fire.

"I'll wait 'til he's older—we have *laws*, you know. Sixteen. 'Til then, I'll have some of the others train him up a little. Nothin' too indecent. He's a sweet-faced lad. Wouldn't want to hollow out those eyes and cheeks too quickly now, would we?"

"You son of...you son of a bitch," Rufus gasped.

The halfling shrugged. Somewhere far below came a loud knocking.

"Ah, that'll be them. Remember now—go peacefully and it'll all be over soon." The halfling turned back and unlocked the door. "And don't worry—I'll take good care of the boy. He'll never want for food or warmth again, so long as he plays his part."

"*No!*" Rufus screamed and drew his knife. He lurched toward the halfling, who turned, surprised by the Magi's sudden speed. Rufus collided with the man and wrestled him to the floor. The halfling was stronger, but in his sudden rage and desperation,

Rufus won out and with a howl, planted the knife into the soft tissue of the halfling's neck. The halfling gave a gurgled scream. Rufus drew the blade out and did it again, stabbing him over and over as blood sprayed out onto his hands and face. "I won't let you!" Rufus cried. "I won't let you!"

The halfling gazed up emptily as the Magi continued to drive the knife into whatever flesh he could reach. The sound was obscene and Rufus was half-blind for the blood in his eyes, running down his face like tears. His heart roared from the exertion of the kill. Finally, he let up, straddled over the murdered man, his whole body shaking. He couldn't count how many times he'd stabbed the halfling but there was little to be recognised of him now.

Rufus stared down at his victim. His stomach summersaulted. With a horrified sob, he pushed himself off and away, dropping the knife and scrabbling into the corner of the room. He left a trail of blood in his wake.

Had he done that? Had he just murdered a man?

Down below, the knocking grew louder and Rufus remembered himself, rising giddily to his feet before doubling over and throwing up, his insides turning. It felt like someone had struck him hard in the stomach. It was a struggle to draw breath. With a determined growl, Rufus pressed himself against the wall and pushed on toward the door.

Throwing himself into the corridor, he heard someone answer the door far below and knew he had no time. He burst into the room where Joshua was sleeping.

His little brother sat up sharply in the bed, ejected from slumber by the loud noise. The Prince took in Rufus's long form, from his wide panicked eyes to his blood spattered front, and began to shake.

"Rufus," Joshua wheezed as heavy footsteps began up the stairs behind them. "Rufus, what's going on?"

"We have to go."

"There's blood on you," Joshua said in horror, and Rufus reached forward and took the boy's hand, pulling him up out of the bed. "Rufus, what have you done?" the Prince choked.

Rufus didn't reply.

"Good evening my lords," Sverrin greeted the assembly from his throne. A hush fell over the gathered Magi. "I appreciate you all coming, especially at such short notice. I've received some excellent news and thought it best to share it with you all as soon as possible. Lord DuGilles, if you please." The King gestured to a Kathrak who stood in front of him, occupying the space of honour.

Zachary recognised the man—Brandt DuGilles, an alchemist who'd been put in charge of the hunt for Rufus. Zachary wasn't sure of his power but was certain at least of his cunning. DuGilles had an impeccable record and his being here didn't bode well.

DuGilles regarded them with a superior air. From beside Zachary, Emeric glared openly back at the alchemist with obvious contempt. Marcel wordlessly put a hand on his apprentice's shoulder, as if to calm him. Emeric tamed his expression, though his eyes remained dark with anger. With a Kathrak father, Emeric perhaps felt the most betrayed and angered by the misdeeds of the alchemists.

"My friends," DuGilles began, addressing them far too easily, "I bring you much anticipated news." He paused. "As you're all aware, I was tasked with pursuing the rogue traitor, Rufus Merle, and for years I've hunted him diligently. Time after time, I got close, only to have him slip from my fingers. He refused all offers for peaceful negotiation and retaliated with force, killing many of my men."

Zachary didn't believe him. Rufus was no killer by nature and would never attack a man unless absolutely provoked—Zachary himself was a testament to that.

DuGilles continued, "Following his disappearance from the cliff-top, we used a source to track where he might go next, warning the citizens of Bethean that he was dangerous, and distributing his likeness on a poster. With the promise of the reward, many joined our noble hunt, just as King Sverrin predicted, and to that we owe our victory. I've just received a message from my men in Lemra. An assassin discovered Merle's location and dispatched him." DuGilles surveyed the room which had grown still. He extended his arms to the congregation. "Celebrate, my friends," he said. "The traitor is dead."

The statement was met with shock, the words tumbling with a dull resonance. DuGilles didn't seem to mind this muffled reception, a satisfied look on his bold face. And then, from amidst the crowd, came the sharp sound of a clap, as one of the young Magi began to applaud. He was joined by another in this unsteady rhythm, and like a fire it ignited the whole room, applause breaking out. The sound grew, the younger men even beginning to cheer.

Zachary didn't clap, and he didn't clap on principle. You didn't applaud the death of a fellow brother. Rogue or not—Rufus was a Magi. His desertion was a tragedy and Zachary refused to celebrate his death.

Emeric, too, had his arms limp at his sides, his mouth parted as if he couldn't breathe. Zachary scoured the room, watching some of his oldest companions join the sacrilege of this rejoicing. Some were candid in their applause, whilst others darted their eyes fretfully, as if afraid to be caught mourning. They remembered Belphegore's apprentice—little Rufus Merle, with his big thoughts, and his abundant heart.

Below the sound of clapping, Zachary heard the door open and saw Belphegore slip out, shoulders hunched. Zachary's heart sank and he turned back to his King.

"What have we become?" Emeric's voice was barely audible over the thundering applause.

120

"What we've always been," Zachary replied. His eyes met Sverrin's. "Monsters."

They'd returned to the forest. It was cold and dark, but protected, at least, by its fierce reputation. Rufus built a fire and burned his clothes, changing into his last set. Then he huddled with Joshua beneath a blanket, letting his natural body heat keep the boy warm.

They'd escaped the brothel by the window and had managed to collect the horse and what remained of their meagre belongings. Up above them, the branches were weighed down with the first fall of snow. When Rufus breathed, it came out in curls of mist. He held Joshua close to him, conscious of the cold air and how easy it would be to submit to it.

Joshua peeked his head up from beneath the blanket. "Rufus?"

Rufus gave him the most reassuring smile he could muster. Joshua curled his hands around Rufus's shirt.

"It's alright," Joshua said and Rufus almost cried. "It's alright, Rufus."

"I know." He kissed Joshua's brow. He was being comforted by a child—*his* child. "Don't fret."

"Where will we go now?" Joshua whispered.

Rufus gazed into the fire. "I'm not sure." He felt numb to the core, as if the cold was inside him, even though he knew he was burning hot. "It may be time to leave Mag Mell. We could take a boat from Killian, or Lemra, cross the channel." Rufus paused. "How's your Réneian?" he teased and Joshua sniffed.

"Not as good as my Betheanian."

"It could improve, given time. Mine too, I'm sure." Rufus closed his eyes. "It would be warm there, the 'Sunny Island'."

"You could find me a Réneian swordsman—to train me," Joshua said

Rufus raised his eyebrows. Réneian swordsmen were

121

considered some of the finest in the mortal lands. Rufus remembered that Zachary had trained under one, and was remarked for his skills because of it. "We'll see," Rufus murmured.

"I'll need a sword for that," Joshua muttered sleepily. "One of my own."

"I said we'll see." Rufus kissed him again and then grew still, letting his brother fall asleep. In the quiet of the night, it felt like the world didn't exist beyond the light of the fire. Snow had a way of silencing everything.

Rufus breathed out and closed his eyes, resting his head back against the tree they'd taken shelter beneath. Tired as he was, Rufus couldn't bring himself to sleep, and he lulled his head and opened his eyes, looking back over their camp.

In the snow, a few feet away, the man he'd murdered lay, face and neck mutilated. Rufus jolted in horror, and then looked again. There was nothing there. Rufus held his breath, searching all around him for any more sight of the dead-man, but there was none. He settled back again, breathing out shakily.

"Your heart is crying again, mo chuisle."

Rufus nearly leapt out of his skin. Snapping his head around, he caught sight of a familiar figure stood in the darkness, her eyes glowing.

"M-Morrigan?"

She stepped into the light, her clothes rustling, though they'd not done so until now. Rufus pushed himself a little straighter.

She'd changed—but then Rufus gathered that was rather her nature. Where once her mane had been fiery red, it was now long, bone-straight and flaxen, and her eyes were golden in colour. Gone was the ferocious lust that had seeped from her, replaced instead by a nurturing calm that settled over Rufus like soothing music.

"Leave me alone," he said. "I don't want anything from you,"

Morrigan sat beside him. "Perhaps not, but what do you need?"

The very cold seemed to be chased away, the extremes of temperature, between his boiling body and the frosty air, nullified. When Rufus looked into Morrigan's face, he thought of the wheat-fields in Sarrin, the sound of Luca's fiddle, Howell's laughter, Fae's eyes, and it made him want to cry in relief. He was so sick of the sight of corpses.

"You're hurt," she said, as if she could see into his aching heart. "What you did today, you did out of necessity."

"How do you know about that?"

"I have been watching over you." She ran her hand down his cheek and her touch was so familiar, Rufus was drawn back to his childhood. Faintly, he could hear his mother's voice, smell her in the air, like a comforting phantom—a promise that she was nearby. It filled him with longing.

He longed for simplicity. Where the complicated things were only in his head and the pages of the books he poured over. He wanted to be young again, and unwise, and full of wonder. He wanted to forget love, and lust, and hardship. He wanted to forget everything—Mielane, Jionat and, for a guilt-ridden minute, even Joshua.

And then the feeling was gone, and with it a hardened guilt came tumbling over his shoulders. Yes, once Rufus had been ignorant and happy, and it had cost him dearly. He'd lost one brother having barely gained him. He couldn't lose Joshua to that same foolishness.

"You're not real." Rufus flung Morrigan's hand away from him. "You're a figment of my taxed mind."

"Of course I am real. Is it so hard to believe that somebody else cares for you?"

"You don't care for me," Rufus retorted. "You're here to use me."

Morrigan didn't react as he imagined she would. Instead of anger, he saw a disappointment in her eye. Her patience unnerved him.

"I *do* care," she insisted, "more than you know. So why must you force yourself? Any more and you will die."

"What choice do I have?"

"You do not have to do this alone." She moved toward him but he flinched back. She grew still, then retreated.

"Why have the gods forsaken me?" Rufus's voice trembled. He wanted to chase after her, he wanted her comfort, but he abstained.

"The gods have not forsaken you Rufus—I am here," she breathed. "I am here and I will help you. If only you will let me."

"No." He shook his head. "You're manipulating me—yes, you are!"

"I offer you an end to your pain, mo chuisle. Whatever your thoughts on that, my intention is true."

"I can't believe that."

"And it breaks my heart."

"Then why?" Rufus moaned. "Why do you tempt me?"

Morrigan's expression became torn. She struggled to find her words.

"Because," she eventually said, "because I have waited a long time for you, and to see you tear yourself apart, when you could so easily be free of all regret…It makes my heart ache."

Rufus stared longingly at her and then at the child in his arms. He shook his head.

"No," he said. "I have to do what's best for Joshua. And that isn't you—it would never be you."

Morrigan's eyes filled with an earnest sadness, but she nodded and stood.

"Then I shall leave you, for tonight. But know that I have not abandoned you."

"I understand," Rufus said with exhaustion.

Morrigan sighed, stepping back out into the shadow.

"No, mo chuisle," she said, "I do not think you do."

CHAPTER 12

Zachary lurked in the doorway of the chapel, leaning against the frame. Belphegore was knelt before the altar, hands clasped together.

Darkness shrouded the room with conspiratorial shadows and the moonlight, silver and eerie, poured through the open window, bathing the statue of Aramathea. At her left, Athea stood, circled by a ring of red candles which were normally lit and burned brightly at the hem of her stone dress. Zachary suspected that Belphegore had put them out—Athea had been extinguished that night.

Zachary came into the room, closing the door behind him, though he'd never seen it shut in his life. Carefully, he approached. "Master?"

"Arlen." Belphegore didn't look around, but gestured for Zachary to join him. "Will you pray with me?"

Zachary deliberated and then nodded. Moving to the altar, he knelt beside his master. Belphegore had aged again, his figure taut, hands frail where his fingers clutched each other in their pious embrace.

"Praying won't return him to us, Master," Zachary said.

There was a long silence and then Belphegore sighed and allowed his hands to drop. He sat back and stared indignantly at the altar. "I know," he rasped.

"Then why did you come here?"

Belphegore hesitated, drawing his hand up to his mouth as if sickened.

"For guidance, perhaps," he replied. "I am no longer sure. My heart is full of uncertainty. I know the truth, yet I am not prepared to believe it. Rufus dead? No—not after all this time. Not like this. I do not dare...I cannot believe it—it's inconceivable." He hesitated. "You are my only remaining apprentice, Arlen."

"I know."

"Perhaps you're the only one who will mourn with me."

"I doubt that." Zachary's voice was barely above a whisper.

Belphegore seemed strangely comforted by the words.

"When will the King announce the news?" he asked.

"Tomorrow. There are to be several executions in the forum, men charged with conspiracy against the throne. The King will address the public then, cut any conspiratorial hope at the bud."

Belphegore's expression didn't change but Zachary got the impression that he winced.

"At dawn?" he asked in a quiet murmur.

"No—in the eve." Zachary paused. "The news has excited him. With Merle gone, those who oppose Sverrin's rule have lost their figurehead. Sverrin is tactical—he'll try to use that to his advantage."

"Yes, I can see that." Belphegore paused, and then cursed beneath his breath. "I must go and convey the news to the Merle family tomorrow. No parent deserves to discover their son is dead through gossip."

Zachary's raised his eyebrows. "You mean they're still in Harmatia?"

"Of course. It is their home."

"Sons of the gods," Zachary choked. "How are they still *alive?*"

126

"Torin and Nora Merle are good, charitable people, beloved by their neighbours. They protect each other in the Southern Quarters—they take care of their own."

"If Sverrin learns they're here, he'll send for them. He'll start a *purge*."

"All the more reason for us to warn the Merle family." Belphegore cast his eyes down, his face stern. "They must leave Harmatia or they could spark a revolution."

"A revolution is coming, regardless." Zachary glanced over his shoulder warily, his chest tight and heart heavy. "I can feel it— this unrest. Merle's death is just the beginning. Sverrin thinks it will weaken the rebels, I fear they'll rally instead."

"I fear you may be right."

"What do we do?" Zachary asked helplessly.

"For now, we must keep the peace—that is our duty as Magi."

Zachary turned back to Aramathea, a lump rising in his throat. He was no traitor—he'd sworn himself to Sverrin and had done so willingly, regardless of everything. But he also loved his people. And it was for them he tried to have a voice.

"What if," he forced out, "what if the peace can't be maintained. What if the people we swore to protect rise up against Sverrin?"

The silence that Belphegore held was like an eternity, and Zachary suffered each second of the quiet thought. Finally his master turned to him.

"In that instance," Belphegore whispered, "you must choose who it is you serve, Arlen." He rested a hand on his apprentice's shoulder and then rose. "I will go to the Merles' house tomorrow at dawn. Will you come with me?"

Zachary wanted to say no but knew it wasn't really a request.

"Yes, Master," he said dutifully and Belphegore bowed his head in thanks.

"Do not stay at your prayers too long, Arlen," he bid and left the room. Zachary remained, lost in thought, before he too rose. As he went to the door, he paused and, looking back at the statue of Athea, lit the candles below her with a wave of his hand, lest someone realise that they'd been extinguished on purpose.

"Even in death, you're still a pain in my arse," he said softly and departed.

Heather Benson was waiting for him at the door when Zachary got home. His nursemaid from childhood, the stern-faced woman now ran his entire household like the captain of a ship, keeping it spotless, warm and always welcoming. Zachary was certain he wouldn't have come through his lonely childhood in Harmatia were it not for the kindly woman, with her deceptively strict voice.

She was in the entrance hall to remove his cloak as soon as he opened the door, her arm outstretched. He unfastened it slowly and looked around the darkened walls. It was well past midnight—he hadn't expected her to be up.

"You should be in bed."

"You left instructions for me to expect you back this evening, so I did."

"It's late."

"It is," Heather agreed, taking his cloak and draping it over her arm. Zachary studied her closely. Her smile was thinner than usual.

"What is it?" he asked her, reaching for her hand. "What's troubling you?"

Heather pursed her lips, reluctant to speak, before inhaling sharply.

"The young master has not come home yet," she said. Zachary scowled and released her, stepping back.

"Why should it matter? The brat can do as he pleases." He began to mount the stairs, Heather close on his tail.

"Three nights now he's not come home until the small hours."

"He's twenty years old—"

"*Nineteen*, Arlen."

Zachary battered away the correction, grabbing a jug of wine which had been put out for him at the top of the stairway—part of his nightly ritual. He poured himself a glass and took a liberal swig.

"You never fussed about me staying out so late when I was his age."

"I have worried about you every night you were late for thirty-one years."

"Then I must be growing old, because I am going to bed *now*." Zachary turned but she caught his arm with surprising speed for a woman of her age.

"Arlen." She didn't beg, but rather told, "He is in the training grounds. Go and get him before he is carried here with a physician. He is not like you—he is not a warrior. Please, if not for his sake, then for my own peace of mind."

Zachary considered his choices and then with a scowl pushed his empty goblet into her hand and took back his cloak. He threw it over himself in a graceful arc, jumping down the stairs.

"The things I do for you, woman," he grumbled. Heather nodded gratefully.

Leaving the house, he walked back out into the castle grounds, crossing the courtyard toward the academy. The moon made the snow glow, giving the castle a dreamlike appearance, spoilt only by the wet crawl that seeped into his trousers. He crossed the grass, wrapping the cloak tighter around him.

He was in a bad mood. Longing for his bed, the day's events had amounted to a gargantuan headache that had him seeing stars out of the corners of his eyes. But Heather asked very little of him, so he couldn't deny her, even if all he wanted was to see an end to this appalling day.

Entering the training grounds, he stopped at the entrance to observe what was going on inside. There were five of them, one in the centre as the others attacked from all angles, throwing magic carelessly against their victim's withering shield. Zachary recognised a few of the aggressors—candidates for the Warriors' Assessment and favoured by many of his fellow Magi for apprenticeship. Zachary wondered idly what those same Magi would think if they saw the students' behaviour now.

The bullies continued their abuse, jeering as the boy in the centre finally grew exhausted. His shield disintegrated and he dropped to his knees, curling protectively into a ball, arms over his head and knees up to his stomach. The bullies, delighted by this submission, forgot their magic and began to kick the fallen boy instead, like common thugs. Zachary decided he'd seen enough.

He struck out his hand and released a highly concentrated blast of air in the centre of the group. The boy huddled on the ground didn't feel its effects, but the other four were thrown backward off their feet.

Zachary clapped his hands, advancing on them.

"I think, boys," he said, drawing their attention to him, "that will be quite enough, thank you."

The bullies mounted to their feet and bowed as they recognised him. From the floor, the fallen victim didn't move, lying very still, as if he expected the onslaught to start again.

"Lord Zachary," one of the gang began, "we were training for the Assessment."

"Oh I am sure you were," Zachary agreed darkly. "Unfortunately it may pain you to know you don't receive extra points for kicking other students to death." Zachary's scanned each of their faces. "In future, I advise you stick to sparring with each other. Are we clear?"

They exchanged a spatter of nods and mumbled agreement between them, before retreating out of the training ground. Zachary waited until they were out of sight before addressing the fallen boy.

"Did they break anything?" he asked.

The boy shook his head.

"No? Then get up," Zachary barked, folding his arms around his chest. The boy stood, a scowl on his face that pleased Zachary. For some reason, it was a comfort to know that he wasn't the only unhappy one. "Why aren't you at home?"

"Is there a curfew?" the boy replied obstinately, his brow pinched. Like Zachary, the set of his face was severe, and the pair shared in their father's hazel-green eyes. Beyond that, their resemblance was fleeting, the boy taking after his mother, with warmer, darker skin, thick brown hair and a more elfin build.

"Don't be a brat, Daniel," Zachary snapped, and the pair began to walk.

Daniel favoured his left leg, but did everything in his power to hide his limp.

"So, is this what you've been doing then, these last three nights?"

"I'm surprised you even noticed," Daniel said flippantly, and he wasn't wrong. Zachary and Daniel spent so little time in each other's company it hardly felt like they lived together at all. They kept different hours, ate separately and, in truth, Zachary knew very little of the boy, other than the fact he studied meticulously, was secretive in nature and seemed to take sick every month with one ailment or another.

"Mrs. Benson informed me," Zachary said. "And *I* can come and go as I please."

"So can I."

"You may stay out if you wish—I could even call back your friends to finish the job. But not before Mrs. Benson sees you. I won't have her poisoning my breakfast with her accusations tomorrow. She seems to think you're being neglected. Am I neglecting you, Daniel?"

"No, sir."

"You have everything you need. You don't want for books or clothes or writing material. You're housed and fed. You're

131

educated. There's nothing you need of me."

"Yes, sir."

"*Yes?*"

"No," Daniel reaffirmed sharply, "I don't need anything from you."

"Ease that tone, brat," Zachary said and Daniel stared sullenly forward. They reached the house and Zachary held the door open, allowing Daniel in first. Heather was waiting on the other side with two cups of hot wine. She fussed over Daniel as Zachary leant back, sipping his drink.

"You're black and blue!" she scolded. "You will report those boys in the morning, do you hear? They cannot get away with this."

"It's fine, Mrs. Benson. Really." Daniel's tone grew softer, embarrassed.

"I'll fetch some ointment to reduce the swelling." Heather ignored him. "You go up to bed. There's a fire lit in your room. Take these soaking clothes off and go and get warm. Off with you." She herded him toward the stairs and he thanked her earnestly. Praises to the little brat—he was polite to the people that mattered at least.

As Daniel disappeared, Heather turned on Zachary who raised his hands.

"I clean my hands of the affair." He downed his drink and then took Daniel's untouched wine for himself. "Let him do as he pleases."

"Healing Septus, Arlen—can you not see he's been beaten?"

"There's nothing I can do unless he asks. Which he won't. So it has nothing to do with me."

"He's your *brother*." Heather took back Daniel's drink before Zachary could finish it. Zachary snorted.

"If I had a gold coin for every bastard my father bore, I would be a rich man. Oh, wait." He paused. "What am I saying? I *am* a rich man."

"Arlen, if this was one of your sisters, you wouldn't stand for it—"

"Yes, but he's *not* my sister."

Heather's mouth drew into a tighter line. "You cannot punish him for what your father has done. It isn't fair."

"I am not *punishing* him, I am being kinder by alienating him." Zachary snatched back the wine and downed it before it could be confiscated again. "You think Rivalen cares about Daniel? He considers *me* dirt and I am his only heir. He may have legitimised Daniel enough to bear the Zachary name but we both know it wasn't out of love or kindness. The fact of the matter is that Daniel's presence—his very *conception*—was only ever meant to torment me. He's less than a bastard sibling, and so long as he remembers that and works hard, he might actually *make* something of his position before my father grows weary of this jest. If Daniel gains a status on the back of his own achievements, our father can't take it away."

Heather glowered, but saw the truth in his words. "He works hard," she eventually said.

"Then he'll have no problem." Zachary started up the stairs toward his bedroom. Heather pursued him slowly. "Wake me at five tomorrow. I have an important appointment in the morning. Set out my uniform and the unembroidered robes—it promises to be a sombre day."

"Are you attending a funeral?"

"There are to be executions in the evening."

"And your morning appointment?"

Zachary stopped mid-step. "You recall Rufus Merle?" he said.

"Lord Odin's other apprentice? The academic one."

Zachary gave a low laugh of surprise. The gods bless the woman for not marking herself at the mere mention of Rufus's name or replying with 'the traitor?' or 'the one-legged necromancer'.

"Yes, the Master's favourite."

"I recall him, yes. Skinny child, clever, kind."

"Yes. Him." Zachary paused again. "He's dead."

Heather stopped short as he continued up the stairs, his pace even.

"Arlen," she said, "I am so sorry."

Zachary faltered at the top step and his grip around the banister tightened.

"Whatever for?" he dismissed and retreated quickly to his room.

CHAPTER
13

⤛⊱⤚

"If pathetic had a face, man, he'd pity-kill you for lookin' *worse*."

Rufus woke with a violent start and sat up so quickly stars exploded behind his eyes, the world blackening around him. It cleared with a white, searing flash, and for a moment Rufus was so disorientated he couldn't breathe. His stomach jumped up, as if he had been punched and he tried to vomit, heaving dryly as he pushed off the heavy weight on top of him.

As the world came into clear focus, Rufus spotted a set of boots close to him, one tapping impatiently. Joshua, now at Rufus's side, whimpered in his sleep and Rufus scrabbled back, trying to sit up. Above him, the Faucon Assassin stared down, arms folded.

"You paint an entirely new meanin' to the word tragic," the Lemra'n slurred.

Rufus tried to breath, wheezing in panic. "Don't…don't come any closer," he rasped, but the assassin ignored him.

"But Athea, leashin' you was *painful*—you're good at hidin', I'll give you that. Still, you can't hide from Death forever. I sniffed out your bread-crumbs eventually."

"Go away."

"Half-arsed fluff-looks aren't goin' to sucker me, you talentless stage-freak, I'm not a half-pint." The assassin sighed. "Look—you can't even dog yourself, how d'you plan on fuellin' my hair this time, eh?"

Rufus pushed himself back further, trying to stand, the nausea sticking to his constricted throat.

"I don't understand you. Just...stop!" His head swam. He wanted to push the assassin out of conscious thought. But the danger was real and Rufus had to face it. With sluggish muscles he raised his arm, his hand outstretched. "What happened... What did you do to Emerald?" Rufus forced himself to his feet, the world tipping dangerous around him. He felt sickly drunk.

"You sound familiar with the lass," the Lemra'n drawled. "Didn't take you for the whorin' sort. Figured you preferred a more masculine hand." He pushed himself away from the tree he'd been lounged against and stepped closer. As he did, the flames in the fire burst up, rearing angrily, though Rufus hadn't consciously called for them.

"Stay back," Rufus ordered, leaning over and shaking Joshua hard. He almost toppled in the action, barely able to stand.

"Woah there—your eyes look like they're goin' to bleed." The assassin eyed him. "Let's take a pause, sit back and play dead a while. You're at the edge of your life."

"Edge or not, alive is where I intend to stay!"

"Bad wordin' from me there," the assassin muttered, pulling a face. "What I mean to say—and I'll speak crystal now, 'cause you're ears are muffled dumb—is I'm not here to bone-pick you. Are we savvy on that?"

To Rufus's ears it was nothing but a rush of nauseating sound. He felt faint again and for a second thought he might fall unconscious, his heart pounding loudly in his ears. The assassin took another step toward him.

"Get away from me!" Rufus rasped.

"Oh for the love of—"

"Stay back! Not a step closer!"

"You're bein' a fool."

"You think I'm going to lay down and die? You think I'm going to let you harm my boy—get back, assassin." He gasped for air, still feeling like his chest was being crushed. "Get back or I'll s-set this whole d-damned forest 'n f-fire!" he stuttered under the strain, his vision swimming. The flames reared threateningly again, pounding with his emotion. "*Back!*"

"Alright. Easy—my hands are puppet'ed, look." The Faucon raised his hands, his expression bemused. "Let's talk."

"Talk?" Rufus gasped. "*Talk?*" he repeated, in a shriek.

"Easy, I'm gettin' you're a tad on the hysterical side, but I'm sure we can come to a compromise here."

"You are here to *kill me!*" Rufus pulled back, dragging Joshua up to his side, though he wasn't sure if the boy was fully awake.

"Piss-pox and plagues," the assassin grumbled. "Listen to me you sugar-powdered prick—if I meant to hurt you, you'd know it!"

Rufus stopped, blinked, then began to laugh hysterically. It grated at his throat and made it difficult to stand but he couldn't stop, couldn't control himself any more. He was one man, a man who'd been put through more than any deserved. He'd had temptation thrown at his feet, false hope dangled before his eyes and he was sick of it all. He was sick of the fear and the anger and exploitation of his misery. An assassin saying he didn't want to hurt Rufus? It was the same damned thing as Morrigan saying she want to help him.

The Faucon gave an exasperated shrug, bewildered. Rufus eyes burned like fire.

"I haven't slept in years," his voice dropped in cold-blooded fury. "*Years,* you son of a bitch!"

"That's toffee-glazed," the assassin said bluntly. "You want me to get out the onions?"

Rufus glared, pushing his brother back slowly as Joshua's eyes flickered open, bleary and confused. The assassin rolled his eyes.

"Where are you goin' now? Look—we stabbed off on the wrong knife, let's try again. My name is Aeron Faucon, and I'm not here to kill you—"

"Shut your mouth," Rufus snapped and the assassin's mouth dipped.

"We can do this with the oil or I can gut you...figuratively speakin', alright?"

Rufus narrowed his eyes and once more the flames burst up, rearing toward the assassin like wild dogs. Aeron raised a shield, stepping back so the fire spilled around him. The horse, from where it was bound, reared in panic, tugging frantically at its binds. With an almighty crack, the branch it was tied to snapped and the horse was gone, galloping off into the forest with a vast majority of their supplies. Rufus didn't even have energy to care and instead ducked down to his little brother. He gripped Joshua by the arms, the boy's eyes glazed but wide. "Run— get to the next clearing. I'm right behind you."

"But—" Joshua's began.

"Do it!" Rufus ordered, just as a hand lashed out, snagging him by the leg. Rufus was tugged back and fell, Aeron ducked low on the floor beside him. The Magi landed heavily, his ribs jolting as several gave way.

"GO!" he shouted at Joshua, as Aeron scrabbled up, pinning the Magi down. The Prince bolted and the assassin grunted.

"Metaphorical death then. I'd better get my pockets lined for this shit."

Rufus gave a roar and, freeing his arm, lurched it around, summoning power to him. Before he could materialise it into magic however, Aeron had caught his arm again, his fingers tight around Rufus's wrist.

It was like the life was being drained from him—his will, his magic, the very element he wielded, being rejected from his own

138

flesh. A deep fatigue came over Rufus and the anger burning through him diminished. He felt like he slipping off into a frozen sleep. What was the point of struggling? No matter what he did everything kept getting worse and eventually he was going to die—one way or another. Why prolong it and waste energy he didn't have, when he could just slip away instead?

Up above him Aeron's face changed. His pupils dilated impossibly, until they extended over his whole eye, making him look like a skull. The assassin's lips peeled back, quivering with sudden pleasure. Rufus was very aware of how hungry Aeron looked. No, not hungry—the emotion on the assassin's face exceeded man's ancient constitution to feed. It was more powerful, darker and older than any mortal being, so old and vast Rufus couldn't even name it. Suddenly there seemed to be no reality beyond him and Aeron, and though Aeron's lips didn't move, Rufus was conscious of a stream of words which emanated, as if they were spoken through the skin. The words possessed him, relaying images and memories he didn't want to see.

Pain, it said, *pain in here. Dark. Forced into darkness. Wanted you to break. Needed you to break. No escape. Couldn't breathe. You thought it—kill me! You thought it. Let me die. Let me die. I want to die. Death. Too strong. Too dark. Can't stop. Can't stop. Have to feed. Too strong. Feed. FEED. TOO STRONG FEED MUST FEED CAN'T CONTROL FEED FEED FEED—*

There was a thump of wood against a skull. The sensation cracked through Rufus as if he were on the receiving end. Aeron's blackened eyes cleared and then he dropped, limp and heavy on top of the Magi. Rufus lay frozen beneath him and gave out a frightened whimper. His body spasmed with gasps as his fear caught up with him and he shoved the assassin off. Joshua released the branch of wood he'd been wielding and helped drag Rufus to his feet.

"W-w-what was that?" Rufus's could hardly get his words out. "W-what the *hell* w-was *that?*"

"Rufus, let's go. Let's go, Rufus. I want to go," Joshua begged, pulling at Rufus's hand, his breathing taut. Rufus nodded faintly, shaking so badly he could barely stand. Together, the brothers clung to each other, and taking what was left of their meagre belongings, they retreated into the woods.

Luca Rossignol woke with a start. For a moment she lay huddled in the warm embrace of her bed sheets, her eyes wide. Someone shifted behind her and Luca relaxed, casting away the tension. She rolled over slowly to the person beside her. Oblivious to her, Ivar Epervier slumbered, his jaw slackened and lips parted. Luca stroked her lover's cheek affectionately, kissing him tenderly on the nose. He made a soft noise and his eyes flickered open briefly, almost black in the faded light. She brushed his golden fringe with gentle fingers and then slipped from his arms and out of the bed. Her bare feet touched the cold stone floor, lit by cracks of moonlight which peered through the shutters.

Her chemise fell just short of her knees and she shivered, crossing silently to the door where a dressing gown hung. She lifted it from the hook and wrapped it around herself, before slipping her feet into a pair of soft, fur-lined boots and lifting the latch of the doorway. The corridor was dark outside but she navigated her way through it easily, passing the children's bedrooms and gliding down the stairs toward the doorway.

Stepping out into the night air, she yawned. Brexiam was silent and still in slumber, and Luca admired the plain beauty of the town.

Internally, however, something stirred—a deep foreboding that wouldn't settle. She could taste it—battle. Its red hue lay upon the air like a heavy scent, filling her. She'd felt it once before, the day the bandits attacked Sarrin twelve and a half years ago. At the time she'd dismissed it as nothing. Now, however, she recognised its dark call and stood, waiting silently for any sign that this was more than her imagination.

A sharp rustle made her snap her head to the side and jump back, her hand immediately flying to her back in search of a sword which wasn't there. Barely a few strides from her, between the trunks of two young trees, a figure lurked, their face concealed by the shadow of their hood. Luca was sure they hadn't been there a moment before.

She disguised her apprehension with anger. "Who's there?" she demanded.

There was only silence and then a voice like honey replied, "A friend."

Luca shivered, her breath catching at the strange beauty the man—for the voice was male—managed to capture with only two words. She composed herself, the wind blowing against her back as she faced him.

"A friend who sneaks through shadows and hides between trees? Aye, that doesn't strike me as at all suspicious."

The man chuckled deeply, his laughter like sweet wine. Luca felt as if she could almost taste his lips in that sound.

"Cap your quick-tongued cynicism—I *am* a friend. That I dwell in the shadows is only because it is my nature, and that I did not wish to startle you."

"Aye," Luca's voice dripped with sarcasm, "because there's nothing startling about a man appearing from nowhere when you think you're alone."

"Let me rephrase," he laughed, "I did not wish to startle you whilst I was in striking distance."

Luca snorted, opening her arms. "I'm not even armed."

"So you say, yet I am reliably informed that the infamous Luca Rossignol can use elemental magic, and I have no defence against that."

Luca took a step forward but the angle of the shadow ensured that the stranger's face remained completely obscured from sight.

"How do you know my name?"

"I would be no great friend if I didn't. I know too your title, Delphi Knight, and I know that the blood of Cú Chulainn runs through your veins—it's why you are awake now under this heavenly sky, when no one else has stirred from their dreams. You can feel it boiling in your blood. Danger. The coming battle."

Luca paused. The man, whoever he was, seemed to know details which only a few were privy to within their circle. Even Luca hadn't discovered her heritage until the dreadful day she'd learnt of Jionat's death. Her parents had imparted the truth of who they were—descendants of the same Delphi Knights who'd come to Harmatia with the Delphi family so many centuries before.

Once, they had served proudly in the open, until a conflict of interest between the Harmatians and the Delphi had broken out. One of the Princes had broken the law and learnt magic. The Delphi Knights had given him an ultimatum—relinquish his claim to the throne or lose his life. The Prince had refused and, as the law required, the Knights had duly executed him.

The outcry in the court had been terrible, people turning their rage on the Delphi family themselves. To protect their sovereigns, the Knights had stripped themselves of their rank and gone into hiding. They'd remained in the shadows since, operating in secret and waiting to one day be called into action again.

"Swallows dance at window sills, they dance, they dance for you..." The stranger sang, as if reading her thoughts. Luca's breath caught. Either a dangerous foe stood within a few strides of her or he truly was an ally. Luca decided to take the risk.

"Tell me who you are," she ordered him. "And why I should trust you. And then I'll consider whether to hear you or not."

"As you wish." The figure bowed, a hand across his chest. "My name is Embarr Reagon, if pleases you, and I am an emissary of the great Lady Niamh."

Luca didn't need to hear past his name. "You're the

Gancanagh!" she blurted. Embarr paused and raised his head. His hood moved enough for Luca to catch a quick glimpse of pair of shining black eyes.

"I am indeed. How did you know?"

"Fae. Fae spoke of you..." Luca drew off. "You're her friend, aren't you?"

"She is as dear to me as the jewelled sky and the brightly moon," Embarr said and there was no mockery or exaggeration in his voice.

"If that's true..." Luca frowned. "Alright, I'm listening." She stepped back and sat on the steps of the house, drawing her clothes around her. Embarr wasted no time.

"Your enemies will be descending upon you in just over twelve hours' time," he said. "Alchemists, soldiers, perhaps even a Magi or two—they mean to deal you the first blow."

Luca sat, stunned. "Where did you hear that?"

"From Harmatia. It was discussed a few hours ago."

"And I'm to believe you managed to trek all the way to Bethean in that time?"

She saw a flash of white teeth in the moonlight, bared in a grin and a moment later, in a flurry of wind, Embarr was gone. Luca jumped to her feet, only to give a short cry as someone tapped her on the shoulder. She spun around to see him stood there before, with another burst, he was gone again, reappearing back between the tree trunks.

"It's a talent I have."

"*How* did you—"

"Gancanagh," he responded matter-of-factly, pointing at himself.

"Oh. Right," Luca said, feeling foolish. "The first blow, you say? Against Bethean?"

"Against potential revolutionists—supporters of the Delphi."

"What?" Luca felt the blood drain from her face. "Does that mean they know the truth?"

"No. Not as of yet. But they have an informant who seems to be privy to a great deal of information. I cannot say how long our secrets will keep. So far, they are unaware that the Prince lives."

"Thank the gods," Luca breathed, and then frowned. "Then why are they attacking? They've given us no reason to go to war and we no sign that we plan to. So why now?" Luca stood, already sensing the dark news that weighed on her companion's tongue.

He was quiet a while, each second of silence drawing out Luca's fears. Finally he spoke, voice soft with mourning.

"Rufus Merle is dead."

The words incited the strangest sensation in Luca. They washed over her like hundreds of gallons of water, but left her light, as if she were falling. She found herself sat on the stair again, staring at Embarr in disbelief. For a moment she couldn't speak, and when she did her voice was faint.

"I don't believe you."

"It's the truth."

"Rufus...Rufus is dead?"

"He was killed by an assassin in Beshuwa."

"No...No, no, no."

"I asked if any children had also been disposed of but none were recorded. I can only assume your correspondents in the area are taking care of the Prince now. Reports are Rufus's body is being brought back to Harmatia."

"Athea have mercy, no...!"

"I am sorry." Embarr sounded it and Luca clamped her hands across her mouth, gasping.

"Rufus," she sobbed. "Oh gods, Rufus. Oh gods, rest in peace. Athea guide you." She buried her face in her arms and cried. "Rufus, my dearest, dearest love, oh gods, I'm so sorry."

"You must rouse the village and gather your weapons—you have no time to spare," Embarr reminded her, forcing her out of her mourning.

"I understand." She wiped her eyes, her voice strangled.

"Everything's changed now."

"And you must be ready for it," Embarr agreed. "Now, I must leave you, before I am missed." He paused and then added, "I am *truly* sorry."

Luca nodded, wiping her eyes again as she forced herself to her feet. "Thank you... Thank you for delivering this news."

The faerie nodded solemnly and then, with another burst of air, he was gone. Luca stumbled out into the street toward the village bell. On her approach, the patrolling guards ran out, alarmed by her appearance. She shouted as they reached her.

"Ring the alarm! There's an approaching army! The Puppet King is coming for us and Rufus Merle is dead! *Athea have mercy, Rufus is dead!*"

CHAPTER 14

Zachary fingered his collar, tugging it away from his neck. Almost immediately, he drew it back around himself as a blast of cold air reminded him why he'd tightened it in the first place. It was perishing. The whole of Harmatia was cloaked in snow and though the skies had cleared up in the morning, Zachary expected they would have more come nightfall.

If there was one thing that could be said about the whole affair though, it was that snow created unity. As the children played, the adults gathered in a combined effort to clear the streets. If the Magi were put to the task, they could have the city cleared in a number of hours, but Zachary doubted Sverrin would send his forces out for such a menial task. Those commissioned for such jobs would be limited to clearing the main road and forum. Zachary made a note to gather some of his men, once he and Belphegore had completed their grim task, and come and make himself useful.

The Southern Quarters were somehow clearer than their neighbouring districts and Zachary quickly discovered why. Several of the residents were using limited elemental magic to melt away and dispose of the snow. Among them, carefully manipulating a flame, was Torin Merle. From a distance, he was such a spitting image of his son, Zachary had to look twice.

On closer inspection, Zachary could see the grey in the man's hair and lines across the face. As Zachary and Belphegore approached, Torin cast a set of keen, green eyes over them, and halloed in greeting.

"Lord Odin, what a pleasure. It's been a long time," he said cheerfully, his cheeks bright from the hard work.

"Please, Torin, call me Belphegore. You know my first, I believe? Arlen Zachary."

"We've met before, yes, briefly." Torin took Zachary's hand in a strong grip and shook it. Immediately, Zachary was aware that Torin knew what had happened between him and Rufus twelve years ago, on the road to Avalon. Whilst there was no forgiveness in Torin's eye, however, there was no condemnation either—merely a sort of patience that confused Zachary. "Do come on in. The wife is making stew—come and have a bowl."

"Thank you but I am afraid we are here on more sombre business," Belphegore said.

Torin faltered, looking between the pair. Zachary got the impression that Torin was weighing his chances. Finally, he gestured to his door, inviting them in wordlessly. They followed him as he entered, calling to his wife inside.

The front half of the Merle home was a tailor shop, the walls lined with fabrics and items of clothing on display. At the far side, a desk stood in front of an open doorway, with a short corridor beyond. At the back was a little kitchen, where the thick, savoury smell of stew wafted out. Torin slid around the desk and the two Magi followed him silently. Zachary had only been in the Merle household once before, when Rufus invited him in while he fetched some work from his room. It was a small but comfortable place, filled with warmth and memories. The wood was etched with echoes of family life.

For a strange moment Zachary felt as if he was standing at a crossroad. He wasn't sure what lay on any of the paths ahead and a deep foreboding told him he wasn't ready to know. The sensation stopped him cold in his tracks and in an instant the truth was on him, like a heavy stone on his chest.

Rufus Merle was dead. Now what was Zachary going to do?

He shivered and Belphegore glanced back at him. "Arlen?" he prompted gently and Zachary came to his senses, following swiftly after his master into the kitchen.

"Do we have visitors?" Nora Merle said as they appeared. She was a stout but handsome woman, with greying auburn hair and a soft shape that made her look a little like a brooding hen. She smiled up to the two Magi, as if defying their presence to be anything less than pleasant. "Lords Odin, Zachary, what a pleasant surprise. Can I get you something to eat?" Her accent was Betheanian and very welcoming. It made Zachary feel all the worse. He stepped toward her and extended his hand in greeting.

"You have a beautiful home," he said, and she took his hand graciously and shook it.

"Thank you," she said, glancing quickly to Torin, who looked grim. "You're here on official business?"

"I am afraid so," Belphegore said heavily. "Nora, Torin, you may wish to sit down. I am afraid we have some bad news for you."

Both parents tensed, and Torin came to Nora's side. Even before anything was said, Torin and Nora knew what had happened. Nora began to shake.

"Rufus?" was all she asked.

"The King," Belphegore struggled with the words, his head bowed. Zachary didn't want to watch, but he forced himself to.

"The King placed a bounty on Rufus's head. The contract was picked up by an assassin in Lemra, who followed your son to Beshuwa..." Belphegore cut off as Torin gave a terrible groan, somewhere between a sob and a choke. "I am sorry," Belphegore forced out, his words rushed. "But he's dead. Rufus is dead. I am so sorry."

Neither of the Merles made a sound, the pair trapped in their misery. Then Torin turned on his heel and put his head and fists against the wall.

"No, no, no, no, no," he whispered over and over. "It can't be. It can't."

"His body will be sent to Harmatia. I will do what I can to have it returned to you, but…He was a traitor of the realm and will therefore," Belphegore exhaled, "will therefore probably be put on display."

"No!" Torin broke out, banging his fist against the wall. "Not my boy, not my Rufus-lad, please not my boy."

Nora didn't move, her eyes cast unseeingly forward, her body shaking.

"The announcement will be made later today." Belphegore continued with the unforgiving truths. "It may stir up old memories and feelings. You should distance yourself awhile. I urge you to take some time away from Harmatia, perhaps go to your family in Bethean. It may not be safe for you here any longer." He reached toward Nora, as if to comfort her, then thought better of it, retracting his hand. "I am truly sorry for your loss." He turned sharply and swept from the kitchen. Zachary followed him, stopping at the end of the corridor in time to look back and see Torin collapse onto his knees, sobbing hopelessly. Nora rose and gathered her husband to her, as if trying to drown his grief in an embrace. The colours seemed to seep from the house, until it became cold and dark. Zachary, aware he was witnessing something he shouldn't, left the house as quickly as he could.

Stepping out into the snow, he managed eight steps before stopping, his whole chest on fire. He froze, unable to breathe, one hand clenched up to his throat as the other grasped for support from the building at his side. Zachary had seen men suffer and die from horrific wounds but there was no greater torture than the loss of a child, and that was more than the Magi had been willing to see.

Belphegore, realising he was no longer being followed, turned back and strode toward his apprentice. He took Zachary by the arm and pulled him straight.

"Their grief is not your responsibility," he said. Zachary inhaled deeply and nodded. Belphegore gave his apprentice a sombre look and with his hand on Zachary's back, guided him back up the street. No more was said between them.

~⁓~

Joshua was dreaming, the world curling around him mysteriously. He was in a forest but didn't recognise the trees surrounding him. They were dark and tall, and covered in bristles. Joshua had never seen trees like that before, outside of books. He reached out to a branch and touched the prickling leaves.

"Who are you?" a deep, rumbling voice rose from behind him. Joshua turned around.

There, between the towering trunks, a large man stood barely three strides from him. He was a frightening figure, battle-worn and muscular, with eyes as black as peppercorn. Joshua's first instinct was that he was a Fomorii—one of a clan of faerie who were, historically, enemies of the Sidhe and, by association, the Delphi. Yet there was a human aspect about him too. He had bold features, dark skin with a slightly cold undertone, and a terrible scar across his throat that led from ear to ear in an ugly grin.

He watched the Prince with the unblinking patience of a predator. Joshua, despite it all, found that he wasn't afraid.

"Who are you?" the Prince asked in turn, and though his face didn't change, Joshua sensed amusement from the other.

"Varyn," the man said. His accent was northern—Kathrak. "You?"

"My name is Joshua," Joshua replied slowly. He'd been trained all

his life to fear the Kathraks but for some reason he felt at ease with this stranger. As if they'd met before. "Where are we?"

"This is my dream," Varyn replied. "You're not part of it."

"No."

"Better question then—how are you here?" Varyn tipped his head forward, putting his hands together. His arms were heavily tattooed with intricate rings and symbols. Joshua eyed them.

"I'm not sure." He sat down. "We must be linked somehow."

"Hm." Varyn came forward and sat silently opposite the boy.

"Are you…a Fomorii?"

Varyn raised his thick eyebrows.

"Your eyes…" Joshua went on.

Varyn's eyebrows rose even higher and his mouth twitched at once side. He huffed and Joshua got the impression he was amused. "Black eyes are common among the Isny."

"You're an Isny?" Joshua felt a wave of relief pass over him. Isnydea was a county in Kathra, in the far north. "So you're human?"

"Didn't say that," Varyn rumbled. He was still watching Joshua unblinkingly.

"Then you are a Fomorii?"

"Didn't say that either."

"Then are you an enemy of mine?" Joshua swallowed.

"Depends." Varyn pulled a knife from his belt. "You something I'd hunt?"

"I'm just a boy."

"Doubt that." Varyn's black eyes gleamed like polished onyx. "Normal boys don't cross into people's dreams."

"I suppose not," Joshua agreed. His gaze darted down to the tattoos on Varyn's arms again—he'd never seen anything like them before. Varyn caught him looking, and extended both arms, to show the full design. "These are common on Isnys too."

"What do they mean?"

"This is rank." Varyn pointed to a circle with three lines through

151

it on his forearm. "These show who I've defeated. This—my faction. Who I belonged to. Where to return me…" He trailed off, and Joshua finally understood.

"You're a slave?"

"Was. Free now." Varyn pointed to the last mark on his right arm, a simple cross. "And you, boy? What are you?"

Before Joshua could reply, a shriek from the air cut over them and he jumped up. Varyn didn't move.

"What is that?" Joshua looked up in time to see something humungous whip through the air above the tree line. It moved so quickly, it was difficult to see. Whatever it was, it was large, black and scaly, with bat-like wings and long tail.

"Dragon," Varyn replied calmly.

"It's…It's huge," Joshua gasped, as the dragon roared, making the earth tremble. "What's it doing here?"

"Looking for me," Varyn said, and he suddenly seemed to be deep in thought. "You need to go. It's not safe."

"What about you?"

Varyn paused and flashed a grin that was more terrifying than the dragon itself. He gave the boy no other response and Joshua found himself falling from Varyn's dream, back into his own.

<hr/>

They'd walked a few miles before exhaustion felled them both. The snow had gathered around them in a suffocating hold, and Rufus used the last of his strength to build them a rudimentary shelter with magic. Then they'd huddled within it and waited until the storm passed. Sometime in the night both tumbled into uncomfortable sleep.

When Rufus woke next, it was to the stark reflection of the sun on the snow. He was so cold he couldn't feel anything of his body. The fire he'd built had long since burned out, unable to suffer the snow any longer. The harrowing wind had stopped and Rufus lay still, his mind an exhausted mess of muted thoughts.

Even so, knew if he and Joshua didn't move soon, the pair of them would to die of exposure.

He forced himself to roll, shaking Joshua, who was clutched at his side. Joshua was pale, his breathing laboured. He needed warmth and shelter soon, or he would slip into a permanent sleep.

"Joshua," Rufus called faintly, his voice hoarse. "Joshua, wake up. Come on." He shook him more forcefully and the boy gave a groan, his eyes fluttering open. His lips were chapped, and he gave a small whine. "We need to get up. We need to go," Rufus said.

Joshua's eyes fell closed.

"Don't go back to sleep. We'll freeze. Joshua—" Rufus cut himself off as from outside he heard a branch crack.

No, he thought. *No, not again. Not now. Please.*

He put a hand to his mouth, trying to hush the sound of his breath. In the snow, their shelter would be disguised, but Rufus couldn't afford to trust in that chance. He gritted his teeth and forced himself up, crawling to the entrance. Joshua opened his eyes.

"R'fus?" he murmured fearfully.

"Stay quiet," Rufus said, almost falling as his vision swirled. He couldn't get into a fight—he would be dead before he had a chance to summon any magic to him. His strength was fading fast but Rufus had to protect Joshua.

He crawled out of their hiding place and forced himself to his feet. The wintery world was stark and seamless, covered in an even layer of snow, so undisturbed and perfect it might have been a dream. Rufus squinted against the harsh light, falling against the shelter as he stood.

He blinked the black spots from his vision, stepping out into the thick snow. To the far right, he could see the tree branch that had been disturbed, a fresh pile of snow gathered below it, where it had been knocked off. Rufus dared to hope that perhaps the weight of the snow had caused the branch to bend and drop its load. He stepped out further, the wet seeping into his trousers and creeping up. The world was immaculate and deathly still all around him. He breathed out, relieved

Then something moved in his peripheral. He turned so quickly he almost collapsed back into the snow.

Stood among the trees, a vast creature was watching him. Three strides tall, with an impossible wingspan and fur as black as coal, the beast towered over Rufus, vibrant green eyes trained on his face. Rufus glanced down to the white patch of fur on the faerie's breast, bright like a star on a lonely night. He didn't dare speak, frozen by the sight of her. She gave a soft laugh.

"I heard there was a drunkard running around in the forest singing dirty songs for the feeorin. I thought I would come check it wasn't you." She stepped forward, her paws crunching in the snow. "So tell me, lowly lord, are you out here for the sport?" She flashed her teeth in something close to a grin. "Or have you simply gotten lost again?"

CHAPTER 15

~~~

He couldn't believe it. For a minute he feared he might have gone snow-blind or was hallucinating, but the texture of the fur and the rumble of her laugh were too real. He stood, gaping, as with a burst of black mist the large cat form was replaced by that of a young woman. She smiled gently at him and Rufus ploughed through the snow towards her. His eyes darted over her face in hesitant awe.

"Fae?"

She tilted her head, the light catching the small line of star-like markings that framed her eyes.

"I have been looking for you for three days. You're not an easy person to find, Rufus Merle." Her voice was warm and mellow, just as he remembered it.

Rufus dropped to his knees and seized her hands, turning them so that he could see the crescent shaped birthmark on her wrist. He kissed it fervently, her familiar smell washing over him, and he broke down into tears. He hadn't realised how heavy the pressure and misery within him were until the dam broke. Suddenly he could barely breathe for his sobs. Fae dropped down, clasping his chin worriedly, her eyes scanning him for injuries.

"Rufus?" she asked. "Rufus, what's wrong?"

"It's you," he gasped.

"Titania man, you're freezing." Fae frowned, putting her hands on his cheeks. "Are you hurt?"

Rufus shook his head weakly, still sobbing. He couldn't express his relief—his cries feeble and long, like a lost child. He covered her hands with his own, gripping them as tightly as he dared, lest she disappear.

"Easy, Rufus, breathe easy. I have you now." She looked up as a small voice interrupted them.

"Papa?" Joshua asked cautiously, stood in the mouth of their shelter.

Fae's eyes widened as she took in the boy, who stared openly back at her.

"You're her," Joshua identified. "You're Fae."

"Yes, I am." Fae released Rufus and moved toward the boy, her footfall so light, she barely sank into the snow. "And you must be the Delphi Prince."

"You know about me?" Joshua slurred, as if he were still dreaming.

"Yes," Fae said lightly, reaching him and squatting down to his height. "My friend Luca told me all about you." She touched his cheek, her expression darkening with concern. "Have no fear of me, Joshua," she said sweetly. Joshua gave a sound of relief and fell forward into her. Fae didn't expect it but took his weight regardless, wrapping her arms around his thin body. She looked back at Rufus who watched, still tearful.

"His breathing is laboured," she noted.

"He's ill," Rufus replied, his voice thick.

"You both are." Fae stood, picking Joshua up easily. He was already asleep, head dropped against her shoulder, as she manoeuvred him onto her hip. "You *fool*, what were you doing out here?"

"I..." Rufus bowed his head, his voice cracking. "I don't know. We had nowhere else. The Kathraks, an assassin…We had nowhere to go. We just ran."

"Straight into a faerie wood? Without any idea of where you were going? You could have stumbled into Unseelie territory! Or been caught in another faerie trap! Rufus, how could you be so *stupid*?"

"I had *nowhere else!*" Rufus cried. The next second the world around him ebbed to black and he tumbled forward. Sharp spots of white filled his vision and he blinked away the familiar, sticky nausea that clung to his head. He coughed, trying to breathe, aware that Fae was at his side, holding him up with her other arm. Her eyes were filled with panic.

"You're not well," she muttered.

"Fae," he moaned. He felt so weak, he thought he might crumble to nothing. His head was heavy against her body but she bore him regardless. "Don't leave. Please don't leave us."

"I am not going to leave you, you twit," Fae said coarsely.

Negotiating Joshua onto her back, she made Rufus lean against him.

"Hold onto my shoulders," she instructed.

Somehow, he obeyed her and in the next second, they were enveloped in black mist. Rufus felt himself rising up into the air as Fae transformed. It was so sudden, he almost fell from her back, but her wings formed a nest around the pair, securing them. Joshua buried his face into her fur with a faint murmur of approval and Rufus held on tightly. Her back was warm and soft, just as it had been the night she'd carried him away from the Korrigans' nest. He'd been cold then too. So very, very cold.

"Where are we going?" he managed to ask, as Fae flexed her wings, preparing to leap up into the air.

"I am taking you home," she said. "We're going to the Neve."

"Zachary!"

The Magi stopped in his tracks and peered wearily around as Sverrin strode toward him down the darkening corridor. Zachary bowed deeply as Sverrin drew closer, his stride hurried to catch up. He looked bright and excited.

"I missed you at the execution this evening." Sverrin motioned for Zachary to straighten from his bow. "Were you heading this way?"

"Yes, Your Majesty."

"Good, I will walk with you." They set off together, Sverrin strangely light on his feet. There was a boyish excitement about him today. "So? Where have you been?"

"I wasn't feeling very well this morning," Zachary said, "and was late to my work as a result."

"I trust you feel better now?" Sverrin pulled a sympathetic smile. "You look a little pale."

"Much better, thank you." Zachary relaxed a little. Sverrin seemed in an amicable mood, and that eased the tension between them. "I apologise for missing the executions," Zachary added.

Sverrin gave him a puzzled look.

"There's no need to apologise." He knocked Zachary's arm. "There was no obligation for you to be there. I merely noticed you were not in your usual perch with Lords Hathely and Fold. Mind, Lord Fold wasn't there either today. I heard he's taken ill. I hope you haven't come down with something similar."

"No, no," Zachary dismissed, "I merely drank too much."

"Gracious, a hangover? I didn't even know Magi could get them. You must have drunk you weight in wine. Is something the matter?"

"Troubles at home," Zachary replied evenly. "Nothing concerning."

"Ah. Your father, is it?" Sverrin asked knowingly and Zachary's gut tightened. For a moment he'd forgotten how much his King knew of his situation. The pair had once shared every secret.

"Yes. He's being difficult."

"If there's anything I can do…" Sverrin offered as they reached the entrance hall. He looked out, deep in thought. "Are you free now?"

"I…" Zachary hesitated. "I have no further duties."

"Will you take a ride with me?" Sverrin nodded toward the stables with a hopeful smile.

Zachary was taken aback. "It would be an honour," he said.

They set off toward the stables, Sverrin shouting ahead to prepare the horses. When Zachary asked after any servants Sverrin might want to take with him, the King laughed lightly.

"I am sure I can manage without."

They set out a few minutes later, their horses trudging through the snow as they exited the city out into the open fields toward the moorland.

The evening was coming in but it was still fairly light, the sky painted in brilliant colours. It was going to be a clear night.

As they rode out, the clock bell tolled. Even now, the sound of tolling bells rallied something up in Zachary and brought him back to the years of the curfew. He recalled the sick excitement of his impatient years, the rush of the transformation and the iron taste of blood. Those were manic times, months of darkness and a hunger he could never quench—a ravenous guilt. Panicked by the sudden noise, a flight of pigeons took off from the tower, soaring over their heads. Sverrin scowled up at them and Zachary frowned.

"Something the matter?"

"Pigeons," Sverrin replied indignantly, eyes narrowed.

Zachary widened his own. "Are they after your crown?"

Sverrin laughed loudly at the sincerity in the Magi's expression, throwing his head back.

"Truly," Zachary continued, straight-faced, "I have an inside man, should you require information."

"You're mocking me." Sverrin's tone was light.

Zachary grinned.

"Sky-rats," the King said. "I don't like them. They're vermin with wings, shitting on my city and giving nothing in return." He paused and added, "But if you have an inside man..."

"Have no fear, my King," Zachary saluted, "if the pigeons conspire it will be nipped in the bud. I shall see to it, with all of the might of the Night Patrol."

Sverrin chuckled and leant back in the saddle, breathing out. "It really has been a long time," he said wistfully. "We used to ride like this so often as young men."

"I recall."

"Do you remember," Sverrin began, laughing, "that summer you and I rode out toward the coast? I decided to cut through that field of flowers, and you followed me even though they were in full bloom."

Zachary snorted, "Oh sons of the gods—that was a bad day..."

"I had no idea you would have such a reaction!" Sverrin's laughter grew. "I remember, I heard you sneezing, and we were halfway through, and I looked back at you—"

"I honestly thought I was going to go blind," Zachary chuckled.

"Red eyes, tears streaming down your cheeks—I swear your entire face had swelled." Sverrin cackled. "You looked so ill. And I remember—I couldn't believe it—and I said 'Healing Septus, what's wrong with you', and you said—"

"I have an itch in my throat." Zachary pinched his nose, mimicking his congested voice. Sverrin exploded with laughter again.

"By the might of Penthar, who knew such an abled warrior could be felled by flowers?"

"I wasn't felled—I kept riding, didn't I?" Zachary said, with false indignation. "I simply couldn't breathe."

"You poor man." Sverrin wiped his eyes, his smile wide. "I caused you so much trouble. Do you recall the first time I convinced you to take me to a tavern?"

"Athea, another disastrous day."

"You got me a tankard of ale and then bought something for yourself. It was very strong, what was it?"

"Poitín."

"Yes, that's right. Except, I ended up drinking it instead."

"Yes, you did," Zachary said, feigning disapproval. "And then proceeded to break into the farmer's field next door and attempt to ride his cow."

Sverrin slapped his hand on his thigh, laughing.

"I did, didn't I?"

"And then I had to explain why the Crown Prince of Harmatia was almost kicked to death by a cow under my watch."

"Such a fond memory..." Sverrin sighed. "And then life became dull."

"Did it?" Zachary asked softly. Dull wasn't the word he would choose. Chaotic, perhaps. Turbulent, exciting, terrible—but never dull.

"It did," Sverrin huffed. "Politics bore me."

"I should rather hope they don't."

"Do they interest you?"

Zachary pouted. "Not particularly. But I'm not the King."

"No," Sverrin said, "and give thanks for that, you'd hate it."

Zachary glanced back at his King as they both drew to a halt at the top of a knoll.

"Your Majesty?"

"Please—Sverrin. I don't want to be King up here."

"Sverrin," Zachary corrected, his expression torn. The Magi realised he wasn't speaking with his King at all, but with his Prince—the boy he'd known and loved. Zachary had been riding with him all along, and it was so strangely familiar, so sweet-tasting, he was filled with a surge of loyalty that made him pause. He raised a hand quickly to his mouth.

"Are you alright?" Sverrin noted the sudden movement.

"Sorry," Zachary said, a little breathlessly. "You were right. It's been so long. I forgot how peaceful it was out here. It's rather moving."

Sverrin hummed in agreement and then grumbled, "They'll probably be running around in a panic by now."

"Excuse me?"

"My court." Sverrin smiled sleepily. "They'll have been expecting me for near a half hour now."

"You mean," Zachary's mouth fell open, "you didn't tell anyone you were leaving?"

"Hmm…" Sverrin gave him a mischievous smile. "How long until they send soldiers out looking for me, do you think?"

"How long until my father writes, telling me to seize the throne before your other cousins arrive?" Zachary retorted.

Sverrin pulled a face of mock-horror.

"Gods, yes. We'd best return before they announce me dead. Again."

"Or accuse me of kidnap," Zachary agreed, turning his horse around.

"Help, help," Sverrin cried dryly. "I'm being held against my will."

Zachary glanced over his shoulder slyly, then with a smirk, spurred his horse into a canter. Sverrin shouted after him as he shot forward, and then with a laugh, followed his example, charging after. Zachary howled out a hunting call to the wind, mindless of the danger of snow or unseen ice. In an instant he was a young man again, free of troubles and invincible.

In his youth, after a tiring mission away, he would ride upon Harmatia always to find the Prince waiting for him. Sverrin would spot him in the distance and wave excitedly, as if seeing Zachary was the best part of his day. And then they would race back to the city together, regardless of how injured or exhausted Zachary might have been. Those were times of pure happiness, with a family on whom Zachary could rely. Marcel with his monotone and unwavering loyalty, Emeric ever fretting but always brave,

Rufus mostly fearful but unequivocally brilliant. And Sverrin...
Energetic, plain-spoken, full of wonder and adventure—these
things were *home* to Zachary. But that was almost fifteen years
ago.

Sverrin applauded as they came to a halt, the pair slumped in
their saddles, breathing hard. The King drew up beside Zachary,
cackling faintly.

"Aren't you supposed to let me win?" he asked and Zachary
shrugged.

The boy he'd known was a thirty-five year old man, still young
to be a King but old enough to have ruled for a decade already. A
decade longer than he naturally should have.

"Alas, I am not so courteous," Zachary responded.

Sverrin dismounted, whistling to the stable boys who hurried
up to reclaim the horses. It hadn't been a long ride but darkness
had descended quickly and, clear as it was, a chill was beginning
to blow through the city, harrowing its stone walls.

"We should do this again." Sverrin clasped Zachary's hand and
clapped him on the back fondly, "I forgot what good company
feels like."

Zachary blinked and realised that, for the entirety of the ride,
he'd forgotten that he was terrified of his King.

"As had I." He forced a brief smile, fighting his sudden unease.

Sverrin beamed back. Zachary cleared his throat.

"The night is encroaching, Your Majesty. As I would rather
not hang upon the gallows tomorrow for high treason, might I
suggest you go and reassure your court I haven't murdered you."

"Gracious, yes, before they build me another grave." Sverrin
winced and started off toward the castle. Halfway up the stairs,
he turned back. "Zachary," he called, "send my best wishes to
Lord Fold, if you see him. Tell him I hope he is more revived
at our next meeting. And the same for you. Be wary of sickness
or old wounds." He paused and something flashed in his bronze
eyes. "They can fester."

And with that he was gone, marching back up to the castle. Zachary stood below, a streak of terror passing through him, before he too turned and moved swiftly toward his own home. His instincts told him to run, but mindful that people in the low light might see him hurrying, he calmed his stride and forced himself to walk with purpose, rather than scurry. He was a lord, a soldier and a Magi, and despite what he'd said, he played the political game every day. Why would Sverrin have asked him out on a ride? To remember old times? Doubtful—that was merely a pleasant outcome, but within the city walls all that mattered was the present. And the present was cruel and demanding.

Zachary threw open his doors, instantly aware that something was wrong. He strode into the darkened hall and listened intently. From the back of the house, he heard a noise. He reached for the sword at his side as he strode toward the sound.

"Heather," he called and there was a soft clatter from the kitchen. He opened the door and blinked into the darkness. At the back of the room, Daniel and Heather were hidden in the corner with the rest of the servants. Daniel had put himself in front of them all and was guarding them fiercely. He relaxed a little when he saw it was Zachary in the doorway. Heather gasped.

"Thank heavens, Arlen, you're back."

Zachary stepped into the kitchen, lighting the fire with a flick of his hand. "What's going on?" he asked, looking at Daniel.

"They came with a warrant to search the house and forced us all in here out of the way," Daniel told him quietly. "They're members of the Royal Guard, I think."

"Right." Zachary exhaled. He turned on his heel and strode from the room, fury in his every step.

"Arlen, you mustn't! Please," Heather begged. Zachary ignored her, going out into the entrance hall.

"Where are they?" he demanded.

Heather and Daniel were at his back. The housekeeper didn't speak, so Zachary locked eyes with his brother.

"Where are they?"

Daniel opened his mouth to reply but a soft thump from the salle above told Zachary all he needed. He started up the stairs two at a time.

Moving around the landing, he threw open the salle door and stepped inside.

"Good evening, gentlemen." He opened his arms wide in welcome. "Can I offer any of you refreshments?"

The guards immediately pulled back from the business. There were six of them, some tearing through the cupboards along the walls, whilst a couple tried to negotiate their way through a door on the far left. Zachary nodded at it.

"I wouldn't bother with that. It leads to my bedroom—I always keep it bolted."

"Lord Zachary." The captain of the Royal Guard approached. "We have a warrant to search these premises."

"May I see it?" Zachary held out his hand and the warrant was begrudgingly handed to him. Zachary studied it closely, squinting as he tried to make out the words. "Ah yes, this is filed under the third law of the Book. Do you know what that means, Captain?"

"I do."

"It means," Zachary continued, "that a generalised search may be issued into a private household. But unlike a search filed under the fourth law, which requires evidence of suspicious behaviour or previous felony, this search can only be done with the upstanding owner's permission. Permission is to be presumed, of course, in the owner's absence." He folded the warrant back up. "I see you took advantage of that clause."

"You are well acquainted with the Book of Law," the Captain sniffed.

"My sister had me memorise it as a child," Zachary said , "lest I get caught out by men who would abuse the less learned."

"Wise indeed." The Captain snatched the warrant back. "As a

law-abiding citizen, member of the Magi and lord of the King's court, we expect your full cooperation with our search."

"And what exactly are you searching for?" Zachary circled the room. Daniel and Heather remained in the doorway, watching the proceedings nervously.

"The Merle family are reported to have absconded from their home a few hours ago. They are important figures in our on-going investigation into Rufus Merle."

"Rufus Merle?"

"Correct."

"The *traitor* Rufus Merle?" Zachary rearticulated.

"As stated."

"The traitor Rufus Merle who was put to death?" Zachary snorted. "The tale seems rather complete to me. What exactly is the nature of the investigation? Has he *necromanced* himself back to life again?"

The guard remained unamused.

"As a law-abiding member of the Magi, we expect your full cooperation."

"And as a law-abiding member of the Guard, I heavily suggest you escort your men from my premises before I have you all arrested for unlawful entry. Your warrant is void without my permission."

"Think carefully on that request." The Captain drew himself up. "It will reflect very gravely upon you."

"And your disrespect will reflect gravely on you in turn, Captain." Zachary wasn't deterred. "Had you conducted yourself with a modicum of respect when you entered my house, you may have found me to be a more hospitable host. And yet you abuse my staff and my brother, take advantage of the law and then make comments on my allegiance? My loyalty to the King goes beyond your comprehension. I have littered Harmatia with the corpses of those who opposed him. And yet you question me, Captain? I don't appreciate it. If you wish to continue this search, I suggest you return when you've learned some common courtesy. In the meantime, get out of my house."

The Captain's jaw clenched. "And if I disobey your request?" he asked, acid in his voice.

"Two words." Zachary's mouth curled into a smile. "Night Patrol."

The reaction was instantaneous. The Captain's face drained of colour. He was of a generation that had known the terror of the Night Patrol, a generation that still dreamt of them on stormy nights and saw them in the shadows of a dangerous street. The identities of the Night Patrol had been kept relatively private, so the Captain had no way of knowing if Zachary was telling the truth or lying. The Magi allowed his eyes to fill with enough blood-thirst to convince him. It had been some time now since Zachary had sunk his jaws into someone's throat but it wasn't beyond him.

"Is that a threat?" the Captain barely managed to breathe, his men gathered around him.

"As you wish." Zachary grinned, his teeth sharp.

"We will go," the Captain said, raising his hands slightly in surrender. "I am sorry, we will go."

Zachary stepped back to allow them through, then stood at the window to watch them all exit out into the courtyard below. When the last had finally disappeared, he allowed himself to wilt, anger and fear filling him.

"That was unwise." Heather took his elbow. "Arlen, you'll lose your head if you're not careful."

"I know." Zachary leant against the wall. His fear wasn't directed to the men who'd broken into his house but rather at the King who'd conspired with them. Sverrin had given them time to get in, Sverrin had *tricked* him. And regardless of how much truth there was in the joy of their ride, it had at its heart been nothing but a shallow scheme.

Zachary thought back to the surge of loyalty he'd felt. It made him sick.

"There's only one thing worse than a madman in power," he breathed. "A madman in power who knows exactly what he's doing."

CHAPTER
16

Rufus missed the journey. Having slipped into a blissful sleep, he only woke on impact as they landed, and was surprised to find that it was dark and late. Fae deposited them both on the hard, icy ground, and then transformed with an exhausted sigh, rolling her shoulders. She must have flown the entire day, carefully and slow, so as not to disturb her precious cargo. Rufus marvelled at her.

In the darkness, he couldn't see much except the tall, looming shape of a castle carved out of the mountain they'd settled on. The front was opened by elegant white pillars which emerged from the rock and swirled up like stone columns of cloud. It was so big, it made him nervous but Fae took him by the shoulder and, hoisting Joshua onto her hip, guided them toward a humongous open doorway.

They walked for what seemed like hours, Rufus bow-backed, bent over Fae so she took the majority of his weight. In her human form, she seemed so much smaller than him, yet so much stronger.

Finally, after sneaking through several long, wide corridors, bathed only in the moonlight which spilled through tall windows high above them, they slipped down into a small passageway to the left. It was dark down here and there was a door, almost hidden around the corner. Fae stopped at it and knocked.

"Boyd," she called softly. "Boyd!"

The door clicked open and a slender young man with a lean, pale face and a shock of pure white hair leant out. Behind him, the orange light of a fire spilled out, casting shadows. He blinked at the group and raised an eyebrow.

"Fae? What in Titania's name—"

"I need your help." Her gaze darted down the corridor conspiratorially.

The young man, presumably 'Boyd', drew back, then nodded faintly, pulling the door open wide. He took Rufus by the other arm, helping Fae carry him in. Rufus could see he was a small man—no taller than Fae herself.

"What happened to them?" Boyd asked quickly. He had a peculiar accent, almost Betheanian but somehow softer, with strange tonal jumps.

Rufus looked lethargically around the room. It appeared to be a physician's chamber, the walls mounted with shelves of bottles and hanging herbs. In the corners, behind drawn back curtains, were several cots for patients. All of them seemed empty and Rufus and Joshua were directed to a set.

"I found them in the snow." Fae laid Joshua down tenderly and then helped Rufus do the same. The feel of the mattress against his back was pure bliss and he sank into it with relief. Fae touched his face worriedly.

"Joshua," Rufus forced out. "His lungs are sickly. He had a high fever, was coughing."

"Alright," Boyd said. He leaned over the boy. Joshua's face, which had been pale, was now flushed. "The breathing is a little laboured but the heart rate is normal. I can treat him."

Boyd moved over and took Fae's place at Rufus's side. Fae settled beside Joshua, stroking his hair soothingly. Joshua moved into her touch with a quiet murmur and she smiled. A feeling of relief washed over Rufus. Fae could take care of his brother if Rufus didn't live the night out. A part of him was certain he wouldn't.

"He's burning," Boyd said worriedly, touching Rufus's face.

"Normal," Rufus slurred. "That's my...my body. Normally."

"It's true," Fae confirmed. "He's an odd one."

Boyd froze and then looked accusingly up to Fae. "You know them," he said.

Fae's mouth drew into a line and Boyd inhaled sharply.

"You didn't just find them in the snow, did you?" He straightened, his back rigid. "You *know* them!"

"I do," she admitted.

"Oh Danu give me strength!" Boyd raged. "This is him, isn't it? This is Rufus Merle!"

Fae gave an exhausted sigh and rubbed her eyes.

"It is!" Boyd squawked with anger, turning on Rufus like he was the one at fault. The physician opened and closed his mouth, gabbling in silence, before directing himself at Fae again. "He's a Magi, Fae!"

"A Magi?" a soft voice interrupted the tirade and Fae sat bolt upright.

"*Kael?*" she gasped.

A young girl stuck her head out from where she was hiding behind one of the curtains. Her curious green eyes met with Rufus's and she tilted her head.

"What are you doing here?" Fae demanded, dragging the girl out of her hiding place.

"I couldn't sleep," Kael whined.

"It's my fault," Boyd said. "I told her to come and see me if she couldn't sleep. Keep her out of mischief."

Rufus looked the girl up and down. She seemed to be Joshua's age, though there was a youthfulness about her that suggested something younger. Fae pulled Kael to her side.

"Why were you hiding?" she asked, a little more gently.

"Korrick," Kael replied and Fae growled.

"He's forbidden Kael from wandering around at night," Boyd said.

"Of course he has. The gods forbid he'd ever treated his own siblings as more than trainees," Fae fumed. Kael leant over and peered curiously into Rufus's face.

"You're a Magi."

"Yes," Rufus replied hoarsely.

"Are you here to skin us?"

"No, Kael. He's a friend." Fae rested her hand on the top of Kael's head.

"Well, the rest of your family might not see it that way," Boyd reminded Fae tightly. "Does your father even know he's here?"

Fae didn't reply and Boyd winced.

"Damn it, Fae!"

"There was nowhere safe in Bethean. They needed medical attention. What was I supposed to do?"

"Well, I don't know—" Boyd threw his hands in the air, "maybe *not* bring a Magi to a household that will collectively want to kill him?" he gabbled. "And now you've made me an accomplice! What am I supposed to do when they charge me with harbouring an enemy of the Neve? I'm only human, they'll eat me alive!"

"No one is going to eat you."

"Impale me then! Over and over! I don't want to be impaled, Fae. I'm mortal and I won't enjoy it!"

"Would you calm down?" Fae shushed him, her arm still wound around the little girl below her. Kael leant toward Rufus and pocked him in the face. Rufus flinched.

"He's hot. Is he broken?" Kael asked.

"Not as much as we'll be when Korrick discovers he's here," Boyd muttered, chewing his thumb. Fae slapped him across the arm. Boyd yelped in pain.

Rufus closed his eyes. "I'm sorry," he choked out. "I don't want to be trouble. If that's what I'll cause, then maybe it's better I go." He sat up. "Just promise me you'll take care of Joshua. I'll—"

He wasn't given a chance to finish. A sudden, crushing pain shot through his chest and he doubled over, like he'd been struck with a mace. The pain was so unbearable for a moment he could barely draw breath against the excruciating pressure. A set of hands dragged him forward and Rufus might have retched, but he wasn't sure. Finally the feeling passed and he was laid down again, his heart-racing. He wheezed, shaking uncontrollably. Boyd grabbed his free hand and examined it, a pensive look on his face.

"What is it?" Fae asked.

"His fingernails are blue."

"I thought it was from the cold."

"He's not cold now." Boyd touched a couple of fingers to Rufus's forehead. "Naturally high temperature or not, this is too high to be normal. Feel for yourself, it's like a furnace."

"But he's not sweating," Fae said.

Boyd's mouth pinched. "No. He isn't. You're not going anywhere," he informed Rufus, before addressing Fae. "Try to speak to your father before Korrick catches wind of this—or worse, Commander Mac Gearailt. I'll do what I can for them now."

"Thank you, Boyd."

"If he's your friend, then he's mine." Boyd moved out of Rufus's line of sight. Rufus heaved a sigh of relief and felt someone squeeze his fingers. He looked down and realised that his hand was tightly clenched around Fae's. He must have grabbed hold of her when he started coughing.

"Korrick will find him if I'm here." Kael slipped from Fae's arms. "I'll go, before he comes looking."

"Thank you, Kael. I won't forget this," Fae said.

Kael leant in toward Rufus and gave him a smile like sunshine.

173

"If you're Rufus Merle, then you saved my sister's life. I'll save you now. Lie silent or they'll find you." She skipped from the room, stopping only to peer at the sleeping Joshua for a moment before leaving. Boyd said something to Fae but Rufus didn't have the energy to make out the words. He gave into his exhaustion, safe at last.

CHAPTER 17

⁓⁓

It was Boyd's startled cry that woke Rufus, a moment's warning before he was ripped out of his bed. Rufus didn't fight against the band of warriors as they pulled him upright, barely giving him time to find his feet before they dragged him out of the room.

It was still dark but the glow of the moon through the hall windows made Rufus's head throb, his innards rolling unhelpfully. He could barely breathe from where he was hanging between two of the Cat Sidhe. They were all so close, so unprotected—Rufus could set them alight where they stood, burn them all with a heat so sudden they wouldn't have time to draw their swords. The idea swam in his mind. If they truly turned on him, it might be his only chance to escape.

They brought him outside to a glamorous courtyard and he rolled his head back to see Athea's star searing in the sky, hot and fierce like a sun. He gasped, choking as the blistering sensation filled his lungs. He could feel Morrigan's touch throbbing on his skin, her hands driving into his muscles as she slipped into his blood. She poured through him, reaching his heart and it felt like his chest would burst open. He heaved and tossed his head, wailing like a man possessed.

"This man is extremely unwell!" Boyd's voice broke through the delirium. "He needs rest!"

"Step aside physician, the Magi is to be burned alive."

Rufus laughed manically and was dropped onto all fours at somebody's feet.

"Lord Korrick, Commander Mac Gearailt's informant was correct—we found this Magi hiding in the physician's quarters."

Rufus's laugher turned into a harsh cough and he slumped back, looking up at the man named Korrick. He was a lordly looking warrior, with tanned skinned, a firm, unforgiving face, and familiar green eyes that held none of Fae's softness. One of her brothers then, Rufus guessed.

"Magi," Korrick said, his voice a deep rumble, "you have slaughtered our kind for centuries. Tonight, I will skin you."

"Rufus," a voice whispered within him, as Morrigan continued to slither beneath his skin. She was close, somehow. He could sense her. *"Breathe, mo chuisle."*

He did so, drawing in deep, wet breaths as his intoxicated blood flowed into his brain.

"I'm not your enemy."

"No?" Korrick raised a golden eyebrow. "How did you come to be here? They say my sister Fae bore you upon her back. Did you enslave her mind?"

"I'd never do anything to hurt Fae." Rufus shook his head. *"Never."*

"You would skin her as surely as you would control her," Korrick said plainly. "Answer me, Magi."

"Show him. Put the animal in his place." Morrigan's forked tongue flickered against his ear. Rufus shuddered in disgust and desire as her arms bound themselves around his chest, squeezing. Rufus closed his eyes. He could see the universe beyond the darkness. The gods whispered to him.

"Korrick Ó Murchadha," he recited, trance like, "Lord of the

Neve, son of Kathel and Saraid, wielder of the sword Fírinne—I am not your enemy."

"You know my name?"

"As surely as you know mine," Rufus slurred.

Korrick was silent. He drew back as another Cat Sidhe approached. This man wasn't like Korrick or Fae, with darker hair and a more angular features. His eyes were a deep shade of blue and they gazed at Rufus with a harsh contempt.

"Reilly," Korrick said, as the newcomer seized Rufus by the face with unkind fingers. "He says he is not our enemy. I am inclined to believe him."

"Then you're as mad as he is," Reilly spat. "His kind murdered your eldest sister, Edana, and now this one seeks Fae." He let go of Rufus in disgust and unsheathed his sword. "Stand and face death, Magi."

But Rufus couldn't. The sky had descended onto his shoulders and he was holding the entire horizon on his back. The stars drove like tiny nails into his shoulders and neck as he bore the weight of the cosmos for the rest of the world. He wheezed from the strain, his tongue so thick it suffocated him.

Boyd was shouting in the distance.

"Commander Mac Gearailt, *please*. I was tasked with caring for this man—he's not well!"

"This rat is an unwelcome guest," Rielly growled. "And you, Boyd Dacey, treacherous human! Whom do you serve, to be treating this Magi?"

"I serve my lord and those of his line. And I honour that in protecting this man. Magi or not, he's a *guest* in the Neve and to execute him would be a violation of the codes of hospitality!"

"You speak out of turn, physician."

"Yet he speaks truth," Korrick said in a rumbling voice. "If the Magi was brought here as a guest by my sister, then he is to be honoured. Only my father or those of his line may revoke that protection. Speak then Magi, claim your innocence."

"Innocence?" The word slipped from Rufus's mouth. He could have cried. "I'm not innocent. I've killed…" He choked, his hands suddenly wet with blood. In an instant he was over the halfling again, his knife embedded in the soft tissue of his neck. In Harmatia, there was a belief that murderers were punished in death by being reborn as their own victims. Was that to be Rufus's fate? To die so horrifically? And did he not deserve it, if it was? "I stabbed him over and over," Rufus gabbled, the blade shaking in his hands. The halfling looked so frightened. "Over and over. Until there was nothing left of his face." He turned to Korrick. "I don't even know if it was to protect anyone anymore. Maybe I just finally wanted to kill someone who couldn't fight back."

"You are not endearing yourself to me, Magi," Korrick warned.

"He's feverish—delirious! He probably has no idea what he's saying!" Boyd wailed. "You can't take value from anything he says."

"Then we cannot believe his innocence either." Reilly raised his sword.

Rufus snapped his eyes up to the man. "I know you, Rielly Mac Gearailt," he hissed. "You are a *false* leader."

"*What?*" Rielly grabbed him by the collar. "What did you say to me, rat!"

"I say it thrice and am bound by my word—I am not your enemy, and you are not mine." Rufus rolled his eyes to Korrick

Rielly threw him down. "He is utterly demented."

"It would seem so," Korrick agreed

"What is the meaning of this?" Fae's enraged voice echoed down at them. Rufus looked up and caught sight of her on a balcony above.

"Did you bring this one to skin and fashion a new coat from, or have you lost your mind?" Rielly drawled and Fae bristled.

"Rielly Mac Gearailt, release them both or, so help me, you will regret it!"

178

Rufus's head snapped up at the word 'both'. He began to search the mass of people who'd gathered around them. Their faces swayed and melted into each other in a whirlwind of colours.

"Joshua?" Rufus cried. "*Joshua?*"

"Reilly, let them go!" Fae repeated.

"So the boy *is* with the Magi? Child or not then, he too is our enemy. He will share in this heretic's fate."

"*NO!*" Rufus screamed.

"Don't you touch a hair on his head!" Fae shouted.

Joshua was thrust forward in the crowd, his eyes heavy with confusion. Reilly took the boy by the wrist and dragged his arm up. The Cat Sidhe drew a knife from his belt, and it was all Rufus needed to see. With a howl, he released the inferno from within him, the flames bursting from his flesh.

"You call me Magi? You forget the meaning of the word! Lay one hand on my brother, *and I will boil your flesh from your bones!*"

The crowd all reeled back in terror, as the balance of power shifted in Rufus's favour. It would be easy now to kill them all. He could shield Joshua and extend the flame, let it burst over him, make the entire mountain erupt—oh, it would be so *easy*. Rufus's mouth curled into a resentful smile, his heart racing with the exhilaration. And then he caught Joshua's eye—and he *saw* him. His brother was so young, so brave in the face of this monstrosity, and yet Rufus could see him shaking, could see the fearful tears gathering in his wide eyes. His mouth moved in a continuous plea.

"No. Please, Rufus. No. Stop. Please, Rufus. Please, stop."

Behind Joshua stood Jionat, watching Rufus with an expression of disappointment, his brow cast down. He shook his head.

"Jionat?" Rufus choked as his brother raised one hand and marked himself across the forehead, leaving a thick line of blood. He marked himself against Rufus.

"Jionat, please, don't…!" Rufus shuddered.

"Rufus," Joshua continued to plead and Rufus's rage withered. The flames died down and Joshua, using his captors surprise to his advantage, wriggled free and threw himself into Rufus's arms. Rufus engulfed him in an embrace, sobbing again.

"I'm sorry," he wept into his brother's hair, "I'm sorry. I'm a monster. I'm so sorry."

Through his tears, Rufus saw Reilly draw back his sword, and pushing Joshua down and out of the way, Rufus threw back his head, exposing his neck in willing sacrifice.

The blade didn't meet its mark. With a clatter, Fae descended down amongst them, putting herself between Reilly and Rufus, her sword drawn. She gave a territorial growl and the crowd shifted, watching keenly.

"You saw his power," Reilly snarled. "He tried to kill us all."

"To protect his charge, you insolent fool!" Fae retorted. "Do you know who this boy is? This is Joshua of the Delphi—the Prince of Harmatia! And you just threatened him with a knife!"

"I don't care about human politics," Reilly scoffed.

"He is of Niamh's bloodline—a Delphi." Fae repeated, "If you try to harm him—if you try to harm either of them—I swear there will be blood!"

"You dare threaten me?" Reilly drew himself up tall. "I am your commander!"

"You're a damned idiot, is what you are!" Fae cried back.

"Enough!" Korrick boomed, and it was like a thunder clap, silencing the pair. "Fae, our father approaches. Let him lay judgement."

Fae drew back, moving to Rufus's side, her hand skimming his shoulder in quiet reassurance. Both Harmatians peered fearfully around to see Kathel Ó Murchadha, ruler of the Neve approach.

He was a tall, fair-headed man, with a similar build to Korrick but a face closer to Fae's, golden and more kindly in its structure. He moved with a slow but powerful gait. Everyone watched him, waiting in silence. Rufus could tell that this was a man equally feared as loved.

"Why do my children bicker so late at night?" Kathel said, his voice clear. He had an accent a little like Boyd's, though much fainter. "Who is this they fight over? Commander Mac Gearailt, an explanation, if you please."

"He is a Magi, my lord." Reilly knelt down in respect.

"A Magi?" Kathel whistled. "In the Neve? That is a serious concern. Korrick, my son, how have you allowed such a dangerous man to be in our home?"

"He says he is not our enemy," Korrick said tonelessly, and while he bowed his head, he didn't kneel like Reilly had.

"And do you believe him?"

Korrick flicked his eyes over to Rufus. His voice was much colder than his father's. "I believe he is a Magi and should be treated accordingly."

"Your prejudice is well based, but is it wise?" Kathel asked calmly. His easy tone made Rufus uncomfortable. "How did the Magi come to be here?"

"Fae brought him." Reilly shot a glance at Fae. Kathel followed his gaze.

"Is this true, my daughter?"

"It is, father." Fae bowed her head.

"And why did you bring him here?"

"Because he's my friend." She didn't flinch at the collective gasp and whispers of the crowd.

"Do you truly believe so?"

"Yes," Fae said without hesitation.

"I see. This is very grave." Kathel exhaled and then turned on Reilly, Korrick and their rabble. "You dishonour me all!" he roared and Rufus jumped in surprise. "How dare you question my daughter's actions? How *dare* you, when she loves this land more than her own skin! If she claims the Magi is her friend, then she speaks with my voice. He is here as our guest, and no harm is to come to him or the boy so long as they remain. Do you understand me?"

Silence greeted him, the rabble all open mouthed. Some dropped their eyes in shame, whilst others shook their heads in disbelief. Nobody dared argue.

Kathel calmed. "Raise him to his feet, Commander Mac Gearailt," he instructed Reilly. "And put that sword away."

Reilly did as he was ordered, a sour scowl on his face. Crossing to Rufus, he pulled him forcefully up. Kathel approached and studied Rufus curiously.

"What is your name?"

"Rufus Merle," Rufus mumbled. His legs were so weak he could barely stand.

"So it *is* you." Kathel smiled. "I have heard your name in the wind—you are a wanted man."

"I am."

"A rogue."

"Yes."

"Some say a revolutionary."

"Harmatia is my country, my home—not Kathra's and their Puppet King's," Rufus said venomously, his eyes blurring. Kathel chuckled and gently bent down to Joshua who clung to Rufus's side.

"I heard Fae call you the Prince of Harmatia." He touched the boy's head. "Yes, I sense the Delphi blood in you. And yet..." Kathel straightened, his eyes locked with Rufus's, "I also heard you call this boy brother. Now tell me, how can that be?"

Rufus swallowed. Kathel's eyes were too bright, and Rufus felt sick looking into them. He tried to speak, but moaned instead. A hot wave of delirium washed over him, his hands and legs going numb as his vision swam confusingly. His knees buckled.

"*Rufus!*" Fae's voice pierced the veil and the Magi collapsed into darkness.

CHAPTER 18

~~~

Cal polished the apple against his jerkin and took a large bite out of it, swinging his leg from where he was perched on the windowsill. In the room below, Liza cleaned her soiled blade with an old cloth, a few strides away from the steadily expanding pool of blood.

They'd cleared the alchemist's building quick enough on Aeron's behest, burning the Kathrak bodies in the courtyard away from sight. The city of Lemra knew well enough the smell of charred human flesh and no one had come by to investigate.

The Faucon themselves were pleased with their new base, taking up residence in alchemist's building. They had been outnumbered by the Kathraks four to one, but had made easy work of them.

Cal sniffed and took another bite out of his apple, spitting a pip out as he rolled his eyes from Liza across to the twitching body, bleeding on the floor in the room behind him. He was a Kathrak messenger who'd had the misfortune of stumbling into their newly conquered abode. Liza had buried her knife in his intestine and dragged him inside to die quietly.

"This one'll be sweeter than the one we kept," Cal decreed,

examining the soon-to-be corpse. "Taller than the other one. He's meant to be tall, isn't he—Rufus Merle? It'll make the glamour stick better."

"Wouldn't 'ave to use glamour and send a fake body if Aeron 'ad done the job," Liza replied haughtily. She wasn't afraid of Aeron, though whether that was admirable or foolish remained to be seen.

"All Aeron said was, we tell Harmatia we cut Merle's knot, kill the Kathraks and send 'em a glamoured body instead. I don't question beyond that." Cal stroked the scars along his cheeks and then jumped down from the window, silent as a cat. He skulked over to the body, circling it. A flicker of life still remained in the Kathrak's eyes, and something deep and ancient stirred within Cal. He felt his eyes darken to black, then caught sight of Liza watching him intently, a kind of hunger in her face. She was part of the Faucon, but not of the bloodline. The spirit of Ankou didn't flow through her veins as it did in Cethin's children. As it did in Aeron and Cal. He looked down to the Kathrak again and the feeling grew stronger.

"You can, you know," Liza urged faintly. "Aeron's not 'ere to call blood right. You can feast."

Cal nodded, a flare of excitement burning through him. Aeron could be greedy with his victims but it was as Liza said— the older assassin wasn't here now. Cal waded into the blood and lowered himself onto his knees. He closed his mouth, which was salivating, and opened the jaws of the ancient inside of him. And then Cal gripped his victim's arms in cold fingers and reached inside of him to the spark that gave him life. He pushed past the waves of terror, pain and resignation that emanated from the Kathrak, and found the white core. It was small, and fading fast, but there was enough to make a meal of and he engulfed it greedily.

By the time he was finished, the Kathrak was limp and dead and Liza was staring at Cal, her eyes dilated. She stepped elegantly up and over the corpse and fell to her knees in-front of Cal, pulling him hard into a kiss. Perhaps she was trying to taste the death on his lips? He didn't know but he welcomed her mouth. The pair tumbled back, pressed desperately into each other.

Below the window, the half-eaten apple lay forgotten, as the stream of blood reached it like a lazy red river, pooling around the sweet core.

～～

"Who is he, Fae?" Reilly paced, his footfalls loud and heavy. Fae watched him idly, her back pressed up against the wall. They were stood in the narrow corridor just beyond Boyd's chambers, away from sight and prying ears.

"A friend," she repeated lazily, for the third time that night, and he turned on her, his hand raised as if to strike.

"No, who *is* he?"

Fae didn't flinch. She darted her eyes up to the offending hand before looking calmly into Reilly's face.

"He was the first man to ever see me cry," Fae stated coolly. "Lower your fist, Reilly."

"Forgive me." Reilly dropped back and tumbled against the opposite wall, staring at his hand as if it had betrayed him, eyes wide. "You know that I would never—"

"Hit me? Why? You do it all the time."

"In training—only ever to better your skills."

"Every second with you is training," Fae spat, "but if you raise your hand to me outside of the arena again, you had better be ready for the consequences."

Reilly didn't reply, his jaw gritted, as if he were struggling to keep in his words. "How can you trust this Magi?" he asked in a strained voice. "After what they have done? They killed your sister—"

"I *know* my losses," Fae cut over him. "But we cannot label a man guilty for his brothers' actions. There are many Magi, some our enemies, others who merely pander thoughtlessly to a cruel practice—but they do not speak for all. Rufus is a good man, and I would wager there are more like him then we are willing to admit."

Reilly shook his head. "Has your bleeding come early this month? Yours always did alleviate you of sense."

"How *dare* you?" Blood rushed to Fae's face as she clenched her fists, enraged by the insinuation.

"Do not raise your voice to me." Reilly wasn't perturbed. "You are a soldier under my command, Fae. Remember your place."

Fae chuckled darkly. "How insecure you are," she baited, "that you need to piss on your territory like a threatened dog and blame words you don't like on womanhood. You wish to throw your title about? Then I will throw mine. This is not the battlefield. Where we stand now I am not your courier—I am one of the ladies of this household and the daughter of your lord. I am the favourite of my Grandmother, and I am also one of your contesters for command, lest you forget."

"And need I remind you, that I have beaten you in every battle we have ever fought?" Reilly was a thumb-width away from Fae's face.

She tried to stare him down, then darted her eyes away. "Then why are you so insecure?"

Quick as a snake, he struck her across the face. Her head snapped to the side under the force of the blow but her body remained rooted to the spot. Reilly pulled back, seemingly surprised with himself. Fae blinked twice rapidly her face stinging, then turned and walked away.

"Fae, I did not mean—" Reilly called weakly after her. "I lost my temper!"

"Like a threatened dog," Fae repeated. "Go back to your kennel, blood-hound. You're as desirable as sickness."

"Fae, please—"

"Don't," she snapped over her shoulder. "I know your true

nature now, Reilly Mac Gearailt. Would that I had the day I married you."

～⁀⌣

The capitol was silent. Small flocks of nervous birds gathered in the hollows of houses, otherwise unoccupied, and the city seemed shrouded in grey, colours leaked from aged stone, dirty and lifeless.

Rufus walked silently between the buildings, moving past the house he'd once called home, though he barely recognised it now.

As he reached the forum, he stopped in the centre. By the sun, it was close to noon. Normally there would be a market here at this time, bustles of people moving in and around as they bartered and sold their goods. Now, there was nobody, empty carts and stalls gathering dust and dirt, their fabric roofs flapping idly like the sails of ghostly ships. It was an old sound and it filled Rufus with dread.

"What are you doing here?" Somebody spoke and from the colourless wall a figure shifted. Rufus turned and, through the grime and pallor of the stranger's face, he recognised him.

"Zachary?" He approached. "Is that you?"

"It's good to be remembered," Zachary muttered, his voice flat.

"You're not so easily forgot." Rufus gestured around him. "What happened here?"

"The city has fallen," Zachary said. "This world is dead."

"The city's fallen?" Rufus frowned deeply. "What do you mean? Where is everybody?"

"Gone. There's no one left."

"What happened?"

"War."

"You mean they abandoned the city?" Rufus shook his head in disbelief. "Everybody?"

Zachary kept his eyes ahead, his face dull.

Rufus felt sick. "Then what about you? Why did you remain?"

Zachary sniffed loudly and gazed up at the dim sky. His skin was the same shade as the stone behind him. "I dedicated my life to

187

this kingdom. My actions shaped it. There's nowhere else I can run."

"And Fold? Hathely?" Rufus pressed. "Zachary, where are Emeric and Marcel? They wouldn't have left you here alone."

"It wasn't supposed to be this way." Zachary ignored him. "But we fashion our own demons, don't we? We make them with our every mistake."

"Answer me, Zachary," Rufus demanded. "Where are Emeric and Marcel?"

"They fell," Zachary breathed. "Hathely there and Fold there." He pointed out into the corners of the forum. Rufus couldn't believe it.

"They're dead?"

"The city has fallen. This world is dead."

"How?" Rufus felt unsteady on his legs. "What happened, Zachary?"

"The Hunt. They tore through Harmatia." Zachary blinked, his gaze distant. "In comparison to them, the Night Patrol were toothless puppies. We were nothing."

Rufus shook his head. He couldn't imagine such a thing—creatures worse than the Night Patrol? Could such a monster be conceived? "The Hunt?"

"The Wild Hunt." The words rang like an ancient prophesy from Zachary's dry lips.

"The Wild Hunt?" Rufus almost scoffed. "They're a myth—an ancient army long dead and forgotten. Why would they attack Harmatia?"

Zachary didn't pay Rufus's words any mind. His eyes were still fixed on the spots where his brethren had fallen.

"Poor Fold..." he said breathily, and his voice shook ever so slightly. "Poor Emeric. He raised the alarm. Left himself vulnerable in order to warn us. They ripped him to shreds. Limb from limb. I never thought Marcel could scream like that."

"Zachary, don't—"

"But he didn't stop—was like a man possessed. Even when they struck him down, he was still screaming for Emeric. I don't think he even noticed he was dying himself."

Rufus clamped his hands to his mouth, his heart clenching. They'd had their differences, but Emeric and Marcel had been his friends once. "Athea, have mercy."

"Mercy?" Zachary seemed to find the word amusing. "Why are you here, Rufus Merle?"

"I don't know," Rufus confessed. "Why are you? You can't be the only one left?"

Zachary's voice was as dry and toneless as the air around him. "Emeric fell there," he said, pointing. "Marcel there, and I..." he gestured to his feet, "I fell here."

The words were soft and they were crushing. Rufus blinked several times, a tight feeling in his chest. "You're...you're dead?"

"We're all dead." Zachary threw out his arms, as if gesturing to an army behind Rufus. There was nobody else there. Zachary let his hands drop. "But we're all alone. That's our curse. That's my punishment. For all eternity, I must remain at my post."

"Athea, that's too cruel." Rufus took a step back. "Who did this to you, Zachary? Tell me. Maybe I can...Maybe I can right it?"

"You mean you don't know?" Again, Zachary looked half-amused. "The leader of the Hunt? Who led the flock to our city?"

"No?" Rufus drew further away, confused and Zachary threw back his head and laughed.

"Why, it was you Merle."

"What...?"

"It was you. You killed us all." Zachary's teeth flashed. "And you enjoyed it."

"Oh Titania, Fae," Boyd peered worried into her face. "You've broken your cheekbone."

"That isn't what I asked," Fae replied patiently as the physician prodded the offending injury. It was swollen, and her cheekbone

189

and eye were black with bruising. "It'll heal quick enough—stop fussing," she added as he scrutinised it.

Boyd drew back, biting his thumb worriedly. "Did Commander Mac Gearailt do that to you?" he asked quietly.

"Are you going to answer my question if I tell you?" Fae rolled her eyes.

"Fae," Boyd sighed heavily and Fae couldn't meet his gaze. "Is there…is there anything I can do?"

"Boyd," Fae said, catching his hand and pulling his abused thumb away from his mouth. "I have faced worse than Reilly in the past and survived. Don't worry. You don't need to bear my burdens." She released him. "Now, will you please tell me—how are our guests?"

"The boy is sleeping peacefully." Boyd led her over to where Joshua was tucked in bed, his breathing long and steady. "His fever broke a little while ago, and already my medicine and healing are clearing his lungs…" Boyd trailed off. "Fae," he said, "last night, I'm sorry I couldn't stop Korrick's men."

"Boyd—"

"You put them in my care, but I couldn't protect them."

"You put yourself between Rufus and Reilly's sword. There is nothing more I could ask of you."

Boyd didn't respond and Fae sighed. Boyd would feel responsible, regardless of what she said.

The physician pressed on. "Anyway, the boy is better. By my estimate he'll make a full recovery within the next few days. He's a real fighter, that one." Once more Boyd trailed off, an apprehensive look in his eye. Fae picked up on it quickly.

"And Rufus? How is he?"

Boyd inhaled deeply. "I did a full examination, as you asked, and…" He bit his bottom lip. "It's…It's not good, Fae."

Boyd gestured for Fae to follow him. He led her to the curtained-off bed where Rufus now lay. The dividers between the beds were especially enchanted against heightened Cat Sidhe senses, allowing for efficient privacy. As Boyd pulled back the curtain, Fae's heart sank.

Rufus was deathly pale. The sheets were tossed turbulently around him and in some places were even scorched. Perspiration gathered across his skin and he twitched, troubled in his sleep by feverish dreams.

"Gods." Fae reached out to touch him but withdrew her hand as the waves of heat warned her that it wasn't wise. He would burn her. "Is it the same illness as Joshua?"

"Yes. A rather aggressive sickness of the lungs. It's fully treatable and given time I think he'll make a full recovery, but…"

"But…?"

"His body is…" Boyd struggled, "failing, to put it simply. He's malnourished, dehydrated, immeasurably exhausted…" Boyd circled the bed. "I fear there may be deeper issues to contend with as well."

Fae closed her eyes, keeping her voice even. She could hear Rufus's wet breaths. "What issues?"

"Some of the muscles in his back and shoulders are inflamed and have been damaged in the past. That could be caused by a number of things, but the scars on his wrists and hands suggest that it may have been caused by suspension by rope. His ribs have a number of fractures and breaks, both healed and new, whilst others, along with his collar, shoulder, wrists, jaw and hands all show signs of being broken in the recent past. He has scars all over his body— cuts, lacerations and…in some places it looks like he's been flayed. And then…then there's this." Boyd leant across and carefully peeled back Rufus's chemise, revealing a sigil branded into the flesh between Rufus's hipbone and belly-button. "This was burned into his flesh."

"But that's impossible, Rufus doesn't…" Fae drew off in horror. "Boyd, this is…All of this…"

"I know." Boyd replaced the shirt, his fingers nervous. "He's been tortured, Fae," he whispered. "Repeatedly."

CHAPTER 19

❧

Joshua stirred at the soft sound of the door opening and blinked his eyes open sleepily. Sunlight danced across the alabaster ceiling above him, bright and promising, and he huffed, blowing his hair away from where it was tickling his brow.

He was lying in a large, comfortable bed, engulfed in the centre of a nest of blankets and cushions so soft it felt like he was being cradled by clouds. Joshua couldn't remember such comfort in his life and he luxuriated in it before turning his attention to the newcomer in the room.

She stood to the side, a small pile of clothes folded over her arm. Her smile was warm and she was as dazzling as the sunlight, though the side of her face was dark with bruising.

"Good morning, Joshua," she greeted. "How do you feel?"

Joshua considered the question. The last thing he could remember was the heaviness of his lungs, terror and the unrelenting cold of the snow.

"I feel much better," he eventually said, eyeing her. "Where am I?"

"You are in my home, in the Neve. Do you know who I am?"

It came back to Joshua suddenly.

"Fae." He sat up, his heart bursting with joy. "Fae! I remember—you saved us. I remember now."

"It's nice to finally meet you." Fae came and sat on the edge of the bed, depositing the clothes she carried and covering his hands with her own. "I fear our first introduction wasn't in the best circumstances. But you seem to recognise me readily enough."

"Rufus told me all about you," Joshua gabbled excitedly. "I grew up on the stories of Sarrin. You're exactly as I imagined."

"Is that a good thing, or bad?" Fae teased.

"Good. Very good," he assured. "Where's my brother?"

"Your brother?" Fae tensed.

"Rufus," Joshua said. The haunted look in Fae's eye told him that her mind had flown to Jionat. "I meant Rufus."

"He's still in the physician's quarters, down the hall. You were recovering, so we thought it best to move you in here where you could rest more comfortably. Rufus needs a little more time."

"Why?"

"Some hurts take longer to heal. You understand, don't you?" She brushed the hair out of his eyes. "He'll be fine. Now, about you calling him brother—is that a term of endearment, or...?"

"Rufus raised me," Joshua said, with a shake of his head. "He's more father than anything else, but...No—he's my brother by blood. Rufus is a Delphi."

Fae grew impossibly still. Rufus had often described how she was able to do this—pause as if caught in time, barely drawing breath. "Then Lady Éliane was—"

"His mother. And Jionat...Jionat was our brother."

Fae's expression fell ever so slightly, as if her chest were tightening, then she masked the grief of the news.

"When did he find out?"

"The night he discovered I was still alive."

"That must have been very difficult."

"He doesn't talk about it. He doesn't talk much about anything

193

like that." Joshua brought his knees up, feeling strangely defensive.

Fae laughed softly, "Yes, Rufus hordes his pain like treasure and buries himself in it. Joshua, what happened to him? His body…" Fae drew off as Joshua shook his head again. "I see. I will have to extract that truth from him. For now, young Princeling, you have been almost two days without eating. So put on these clothes and you and I shall go to the kitchens."

The thought of food hadn't occurred to Joshua but at Fae's suggestion, he realised precisely how hungry he was. It wasn't so much a feeling in his belly, as a numbed sensation throughout his body. He felt gutted of energy and was eager to replenish it. He got out of the bed, wobbling on shaky legs. Fae steadied him, stepping back to give him room as he straightened.

"Don't rush," she berated. "We have all the time in the world—the kitchen isn't going to disappear." She paused and then took his hands, turning them over curiously as she spotted something. "These calluses…"

"I lost my bow in the woods," Joshua said. "It was getting a little small for me anyway."

Fae broke into a smile.

"Rufus raised an archer?"

"He said it was for catching food and protecting myself." Joshua took the clothes, looking over them. "Archery is easier than the sword to practise alone and on the move." A thought occurred to him and he peered over at Fae. "Wait, I can learn it here. The sword, that is."

Fae raised an eyebrow. "Is that a question, or a demand?"

Joshua righted his tone, extending his senses toward Fae as he tried to read her. She was already warm to him and a great deal more amicable to the idea of battle than Rufus would ever be. Joshua also knew, from the stories alone, that Fae had a will of iron and making demands of her would in no way win him favour.

"I'm sorry," he said, "I don't mean to get ahead of myself.

We've only just arrived and I'm asking for favours. I don't want you to think I'm ungrateful."

Fae raised a knowing eyebrow—she knew he was playing to her goodwill but the effort seemed to please her.

"You don't need to be sly with me, Joshua. Jionat was stark in what he wanted and bold too. I will allow it of you. You look so much like him…" she trailed off sadly. "I have no intention of uprooting you within the foreseeable future. The Neve is safe and so long as you need such a place, you are welcome here. If you want to learn the sword in that time, you will. Great Danu knows we have the facilities. I will ask my brother Korrick if he would be willing. He was my mentor and, for all his faults, he is a good teacher."

Joshua felt excitement well up through him. "You would do that? For me?"

"I wouldn't have offered it otherwise. As for the bow," Fae continued, "I will see to it you have another to replace the one you lost. I am an archer myself, you know."

"I know." Joshua grinned. "Everything I learnt about shooting, I learnt from stories about you. I guess in some ways, you were my teacher."

Fae, for the second time, appeared a little stunned. She righted herself.

"In which case, little Prince," she patted his hair, "I expect nothing less than perfection from you."

Zachary didn't knock before entering and Marcel didn't bother to greet him, neither in the mood for courtesy. Marcel was bent over the desk, drawing up a diagram with a patient precision that would have driven Zachary mad. He strode over to his second in command.

"Where's Fold?"

Marcel nodded toward the next room. There was a stiffness in his plain expression—he was worried.

Zachary lowered his voice. "How is he?"

Marcel shot Zachary a 'how do you think?' look, his eyebrows cocked. Zachary threw his hands in the air and leant back against the table.

"There's been word of a sickness in Bethean—a relapse of a winter infection that affects the lungs. They think it was brought on by the snow. A fever, coughing, delirium—even the strong are falling prey. Do you think Emeric might have taken ill with it?"

"I think he is too sick to be here today," Marcel replied stiffly.

"The King noted his absence last time. Any more and he'll be suspicious," Zachary said.

Opposite them the door opened and Emeric came back in. He looked awful—gaunt, shaken by weakness and pale as a ghost. Dark lines marked his eyes and his lips were grey. Zachary twitched a half smile in greeting. Emeric tried to return it.

"How long?" he asked, taking small shaky steps toward them.

"Oh, we'll go in another fifteen minutes." Zachary moved forward to steady him, "Sit—you look ready to drop."

"I'm fine," Emeric sighed. "Only tired—sleep has been evading me as of late."

"Then you must drink." Zachary peered into his wax-coloured face, trying to make light of the situation. "Drink until you can't remember the problems that keep you up."

"Would that I could keep enough wine down." Emeric wilted a little and Zachary tightened his grip on the younger Magi's arm. Marcel came and joined them.

"It will be over soon," he reassured tenderly.

A knock from the door made them all jump—hardened warriors leaping like frightened kittens at the slightest provocation. Zachary eyed the door.

"Come in," he called in Marcel's place. Even before the door opened, Zachary saw his second in command relax knowingly, recognising the foot-fall. A woman entered the room, sweeping in grandly.

"Béatrice," Marcel greeted.

"My sweet little brother, my darling cousin," the woman, Béatrice purred, her voice deep and throaty. Zachary smiled to himself. Marcel's sister, older by only a few years, couldn't have been a more contrary person to her brother. For all Marcel's Harmatian-born fair features, she'd inherited in full their mother's Réneian looks. With thick, luscious hair, streaked now with silver, she had dark, sunny skin and a pair of Réneian 'yeux garnet'— deep, almost maroon eyes, the colour of garnets. Unable, unlike her brother, to do magic and retain her youthfulness, Béatrice had aged beautifully into her mid-forties and was an enviably handsome woman, not least for her charisma.

"Arlen." She greeted him fondly. His name always sounded a little peculiar on her lips with her accent. She made no effort to pronounce it the Harmatian way, like Marcel did, but said it as 'Ah-ruh-len', her 'r's deep and throaty.

"Béatrice." Zachary tipped his head and stood back as she waltzed into the room, coming to Marcel's side. She kissed him fondly on the cheek and wiped away the lipstick stain with the pad of her thumb. Marcel gave her an exasperated look, but didn't bat her hand away.

"Qu'est-ce qu'il y a?" He asked, switching to Réneian.

"I have news," Béatrice said coyly, keeping to the Common Tongue. Whatever she'd come to say, she wanted them all to hear it. "It concerns the King's meeting, if you would like to hear." Béatrice turned to look at Zachary and Emeric, her dark, almond eyes cunning. Were she capable of being a Magi, Zachary would have snatched her up for the Night Patrol long ago. It was a blessing that she wasn't however, because Zachary rather suspected that, given half the chance, she would have overthrown him as captain.

"We're listening," he invited.

"The purpose of the King's summons," Béatrice said, almost gleefully, "I have discovered its true nature."

"Is it not about the Merle family's disappearance?" Emeric asked, looking decidedly unsteady on his feet, his hand against the table.

"Non, non, non—it is much more exciting than that," Béatrice purred. "Guess what I saw being brought into the throne room only a few minutes ago?"

Marcel exchanged a look with his sister, and his frown deepened. He mouthed something to her, and she nodded.

"Oui, c'est ça," Béatrice said, her voice lilting. "They have arrived with Rufus Merle's corpse."

Any colour left in Emeric's face drained. He made a quiet choking sound and staggered, his legs buckling. Zachary reached for him but Marcel was quicker, grabbing Emeric around the waist before he toppled over. Béatrice took him by the other arm and they guided Emeric to a chair, lowering him gently down. She scrutinized him, kneeling down at his side.

"Mais mon chéri, you are still not well, are you?"

Marcel clenched Emeric's shoulders, his knuckles white. Emeric composed himself forcefully, giving a grim smile, though he was utterly grey.

"Forgive me, I'm fine," he said. "I'm fine," he repeated to Marcel, who drew back, uncertainty in his step. Zachary realised he'd stopped breathing entirely.

"Je suis vraiment désolé," Béatrice offered her condolences. "I know that Rufus was a dear friend to you all."

"Damn him, no!" Zachary burst out before he could check himself, smacking his hand against the wall. Emeric jolted and somehow went even paler, trembling. Zachary inhaled sharply through his nose and let out a shuddering breath. "He was not—" he cut himself off, trying to control his sudden anger. "He wasn't our friend. Don't you dare say otherwise. Not now." He glared at Béatrice who met his gaze without fear. Marcel stepped between them, half-shielding his sister. He stared Zachary down, as if expecting him to spring.

Zachary raised his hands to show he meant no harm and retreated toward the side table. There, a jug of something amber and strong smelling was waiting beside a set of crystal glasses. He poured himself a generous glass and Béatrice stepped out and around Marcel to join him. She poured herself a more modest glass and stood silently in his company.

Behind them, Marcel slowly sat beside Emeric and took his hand, kissing the back of it.

"You cannot change the truths of the past, Arlen," Béatrice whispered to Zachary.

"If you believe that, then you haven't been paying attention to our political history," Zachary said dryly and Béatrice chuckled.

"Lying and changing are different things. I know you are trying to protect them and trying to protect yourself, but we both know you are far too sentimental. For all you say, you grieve as much today as Emeric does. Because Rufus *was* your friend and you cannot deny yourself that."

"Watch me," Zachary said, a little too fiercely. Béatrice gave him a knowing look. It irritated him.

"You are a good man, Arlen, and a greater leader for the diligence you give to your men. But you cannot be loyal to two who call each other enemy—it will tear you apart."

"I'm not. Sverrin is my King."

"And Rufus Merle was your brother."

Zachary closed his eyes.

"You have a talent," Béatrice went on, "for disguising your heart but do not try so hard to be deceived by your own lies. It will make you head-sick." She glanced over to Emeric. "Be careful, and be kind. It will become a rarity soon, I fear."

Zachary nodded mutely. Béatrice finished her drink and moved across to the door, stopping to kiss Emeric on the cheek as she passed.

"Good day to you all." She curtsied. "Et soyez courageux," she added in Réneian, biding them all courage.

As she left, an uncomfortable silence fell among the men—Emeric with his eyes cast vacantly to the floor and Marcel still hovering tensely. Zachary refilled his glass.

After another five minutes of silence, they all collectively stood, leaving their posts. Marcel and Zachary took positions either side of Emeric, quiet supports as they moved off together.

They made their way through the castle, down the long corridors. Zachary counted the echo of their footfall, which beat and clattered on the stone like a death rhythm as they made their way to the throne room.

Even before they'd reached it, the unholy smell of cold, rotting blood and preserving balms filled the hallways. Emeric retched discreetly again as they entered and they moved to their usual place in the corner of the room, to the left of the King.

In the centre, where the putrid smell originated, a wooden box had been laid out before the throne. Sverrin was staring at it intently, unmindful of the stench, maybe even enjoying it a little, his eyes alight. To the King's right, DuGilles was sharing a quiet joke with Reine, who had a handkerchief to her face but did nothing to distance herself from the cause of the smell. Belphegore was nowhere in sight. Perhaps he too had been given some advance warning and had chosen to risk Sverrin's anger and stay away. Zachary felt rather abandoned by that.

When the last of the Magi had entered and were stood among DuGilles's alchemists, two servants came cordially forward and stood at both ends of the coffin, waiting.

Sverrin stood. "My loyal subjects," he addressed the crowd, "faithful soldiers and courtiers, I present the man who betrayed you all." He gestured to the servants who dutifully removed the lid of the coffin.

Many of the Magi flinched back as the full weight of the sickly smell filled the air. Zachary wasn't so weak of stomach—death and gore didn't frighten him. Looking into the coffin however, he didn't need more than a few seconds before he was forced to turn his gaze. He'd seen enough. The man inside the box was a wasted mess—bloodied, with a sunken face that seemed strangely inhuman, tipped back and twisted as if he'd been frozen in the midst of a great agony. But below the horror and anguish, there was at least half a man, and it hadn't been so long that Zachary couldn't recognise Rufus in those features.

As if Sverrin couldn't trust the judgement of his court, he gestured to DuGilles, who leapt down excitedly. He began to circle the coffin, examining Rufus keenly, ignorant of the fumes. At last he drew back from his morbid study, bright-faced like a child on his birthday.

"It's him," he announced and a cheer rose from the room. That, more than the carcass, was nauseating.

"As a traitor then, his head should be put on display, do you not think, mother?" Sverrin reclaimed his throne, relaxing back. Even from behind her handkerchief, Zachary knew Reine was smiling.

"I quite agree, Your Majesty. You will excuse us, Lord DuGilles, but tradition must have a Harmatian take that trophy," Reine said.

DuGilles bowed graciously. "And who'll have that honour?"

Zachary's heart sank even before Sverrin's eyes found him. They held each other's gaze and Zachary nodded shallowly. Sverrin's face broke into a fresh smile.

"Lord Zachary, in the absence of Lord Odin, the duty should fall to you. Now is your chance to redeem us all for your brother's sins."

From the side, Emeric and Marcel both grew taut and Zachary watched as the Magi around him parted, creating a corridor of faces down to Rufus's coffin. Zachary didn't allow himself to hesitate, stalking forward.

As he approached, a servant offered him an executioner's

sword, which he took with relief, glad to keep his own in its sheath. The servants removed the sides of the coffin which came off in panels, so that Rufus was fully exposed.

Zachary stared at his brother long and hard. Then, drawing the sword back, swift as an avenging god, he beheaded Rufus without a word. Because Béatrice was wrong—Zachary *was* good at disguising his heart but in this instance there was nothing to hide. He had to believe that. The alternative was too frightening. He was loyal to Sverrin.

Zachary held the head up for the crowd and didn't shy away from the cheers as they applauded and rejoiced. He did a full circle and then threw the head to the foot of Sverrin's throne.

"Long live the King," he said and the chant rose up into the roof as Zachary descended back into the mass and disappeared from sight.

CHAPTER
20

The water tickled his feet as the waves breathed in and out, the bone-dust sand warm against his back. Rufus had no idea where he was and he lay puzzling over it for a long time before finally driving himself to his feet. He was on a beach of some kind, an endless stretch of white sand, water and horizon.

Jionat sat a few strides away, his stormy eyes cast over the ocean, arm rested on his knee, which was drawn up to his chest.

"You," Rufus said, by way of greeting, and Jionat huffed, blowing a curl from his line of vision.

"Yes, yes," he replied. "It's me. Your sadistic subconscious, come back to haunt you with the face of your biggest regret." Jionat paused and rolled his head toward Rufus. "You've had a lot of voices whispering in your head recently, haven't you? It's not turned out so well. Are you ready to listen to what I have to say yet?"

"Do I have any choice?"

"Not if you want to survive..." Jionat drew off. "But before we begin, here's a question for you—have you ever even been to the beach?"

"No," Rufus said, sitting beside him. "Why—is it significant?"

"Is it significant? Athea have mercy, do you think I'm the only part of your subconscious you've conjured?" Jionat said. "This is your mind, Rufus. I'm only one layer of it—the part that keeps you alive when you're under threat. But this—this is all you. Now last time we met, we were in Sarrin. That, I understand—good memories are an excellent place to hide. But the beach?" He smirked, looking menacing. "Now there has to be a meaning behind that, something very important."

"I have no idea," Rufus admitted.

"Come on, Rufus!" Jionat snapped, making him jump. "You're the captain of this ship. If you've never been to a beach, then you must have imagined it." Jionat pointed down to the sand. "There's a reason we're here. A reason you brought us here—so what's the significance of the beach?"

"I don't know. Why can't you tell me?"

"You're not listening." Jionat gesticulated angrily. "I'm a part of you—a courier between your conscious and unconscious mind."

"What does that mean?"

"It means I have access to everything you've ever learned. Every memory. Every sensation. An archive of everything that makes you who you are. But my usefulness is dictated entirely by you and what you know! So for Notameer's sake—ask yourself why are we here?"

"I told you—I don't know!" Rufus tore his hands through his hair. He heard Jionat inhale sharply and braced himself for an outpour of shouting, but there was nothing. Instead Jionat exhaled over a long count, as if expelling his temper, and when he spoke next he was calm.

"Clearly you're not ready to face that yet. Fine. There are other things we can discuss. Other ways I can make myself useful."

"Useful?" Rufus spat, his face buried into his hands. His whole head was aching. "You're just a riddle that's answer is another riddle."

"Would you stop your self-pitying and start using your brain?" Jionat groaned. "You've read a thousand books, you have all the knowledge you need to solve this. So take your head out of your *arse and start asking the right questions."*

Rufus gritted his teeth and stood, running his hands through his hair.

"The dream I had before this—with Zachary in Harmatia... Was that a vision?"

"Of sorts," Jionat replied. "The Delphi get their powers through a connection between the different realms. The problem with your unconscious mind, Rufus, is that it isn't only full of old memories, it also contains memories of events yet to pass. For some, like Jionat and Joshua, these are clear—they rise to the surface undisturbed. You haven't developed that ability yet, so the messages are interpreted by your subconscious into dreams instead."

"He talked about the Wild Hunt." Rufus tugged his fringe. "What do I know about the Wild Hunt?"

Jionat's expression became blank, as if he were recalling something. When he spoke it seemed to be in verbatim. "The Wild Hunt. They were formed from an ancient hunting tribe of Fomorii, who were sworn enemy of the Sidhe. They learnt to use magic to change their physical forms, a technique which inspired the Night Patrol. These beasts scoured the land, destroying everything in their wake, an unstoppable force of darkness that threatened to eradicate all life. Story tells that the Soldier God, Penthar, in order to protect the balance, had six mighty swords forged with the powers of his brothers and sisters, and met the Wild Hunt in battle, defeating them. Though slain, they say the Wild Hunt remain in spirit, dormant and waiting to be called to the hunt again by their Queen Nicnivin, Ruler of the Unseelie."

"I thought it was only a story," Rufus said weakly. He remembered his mother's tales now, her warnings about the Unseelie, those faeries who didn't adhere to the Betheanian treaty and had formed their own malevolent court. Things like the Wild Hunt had seemed like a hellish nightmare but Rufus had never forged any strong belief in them. "Zachary said I led them," Rufus continued, uneasily. "He said that I destroyed Harmatia. Why would I do that?"

"Of course, because what have you got against Harmatia?" Jionat drawled, and Rufus's mouth dropped.

"I don't hate them enough to destroy an entire city!" he choked. "To be capable of that, just for revenge—how far gone would I have to be?"

"When you're part of the Wild Hunt, you lose the parts that make you vulnerable—your kindness, your pain, your sense of right and wrong. Actually, I think that's the point," Jionat replied starkly and Rufus began to pace.

"But why would I even be part of the Wild Hunt to begin with? I'm not a Fomorii."

"It's not about that, it's about power."

Rufus pushed his fringe away from his forehead, running his fingers through his hair as he paced back and forth, Jionat watching him.

"You could, you know," Jionat eventually said.

"Could what?"

"Lead the Wild Hunt."

Rufus stopped short. "Why would you say that?"

"Why would you?"

"Would you give me a clear answer for once, Athea damn you!" Rufus snapped, and Jionat raised an eyebrow. In an instant he was in front of Rufus, uncomfortably close. A dangerous aura rose from his body, his eyes boasting an impossible depth, his face dark with anger.

"There's your answer," he hissed, and Rufus trembled at the change, jerking back. "Your anger. You have so much of it—so much fear and resentment which you try to bury. But you forget that beneath the civil layers of your bookish charm and morals, you're a being of power and emotion. You're part of Athea." Jionat snapped out his hand, catching Rufus by the wrist and drawing him in. "You can't run from me," he said, his eyes burning red, "I'm in you, I am you." He thrust his hand forward, slamming it against Rufus's stomach. Beneath Jionat's cold fingers, a brand began to burn into his flesh and the shock and pain of it brought Rufus to his knees. Jionat didn't relent.

"Stop…please s-stop!" Rufus begged.

Jionat seized his face. "You don't burn, yet they did this to you— they hurt you and you're reminded of it every day. Every day on the run, giving in further to instinct in order to survive. Is it really so far-fetched that you might succumb to your worst nature? That the anger would grow too large for you to contain any more? After all, it's already slipping out." Jionat stepped to the side and on the sand behind him lay the murdered halfling.

Rufus covered his eyes, turning away, but it did him no good. "I had to protect Joshua."

"You could have incapacitated him. You didn't have to stab him over and over."

"He used me—blackmailed me!"

"You offered yourself—you were willing."

"I didn't want to kill him!" Rufus gabbled, heaving for air.

"So why did you?"

Rufus shook his head, clawing at his eyes. A moment later, strong fingers were pulling his hands away from his face.

Jionat's eyes were sympathetic. "I know why you did it," he said in a quiet, calm voice. "And the guilt you feel now should relieve you—because you're still capable of feeling it. You're still fighting to be a good man—that's why I'm in here, and you're in charge." He sat back in the sand, looking up at Rufus. "But be careful Rufus—that little voice that has weaponised your anger is tipping the balance in my favour. If you give in to that carnal oblivious, then I'll lead the Wild Hunt into Harmatia myself." His eyes flashed. "So before that happens, I suggest you really start thinking about how to take back control."

"I don't know. Tell me, please tell me." Rufus shook, and Jionat looked up at the sky, and then around to the water and sand.

"You need you work it out," he said absently, "the significance of the beach."

They returned to Zachary's house at his request, Emeric dragging behind. Marcel led him wordlessly and Zachary stalked ahead, calling out to Heather to fetch his strongest brandy and to bring him a bowl of water, so he could wash his hands. She complied without question, sending a servant for the drinks whilst he heated the water in the washing bowl and scrubbed his hands clean of death. Marcel and Emeric finally followed him into the house, and he shook his hands dry and dismissed all the servants, gesturing for his friends to go through a door on the far left.

The three passed through a lavish dining room into the library which was equipped with comfortable seats and four large south facing windows that looked out over the castle gardens. These were shuttered now and a fire had been lit in the large fireplace, cracking and burning brightly, the only source of light in the room. It cast a halo over the chairs that were huddled around it, making them look comfortable and beckoning.

Marcel paused in the doorway and raised his eyebrow, looking across the room.

"You seem to have gained an unlawful tenant," he noted, nodding toward the slumped figure of Daniel, who was strewn over one of the desks, his head resting in the pages of an open book, quill slack in his hand. Zachary didn't have the energy to scowl.

He walked to Daniel's side, scrutinising the boy. Heather entered, carrying the decanter and three glasses on a tray. She faltered at the sight of Daniel, glancing almost fearfully between Zachary and his men. She didn't know their temperament. Zachary frowned and gently touched a hand to his brother's shoulder, rousing him.

Daniel's green eyes were colourless in the firelight, and he blinked lethargically, sitting up, head nodded forward in fatigue.

"I think Daniel has done quite enough studying for the evening, don't you, Heather?" Zachary said and Heather set down the tray and bustled the boy out of his chair. Daniel looked between the men in confusion. He gave a sluggish bow to Marcel and Emeric, mumbling an apology and goodnight, before allowing himself to be coaxed from the room. Zachary moved to the chairs and poured his friends each a generous glass of brandy.

"I had no idea you were housing a student from the academy," Emeric said as the door closed behind Heather. "Do you intend to apprentice him?"

"I don't want an apprentice," Zachary dismissed. "Even if I did, he's studying to take the Architect's Exam soon. Then I believe he intends to study to become an ambassador. I would hardly be appropriate."

"Ambassador?" Emeric whistled weakly, taking a seat beside Marcel, who was already helping himself to his drink. "He seems very young. Can't be older than twenty?"

"Nineteen," Zachary said.

"And he's hoping to take the Architect's Exam already? What's the average age for that? Twenty-five ? Thirty? He's ambitious."

"A family trait," Zachary grunted, dropping into his own chair and sipping his drink. Marcel peered over his glass, his eyes the same colour as the brandy.

"A relation?" he asked. "Cousin?"

"No," Zachary snorted. "Brother."

Emeric choked on his drink and Marcel placed his glass down quickly. Zachary chuckled softly at their surprise.

"A brother?" Emeric leant forward. "You never told us you had a brother!"

"Didn't cross my mind," Zachary half-lied. "I am rather prone to forgetting myself."

"Forgetting?" Emeric spluttered. "How do you *forget* your own brother?"

"Oh please, Fold—I have sixteen known siblings." Zachary

209

shrugged. "Occasionally I struggle to keep track of them all."

"Sixteen?" Emeric balked and Marcel reclaimed his drink from the table.

"Bastards," he guessed.

"As you say. Rivalen's bedded almost every servant he's ever employed. I have fifteen sisters and one brother. There may be others, but…" Zachary waved indifferently. "I am the only legitimate one. He's given the Zachary name to both Daniel and Katrina though."

"Katrina…She's your eldest sister, isn't she?"

"The only one he's ever loved." Zachary tipped his head back to the ceiling.

"I've never understood it," Emeric finally said, refilling his glass. "You have such a strained relationship with your father, why didn't you take your mother's name instead?"

Zachary's lips twitched into a half-smile and he raised his glass. "A toast," he proposed. "To our glorious King?"

"To dysfunctional families," Marcel countered.

"To Rufus," Emeric suggested quietly, his words met with silence.

"To Rufus," they finally agreed.

They all drank deeply, Emeric drained his glass. Marcel pulled out and considered his pipe. For once the blond didn't seem in the mood to smoke. Rufus's fate weight heavily on all three of them.

"That damned fool." Zachary stared into the fire. "He should have come home when he had the chance. He didn't have to die like that—run off the road like a fox."

"A fox was always his nature," Marcel murmured. Emeric refilled his glass again. A knock came from the door and Heather stepped into the room, carrying another decanter and a bowl of salted bread crust.

"In case you finish the first." She held up the alcohol. "And for when you do." She placed the bread down.

Zachary took a swig of his drink and smiled stupidly up at her. "What would I do without you?"

"Suffer," she replied matter-of-factly and he cackled.

"To bed with you, it's late," he ordered. "You need not wait up for us delinquents."

Heather bowed to them all, bidding them goodnight. Zachary plucked some bread from the bowl and put it in his mouth. Marcel, after much consideration, began to stuff his pipe with leaf, whilst Emeric took another drink, staring drowsily into nothing.

It was he who eventually broke the silence. "Do you remember our first assignment together?"

"Oh stop it." Zachary scowled. "We are not old men reminiscing."

"I feel old," Emeric whispered. His words echoed through Zachary with a dreary familiarity.

Zachary put his head in his hands. "If I recall," he relented, "we were asked to investigate a town supposedly overrun with bandits. Merle was there only as our medic but it was he who conned us into their midst. Pretended we were minstrels of all things."

"You know, I hadn't known he could play the fiddle until that day," Emeric sniggered. "Or that he was a lover by nature, until he started wooing the leader's chosen bride for information."

"Wooing you say." Zachary barked a laugh. "The way she looked at him, you'd have thought he was an incubi. A few minutes more and she'd have stolen him to her bed had the leader not arrived. Oh, but that bastard must have been seven foot tall."

"Eight," Marcel corrected.

"Hands made to strangle tree trunks." Emeric poured himself a new glass. "That had Merle running."

"Round and round the tavern, flapping uselessly like an inebriated gosling." Zachary twirled his finger.

The three chuckled at the memory before petering out. Emeric downed his glass and refilled it, and Marcel eyed him. Zachary stood and moved to the fireplace, dusting his hands across it, the heat beat against his legs.

"They searched your homes as well, didn't they?" he said faintly. Emeric retreated further into his chair.

Marcel didn't hesitate. "Yes."

"Yes," Emeric added timidly.

"How comforting it is to know we are loved so equally." Zachary kept his back to them. "Our King is a fair man."

"Consistent is the word." Something akin to anger slipped into Marcel's words, and it was strange to hear in the usually blank palette of his voice.

"Consistent," Zachary repeated. He recalled the ride with Sverrin and rested his head against the wall, reminding himself to breathe. Reminding himself of what it had felt like to remove Rufus's head, the weight of his rotting skull. Zachary wanted to wash his hands again.

"We should have never brought Sverrin back." The words were so faint Zachary could have pretended Emeric never said them. But he did and Zachary turned on him so sharply he almost felt his neck crack.

"Bite your tongue!" he barked. "Before you give someone an excuse to behead you."

Emeric shrank back at the venomous tone—but *Athea*, Zachary didn't want it to be Emeric's throat he was ordered to sink his teeth into. He didn't want to hold up Emeric's head to the cheer of traitor.

Marcel stood as Emeric dropped his head into his hands, his shoulders hunched. Zachary slumped, pinching the bridge of his nose, his eyes cast over Emeric's empty glass. How much had they let him drink? A Magi normally had a strong immunity to alcohol but with Emeric as he was...

Marcel helped Emeric out of his chair and Zachary extinguished the fire with a wave of his hand. He stepped toward

212

his friends.

"I have spare rooms," he invited. "Stay here—there's no point walking home now. Take him upstairs. We're safe here."

Marcel nodded a quiet thanks and led Emeric from the room, his hand firmly on his apprentice's shoulder. Zachary directed them up the stairs and toward a spare bedroom. At the door he extended his hand to Emeric, as if to offer comfort, but retracted it silently. He struggled, looking helplessly at Marcel, who returned the troubled expression. Zachary stepped back.

"Put him to bed," he said wearily.

Marcel gave another appreciative nod and pulled Emeric into the bedroom, closing the door after him. Zachary turned and leant against the wall, his eyes closed. For an extended moment there was only silence, then he heard the soft breaks of the first sobs, muffled in an embrace. The bed creaked under the weight of a human body and the sobbing continued, harmonised by a gentle murmur of comforting words, too quiet to discern. Zachary rubbed his forehead. Poor Emeric. Foolish Emeric. He'd always liked Rufus the best.

Damn you, Merle. Zachary pushed away from the door. *For exposing us like this—damn you!*

CHAPTER
21

Rufus watched Boyd for several minutes before announcing his consciousness. "Boyd, is it?"

The break of the silence surprised Boyd so badly, the physician jumped a foot in the air, knocked several bottles from his work desk and proceeded to fall back over his own chair.

An elegant introduction.

"You're awake!" Boyd scrabbled over, thrilled.

"Evidently." Rufus's voice was coarse but though he felt weaker than a drenched butterfly, his head was clear. "It's Boyd, isn't it?" he repeated, studying the physician. Something of the man seemed familiar, but Rufus couldn't place what. Boyd came to his side.

"That's right." He checked Rufus's temperature with the back of his hand. "How are you feeling? Any pain? Nausea at all?"

"No. I feel better. Clearer. How long…?"

"Several days. You've been very unwell. D'you remember anything?"

Rufus closed his eyes. "Fae…She found us in the snow. Then we were here. After that, very little. It feels like a nightmare."

"A nightmare is accurate—you came close to death."

"Was I that sick?"

Boyd shook his head. "Much worse than that—you were discovered. Commander Mac Gearailt was ready to flay you both alive, until Lord Kathel stepped in."

Rufus frowned, rubbing his eyes, and then jolted. "Joshua?" He grabbed at Boyd's arm. "Where's Joshua?"

"He's absolutely fine, don't fret," Boyd reassured. "Quite recovered, I'd say. Fae's been taking very special care of him. He'll be down here soon, I expect—he comes by every few hours or so to see how you are."

Rufus nodded, moving his hands down from his face to massage his stiff neck and shoulders.

"Is that sore?" Boyd leant forward. He touched his hand to the tense muscle and concentrated on it. A warm, familiar feeling filled Rufus and he sat upright.

"You're using magic!" he gasped. Boyd stared at him blankly. "Yes."

"No," Rufus corrected, "you're using *elemental* magic."

"Yes."

"You're human?"

"Well, I think you can probably guess my answer."

Rufus scrutinised the physician. "What's a human doing in the Neve?"

"What's a *Magi* doing in the Neve?" Boyd retorted primly, removing his hand.

"Apologies," Rufus said sheepishly. "I only meant to say... Where did you learn to heal like that? Those techniques aren't even taught in the academy."

"You Magi." Boyd rolled his eyes. "You think you're the only ones who know how to use elemental magic? Like it wasn't the Sidhe who taught it to you."

"The Delphi—"

"Are descendants of Niamh, Lord Kathel's mother." Boyd returned to his desk. "I learnt to heal directly from the source, thank you very much. You're welcome, by the way."

Rufus rested back against the pillow, already feeling exhausted. "Thank you, I'm very grateful," he said in a tone of defeat.

Boyd peered around at him. "You did well, though," he announced, "taking care of the Prince, given the circumstances. He might well have died but for your care. He was already over the worst of it when you brought him to me. Strong boy. Weak lungs, though."

"Yes, ever since he was a child."

"Not to worry, he can strengthen them, over time." Boyd turned back to the desk. "And he'll need to, if Korrick starts training him."

"Who starts training who?" Rufus sat a little straighter.

"Well Korrick hasn't agreed yet, of course, but once the politics are dealt with, he won't be able to resist, I know it," Boyd continued, oblivious. "Most boys get excitable when given a sword, but Joshua's a natural."

"You gave him a sword?" Rufus choked, just as the door opened and Joshua came bouncing in, followed by Fae. At the sight of Rufus, the Prince gave a cry of delight and dove straight toward him, launching himself into his arms. Rufus welcomed him, despite all his aches and pains.

"Rufus, you're awake!"

"Did you think you'd be so easily rid of me?"

Joshua grinned across to Fae and Boyd. "I told you he was invincible!" he said. "Rufus just can't die."

"Not for lack of trying." Fae crossed the room and laid a gentle hand on Rufus's knee. Something of her touch seemed hesitant, as if she was unsure of him. "You gave us quite a scare, my friend."

"You've seen me worse."

"That doesn't console me." Fae perched on the edge of the bed, pulling Joshua away from where he was now starting to suffocate Rufus. Joshua settled between them.

"Rufus, Fae says they're going to teach me to fight! They've given me a sword to train with."

"So I've heard." Rufus's mouth formed into a line. "A prior discussion with me on the matter would have been appreciated."

"You were twitching and indisposed," Fae dismissed. "I took liberties of guardianship."

Rufus frowned, looking at Fae a little closer. There was a faint mark of a dark blue hue across the plane of her cheek.

"Fae?" he asked, "what happened to your face?"

"I was born like this," she replied instantly. "Two eyes, a nose, a mouth—I know it's distressing for you."

"She broke her cheek bone," Boyd said and Fae shot him an absolutely filthy look. Boyd turned away hurriedly, ducking back toward the work at his desk.

"You didn't have that injury when you saved us," Rufus said. "What happened?"

Fae considered her words carefully.

"I had a disagreement with a dragon," she eventually decided and Rufus could have believed that. "Though the same might be asked of you." She poked him obtrusively in the face, making Joshua giggle. "You look precisely the same as when I saw you last—that was over twelve years ago."

Rufus detected a note of mistrust in Fae's light actions. "I'm a Magi," he said. "What's a decade to me?"

"Perhaps, though *that*," she moved her finger up to the scar on his brow, "ages you."

"I'm thirty-five, I'd hope *something* ages me. I don't want to look like an adolescent for the rest of my life." Rufus rubbed the scar with a growl.

"I didn't say you looked like an adolescent. More like…an old, young man."

"My shrinking self-confidence thanks you."

"Rufus." Joshua grew impatient, bouncing up and down. "When are you going to be well enough to come out and see everything?"

"Give him a few days," Boyd said from his table. "He's not as spry as you are."

"How dare you," Rufus objected, as Fae laughed. Once more Rufus noted a tightness about her that made him uneasy. Something was wrong.

"Boyd, Joshua," Fae maintained a forcefully bright tone, "could the pair of you go and fetch something for Rufus to eat? He must be famished."

Joshua leapt from the bed enthusiastically.

"Certainly." Boyd looked between Fae and Rufus. "Come along now, Joshua," he ushered and the Prince ran energetically after him. Rufus hadn't seen the boy so happy in many months.

The door closed leaving Rufus and Fae alone. Without their audience, Fae's expression grew more serious and she stared at him, long and hard. He was uncomfortable beneath her gaze, his stomach churning. She stood abruptly.

"Fae?" Rufus asked, as she crossed to Boyd's desk, plucking one of the candles from the candelabrum. "Fae, what are you—ow!" Rufus cried out as she seized his wrist. "Ow! What are you doing?" He tried to pull away but she gripped him firmly, holding his hand over the flame. Rufus grew still, allowing her to observe the harmless flicker of the fire against his skin. Finally satisfied, she released him, and he hugged his arm to his chest. Fae replaced the candle and once more resumed her staring.

"Are you..." Rufus began quietly. "Are you going to kill me?"

Fae raised her eyebrows. "Rufus," she sat down heavily on the bed, "you are still breathing because I intend for you to keep you doing so."

"Oh." Rufus looked down at his arm. "You just had to be sure it was me."

"Boyd gave me some information which was...contradictory." Fae sounded tired, her voice heavy.

Rufus felt his gut tighten. The brand on his stomach burned faintly and he ran a nervous hand through his hair.

"In fact," Fae continued, "there has been a great deal these last few days which has been difficult to swallow."

Rufus didn't have to guess. "You found out that I'm a Delphi."

"Joshua explained it to me."

"I'd have told you."

"You were otherwise engaged, I understand," Fae said. "I sent word to Luca to tell her that I had Joshua—don't worry," she added, as Rufus made to object, "I made no mention of you. If the letter is intercepted, people will merely think it's two friends idly chattering about a beloved nephew. You are quite safe."

"How did you find us?" Rufus asked. Fae's mouth curled into a small smile.

"The feeorin," she said. "You earned their favour with your songs. They kept an eye out for you, steered you clear of glamour traps and the like. They guided me to you when they thought you were in danger. Had they not, you would both be dead." Fae's expression sobered. "Rufus, what happened? The last I heard, you were with the Delphi Knights. I thought you were safe. And then I find you like this—covered in scars, broken bones...*burned*. Rufus, you don't—"

"I know," Rufus said a little too forcefully. He refused to meet her gaze and covered the brand, squeezing his abdomen as if trying to protect it. "It's complicated."

"Then explain it to me."

"I don't want to talk about it."

"I do," Fae pressed. "Do you know how worried I was? Do you know the risk I took when I brought you here?"

"And I thank you for that, but what happened..." Rufus swallowed dryly. "It's not important now."

"Rufus, you *stink* of blood and it's not all your own. You said some alarming things in your delirium. I need to know what's going on—"

"And I said it wasn't important, Athea damn you!" Rufus snapped, his temper rearing. Fae jumped back in surprise at the sudden change of tone, her eyes widening. Rufus thought she might reach for a weapon but she kept her hands in her lap. She appeared to have stopped breathing entirely. Rufus panted and clasped his stomach, hunching over himself as the burning pain intensified. He breathed out long and hard—the pain wasn't real, but he felt it nonetheless.

Fae touched his hand hesitantly. "Alright," she said calmly. "Breathe. We'll discuss this later."

Rufus glanced up into her face. He expected her to be angry but her expression was unreadable, almost guarded. He made to apologise but could only manage a soft groan. He couldn't tell her what had happened—he couldn't bear to. It was shameful, it hurt too much.

Slowly Fae settled back on the edge of the bed. They sat together in silence until Boyd and Joshua returned with the food.

"That whoopsie-bashin', pasty son of a miller's turd!" Aeron growled into his drink, rubbing the back of his aching head. Rufus Merle had disappeared, taking the half-pint with him, and Aeron was rapidly losing his patience. He'd followed the Harmatians' trail through the wood for many miles, until it had disappeared as suddenly as if Rufus had simply taken flight. At that point, unable to find any other clue, Aeron had returned to Beshuwa to recuperate.

He downed his drink and closed his eyes, deep in thought. Lemra was a long way back but he had no reason to stagnate in Beshuwa any longer. He needed to make a decision. After all, who knew where the Magi had gone?

Standing, the Lemra'n crossed to the mirror which was leant against the wall. He'd covered it with his cloak, because, as all good merchants of death knew, mirrors could trap souls and be used as doorways for all sorts of things. Aeron removed the cloakand knelt before the polished looking-glass. He took a dagger from his boot and stroked it across his palm, allowing blood to well into the bowl of his hand. He let it gather there, then pressed his bloodied hand to the mirror.

Closing his eyes, he allowed his human body to slump, letting the demon inside of him rise and push forward. When he opened his eyes, his pupils had dilated impossibly, the darkness within swimming to the surface of his skin. He drew a spiral with his blood on the mirror, then a triangle within it. "Birth, Life, Death, I am your master," he chanted and then, taking his uninjured hand, he delved his fingers through the centre of the spiral, into the mirror. They slipped through the surface like it was made of water.

Immediately, he felt his human flesh begin to reject the new realm, twitching and jerking, but he didn't retract his hand.

"Piss off," he ordered the spirits who immediately appeared in the mirror, scratching at the surface. "Cethin," he called, extending his will. "In the name of our forefather Ankou, I call to you—Cethin. *Cethin*," he said between gritted teeth. From with the mirror a hand grabbed hold of his wrist and tugged hard, trying to pull him in. Aeron pulled back and ripped his hand free of the mirror.

Cethin appeared in the obsidian surface and Aeron bowed his head. "Father."-

"Aeron," the old man greeted, his silvery hair misty in the darkness. The realm of the dead always made him look withered, white-faced and skeletal. "You have failed."

"Merle's trail disappeared. I can't find a single bread-crumb."

"What of the Harmatians?"

"The integrity of the Faucon stands—Cal's pint'ed some blood for me, sent home a glamoured body. As far as Harmatia's concerned, I've reaped Merle's sorry knot."

"That's not good enough." Cethin wasn't impressed. "Should Merle reappear before we are ready, it would be problematic for us all."

"Rah, I know." Aeron sulked. He glanced down and saw that his hand was still bleeding. He narrowed his eyes and stared at it, concentrating. Black tendrils wove out from the blood-flow, like an octopus emerging from water, and needled the severed skin together with silken, smoky strands. "There's somethin' else."

Cethin waited for Aeron to elaborate.

"I almost got Merle, but when I did, I smelt the she-war. Morrigan's marked him."

"So she's finally made her move," Cethin murmured. "What does she want with him?"

"He's Athea's glove." Aeron shrugged. "And he's got anger in him too, sweatin' torture—skin smells of burnin'. We know she's been playin' the long-game with this one and now he's perfect for pickin'."

"If Morrigan has him," Cethin said, "you must go to one above her."

Aeron almost winced. He'd expected it but that didn't make him any happier about the order. "You want me to seek out Nicnivin?"

The Queen of the Unseelie Court was a figure of terror and Aeron was well aware that, should he walk into her court uninvited, she might very well take his head as an ornament for her dining table. Credit to the woman—she knew how to keep up appearances.

"Shed your mortal body—go as the blood of Ankou. She will receive you then."

"Stands to reason." Aeron picked dully at the fresh, black stitching across his palm. "But if Morrigan *has* got Merle, then I'm not goin' to be able to touch him."

"Merle is of no consequence—it is the *boy* we need. I went to great pains to have the Faucon name whispered into DuGilles's ear so that we might get to them first. Merle's falsified death gives you time but not enough to be idle. You need to find them." Cethin paused and then looked to the side of him as if someone was calling. "Do not fail again, Aeron," he warned.

Aeron nodded. Reaching forward, he smeared the blood-spiral, breaking the connection. Cethin disappeared and immediately the room brightened.

Aeron went to the bed and dropped down onto it. "Time to shed this organ-bag then." He whistled harshly at the door. "Whore!"

"What?" came the abrupt response.

"I'm goin' to sleep for a few days!" he shouted down to her. "Leave me be, and don't sex me up neither. And—uh—if I stop breathin', that's normal!"

"What?" she called again.

He fell back against the pillow. "Death," he mumbled softly, "this is just a bitch."

CHAPTER 22

⁓⧽⧼⁓

He dreamt of the cold, red-darkness and, as usual, woke screaming. By the time Boyd skidded across to the bed in a blind panic, Rufus was able to stifle his cries into heavy breaths. The high, frightened energy sapped out of him and he slumped, dropping his head into his hands.

"Rufus? Rufus?" Boyd rubbed a comforting had across his back. "You're safe. You're safe."

Rufus gave a jerky nod, his face damp in his hands as he tried to regulate his breathing, his throat and stomach burning. He felt as if he'd run a great distance.

"Are you in pain?" Boyd asked.

"Ni-nightmare," Rufus tried to assure, his voice hoarse as he wheezed. The dreams, which had been a regular bane, would come back for him every few weeks or so, usually just when he thought he was rid of them.

"What was it about?" Boyd maintained his even tone, quiet and comforting.

"Nnnn…" Rufus stuttered, his fingers slipping up into his hair. He gripped his fringe, pulling at it hard. "Nothing," he forced out, jaw clenched. "Don't remember."

By the narrowing of his eyes, Rufus knew Boyd caught the lie, but the physician said nothing of it. He continued to rub soothing circles across Rufus's back and the Magi felt the warmth of magic ebb from the physician's hand. Whether Boyd did it consciously, Rufus didn't know, but already he'd come to admire the level of sophistication Boyd possessed when healing. Rufus had only ever seen such mastery from Morgo Edwin, leader of the healing sect, and he was over a century old.

"Speak with me," Rufus said softly, still reeling from the dream. "Distract me."

Boyd removed his hand and stood awkwardly, chewing his thumb, before fetching a chair and sitting at Rufus's side. "Well that rather puts me on the spot. I'm not sure what to say," he admitted.

"I'm sorry for waking you."

"It's alright, you didn't. I was busy reading."

Rufus, pleased to talk of books, craned his neck over to the one Boyd had left on his chair. "What is it?"

"It's a book on anatomy." Boyd fetched it and showed it to Rufus. The inside was full of gruesome drawings and Rufus raised his eyebrows. Boyd exhaled contentedly, his eyes gliding over the illustrations with an odd fondness. Rufus felt a bit queasy.

"This is somewhat heavy for a nightly read, isn't it? The human body must intrigue you."

"You mean it doesn't you? What, with all its intricacies?" Boyd took the book back, flicking through the pages. "I must confess," he said quietly, "post-mortem examinations are somewhat of a hobby of mine. Drawings are insightful but to plunge your hands into the body and hold the heart, liver, and stomach for yourself..." he drew off, dreamily. "Well it's really quite unparalleled."

Rufus gulped. "Athea have mercy, you're a *ghoul*."

Boyd seemed to emerge from his reminiscing, smiling. "I've never killed anyone," he said brightly. "I'm simply intrigued."

225

Rufus watched him cautiously. "Reading such gruesome things before bed—does it not disturb your sleep?"

"Well fortunately for me, that's not a problem I have to contend with."

"You never have nightmares?"

"No, I simply don't sleep."

Rufus giggled weakly and then reconsidered Boyd's serious expression. "Wait, really?"

"Yes...?"

"You don't sleep *at all*?" Rufus demanded, flabbergasted.

"Well, I can," Boyd sniffed, "but I find it to be rather a waste of time. I tire, of course, but so long as I rest occasionally, there's no need to take huge chunks out of my day, is there? I think the last time I slept was..." he counted back, "Well, it must have been three years ago."

"Three years?" Rufus coughed. "How? I thought you were human. You don't sleep?"

"And apparently you don't burn," Boyd replied dryly. "What a complicated pair we make."

"How can a man go three years without sleeping at all?" Rufus persisted. He'd seen men after three days without sleep— paranoid, irritable, exhausted. "You would die."

Boyd sighed. "It's complicated." He fixed his eyes on the bookshelf opposite. "Where do I begin? D'you understand the concept of the soul?"

"The spark of life which animates the body, yes," Rufus said.

"And d'you know what Sidhe are, in that respect?" Boyd asked slowly. When Rufus didn't reply, he explained. "The Sidhe are the descendants of the Tuatha de Danaan, who came from the heavenly plains. Sidhe are pure, physical souls. Unlike humans, they don't have a mortal body to animate, they simply exist on their own. That's why some faeries seem lighter than humans, of a less tangible substance. D'you understand?"

Rufus nodded.

"A human, then, is made of two things which balance together. The first is the soul, which is the spark of life—your character, your emotions, your intelligence. The second is your mortal flesh, which gives you your sense of mortality. It limits your strength, makes you hunger, sleep, feel pain." Boyd stopped again, as if uncomfortable. "Most Sidhe believe that the mortal aspect is a weakness, but because it's mortal, it gives a sense of time. That sense creates responsibility, it lets you learn to harness the more raw aspects of your character, and most importantly, it teaches you to adapt. That's why the Sidhe sometimes act like children, caught in one moment of existence, whilst mortal men become wise and fruitful."

"I'm not sure I understand where this is going," Rufus confessed.

"For faeries, such as the Cat Sidhe, who are a mixed breed," Boyd continued, "that ratio balance of soul and mortality is tipped more toward the soul. They can still die, but they're stronger and less limited by their need to sleep and eat. It also means they heal quicker. If I were to quantify it, I'd say approximately six-tenths of their being is made up of their soul. D'you see?"

"But what does that have to do with you?"

Boyd breathed deeply. "In order to make me the most sufficient version of myself, able to work longer, to perform magic better, the goddess Niamh changed the balance of my soul and mortality. Where once they were equal in standing, I am now almost entirely made of my own soul." Boyd toyed with his white hair, as if surprised by it. "Of course, she couldn't remove all of my mortality. You see, most human souls can't exist without their fleshy tether. But she carved away enough. I suppose, in that sense I might be called a faerie, in the rawest form."

Rufus sat in silence, stunned. He opened and closed his mouth. "How…?"

"Well, she's a goddess, of course. Many centuries old. She has her ways."

"Was it painful?"

"I don't know." Boyd kept his gaze to the floor. "I can't remember. I was only a baby."

"Then how could you consent to such a thing?"

"Consent?" Boyd laughed. "You don't honestly think I came to the Neve of my own volition, do you?"

"You mean...you're a *slave?*"

"Now I don't like that word." Boyd looked away. "It implies I can't leave. I jolly well can leave, and whenever I want too! It just so happens I *don't.*"

Rufus felt like his head was spinning. He shook it, almost as if to expel a dream. "Then how did you come to be here?"

"I was sold to Niamh to repay a debt, and she gave me to Lord Kathel to be his physician." At Rufus's astonished expression, Boyd expanded. "My ancestors are from one of the lands beneath the sea. They took a favour from Niamh many years ago—a hefty one, I might add. They desired riches, comfort and a good family name. And in exchange they promised her the first born of every generation of our family—I so happened to be one such firstborn."

"You're a changeling." Rufus realised.

"That's it." Boyd nodded. "I was swapped in my crib. I can't say with certainty whether my parents knew of their forefather's debt, but a promise with one of the Tuatha de Danaan is not to be broken lightly. They paid, knowingly or not."

"That's barbaric."

"Rufus," Boyd chuckled faintly. "They're *Sidhe*." He shrugged, almost sadly. "What exactly did you expect?"

Rufus was lost for words. Of course, all that Boyd said rang true, and a part of Rufus had always been aware of it. The Sidhe were incapable of telling lies and held treaty with Bethean, but they could be as cruel as any mortal. In many ways, they could be even crueller.

"I shouldn't have said anything, I can see that now." Boyd

fretted, his brow dipping. "You're upset."

"I simply…I thought better of Fae."

"This is not a stain on her—she's my friend, not my captor." Boyd stood. "Now is not the time to be dwelling on such things, either way. You need rest, Rufus. For all my lack of sleep, I know how crucial it is, and you're not getting nearly enough. I think I'll fetch you something to help you rest."

Rufus didn't like the idea of being drugged but the relief of deep sleep was a strong temptation. "I'd appreciate that."

Boyd scoured the shelves around the room and returned with a bottle of clear ointment. "I would usually prescribe three droplets, but for you, take seven." He measured them out into a small dish. Rufus took it with agile fingers, sniffing it.

"How strong is it?" he asked. Boyd simply smiled and Rufus grimaced. "Don't remove my kidneys while I sleep."

"Now there's an idea." Boyd's sleepless eyes were oddly frightening in the dark.

Rufus emptied the contents into his mouth and settled back against the pillow.

"Sleep well."

"Stay away from me," Rufus warned. He was asleep before Boyd finished laughing.

~※~

"You are the most needlessly frustrating man I know!" Fae ranted. "Over-bearing, supercilious, condescending, arrogant, prejudiced—"

"Are you quite finished?" Korrick growled from where he sat, sharpening his sword. Fae shot him a venomous look.

"I am still at the top of my list." Fae shot him a venomous look. "Reconsider!"

"No."

"Korrick!"

"I will not."

229

"You're being purposefully unreasonable. This is ridiculous!"

"If it irks you," Korrick sighed, "have Reilly order me to do it. He is your husband, after all."

"Don't be difficult, Korrick." Fae dropped down into a chair, her arms tightly folded. She'd always felt small beside her brother, not least because he was older than her by a century. "I am not asking for any favours from Reilly. And why should it matter? It's nothing to do with him."

"Reilly Mac Gearailt is the commander of the Neve army. I train new soldiers on his behest. If *you* were commander, Fae, I would do as you asked, but you forfeited that right."

"I won't hear another word about that," Fae snapped. "It's none of your business."

Korrick was silent and Fae watched him disdainfully. She had mixed feelings about her brother. He'd been too distant with her as a child for her to love him as she did her little sister Kael, and her younger twin brothers, Eadoin and Arton. Though some decades older, Fae was even still close to her other brothers as well—Amergin and Calder, and even Sloan and Quinlan. Korrick had never made any similar effort to know her as a sibling.

When it came to training Fae, however, Korrick had risen to his duty, invested by her enthusiasm and natural skill. She'd despised him as a brother, for his coldness and overbearing nature, but as a mentor she'd grown to love him deeply.

Through their swords they shared a connection that Fae knew was unique to the pair of them. Fae was one of the finest students to come through Korrick's schooling, and she owed her every skill and ability to him. Joshua could have no better mentor.

"Why?" she pressed. "Why won't you train him? If you can give me one good reason, then I will do as you say and go and humble myself to my husband."

Korrick studied her pensively. "Why are you so devoted to this Magi?" he asked, and Fae cursed, kicking his desk.

"Oh Great Danu, give me patience—Korrick, this has nothing

to do with him."

"Answer my question."

"Does no one understand the concept of friendship anymore?" Fae demanded. "Rufus saved my life. Yes, I find him to be secretive, suspicious in nature and occasionally disagreeable, but I trust him entirely. That's not what I am here to talk to you about."

Korrick rested his head in his hands. His fingers were strong and scarred, hardened with calluses like Fae's.

"I have thought long and hard," he eventually said, "about why you have not accepted your potential as a Chosen yet. I think at last I understand."

Fae's heart sank. "Korrick, now isn't the time."

"You love humanity too much."

"You can't love humanity too much." Fae exhaled. "But that's not something I would expect you to understand."

"Fae, you have the potential to transcend all of this. To forgo your mortality, any weakness you retain, but you linger. You linger for them." Korrick stood. "What endears you to this Prince? Do not invoke Niamh's name to guilt me—this is nothing to do with his heritage," he added as he saw Fae make to speak.

She paused, grimacing. "It's a personal matter," she finally admitted. "But it's also a political one—and believe me when I say the two are tied. I want peace in Harmatia, I want to help build the vision a friend of mine once had for his kingdom." Fae gazed solemnly at him. "You must teach Joshua, Korrick. He has learnt to think and love from one of the greatest men I know. Now he must learn to fight." Fae knelt at Korrick's feet. "I don't ask this as a sister, but as your pupil. You taught me to trust my instincts and they led me here."

Korrick didn't speak for a long while. Finally, he sighed. "I have one condition."

Fae rose. "Name it."

"He must pass a test of my choosing. He will not have the

stamina or natural talents of our brethren, and must therefore prove himself in another way. If he can pass my test I will train him, but if he fails he loses all right to that privilege."

Fae bowed in gratitude. "It will be done," she said. "And he won't fail."

"We shall see."

Korrick returned to his sword, his long face sombre and grim. He waved distractedly at Fae to dismiss her, and she left the room. It was too late now to go and speak with Rufus. She would convey the news in the morning. He wouldn't be happy, she suspected, but he would come to appreciate this favour one day.

CHAPTER
23
~~❧~~

Rufus woke feeling groggy, but rested. After ensuring that Boyd hadn't removed any of his internal organs for examination, he bartered permission to leave his bed and have a much needed bath.

The water was almost at boiling point as Rufus slipped into it, enjoying the scalding heat against his aching muscles. His ribcage, in particular, had been bothering him, and the bath relieved some of the pressure.

"Well several of them are broken, aren't they? Of course it's going to hurt," Boyd said.

"I didn't realise they were broken," Rufus admitted, scrubbing himself clean with the brush. Boyd stood in the doorway with Joshua, his eyes narrowed. "I can't always tell anymore."

"You mean to tell me you've been running about with broken ribs, unattended for days?"

"He probably got them when he fell off the cliff," Joshua declared and Boyd turned on Rufus in horror.

"You fell off a cliff?"

Rufus pulled a face. "I didn't fall. I jumped."-

"You *jumped* off a cliff?" Boyd wasn't comforted by this

apparent improvement.

Rufus sighed and slipped back into the water, submerging his head. He lay there as long as he could, enjoying the heat around his face. When he resurfaced, it was to find Boyd had stepped over and was peering over the edge of the bath at him. Rufus balked.

"What?"

"Thought you might have fallen unconscious there and drowned. You can hold your breath for a very long time," the physician said, impressed. "Or are you simply trying to kill yourself in another way?"

"Oh for Notameer's sake," Rufus growled, "I jumped off that cliff to escape the alchemists. Besides, the fall only fractured them—it was probably that Lemra'n assassin who actually broke them."

"When he threw you off the horse or when he got you in the woods?" Joshua asked cheerfully. Rufus scowled.

"Look, would the pair of you go away? I'm trying to wash and I don't need to be under surveillance."

"But what if you slip and crack your head open?" Boyd asked.

"That's a risk I'm willing to take." Rufus splashed some water at the physician, who retreated. "Now leave me alone. I want to relax and your presence is disconcerting."

"I've already seen you naked," Boyd said. "You have absolutely nothing to hide from us."

"I'm not body-shy, I just don't want you here." Rufus narrowed his eyes. "Examining me—as if I were a piece of meat for dissection."

Boyd barked a laugh. "Fine! Well, come along then, Joshua," he declared, "let us leave our distrustful friend to wash, shall we? We'll check back in a few minutes to make sure you haven't drowned."

"Fine," Rufus growled, taking what he could. "Go away now."

"See you in a minute," Joshua chirped, skipping from the

room, with Boyd just behind him.

Alone at last, Rufus shifted back into the bath and sulked, the water steaming around him. He pushed his fringe away, leaning back as the sweetened water dropped down from his forehead, round the hollow of his eyes and disappeared into his beard. He needed to groom himself, he looked terrible.

There was a knock from the door and he groaned, "It's been thirty seconds—I haven't even had a *chance* to drown yet, Boyd."

"Well that's a relief," Fae's voice replied through the door, "but it's actually me."

"Fae?" Rufus sat up.

"May I come in?"

Rufus looked between the bath and the door, debating with himself. He wasn't sure how he felt, after last night's news, but he owed it to Fae not to be an ungrateful guest. He cleared his throat. "You realise this is a washroom."

"I am aware."

"And that I'm washing."

"Gracious, is *that* the purpose of the room?" Fae's voice was muffled through the door.

Rufus couldn't help but smile. "In which case, enter at your leisure, but it may cause you some distress to know that I'm naked."

Fae laughed, "I have already seen you naked."

"Apparently everybody has," Rufus mumbled.

"Just stay in the bath and it won't be a problem." Fae opened the door and slipped in, her face bright. "Good morning."

"Good afternoon," Rufus corrected. He could feel the shift of the reigning gods outside, and noon was already upon them.

"How do you feel today?"

"Cleaner." Rufus skimmed his hand across the surface of the water. "I say," he noted, "you're wearing a dress."

Fae looked down at herself with a vague horror. "Titania, I was tricked."

Rufus tittered dryly. "I haven't seen you in a dress since Sarrin."

"You haven't seen me since Sarrin."

"I have. In here." Rufus tapped his forehead grimly. "What do you want, in any case?"

"To speak."

"If that was all, you could have waited until I was finished. So it must be important," Rufus said glumly. "I presume it's to do with training Joshua?"

Fae folded her arms. "My brother, Korrick, has agreed to teach him."

"Excuse me if I don't fling myself about the room in jubilation."

"It's nothing to turn your nose up about—Korrick is the finest teacher in the Neve. He made me the fighter I am today. Joshua would be privileged to learn under him."

Rufus grunted, splashing water onto his face and rubbing his cheeks. "I'm sure," he mumbled and then dropped his hands, ashamed. "Thank you," he forced himself to say. "It can't have been an easy task convincing him."

"It wasn't, but he's willing to do it on a condition."

"A condition?" Rufus's breath caught. Something hissed in his ear, like an advisor leaning over to whisper a warning.

Ah—a condition, is it? the dark thoughts said. *So there's the snag.*

"It's nothing to worry about," Fae said and Rufus almost stood.

"Oh no," he pointed accusingly at her, "I know what you Sidhe are like. Given half a chance you'd trick us out of our virtue, fortune and freedom—don't take me for an idiot!"

Fae blinked. "*Excuse* me?"

Innocent face, Rufus thought, looking into her brilliant green eyes. *Lovely face—but I'm sure Niamh looked lovely too, on the day she bartered for her slaves.*

"I know the truth," Rufus said, "the truth about Boyd. That he was stolen away because of an archaic debt that his family may not even remember. That he was fundamentally changed in order

236

to be more useful to you." Rufus rose from the bath hurriedly. He could no longer relax—he was burning with anger. "So don't tell me it's nothing—I don't care for your definition of nothing."

Fae opened and closed her mouth, speechless for a moment. "How dare you?" she finally gasped. "I saved your lives, you ingrate."

A life saved—a debt owed, the dark thoughts purred.

"Yes," he said, "You did. But for what price?"

"Rufus," Fae laughed incredulously, her eyes wide, "I'm not presenting you with a bill."

"Stop joking with me!" Rufus roared and Fae stepped back.

"Calm down." Her eyes flashed.

"It's Joshua, isn't it?" Rufus ignored the warning look in her face. "That's what you want, don't you? Oh Athea, how could I be so blind? Of course that's what you want!"

"Rufus, I don't—"

"I can only imagine what sway Avalon would hold over Harmatia then!" Rufus's voice rose, cracking slightly. "You pretend to extend the hand of friendship but you're just trying to buy him to your side with your training, and your promises, and *your bloody swords!*" he roared, advancing on Fae. "Well I won't let you!"

Fae slapped him so fast he was sprawled on the floor before he realised he'd been struck.

"Have you gone stark raving mad?" She towered over him, and he stared up at her, cradling his cheek. All at once, he felt very frightened.

What had he just done? Where had that momentous anger burst out from? He'd been willing to talk, to listen, to hear what Fae had to say, and yet somehow in the moment none of his rationality had mattered. He'd felt only rage. Rage and suspicion.

Rufus had never been so powerless against his own temper, never lost it so quickly without control. What if he'd taken it to the next level? What if he'd *attacked* Fae?

Fae's eyes roamed down his body, lingering on the scars, and for the first time Rufus was embarrassed by his nakedness. He tried to cover himself, and Fae offered him a hand and pulled him gently up to his feet.

"Forgive me, I shouldn't have hit you."

"I deserved it," Rufus mumbled, rubbing his cheek. The pain had steadied his senses, bringing him back under his own control. He pulled his hand free of Fae's and grabbed his towel, covering himself. "How could you do it?" He kept his eyes to the floor. "Steal a child away from his family? Trick someone out of something so precious?"

Fae drew back. There was a shame in the set of her shoulders. "My grandmother is of an ancient race—she knows a different morality. Those humans agreed to the debt of future children— they signed that contract knowingly. Did they have the right to do so? Perhaps not, but Niamh's conscience is clean. Do I agree with it? No. And I have spoken against it, but… regardless of how he came to be here, this is Boyd's home now. And so long as he wishes to call it such, it's where he belongs."

"But it shouldn't be a reality," Rufus argued. "You shouldn't allow it to happen."

"And how do I stop it?" Fae threw her hands in the air. "How can I defy a god?"

"*I* did," Rufus said and Fae gave a sharp laugh.

"Great Danu—why can we not have a single conversation without you ending it in an argument?"

"I didn't start this!" Rufus cried.

"What have I done to earn this distrust?" Fae sounded tired and Rufus closed his eyes, running his hands through his hair. "A few days ago, you were kneeling at my feet, weeping at the sight of me, begging me not to leave you. And now you're throwing accusations at me as if I were your enemy."

"I've trusted," Rufus's voice rose again, that same anger flaring, "I've trusted over and over. My friends—my own kingdom betrayed me! When they took Jionat—" Rufus choked off, and he saw Fae flinch. "I've loved. I've—" again, Rufus couldn't finish his sentence. He gestured miserably. "And they've taken everything—*everything*—because I trusted too much to heed the signs. So tell me, how do I trust you, when you're more a memory to me than a reality?" he gasped. He'd never seen Fae look so hurt, her mouth parted in silent dismay. "You told me once that you'd been betrayed by those you played with as a child. I know you don't trust me either."

Fae blinked and looked away, as if the breath had been knocked out of her. "What a relief it is," she said bitterly, "that you are here to tell me my mind."

Rufus couldn't find the sufficient words to respond, so they both stood in silence, the heavy words hanging between them. Rufus turned his back on her.

"What was the condition?" he asked hoarsely. "Korrick's condition for Joshua?"

"He wants to test him—see that he's fit for training. Joshua may forfeit or refuse at any time." Fae paused. "We won't be enslaving him today."

Rufus closed his eyes in shame.

"That's all I wanted to tell you. Good day, Rufus." She turned swiftly and left the room, slamming the door as she went.

~⁂~

Fae stopped outside the washroom, trying to catch her breath. She was so angry she almost couldn't see straight, but she held it in, resisting the urge to rip the door back open and give Rufus a piece of her mind.

"He doesn't mean it," a voice piped up beside her. Fae was so consumed with her thoughts she hadn't noticed Joshua waiting outside. She jumped and turned quickly, masking her expression. It wouldn't do for Joshua to know how much Rufus had upset her.

"What are you doing here? I saw you with Boyd."

"I told him I forgot something in my room. I wanted to speak with Rufus. We haven't had any time to ourselves since he woke. I wanted to tell him it was my idea to train—that I was the one who suggested it." Joshua glanced down at a black book he held in his hands.

Fae followed his gaze. "That book." She jolted with recognition. "That's Jionat's book of dreams."

Joshua held it up for her, "It's the only thing I managed to keep hold of after we were attacked. I never leave it far." Joshua's eyes were wide and very sad. "Rufus doesn't mean it, Fae. He does trust you, I know he does—or he wouldn't let me out of his sight. He's just frightened."

"Come on," Fae sighed, and she steered him away from the washroom. They walked together, side by side. "I rather fear that Boyd has unintentionally fed your brother's paranoia. But Rufus is a little justified," Fae admitted reluctantly, "even if he's being incredibly rude."

"It's because of the Crow woman," Joshua whispered, almost nervously. Fae peered down at him curiously, the Prince hugging the book to his chest, as if he thought someone were about to swoop in and snatch it away.

"The Crow woman?"

"I shouldn't talk about it."

"Speak your mind," Fae urged.

Joshua drummed his fingers nervously. "The Crow woman. She visits us. Rufus doesn't think I know, but I do. I saw. In here." He tapped his forehead, and Fae was strangely reminded of the way Rufus had made the same gesture only minutes before.

"You mean you had a vision?" Fae asked gently.

"My sight isn't as good as Jionat's was," Joshua mumbled into his collar. "But I see things sometimes. And I see people for what they are. It's hard to describe." He seemed to grow uncomfortable, tugging at his own fingers and glancing over his shoulder down the empty corridor.

Fae drew him into her side. "Tell me about this Crow woman."

"She first came after we were chased out of Beshuwa. I was asleep and she appeared to the camp. She said she wanted to help us but she wasn't good for Rufus. She did something to him." Joshua frowned deeply, as if trying to recall it all. "She wanted Rufus to have sex with her."

Fae's eyebrows shot up. "And did they?"

"No." Joshua bit his lip, once again glancing worriedly around. "He would hate it if he knew I saw, so I didn't say anything. They didn't have sex but she tried to compel Rufus with magic. I could feel it in the air—it was toxic. She was *bad*, Fae. Rufus refused her, but even when she left, she didn't really leave him. And then we met the halfling, and Rufus—Rufus went with him, and—"

"Slow down, slow down." Fae stopped walking and knelt before the boy. Joshua chewed his bottom lip. "This Crow woman. You say she tried to force Rufus with magic?"

Joshua nodded his head and Fae pursed her lips. There were a handful of faeries who possessed that kind of power, though what they would want particularly with Rufus…

"What about this halfling?" Fae asked.

"He was a Gancanagh. He recognised Rufus. Said he'd give us room for the night if Rufus went with him." Joshua began to tremble. "They thought I was too sick to understand, but I knew. I knew what they were doing."

Fae felt her chest tighten. The conflict in Joshua's expression was overwhelming—Lords knew, Rufus was a secretive man, and it couldn't be an easy thing for Joshua to breach such a trust and reveal these sensitive truths.

"Speak, Joshua," Fae bade him, brushing his hair from his eyes. "I will guard these secrets with my life. You don't have to fight them alone."

Joshua sniffed. "Fae, I'm scared. When Rufus returned, he was covered in the halfling's blood. I could see the Crow woman under his skin. She's still there now—eating away at him, fuelling

241

his anger, *blinding him*. You have to get her out." Joshua's hand clenched around Fae's wrist, his eyes wide and unfocused. "Get her out or something bad is going to happen."

"How do you know, Joshua? Have you seen something?"

"No," Joshua moaned and opened the book of dreams. "Jionat did."

Fae glanced down at the page and for a moment, the familiar pencil strokes caught her off guard. She'd once heard that an artist lived in his every mark, and that was true of Jionat's drawing. She could see him in the arch of the pencil work, in the impatient shading, and the bold lines. And then she saw the picture itself and she realised why Joshua was so frightened.

"Morrigan," she choked. Joshua seemed to sense her apprehension and his fingers tightened around the book. He was an astute boy. Fae forced down her fear—it wouldn't do to upset him. "This is the Crow woman?"

"She wore a disguise." Joshua turned his eyes down to the drawing. The woman depicted cut a fierce figure, with wild, dark hair and penetrating eyes, clad in black armour that seemed to be moulded from feathers.

"Yes, and I'm sure she had many pretty things to say," Fae murmured.

She recalled the way the Korrigans had captured Rufus so long ago. It couldn't be a coincidence that their patron goddess was stalking him now. Was Morrigan controlling him? Rufus was certainly exhibiting all the behaviours of being under her thrall—aggression, anger, sudden fits of agitation and anxiety. But no—if Morrigan had control of Rufus, he would be marked. There would discolouration on his skin, a dark shape across his chest—Fae would have seen it in the washroom.

"You say Rufus refused her?" Fae gave a bitter laugh. "He really did defy a god. But Morrigan won't have left it at that."

"You can't tell him I told you."

"Joshua, this is extremely serious. If Morrigan is targeting

Rufus, I need to talk to him."

"He has to tell you himself," Joshua pleaded. "I only told you so you would know. Fae, promise me. Please."

Fae struggled and then sighed. "Very well, Joshua," she granted. "I won't say anything to Rufus for now, but I can't promise not to investigate the matter myself. In the meantime," she touched his cheek, "I don't want you to worry—I won't let any harm come to Rufus. I'll protect him."

"Even after everything he said?"

"Especially after everything he said," Fae assured. "There is nothing I love more that proving that man wrong."

This time Joshua giggled, a little of the tension leaving his body. Nobody so young should have to bear such a heavy burden—it wasn't Joshua's place to take care of Rufus. Fae was sure Rufus would be mortified if he learned how much Joshua knew. She forced her smile.

"There you are!" Boyd rounded the corner. "You said you were going to your room!" he berated Joshua.

"Sorry, I kidnapped him." Fae seized Joshua and pulled him close to her dramatically, making him giggle again.

Boyd seemed unconvinced, his arms folded. "You're wanted as well," he warned Fae. "Amergin found me on the way here, he says Commander Mac Gearailt has an errand for you."

"Of course he does." Fae rolled her eyes, muttering under her breath. Reilly had seen to it that her days were lined with menial tasks, and though he never admitted to anything so petty, she knew he did it in order to lessen her time with Rufus and Joshua. This might not have bothered Fae so much, were it not for the fact that her brothers were also avoiding her, wherever possible. They used Boyd and the servants to pass messages, and refused to meet her eye or speak if they met in passing. Her decision to bring Rufus into the Neve hadn't been popular, but over time, they would forgive her.

"I had better go and change." Fae felt Joshua grab the skirt of her dress. "Joshua, forgive me, but I have to go."

"I know." Joshua released her reluctantly. Boyd stepped in, putting on an air of indifference.

"Now Joshua, I thought you might like to know," he sniffed, "I was just outside a minute ago and it seems the gods of winter are yet lingering."

"What do you mean?" Joshua frowned. Fae felt her heart lighten.

"What I mean is we've had another heavy bout of snowfall," Boyd said and Joshua straightened, an excited glint in his eyes. Boyd exchanged a quick smile with Fae. "The mountainside is absolutely *covered*."

CHAPTER
24

They were lounging in the Magi common room in a rare display of relaxation, when the disturbance came. A pair of sniggering men sauntered over to where Zachary and Belphegore sat, and Zachary knew immediately, by the way their eyes darted over to him and their smiles elongated, that they'd discovered something scandalous. He wondered, dully, what he could have done this time to ignite their amusement.

"My Lords Odin, Zachary," the front man, Radford, bowed, saying Zachary's name with more mockery then respect. Radford and his circle had been at the academy with Zachary, and had mocked and bullied him viciously in his youth. Their relationship hadn't much improved in the growing years.

"Lord Radford, Lord Mallinson," Belphegore began wearily. "How may we be of assistance to you both?"

"We apologise for the disturbance," Mallinson said in a deeply unapologetic voice, "but there is a boy here to see you, Lord Zachary."

"Me?"

"I confess," Radford barely seemed able to contain himself, "I had no idea you had a son."

The words caught Zachary off guard and he found himself throwing his mind back, trying to recall exactly how many years it had been since he'd actually had sex. It took him a moment to realise what they were really talking about, and he looked past them all to the doorway, where Daniel was just visible beyond a cluster of Magi.

"Oh for Notameer's sake," Zachary grunted, putting down his glass forcefully as Belphegore sat up, intrigued.

"Arlen, what are they talking about?"

"It's nothing," Zachary stood, and then added, "and I don't have a son, Radford."

"A bastard then," Radford corrected carelessly.

"Oh he's a bastard," Zachary agreed venomously, "but he's not mine."

Moving up and toward the doorway, Mallinson and Radford followed after him like a set of malicious geese, Belphegore in tow, his interest piqued.

From across the room, Zachary caught eyes with Marcel, who tipped his head, wordlessly asking if everything was alright. Zachary gave him a curt nod.

Reaching Daniel, Zachary found another of his childhood bullies waiting at the boy's side, looking strangely pleased with himself.

"Not much resemblance, I must say. Fortunately, he must take after his mother, eh?"

"And thank Haylix she's prettier than yours, Milton," Zachary snapped, his temper getting the better of him. "Daniel, get out, now."

Daniel bristled.

"Arlen," Belphegore chided.

"I will not—" Daniel began.

"It's not up for debate. Get out," Zachary repeated sharply.

"It seems that all the Zacharys are destined to hate their sons," Radford scoffed, and Daniel looked at the man with such disgust,

Zachary almost felt better.

"You think he's my father?" Daniel recoiled.

"You announced yourself as a Zachary." Milton turned on the boy, riled by his tone.

"Octania's spark, you're right—if only a father could permit his name to more than one child," Daniel snipped.

"That is a Magi you address, boy—watch your tongue!" Radford stepped in, his hand raised as if to slap Daniel. Zachary seized his wrist.

"Don't," he snarled.

Belphegore raised his hands. "That is quite enough of that," he said, taking easy control. The men stepped clear of Daniel, who hadn't moved. "This is clearly a family affair. I thank you, my lords, for bringing the boy's presence to our attention, but Arlen can take it from here. Good day to you all."

The three Magi looked between one another and then, under Belphegore's prompting, dissipated, shooting Zachary and Daniel scathing looks as they went.

When they were clear, Belphegore relaxed. "A brother, Arlen?" he asked disparagingly.

"My father'll fuck anything with a pulse," Zachary muttered into his hand, rubbing his mouth.

"Doesn't explain how you were born," Daniel mumbled back under his breath, too soft for Belphegore to hear. Zachary snorted.

"You must be new to the academy or else I am going senile. Daniel, was it?" Belphegore asked, extending a hand. For the first time Daniel seemed to realise whom he was being addressed by. He bowed, looking unsure of himself, and awkwardly took Belphegore's hand.

"Yes, my lord. I came to study in Harmatia a few months ago, in preparation for the assessments."

"I see." Belphegore smiled kindly. "It is a pleasure to meet you. It would seem you inherited the same predilection Arlen has for picking fights."

"No, my lord." Daniel shook his head. "I don't like to fight."

"In which case, you might be a little more wary of your tongue, or you may find it will get you into trouble."

"I apologise, my lord. I'll hold my peace in the future." Daniel looked suitably embarrassed with himself.

Belphegore gave Zachary a meaningful look. Zachary gave an exaggerated shrug in response and, taking Daniel by the arm, dragged him from the room, out of the way.

"What are you doing here?" Zachary hissed when they were clear of prying eyes.

"I needed to speak to you."

"And it couldn't have waited until I was home?"

"With the hours you keep, not if I wanted to catch the evening courier." Daniel was unperturbed by Zachary's tone. "Thank you for not letting him hit me," he added in abrasive thanks.

"Fine then," Zachary sighed. "What was so urgent that it couldn't possibly wait? You want to send a message, what has that to do with me?"

"I need your blessing."

"Blessing? Sweet Haylix, are you getting married?" Zachary mocked.

Daniel rolled his eyes. "Re'th kyjyewgh hwi," he muttered quietly in Althion.

"Watch your language," Zachary snapped and, at his brother's surprised expression, reminded him, "We were *both* raised in Corhlam, Daniel—I can speak Althion as well as you."

"I've never heard you use it."

"A mother tongue doesn't fall so quickly from the mouth. But nobody speaks it in the capital, so unless you want to mark yourself out even more, keep to the Common Tongue. Now what is it you want? You're wasting my time."

Daniel opened his mouth to reply and then froze, going taut and hunching over himself, as if he'd torn the muscles in his stomach. He gave a hiss of gurgled pain, his teeth gritted.

Zachary blinked. "What's wrong with you?"

"Nothing." Daniel forced himself to straighten but Zachary could see it caused him great pain. He kept his expression the same, despite the fact he was shaking. "I need your blessing to invite a guest to the house."

"A guest? Do you even *have* friends?" Zachary raised his eyebrows and Daniel huffed impatiently.

"My mother," he said.

Every limb in Zachary's body locked into place. He stared, long and hard at his brother, caught off guard. "Your mother?" he eventually repeated.

"I need to see her." Daniel suddenly looked drained, slouching against the wall. Zachary's first instinct was to forbid the request, but his sensible mind caught up with him. If he forbade Daniel, the boy would merely go and invite her anyway. Knowing their father, Rivalen, would undoubtedly pander to Daniel's wishes, if only to spite his eldest son. Zachary couldn't afford to show his hand now.

"Are you writing to our father and asking his permission?"

"Yes."

Zachary turned away, trying to compose himself. "Very well. Tell him I would be happy to accommodate your mother a few weeks, at her leisure. If you need to see her, she must come. In fact, tell him I insist upon it."

"You...You do?" Daniel blinked, perplexed.

"I do. Now go and send your damned letter, and Daniel— if you disturb me again at my work," Zachary turned his back on the boy, "I shall see to it you never become a Magi. Do you understand?"

Daniel blinked rapidly. "No, I don't." His surprise was replaced once more with anger. "You make absolutely no sense. Defending me one minute and casting me out the next."

"This is a friendless city, brat, and until you learn to play by its

249

lack of rules, you have no place in it. Now go, and Athea forbid I see you again today."

"I'm glad to quit your company," Daniel growled and stormed away.

Zachary watched him go. Behind him, Marcel shifted out from where he'd been lurking close by.

"I thought I recognised him," Marcel drawled and Zachary's eye twitched. "He is Isolde's son."

"For once in your life, Hathely, you are talking too much," Zachary warned as his second in command moved to his side, the pair watching Daniel disappear down the corridor.

"Does he know?" Marcel asked faintly.

"No." Zachary closed his eyes. "Nor will he ever, if his mother has any shame and I retain mine."

Marcel touched a hand lightly to Zachary's back, making him jump, uncomfortable with the sudden, uncharacteristic contact. He didn't like to be touched, especially not there.

"That is not shame," Marcel said.

Zachary clenched his fists. "And that's not for you to decide," he retorted, pushing past the blond and going back into the common room. "And if you're as clever as you're supposed to be, you won't bring it up again."

Marcel replaced his pipe wordlessly into his mouth, and they went silently back to their places in the room.

~≈~

Rufus watched from the window as Boyd ran furiously through the garden outside, shouting after Joshua, who was piling through the snow with unadulterated glee.

"A bag of gold says you can't catch me, Boyd!" Joshua taunted, and Rufus lowered his head into his folded arms, propped up against the window sill, watching with a melancholic pleasure. It was good to see his brother playing, though Boyd looked positively manic.

"Stop! You're killing me! Please for the love of Titania, stop—you're getting soaked!" Boyd was half-sobbing as Joshua grabbed a fistful of snow and threw it at the back of the physician's head. "I am a man of medicine, not a plaything—please!"

Rufus's smile elongated and he closed his eyes, resting his cheek on the stone ledge. He could almost sleep like this, ready to drift off. All at once, however, he became abruptly aware he was no longer alone. With a sharp jerk, he sat upright. A man was stood at his side, staring at him with a mixed expression of curiosity and heavy disdain. Rufus scrabbled to his feet.

"Reilly Mac Gearailt." The man thrust his hand into Rufus's chest.

"What? Oh! Er—R-Rufus Merle," Rufus stammered in return as his hand was crushed in a harsh grip. "Ouch," he added blandly. Reilly released his hand.

"You do not remember me?"

"I...No?"

"We met the night you arrived. You called me a false leader."

"Did I?" Rufus gave a nervous chuckle, shifting back slightly as Reilly took another step toward him. "Well, that...er, that was silly of me, I'm sure. I wasn't in my right mind. No doubt I said many unwarranted things." He paused. "Mac Gearailt," he repeated, trying to remember why he recalled the name. "Oh, that's right. Boyd mentioned that you wanted to flay us alive... Oh."

"Relax, Magi." Reilly kicked Rufus's empty chair out of the way. "I am bound by the law of my lord." He loomed predatorily, blocking the doorway. "How do you feel?"

"Threatened," Rufus replied, his skin crawling as Reilly laughed, moving in even closer.

"Do I make you uncomfortable, Magi?"

"Exceedingly." Rufus took another step away and his back met the wall. He flattened himself against it. Reilly's lips curled up, pleased by this fear. Neither moved for a long moment, and then finally Reilly pulled away, allowing Rufus to relax.

"Thank you," Rufus murmured.

Reilly turned to the window, his arms folded. "Tell me," he said stiffly, "what is it about you that attracts my wife?"

Rufus stammered, confused. He searched the room for some hidden woman he may have missed, but saw no one else. "I beg your pardon?"

"She devotes so much time to you, to your needs. Tell me, *Magi*," Reilly curled the word around his mouth like it was an insult, "what is so inspiring about you that she would do so much?"

"My delicate features and poetic nature?" Rufus suggested, bewildered. "I'm afraid I don't know what you're talking about. If you're having marital problems, I suggest you take them up with your wife."

"You think yourself a funny man?"

"I think myself an honest one. I've not been advertising—there's no further thought from my mind. Nor have I ever been an adulterer. I've not lovingly shared a bed with anyone in many months, and the last woman I had a meaningful relationship with died fifteen years ago. You must be mistaken—" Rufus made to walk around Reilly, but the Cat Sidhe pushed him back.

"I didn't say you were sleeping with my wife, nor do I care. I asked why she was devoted to you. Why is she prepared to throw so away much, even push her loyalties to the limit for you?"

"I really have no idea what you're talking about." Rufus tried to wriggle past but Reilly piled against him, pushing him back against the wall. Rufus's body protested the abuse and he gasped in pain. Reilly didn't seem to care.

"She cried before you!" he hissed. "She has never done so in front of anyone else. It is not in her nature. So why you? When I was with her from the start, when I saw her...Not even when..." Reilly broke off. "What have you done, to earn Fae's loyalty?"

"Fae?" Rufus stilled. "Fae's your *wife*? When did that happen?"

"She has been married to me for over fourteen years."

"That would mean she was...when we met." Rufus shook his head in disbelief. "She was married. I had no idea. But," Rufus frowned, "there are no children?"

Reilly's expression twisted angrily. "We Cat Sidhe do think of other things than procreation. We're not vermin."

Rufus battered the comment away distractedly. "Apologies for your clear lack of sex but Fae has always given the impression of *wanting* them. She was so good with my cousins, so sweet-tempered. I was sure she would have...Or adopted..." He paused, sweeping his eyes up to Reilly's. "Perhaps she didn't want to inflict you on any child," he said. Reilly released him and went for his sword.

Before anything could escalate further, the door burst open and Boyd skidded into the room, slipped on his own wet shoes, and toppled face-first onto the floor. Rufus and Reilly stared at him in silence, both as shocked as the other. When the physician didn't move, Rufus spoke.

"Boyd, are you hurt?"

"No." Boyd's voice was muffled by the stone. "No, I am quite well." He winced, rolling onto his back so that he was sprawled, looking up at them. He noticed Reilly for the first time and balked. "Oh, Commander Mac Gearailt, I didn't see you there. Excuse me." He forced himself to his feet, brushing himself down, his eyes averted. He began to chew nervously on his thumb. "Ur, Rufus, I may need your help. We were playing a game, and he went to hide, and—well, I've lost Joshua."

"Already?" Rufus asked dully. The physician pulled a face.

"You mean to tell me there is a human child running amok in the grounds?" Reilly demanded. "You never tire of being a disappointment, do you Physician Dacey?"

Rufus saw Boyd bristle, but the physician clearly wasn't foolish enough to retort. He mumbled something, shuffling his feet. "I'll find him."

"Yes, you had better. I don't need some Harmatian Prince disturbing my troops in their training."

"I'm sure he won't...that he hasn't..." Boyd continued to mutter. Rufus moved past the pair and out of the door, ignoring them both. His mind was occupied by his discovery—Fae, married? From what Rufus had already discerned of Reilly, the match seemed absurd. Perhaps, Rufus reasoned, he was prejudiced, but when he thought of Fae in love, all he could see was her dancing with Jionat during the Summer Festival. When Rufus tried to imagine Reilly dancing, he couldn't picture it.

I called him a 'false leader', Rufus thought. *I wonder what I meant by that.*

He reached a heavy side door and stepped out into the frosty courtyard. The world beyond was a white wilderness. He paused, struck by its silent beauty. The never-ending sky and the jagged mountains were infinitely more beautiful than when he'd been looking through the window.

The bright, cold air seemed to revive him and he stepped out into the snow, which crunched satisfactorily beneath his shoes.

"Joshua?" he called faintly, knowing his brother wouldn't respond, not when he was feeling so playful. "Ready or not then," Rufus set out, "here I come."

～～

The field was frozen when the Hunter reached it. From a distance, the sun had deceivingly lit it gold, making it look alive with long stalks of corn. If it had been once, the snow had long killed anything food worthy. The vast man stumbled across the white expanse, a dark spot in plain sight. His hands were stained, his clothes caked in dried blood, and he had a look about him—a severe ferocity that would stop a feral wolf in its tracks.

Now, however, Varyn was being hunted. His obvious Isny features—the dark, bold face and eyes the colour of coal—were always enough to make him stand out, but it was his tattoos which had betrayed him this time. The tattoos that marked him as property of the Shin.

Even as a free man, there was no place for an ex-Shinny this close to the King's city. Varyn should never have come. He cursed as his legs gave away beneath him.

Not here, he thought, *not now.*

Behind him he could hear the thundering of horses' hooves, and he knew it was useless. There was nowhere to hide for miles—the landscape was as open as the sky. He wasn't in the mountains here, he was on the treacherous Kathrak plains of South Meare, too close to Sigel'eg for his own good. And for him they *were* treacherous, more than the perilous mountains and coasts of Isnydea, which had claimed hundreds of lives.

Varyn tried to stand, but the pain came over him again and he collapsed, his strength seeping away. Once, long ago, he'd made a wish that when he died, it would be on Kathrak soil, and that he would leave behind something to be remembered by—an achievement, a memento of good. Something to prove that his life had value.

As King Bozidar's men surrounded him, sprawled against the frozen grass, Varyn consoled himself that at the very least one of those wishes would come true.

"Well run, Hunter," the leader of the group said. He was a young lieutenant with a scar down his face. "You gave us a merry chase. But it would appear even you cannot outrun a horse forever. Get him up."

Two of his soldiers got down from their horses and forced Varyn up onto his knees. He stared dully at the Lieutenant, who watched him with glee. This idiot thought he'd felled Varyn. It made the Hunter want to laugh. It was no mere man who'd brought him to his knees—it was magic, a curse, a woman...

"So this is the one they say has 'dragon blood', is it?"

Varyn groaned. They said many things about him but the

worst were the things which were true.

"Then you can all call me Dragon Slayer." The Lieutenant dismounted his horse. On foot, he wasn't so tall.

Varyn grumbled. He was worth too much gold to be killed by some fresh-faced soldier, still green and bloodthirsty. The Lieutenant's men came to the same conclusion, and one spoke up.

"The King will want him alive, Sir."

The Lieutenant's expression twisted and he drew his sword angrily. He placed it against Varyn's cheek. The Hunter didn't flinch as the blade cut into the skin. "You've gone too far this time, Hunter," the Lieutenant said, maintaining his sneer. "Killing one of the King's men."

"Was already dead," Varyn spat, though he knew there was no point explaining. These men were too far south to know about the monsters that dwelled in the shadows. This fool probably thought that the Elves were nothing but stories wet nurses used to scare children. He'd never seen a dragon, or a draugr, or a huldra—he didn't know the fear of the demons and spirits which plagued villages all along the coast. Varyn did. Varyn had known these monsters from childhood.

"Already dead, you say?" The Lieutenant laughed. "Is that how he's been able to fuck his wives and whores these last few months? Because from all accounts, that is the mark of a man very much alive. Or do mean that he was possessed, as you claimed when you murdered him?"

He had been. Varyn had never seen such an aggressive possession in his life. The host had been rotting from the inside. When Varyn had cut him up, his intestines and bowels had been black.

"Ask the wives. They'll tell you," Varyn growled.

"Hysterical women don't make for valid witnesses," the Lieutenant replied. "Even so, you might have been considered innocent, until you decided to flee. That, we tend to mark as the action of a *guilty* man."

Varyn gritted his teeth, opening and closing his fists. "I had to. For everyone's safety. It's coming."

"What's coming?"

"Dragon."

The Lieutenant exploded with laughter. "A *dragon*? In Sigel'eg. This tale gets better and better."

"It's hunting me and it's close. There's no time. I have to go far away."

The Lieutenant only laughed harder. "And how do you know it's coming? Last I checked the skies were clear. Anybody else seen a dragon swooping around? Be hard to miss."

Varyn was running out of time, his patience wearing thin. "I can sense it."

"You can *sense* it? That's convenient," the Lieutenant drawled, and at Varyn's serious expression, raised an eyebrow. "Don't tell me you honestly expect me to believe you have dragon blood in you?"

"Take me to the city, it kills you all. Let me go, no one else dies." Varyn turned to the other soldiers. Surely there must have been at least one among them who remembered the warnings and tales of their ancestors? Who knew that dragons had flown down this far south before, in search of prey, and the devastation they'd left in their wake. Nobody met his eye.

"Your children's stories may well work north of the capital, Hunter, but here they will not," the Lieutenant said. "You killed a King's man, tried to flee, and now you will pay for it. What do you say to that?"

A shot of pain passed through Varyn, from deep within his belly. He tensed, and then, unable to repress the clawing agony, cried out, grinding his teeth together. The Lieutenant watched, confused, as Varyn hunched forward, easily resisting the soldiers' hold as they attempted to straighten him again.

"Something's wrong, Sir," one of the soldiers said.

257

"He's faking," the Lieutenant snarled, and Varyn groaned again as the pain persisted. He could no longer feel his legs. The pain would only get worse from now, he knew.

"I think not, Sir," the soldier said. Varyn could feel the blood draining from his face. Such pain couldn't be faked. The Lieutenant grew impatient.

"Get him up! We're returning to the city."

The two soldiers attempted to drag Varyn to his feet, but the Hunter couldn't stand and he sagged between them.

"The gods curse you—stand, Hunter!" the Lieutenant barked, and amidst his pain Varyn wished he could obey this order. If he could stand, he could fight—if he could fight, he could just as easily run and escape. "Damn it! Put him on the back of the horse if you must, we return—now!"

Varyn was heaved up and thrown across a saddle, a soldier mounted behind him. The Lieutenant turned his horse back toward the distant city and gestured for his men to follow. Varyn closed his eyes and, as the pain increased, wondered if he'd ever open them again.

CHAPTER
25

~∗~

"What are you doing?"

Joshua jumped a foot in the air and almost toppled off the branch he was balanced on. The tree had proven to be a perfect hiding spot from Boyd, covered in snow as it was, and with such a thick coat of leaves it was like sitting in a tent. The Prince had been so preoccupied with keeping quiet and not being seen, he hadn't heard someone else enter his leafy domain.

The girl was a few branches below him and had wide green eyes that glowed like an animal's in firelight.

"Hiding," he answered, keeping his voice low. He peered curiously at the girl. He hadn't seen anyone of his own age since arriving in the Neve, though logically he'd known there must have been other children around.

"Why?" The Cat Sidhe tilted her head to one side, blinking languidly. She had amiable features, a round face and slightly upturned nose, like a kitten.

"For fun." Joshua shrugged, "What are you doing here?"

"I'm hiding, too." The girl gave a sudden, wide smile that Joshua returned, unable to help himself.

"Who from?"

"My brother, Korrick." She pulled herself up higher, so that she was closer to Joshua. She was a little shorter than him, though they appeared to be close in age. They studied each other curiously. "You're the Prince of Harmatia," the Cat Sidhe eventually said, as if there were other human boys running around the Neve.

"My name's Joshua."

"I'm Kael Ó Murchadha," she replied. "My sister's friends with the Magi. Shall we be friends too?"

Joshua blinked rapidly, delightfully taken aback. Looking into Kael's eyes, the Prince had a clear sense of the girl. She was excitable, sweet-tempered, younger than she appeared, and of an optimistic temperament. Joshua had started to forget what optimism looked like after so many years on the run, having to be suspicious of everyone.

"Yes, I'd like that," he said, and Kael's smile grew wider still. "Why are you hiding from Korrick? Are you playing a game too?"

"Korrick doesn't play games," Kael said sullenly, pulling herself onto the branch beside Joshua. "He was making us study the history of the Sidhe and the Fomorii. It was boring. I climbed out of the window."

"Hah!" Joshua laughed loudly, and then covered his mouth, conscious that the leafy walls around them didn't conceal their voices. From beyond their sanctuary, Joshua heard footsteps in the snow, and a moment later the branches were parted and Rufus had stuck his head in. He looked up and raised an eyebrow at the pair of them.

"Joshua, Boyd is very upset and looking for you," he said, and Joshua giggled. Rufus turned his attention to the girl. "And this would be?"

"This is Kael. She's hiding from Korrick."

"And you're aiding and abetting her?" Rufus's voice was light, but the joviality was skin deep. His smile was tired and Joshua could see a frightening fatigue still clung to Rufus, as if he'd been drained of life. "Where do you get this outlandish behaviour from, Joshua?"

"Probably my outlaw father."

"Ah. Very true. As you were, then." Rufus winked at them, and pulled his head back out from the tree to the sound of their laughter. From outside, Joshua could hear Boyd shouting.

"Have you found him?" The physician sounded panic stricken and Joshua almost felt guilty. Through the leaves, he saw the vague outline of Rufus shrugging exaggeratedly.

"We'll have to move on—he could have gotten anywhere by now." Rufus moved off through the snow, Boyd stumbling after him, complaining loudly.

"Wait...wait me for me, Rufus! I'm tired. Rufus, wait!"

"You're worse than a child, keep up." Rufus's voice faded away as the pair departed one after the other.

"Your father was an outlaw?" Kael asked, abashed. "So you're not the Prince of Harmatia?"

"No, no—I am the Prince." Joshua quickly raised his hands. "It's just I never knew my father the King. I was raised by Rufus. That's who I meant. He's the outlaw."

"Oh." Kael gave a nod of understanding. "Is that why nobody's happy he's here?"

"I think that's the least of it." Joshua had noticed it as well— the quiet whispers that followed him wherever he went, the haughty stares of anyone who spotted him. They all knew he'd flown in with the Magi, and had made their judgements. Joshua had forced himself to be cheerful even with this cold reception, if only for Fae's sake. With Rufus in his misery, Fae ought to know someone appreciated her for rescuing them. But it was getting hard to maintain. Joshua wished everyone would just speak and settle their differences once and for all, instead of hiding behind false courtesy and prejudgements.

"Adults are so needlessly complicated sometimes," Joshua said, more to himself, and Kael hummed in agreement.

"It's because they think too much. Father always says too much worry, and no play, makes the creative mind wither away," Kael offered wisely.

"And too much play makes you foolhardy and stupid," a sudden voice boomed, and before either of them could speak, a set of hands had reached into the tree and snatched Kael by the wrist. As she was ripped out, Joshua grabbed hold of his new friend by the waist, and the pair were dragged away from the branch together and deposited hard into the snow.

Blinded by the sudden brightness, Joshua sat up, blinking hard, the sun directly in his eyes. A tall, imposing figure moved in front of it, casting a shadow over them both. His face was stern and unforgiving—long with a square jaw and a tight mouth that had no laughter lines. Even without introduction Joshua knew exactly who he was.

"This is what you forsake your studies for, Kael?" Korrick demanded loudly, and from around the corner, Boyd re-emerged and spotted them. The physician's face went as white as his hair, and he stumbled quickly toward them. Korrick seized Kael roughly by the elbow. "Physician Dacey," he addressed Boyd, "I expect you to keep a better eye on my sister's ward. As for you Kael—you have better things to do than play with this human." He pulled Kael so sharply upward, the girl almost fell.

"Please, brother, I was only—" Kael began, but Korrick spoke over her.

"Your cousins and classmates all study meticulously whilst you, a daughter of the Ó Murchadha clan, waste your time. You are a dishonour to our father and mother. Do not bring further shame to yourself with empty excuses."

"Wait!" Joshua cried. "Please, she was only keeping me company. It wasn't her fault, it was mine."

"I have no doubt of that." Korrick responded sharply and Joshua felt his cheeks burn with embarrassment. He could see a strict hue around Korrick, an aura that dictated the man wouldn't stand for any nonsense, and wasn't inclined to be kind either.

"Lord Korrick," Boyd said, "Joshua and Kael were only playing—"

"You are not here to give an opinion," Korrick snapped.

Boyd ducked his head. "No, my lord, but all the same—"

"There is nothing beyond that." Korrick towered over Boyd. "Know your station, Physician Dacey. Unless this portends to some medical issue, you have no leave to speak at all."

"Yes, my lord," Boyd said softly. Joshua saw red.

"You can't speak to him like that!" The Prince dove forward, putting himself between Korrick and Boyd. Korrick raised his eyebrows in amusement, though his mouth remained tight and grim.

"Ever the sacrificial one, aren't we?"

"You trust your lives to Boyd when you're at your worst. Why should you treat him as any less important now when you're healthy? He's not something that's only valuable when it's useful! He's a man, and he has a good heart and soul, and is equal to you in every way!"

"Equal?" The amusement spread in Korrick's eyes, but it wasn't malicious. "You think humans and Sidhe are equal?"

"Of course we are!" Joshua's face burned with fury. All the anger that had been building in him for so long was suddenly at his fingertips like a weapon. His anger at the injustice they'd faced, at the Kathraks for their relentless hunting, and at Rufus for his unkind words to Fae. It flooded through him and he directed it at Korrick. "We're here speaking, aren't we? The same tongue, the same words! We can both think and rationalise, though you seem to lack any ability to feel!" He thundered a fist against his chest. "How, then, are we not equal? How are we not the same?"

Kael and Boyd were struck dumb by the angry display, mouths slack, but Korrick remained unaffected.

Joshua breathed in deeply, trying to even his voice. Anger wouldn't impress this man—he could see that now. "People like

263

us, we were given our titles at birth. But honour, nobility—we have to earn those! And if you can't even respect your own people, then you don't deserve to be respected back. Not by me, not by them."

"You would do well to talk less," Korrick said, his tone final. "You speak very prettily about honour and nobility, but you have never commanded men. You know nothing of discipline. You marked my orders to the physician as a lack of respect but they were a mark of authority, not superiority. And I am the authority in these grounds. You may not find me kind, but kind men do not win battles."

"That's because kind men don't start them," Joshua snapped, and a hand landed on his shoulder.

"One doesn't have to start a battle to have to fight it." Rufus's fingers were firm. "That's quite enough, Joshua. Apologise."

"But Rufus!" Joshua squirmed, looking around.

"Apologise. I know you were trying to defend your friend but Kael was disobeying Lord Korrick, and he's a master in this house, someone to whom we owe our gratitude. Don't make me say it again."

Joshua felt a burst of betrayal but obeyed none-the-less, bowing his head. "I apologise for speaking out of turn." He kicked his feet.

"This Magi speaks sensibly," Korrick said. "You would do well to listen to him and stay out of my way."

Joshua gritted his teeth, humiliated. Rufus's hand didn't leave his shoulder.

"Equally," Rufus replied in Joshua's stead, to their surprise, "you might do well, Lord Korrick, to remember that you're speaking to the last of the Delphi line and the heir to the Harmatian throne. He may have apologised for his conduct, but nothing of what he said was unjustified—idealistic, perhaps, but not wrong. I might also remind you that whilst you can be as haughty as you wish, he—a twelve year old—was still courageous enough to stand between you and his friends, in order to protect them." Rufus didn't raise his voice but it was strict, and something of his manner pushed the topic to a natural end.

Korrick inclined his head, his eyes cast down to Joshua.

"It is noted," he finally agreed.

Rufus moved his hand from Joshua's shoulder to the back of his head. Joshua's anger at his brother dissipated.

Korrick turned to Boyd. "Physician Dacey, it is not your place to defend Kael when she is being a nuisance. That being said, I apologise for my abrupt tone."

Boyd looked so shocked by the apology, Joshua almost laughed. He resisted the urge.

Korrick returned his gaze to Joshua. "Your name is Joshua, correct?"

Joshua nodded.

"I have no patience for impertinent students, Joshua, but your bravery in standing up for what you believe is admirable. I trust Fae has explained the conditions of my training you?"

"You want to test me first."

"That is correct." Korrick placed his hands together. "And I see now the appropriate nature of the test. Tomorrow at the fifth hour, have Fae bring you to my training grounds. I will determine then whether you are worthy of my time or not."

And with a sharp gesture for Kael to follow, Korrick turned and strode away.

Kael reluctantly trailed after him, stopping only to turn back and wave enthusiastically at Joshua. "Joshua, don't worry, I know you'll pass the test! And when you do, we'll be training together." She grinned, then ran quickly after Korrick.

Boyd exhaled heavily. "Somehow, you tamed the storm," he said in disbelief.

"Did you manipulate his emotions?" Rufus asked softly.

Joshua frowned and shook his head. "Someone like that," he muttered, "I don't think it would be possible."

"I heard there was a commotion in my absence."

Rufus looked up glumly from the table, his thoughts far away. Fae was in the doorway. Rufus got the impression she'd been standing there a while, deciding what to say. She was wary of him, probably still a little angry too, but her light words were an offer of peace. He accepted them gratefully.

"Your brother's a frightening man."

"Yet you escaped unscathed. From what Boyd tells me, I think Korrick was even a little impressed with you."

"With Joshua, maybe." Rufus gestured to a chair on the other side of the table. Fae sauntered forward and took a seat. Her eyes didn't leave Rufus and he found it hard to look back at her. He swallowed dryly. "Listen, Fae—"

"Rufus, if you try to apologise to me about this morning, I will remove your ability to see," Fae said promptly. "I won't accept anything of the like until you are ready to be completely sincere. And by the darkness that lurks over you, I would wager that you aren't. Not yet."

Rufus opened and closed his mouth, then bowed his head in thanks. She was right, of course. He maintained some reservations and he didn't want to give a superficial apology. Better to wait until it was completely heartfelt. "Thank you."

"Clearly there are many things weighing on your mind—I have an idea of some, but I won't press until you are ready to share." Fae had obviously thought a great deal about her words, for she said them with a rehearsed ease. "There is one thing I will say, Rufus—one thing of which I need you to be clear." Her voice rose and Rufus looked up. Her eyes were sharp. "Never, *ever* use Jionathan's death to guilt me again."

Rufus blinked, astounded. "I wasn't—"

Fae didn't let him finish, "Because as close as you were, I loved him too. I loved him and I had to discover his death by word of mouth, days after it happened, by which time you too, were gone. So, as great a tragedy as it was to you, you must understand that on the day Jionat died, I lost both of you. I lost you and I was alone." She never looked away from his face, and he stared into hers. "You were never alone," she said.

Rufus couldn't find any words, so he reached forward and took her hand instead. He shook her fingers in a worthless attempt at comfort, and she watched the display with a faint smile.

"You must be exceptionally bored, sitting in here," she eventually said. "What are you doing?"

"Hiding."

"From whom?"

"The wanderers."

"The who?" Fae asked, arching an eyebrow.

Rufus leant in conspiratorially. "They move down the corridors, sweeping to and fro like a lazy river—but they've no destination, and their eyes are beautiful and vacant."

Fae blinked at him, before frowning with realisation. "You mean the Sidhe tenants who live with us on the mountain? My extended family?"

"Is that who they are? They look sickeningly content with everything. I don't like it." Rufus had recognised them as full-blooded Sidhe the moment he saw them. There was a translucent element about them, as if they were made of a lighter substance, and they were tall— so tall, the women at least eye-level with him, and the men over a head taller. They walked as if they were dancing on the air, without a care in the world. Rufus had found them so unnerving, he'd done his utmost to avoid them.

Fae laughed. "Yes, they do rather live in their own world. They do as they please, when they please—they have no sense of time at all. It's funny what a difference mortality can make…" she trailed off. "You don't like them?"

"They seem detached. But perhaps I'm too earthly for my own good."

"Perhaps. Perhaps we both are..." Fae dropped her gaze to the table, drawing off into silence.

Rufus glanced down to where she was looking, and realised he was still tightly holding her hand. He released her, and she quickly withdrew her fingers and stood.

"Regardless, I didn't come here to dwell," she said. "To ensure you don't die of boredom, I have found you a pretty distraction to occupy yourself with, while Joshua trains."

Rufus narrowed his eyes in exaggerated suspicion. "A pretty distraction?" he repeated slowly, standing cautiously. Fae rolled her eyes.

"No, it's not someone for you to steal to your bed. You can do that at your own leisure."

Rufus gritted his teeth and ran his hand up through his hair. Morrigan's hands on his body flashed in his mind, and then the halfling, blood pouring from the open wounds on his face and neck as Rufus stabbed over and over. "Ah—no," Rufus said quickly, swallowing the bile that rose in his throat. "No, I'm actually...I've rather lost my taste for that kind of companionship. For the moment."

Fae grew impossibly still, and Rufus panicked, trying to discern the meaning behind her expression. He couldn't be sure if she was surprised by his words, or whether her furrowed brow indicated she was angry at herself for mentioning it. As if she knew about everything.

Fae realised she was staring and looked away so abruptly, it was as if she were trying to retract her own expression. "A pity," she spoke too loudly, "I am sure there is many a partner in the Neve who would have enjoyed your company."

"Is Boyd among them? Because if my mood changes, I may make some effort," Rufus half-joked, allowing Fae to push the conversation on.

"In that pursuit, you would be wasting your time."

"Men don't interest him?"

"Sex doesn't interest him. At all." Fae gestured for Rufus to follow her. "Once, a group of—what did you call them?—wanderers discovered he had no sexual inclination, and thought to educate him. Boyd was happy to go along with the experiment, until it went beyond kissing. Then I had to rescue him from the unwanted affection. He has remained happily disinterested since."

"Is it because of Niamh's alterations?"

"Not that I can see."

"Curious," Rufus pondered. "If I keep to my abstinence, we might be perfect for each other."

"Rufus," Fae said seriously, "Boyd is easily agitated, and you are an exceptionally worrisome and stressful person. You would break him, and he would remove your intestines in return. Better remain as friends."

Rufus laughed nervously, sticking close to Fae's side as she guided him through the corridors of the Neve. "Fae, where are you taking me?"

"I told you—a distraction." Fae flicked her hair over her shoulder and slowed as they reached a grand set of double doors. "Because for all our talk of sex, I know your true temple." She thrust the doors open, stepping back.

Rufus peered in curiously and froze, his mouth going dry. He took a few tentative steps forward and then grew still again, fearful of breaking the wondrous illusion. When the room didn't disintegrate away, and he was sure it was real, he chanced a quick look at Fae, like an excitable puppy. Fae laughed as Rufus gabbled wordlessly. "Rufus, it's only a library."

"O-only a library?" Rufus gaped. It was the most beautiful room he'd seen since he'd left Harmatia. Whilst not as large as the Great Library there, it was still a fair size—tall, with a similar glass dome in the roof at the centre, and shelves upon shelves of books.

Rufus had once heard that the Harmatian Great Library was

designed after a Sidhe Library in Avalon. This one, too, seemed to have echoed the architecture, and for Rufus, it seemed just a little as if he were returning home to happier times.

"You're permitted to read whatever you wish," Fae continued. "No book is safe from you."

"I...This is..." Rufus felt on the verge of collapsing, his legs weak with gratitude. He couldn't recall the last time he'd read a book. "Fae," he eventually forced out, "I don't much like my chances against your husband, but will you marry me?"

Fae, who'd been smiling, grew still. Rufus strode quickly toward the closest bookcase and began to flitter across the titles, like an anxious bird, spoiled for choice. *The Ancient History of Mag Mell, Ballads of Ériu, Sidhe Bloodlines & the Chosen*—Rufus pulled them all from the shelves. From the corner of his eye, he saw Fae blink slowly, looking stunned.

"Reilly?" she mouthed, as if she'd forgotten her own husband, and she clasped her left hand, which was ring-less. Rufus had wondered about that. He turned, his arms now laden with books, and watched her. She noticed him looking and forced a smile. It fell quickly as they maintained their gaze. Rufus felt a rush of emotions fill him, unleashed by the height of his gratitude and appreciation. He wanted to cross the space between them and throw his arms around her, or perhaps sink to his knees and clasp her hands, as he'd done when she found them. Neither action seemed appropriate however, so he remained where he was.

"Fae."

"Don't apologise." Fae seemed a little breathless. "Don't apologise because you're momentarily happy."

"I won't." He stepped toward, but stopped himself before he could get any closer. "But...you know, don't you? You know I trust you."

Fae didn't reply. Rufus swallowed.

"I wouldn't let Joshua out of my sight, otherwise."

"Rufus..."

270

Rufus tightened his arms around the books he'd piled into them, cradling them to his chest like children. He'd missed the weight of books. They made him feel strangely complete, like if he held them tightly enough they would fill the parts of him which had been carved away. "But we're not children anymore, Fae. This isn't Sarrin. And things have changed. I've changed."

"I know." Fae's voice was hollow.

"You and I've both forgotten to share certain things." Rufus dropped his eyes purposefully to Fae's empty hand, and she tensed. She clenched her fingers and then relaxed them with a faint, humourless laugh. She nodded. Rufus took another tiny step toward her. "But no matter how complicated this is, never doubt my gratitude."

"Again, Rufus—it's only a library."

Rufus gave her a pointed look and Fae ducked her head and turned toward the door.

She was as closed off and guarded as him. "I need to go. Stay as long as you wish." She paused in the doorway. "You're welcome," she whispered, lingering, before, with a sudden urgency, she sped from the room.

CHAPTER 26

"Cull fish and neck breaks. Where are you trippin' to now, you damned house-cat?" Aeron demanded furiously as the faerie ahead of him growled, flashing its yellowing teeth.

Far from being a cat, it was large, and canine in shape with eyes like fire. The creature was one of Nicnivin's hunting hounds and had met Aeron on the edge of the Unseelie territory, sent to guide him through the woods. It clearly wasn't happy with the task, because it had taken Aeron down the longest, most convoluted path it could, through bogs and thickets.

Aeron gave the faerie a kick on the backside and laughed as it roared and leapt right through him, tearing through his translucent skin. Landing face first on the ground behind, the faerie scrabbled away, thrusting its snout between its paws with a yelp. "Rah, didn't head-scratch that you'd like that, eh Shuck?" The assassin whistled between his teeth and set off into the impending darkness. He knew they were getting closer by the unearthly prickling that moved down his soul-skin.

He'd left his mortal body in Beshuwa and walked now as a half-spirit. It was the only way he could hope to enter the Unseelie territory without being torn apart. Of course, he could only survive for so long like this—soon he would need to return to his fleshy tether. For now, however, it served him to be less than mortal.

He whistled again, and the Shuck rose to its ragged feed and padded forward, jaw hanging open so that saliva, blue and fiery, dripped from its rolling tongue. Aeron followed fearlessly after it into the perpetual black.

For several minutes they walked, the silence broken only by the thud of the Shuck's paws. Aeron listening keenly to the world around him, trying to judge how far they were. From somewhere ahead, he heard low moans of pleasure and knew they were arriving at last.

The moans got louder as they approached, coupled with the clinking of goblets, and finally the wet smack of bodies. Aeron licked his lips, and as they passed beneath the sagging branches of several dying trees, they came upon a huge throne.

It was carved like a great monument out of the bones of something ancient and humungous. Along the top, figures were stretched, drinking and smoking, all caught in the frenzy of sex. Aeron salivated at the carnal beauty of the display and the Shuck slunk past him and lolled at the feet of a tiny girl who sat in the centre of the orgy.

She looked like a child of no more than eight, and sat with such a careless gaiety, she might have been in the middle of a flowery field. Her skin had the bluish undertone of a dead thing, her eyes were entirely black, and her hair fell down to her collar in a tangled mess of thick brown locks. Her chest, flat as her stomach, was covered by a white chemise that was much too big for her petite figure. It fell down to her knees, covering her thin legs.

She stretched her leg out and patted the Shuck with her foot fondly, the faerie rumbling an approval.

Aeron approached cautiously and she directed her attention to him, considering him long and hard. Finally she slid from the throne, her chemise rolling up. She was completely naked beneath it. She padded over to him and thrust out her arms expectantly, an impatient demand for affection. Aeron took her in his arms, lifting her up to his head-height. She wrapped her legs around his waist, her thighs squeezing his ribs.

In an instant Aeron felt her full weight. Her legs, which ought to have been weak, were powerful, her fingers which should have been small, were long and strong, and her breasts felt full and tender where there were none. If Aeron closed his eyes, he was holding a woman, and it sent his sensible mind reeling. Here in the Unseelie Court, the monsters had many faces, and each of the senses could betray each other.

Thankfully she didn't speak—Aeron doubted even he could have survived that.

He released her and let her drop carefully to the ground, a child again. Dutifully, he knelt and grovelled before her.

"Hail Nicnivin, Ruler of the Dark, daughter of Domnu, fairest of the Fomorii."

The Queen of the Unseelie Court smiled with unadulterated pleasure.

～⁂～

This time when he woke, Boyd wasn't there to tear him from his dreams. Rufus gasped for air, his throat raw from screaming, and toppled from the bed, weak and bleary. Boyd had dosed him with a sleeping potion, and Rufus swooped dangerously as he stood, his body unprepared. He collided with the wall and crumpled against it, sliding to his knees.

The dream had been an amalgamation of horrors and sensations, starting and ending, as they always did, with the cold, red-darkness.

This time, however, Mielane had been there, but not as she once was. The Bean Nighe had sat washing her stained clothing, the river running red with the weight of so much blood. There seemed no end to her task, clothing piled around her, red and wet as she scrubbed. Rufus had understood his part in her chore. She sang as she washed, but it sounded more like a scream. Had she been capable of it, there would have been tears on her face.

"Look at all these people I'm going to kill," Rufus had said, and he'd been pleased by the prospect—proud even, Morrigan's arms wrapped around him, rocking him lovingly from side to side.

"I don't want to kill anyone." Rufus closed his eyes and hit his head against the wall. "I don't want to kill anyone."

"It's a little late for that." Jionat's voice echoed behind him, and Rufus shook his head. "You can't deny what you suspect—that Mielane didn't stay for love of you. She stayed to foretell all the death you would cause."

"No, no." Rufus juddered, not daring to look over his shoulder, where Jionat loomed over him, his arms crossed. "You can't be here. You're not here."

"Did you think a few books would keep me at bay?" Jionat snorted. "Do my warnings mean nothing to you?"

"Please." Rufus drew his head back and struck it hard against the wall again. "Leave me alone. Please leave me alone."

"You *are* alone." Jionat dropped down beside him, his arms around Rufus's neck, as if he meant to strangle him. "That's the problem!"

Rufus sobbed harder, tearing his hands through his hair. He tugged his fringe and rammed his head against the wall again. The coarse stone began to tear into his skin, but he couldn't stop, driven by desperation. He felt like a trapped animal chewing through its own leg to escape. "No, no, no. Go away. Go away." He crashed his skull against the wall harder, and the force knocked his teeth together, sending pain through his cranium and down his neck. It made his ears ring and he saw white. He wrapped his arms around his head, cradling himself. "Please, please go away."

From behind, the door opened and Boyd stepped in, his skittish walk easily recognisable. He grew still, and then ran to

Rufus's side.

"Rufus?" he said with alarm, kneeling beside him.

Rufus closed his eyes, his head against the wall.

"Are you alright?" Boyd whispered.

"I was just admiring the stonework," Rufus mumbled, "with my face."

He heard Boyd give a worried titter, and the sound triggered something in Rufus. Boyd's voice grew panicked as fat tears began to stream once more down Rufus's face.

"Rufus? What's wrong? Rufus? Rufus?"

Rufus shook his head and sobbed, his whole body shuddering from the sudden force. Boyd gabbled, flustered and anxious, but Rufus couldn't make out any of the words as waves of grief and panic overwhelmed him again. Unable to speak, he tipped into Boyd, his shoulder rested against the man's chest, and wept openly. Boyd's incessant chatter died down to a soft murmur, and he hesitantly patted Rufus's back.

"You're safe now."

Rufus didn't have the heart, or ability, to correct Boyd. Yes— he was safe. It was the rest of them who weren't.

CHAPTER 27

Joshua found himself in the dark forest again, stood in a glade of thick, needled trees, frosted with snow. The earth was dry and cold, and there was a stillness and serenity to the air that made him feel he had no right to move or speak. Through the fence of trees to the side, he could see a vast lake down below, glittering an impossible blue. It looked so welcoming he was tempted to run down and throw himself in.

On the ground in front of him, the Isny Hunter, Varyn, was chained and shackled. "Beautiful, isn't it?" Varyn looked up at Joshua, his eyes narrowed to slits, as if he were in great pain.

"Where are we?"

"La'Kalciar."

"The Lake region?" Joshua's knowledge of Kathrak geography was limited, but he knew the four main provinces.

"My home."

"I thought you were from Isnydea?" Joshua took a seat opposite the man, examining the thick black chains which bound him, like a mighty beast caught in a trap.

"Isnydea?" Varyn chuckled, the sound a soft rumble in the back of his throat. "The land of the damned. It's not home for anybody."

"Because of the Fomorii?"

"Because of the Shin." Varyn gritted his teeth together, hissing. He doubled over, the chains around him seeming to grow tighter. They cut into his skin. Joshua hurried to Varyn's side and tugged at the binds, trying to loosen them. They fed into the earth, like tree roots, and wouldn't give-way to Joshua's meagre strength.

"Don't bother," Varyn said, but there was an odd fondness in his gravelly voice. "You can't break them."

"I can try." Joshua heaved with all his might, and his hands slipped on the cold metal. He fell back with a grunt, palms grazed and bleeding.

"See." Varyn settled in his hunch, his eyes rolling across to where the lake was still just visible to him. "Twice now, you've invaded my dreams. Why are you here?"

"I told you—I don't know." Joshua rubbed his scuffed hands down the front of his shirt, blowing on them. They stung so badly, he was almost certain he was awake. "Why are you chained down?"

"Doesn't matter."

"Maybe I can help you?"

"Doubt it." Varyn almost sounded bitter, but there was no depth to the words.

"Where's the dragon?" Joshua asked cautiously. "Is it gone?"

"No, it's close. Resting. They do that before they attack. That way they can go for days." Varyn's eyes didn't leave the lake. There was a longing in his expression, as if he were missing something. Joshua peered into his face. Perhaps it was the nature of the dream but he could discern nothing from his usual empathetic skills. It made the boy feel oddly powerless, even though Varyn was chained down.

"You're not really here, are you? In La'Kalciar."

"No."

"But the chains…" Joshua scrutinised them. "They're real?"

"Some things you don't escape, even in dreams."

"What happened?"

Varyn glanced down at himself and gave that soft grumbling

chuckle again. He seemed to have nothing left to lose. "I'm dying."

Joshua's heart jumped in alarm. "Dying! How?"

"Was cursed…I committed a crime. This is my punishment."

"What did you do?"

"Killed a man."

Joshua lowered himself to the floor slowly, sitting cross-legged. "And the dragon?"

"It's followed me for years. I kept moving, but now…" Varyn gave a half-hearted tug at his chains. "You say we're connected. Why? I'll be dead before summer."

"You don't know that."

Varyn tore his eyes from the lake and peered into Joshua's face. "Do you?"

"Athea, why are adults so morose?" Joshua growled. "It's like you thrive off it. Is having a little faith, a little hope, so difficult for you all?"

"Joshua." It was the first time Varyn used his name. Joshua had presumed he'd forgotten it. "The Isny don't have room to hope. We can't."

"Really?" Joshua asked. "In that case, what are you doing here?" He gestured to the beautiful view of the lake.

Varyn's obsidian eyes widened a fraction and then he made a sudden, very sharp noise, that sounded like a clap. Joshua realised it was a laugh.

"Hah! Smart boy. Harmatian, are you?"

"How did you know?"

"Frail looking. Fair. Pompous accent. Sound like a friend of mine. Maybe you know him?"

"I doubt that."

"Hm. Yes." Once again Varyn's eyes trailed off down toward the lake. "He lives down there. Isaac, does."

"Who is he?"

"Magi. Good man. The best man." Varyn might have sounded sad, but he didn't betray himself. "You should go," he eventually said, "All your talk...Sounds like someone needs you more than me."

Joshua hesitated. As strange and frightening as Varyn was, the Prince didn't want to step out of the dream yet. He felt an overwhelming sense of companionship with the man. "Will I see you again?"

"You step in and out of my dreams. You tell me."

Joshua nodded slowly. "Don't die yet."

"Can't promise." Varyn gave him a wry, ugly smile, which seemed more like a grimace. He appeared to be in tremendous pain. "Go, boy, get gone. Air's changing—won't be near as nice in a minute."

Joshua had noticed it too—the temperature had dropped, and there was a stale smell floating through the trees. Everything began to darken and Joshua got the impression that Varyn was waking up. The Hunter wilted, haggard and shaken, his energy drained.

Joshua watched hopelessly. "I'll come back!" he promised. "Keep fighting. Please, keep fighting."

Varyn gave one last rattling chuckle and Joshua felt the world slip away from him.

∞

Joshua's eyes fluttered open to find Rufus lying beside him, arms folded, fully clothed and ready for the day. He'd been calling Joshua's name very faintly, gently rousing him.

"Were you dreaming?" Rufus asked and Joshua buried his face further into his pillow, nodding sleepily. In the haze of his fatigue he noticed some dark bruising across the top of Rufus's head. He reached up to poke it carefully.

"Wha' happn'd?" he asked in a sleepy mumble.

"Nothing to worry about." Rufus rested his hand in Joshua's mop of curls, tenderly brushing them out of the boy's face.

"Rufus?" Joshua pushed himself up, his mind focusing. A dark, tired energy clung around Rufus, stronger than the day

280

before. Joshua drew in a deep breath. "Rufus, what's wrong?"

"Joshua," Rufus said softly, "listen to me. I know that you can *sense* it—that I'm…not quite right. Your ability as an empath is growing stronger every day, but I need you not to worry."

"But—"

"You have Korrick's test today, and all being well, you will begin your training after. You must focus all of your energy on that."

"But—" Joshua tried again.

"I know you're frightened." Rufus frowned. "But it's not your responsibility to take care of me. I'm your brother…your *father*. I've burdened you with enough." Rufus leant forward and kissed Joshua on the forehead. "Whatever happens, I need you to be well. You're capable of so much. Don't let my failings divert your energy. Not my sins or my negativity." He gazed down at Joshua with a sad fondness. "I'm so proud of you, Joshua."

Joshua didn't like the almost unspoken farewell in that statement. He tried to make light of it. "Even though you don't like the idea of me training?"

"Yes."

"And that I went behind your back to do it?"

Rufus smiled. "Even so." He rolled off the bed and stood, brushing himself down in several sharp strokes. "It's almost time—you'd better get up."

Joshua obeyed, though he could have gladly slept another hour. He suspected that, should all go to plan, Korrick wouldn't stand for any late mornings. Joshua would have to get used to the sunrise—a daunting prospect.

He changed hurriedly, debating whether or not to tell Rufus about his strange dream, and the Hunter named Varyn. Stealing a glance at his brother's bruised face, Joshua decided to keep it to himself. Rufus's thoughts were like a physical weight on him, and Joshua didn't want to add to that. His encounter with Varyn would keep for now—besides, Joshua wasn't sure he could explain it, even if he wanted to.

As he dressed, Rufus strung his new bow for him. Fae had lent it to Joshua on the understanding that he practise with it every day. It was as small as his previous one, but curved around at either end to give each shot more impact. To begin with, Joshua had struggled with the new weight on the drawback, but he was slowly acclimatising to it.

Dressed and armed, Joshua and Rufus departed the room together, and met Fae in the corridor. Boyd loitered nearby, chewing his thumb. It was a wonder he hadn't worn it down to a knuckle.

Fae took one look at Joshua's pinched, nervous expression and took his hand. "You will be fine," she reassured. "I assume you won't be wanting breakfast?"

"You assume correctly." Joshua wasn't sure he could stomach anything more than a glass of water. Fae moved her hand to his shoulder, and kept it there as they moved on, a silent and confident comfort. Boyd trailed after, looking discontent and worried, though he offered Joshua a wan smile when the boy caught his eye.

They found Korrick out in the training grounds, which were dusted white with dew. The sun hadn't risen yet, but there was a pre-dawn greyness in the sky that lit the mountains. The air was still and tepid, promising to flourish into a hot day.

Korrick acknowledged them wordlessly with a solemn bow of his head and, as they got close enough, turned on his heel and began to lead them away. Joshua felt Fae hesitate for a fraction of a second, and it doubled his nerves. Wherever Korrick was taking them, Fae hadn't expected it.

"It's warmer today," Joshua broke the silence. His nerves were getting the better of him. "And it seems the snow's melting."

"Spring is returning," Rufus agreed faintly, nodding toward where a cluster of snowdrops nodded lazily at them in passing, caught in a stray breeze.

"That's the way it is in the Neve," Fae kept her eyes ahead. "Shrouded in snow one day, and then lounged in green the next. I was down by the coast a few days ago—you would think it was summer there already."

They went on, a sudden wind blowing up ahead of them as they moved through a collection of tall, bleak trees, which swayed like the masts of ships. The wood groaned ominously, and Joshua tried not to be troubled by it.

"Korrick, where are we going?" Fae finally lost her patience. "There are no training grounds out here, only…"

She drew off as they stepped out from the trees. The group came to a stand-still. Up in front of them, the ground broke away over a sudden, sheer drop. Korrick went to the edge of the ravine, unmindful of the great height, and drawing out his own bow, he nocked an arrow and shot it. It struck a tree on the other side and Korrick replaced his bow. At his side, a rickety old rope bridge was the only crossing over the divide. Even before Korrick had said anything, Joshua knew what he was going to be asked to do. So did Fae.

"Korrick, have you *lost your mind?*" She stormed ahead. "Nobody has stepped across that thing in decades. It can't bear the weight of a man."

"Some of the planks are rotted through, certainly," Korrick conceded, "but others are steady, if you are nimble enough. The right footing and you should be able to cross safely." He turned to Joshua. "Are you willing to face the risk, to fetch me that arrow?"

"This isn't fair!" Fae said. "What do you hope to learn from such a foolish venture?"

"He is a Prince, as you all seem so keen on reminding me. One day, I presume he means to be King, which means he must command. To do so is to put not only his life at risk, but the lives of others too. Every decision he makes will have its consequences."

Joshua looked back across to the bridge and edged closer toward it. A bout of dizziness came over him and he stepped

283

back, nauseous with vertigo. He closed his eyes, trying to battle through the sudden charge of emotions that filled him. He was angry at Korrick for putting him in such a position, resentful with himself that he wasn't capable of simply charging over the bridge without hesitation, and fearful. Fearful of what it could mean if he *did*.

Furiously, he fought back his tears, scrabbling for courage.

"Will you do it?" Korrick asked.

"Obviously he won't—this is utterly ludicrous!" Rufus spoke for the first time, his voice raised in anger. His brother's tone bought something up in Joshua, and he was suddenly faced with a new perspective.

Rufus had sacrificed so much in Joshua's name—his chances of love, safety, comfort, and even a home, all so Joshua might have a brother and a father to raise him. Korrick was right—one day, Joshua would be called on to make similar decisions. He would have to make sacrifices and choices for his people, and each of these would have consequences.

Joshua understood. The bridge was a metaphor for that, and perhaps then it was best he hadn't simply run over it. Each step had to be considered carefully, each risk calculated. He could walk away from the ravine and decide to forfeit the training, but that would be disregarding the worth of what Korrick could teach.

For the first time, it dawned on Joshua his skills in battle went far beyond him, and Korrick had chosen this test specifically for that reason. He wanted to see what kind of ruler Joshua would be—one who was wise enough to preserve his life at the cost of something great, or one who took risks to achieve something more. "My conditions are clear. He must pass my test to earn my tutorship."

"You're stark raving mad!"

Behind him, the squabbling continued and Joshua saw his chance. He stepped up to the edge of the bridge and looked out over it. It rocked dauntingly but Joshua felt his resolve settle.

He studied the planks of wood, looking for rot or signs of damage. A few were cracked, others weather-beaten and frail, but Korrick was right—if Joshua moved carefully, if he was nimble and smart, he would make it across the bridge. He swallowed, licked his thumb and drew a line across his forehead, offering a prayer to Etheus for luck, then Malak for steady-footedness, and then finally Athea, just in case he did fall and no one was able to recover his body.

"—totally unreasonable request!" Rufus was still saying, so preoccupied with his anger he didn't see his brother step out onto the bridge.

The rope banisters creaked as Joshua took hold of them, bearing his weight. He swallowed dryly and took another step, and then another.

It was Boyd who noticed first and gave a cry of alarm which was quickly echoed by Rufus.

"*Joshua!*" Rufus shouted in horror but Joshua didn't dare look back. Turning would tip his balance and he had to concentrate on his every step, or the bridge would kill him.

"I won't let you conquer me," Joshua told the wood fiercely, and knew that both Korrick and Fae heard him.

"Joshua, come back!" Rufus pleaded.

Joshua shook his head. "I have this." His voice juddered. "Believe in me."

"But—"

"Please," Joshua begged, almost losing his nerve. He couldn't cross the bridge without Rufus's support, and from his silence, Joshua sensed that Rufus knew that too. The bridge rocked a little, trying to deter his courage, but Joshua simply remained where he was until the ropes grew still again. He continued on his way, the wooden planks creaking disconcertingly as he passed over them.

The tension was tangible in the air, and with it came the tightening of his throat as Joshua lost the pace of his breathing.

He'd struggled with his lungs all his life, in particular during times of stress and fear. He'd come to learn a method to combat this.

"One step is more than another two back," he sang, falling back on the old marching rhyme of his childhood. Howell, Rufus's last lover, had written it for to Joshua. The Prince was young at the time, but he remembered the man vividly. There had never been a shortage of laughter when Howell was around, nor of songs. "Two steps is further yet, courage little sap. Three steps, you're almost there, your heart is singing strong. Four steps is a milestone, keep your gait so long." He counted with each step as he took them. "Five steps and rest, you've conquered this hill. Six steps and seven you've not far to go. Eight steps is close now, the pear upon the tree. Nine steps you've come to, final challenge see."

The end of the bridge was near, but Joshua resisted the temptation to speed up and dart toward it. "Ten steps," he said breathlessly, a stride away from the end, "your journey's end, I take my hat off to thee. The song of the rambler commence again at the count of one, two and three."

He jumped the last plank and landed on the other side of the ravine. Even from the distance, he heard Rufus and Boyd both moan in relief.

The ground seemed to wobble beneath Joshua's feet, and his ribcage felt like it was trying to suffocate him. Joshua resisted the urge to drop down and hug the ground. He inched unsteadily over to the tree.

Clasping the arrow with both hands, he ripped it free and reached back for his bow, ready to shoot it across. Something made him pause—Korrick's test was more a mind game than a physical exercise, and simply shooting the arrow back seemed a rather easy end. If the examination was a metaphor for the leader that Joshua would be, then it seemed to show a lack of confidence to try and return the arrow before even attempting to return himself.

The purpose of the whole thing had been to earn Joshua his right to train. The arrow had no significance without him.

He loaded it into his holster, among his own arrows, and turned back to the bridge. He considered giving himself another minute to recover but knew his nerves would only sustain him for so long.

He stepped out, darting his gaze quickly up to the group on the other side. Rufus had his arms folded so tightly across his chest, it was clear he wasn't breathing. Joshua wasn't sure he was either. He peered down into to the ravine below and regretted it, forcing his eyes up.

"You're almost there." Joshua forced himself to walk on, picking his feet over the planks. "You're almost—" He was cut off by the loud groan of wood behind him. He snapped his head around in time to see the posts that held the rope taut were straining against their supports. Even as Joshua watched, the supports began to crack, and the posts bent forward, the bridge dropped a few strides down with a jolt. Fae gave a short scream, and Rufus bellowed.

"JOSHUA!"

Joshua gripped the rope banisters tightly, the bridge rocking from the sudden motion. He gave a terrified whimper, looking back around to the path ahead.

"Athea, I don't want to die. Please don't let me die," he begged, his legs going weak.

"Joshua!" Rufus was stood at the mouth of the bridge, leaning out to him. "Slow and steady, alright? You're not going to fall. I won't let you fall. But you can't stop now." Rufus squatted down so they were eye-level. "You're so close." He reached out even further. "Come on."

Joshua didn't move, tears blurring his vision. "Papa," he moaned and the bridge slipped further, sagging. Joshua clung on for dear life, his feet slipping on the wood. He planted a foot on a rotted plank and it fell through. Joshua scrabbled upright, gasping and close to sobs.

"Keep moving!" Rufus shouted. "Joshua, *please!*"

Joshua screwed his eyes closed, took a deep breath and inched forward.

"That's right," Rufus encouraged.

Fae's voice joined him. "Have courage, Joshua. We're right here."

Joshua took another step, forcing his eyes open. "Rufus, I'm scared."

"I know, but don't stop." Rufus voice was strained, but even. "What were you singing earlier? On the way up?"

"The—the song of the r-rambler." Joshua took another step.

"I recall it. It was one of Howell's, wasn't it?"

Joshua sobbed, as the posts slipped further forward, the supports bending. If they snapped, the posts would have nothing keeping them upright and would unearth themselves. The entire bridge would collapse.

"Sing it again." Rufus inched as close as he could without stepping onto the bridge. "Come on."

Joshua didn't dare release the rope banisters to wipe the tears from his face. He took another unsteady step, the wood below him almost giving way to his weight. "One step is more than another two back," he sang, his voice wobbling.

"Two steps is further yet, courage little sap," Rufus joined in and Joshua continued to slowly edge forward, the wood creaking obscenely. "Three steps, you're almost there," Rufus almost spoke the lyrics, "your heart is singing strong. How does the next one go?"

"F-four st-steps is a milestone—ah!" Joshua's foot went through another of the planks as it snapped beneath him. The whole bridge shuddered as Joshua lurched back, trying to stop himself falling through.

"Keep going!" Fae cried out.

"Four steps is a milestone, keep your gait so long," Joshua whimpered, stepping over the missing plank. "Five steps and rest, you've conquered this hill..."

"Six steps and seven, you've not far to go!" Rufus encouraged.

"Eight steps is close now, the pear upon the tree," Fae joined in, recalling the verse. Her voice was sweet and Joshua moved toward it.

"Nine steps you've come to, final challenge see." Joshua's throat was so tight the words came out in squeaks. Rufus's outstretched hand was only a few strides away from him. Another few steps and he would be in reach.

There was a monstrous crack, and Joshua jerked and twisted in time to see the posts behind him both splintering at the same time. The bridge dropped even further, the rope snapping taut. Joshua turned back and saw Korrick watching him intently.

"Jump," Korrick instructed calmly, as Joshua heard the wood give one last whine. The boy squeezed his eyes shut tightly, and planting his foot on one last precarious plank, he lunched himself up into the air just as the bridge snapped and fell out beneath him.

Rufus and Fae seized him by each arm, and drew him rapidly up onto the safety of the other side.

Joshua collapsed onto the ground, taking tufts of grass between his fingers and tethering himself down. He lay like that, heaving, before, with a shaking arm, he reached back, took the arrow out of his quiver, and, without looking up, tossed it vaguely in Korrick's direction.

"Take your *fucking* arrow." Joshua pushed himself up, glaring angrily at Korrick, "I hope it gives you the answer you're looking for," he said fiercely, his arms barely supporting his weight.

Korrick gave him a half, almost amused smile. "Yes, it has." Korrick shared a silent exchange with Fae, who was staring at him pointedly. He turned away. "Be sure to arrive promptly at the training grounds tomorrow. I do not delay my classes," he instructed and, without another look, strode away.

Joshua dropped his head back onto the ground, sobbing in delayed terror, his emotions overwhelming him. Rufus dragged him up and into his arms, rocking him from side to side.

"Well done, well done my little warrior Prince." Rufus cradled Joshua's head as the boy buried his face into his shoulder. "Well done...And for the love of Athea, promise me you will *never* do that again."

Through his watery eyes, Joshua could see Fae and Boyd had also sat down, looking as exhausted by the ordeal as he felt.

Joshua managed to laugh, tears streaming down his cheeks. "I promise," he agreed. "I *absolutely* promise."

CHAPTER
28

Zachary woke with an intense feeling of unease. He lay very still in his bed, eyes closed, listening to the silent room and trying to discern the cause of his distress. It was peaceful, the creeping sunlight making his eyelids light up red. Outside, he could hear birdsong, and there were children playing somewhere in the garden. By all accounts, he should have felt relaxed, but he couldn't shake the feeling that something was wrong.

From downstairs, he heard the front door close, and he tensed, his eyes flying open. There were no voices, so someone must have left rather than entered. The servants used another exit, so either Daniel had stepped out to go to the Great Library, or someone had come calling. No doubt it was something perfectly innocent, but Zachary rolled from the bed nonetheless, his nerves jittery.

He pulled on his trousers, shoes and a chemise, and crept soundlessly to the door, stepping out onto the landing. Peering over the balcony he spotted Heather at the doorway. Her back was to him, apron clenched in her hands. She sighed, and turned, jumping as she spotted him.

"Good morning." She curtsied. Zachary scanned the rest of the entrance hall, but it was empty. "I did not expect you up for another few hours."

"What's going on?" Zachary ignored her niceties, concentrating on her hands, which were still bundled into her apron. She noticed his gaze, and released the crumbled fabric, smoothing it back over her lap. "Who was at the door?"

"It was a messenger, he bought you a letter. I put it on the dining room table for you."

"A letter? From whom?"

"By the hand, I would say it's come from Lord Thornton."

Zachary felt himself relax a little. "Thornton?" It had been some time since he'd had word from his friend in La'Kalciar, but Zachary's conversation with Marcel had prompted him to think more often of Isaac. "I'll take that letter now then." Zachary started down the stairs.

"Lord Rothschild also came by but I told him you were unavailable." Heather followed Zachary as he moved into the dining room, taking up his letter.

"Rothschild again? I am starting to regret allowing him into the Night Patrol. He's too ambitious. He's vying for Hathely's position at my side."

"That is ambitious," Heather agreed.

"Sycophantic, position-grabbing tendencies aside, he's a good soldier." Zachary inspected the handwriting and the seal on the letter and, confirming it was Isaac's, he slipped his finger under the wax, and pulled it open. He read eagerly. "Thornton's well. He's travelling down to Sigel'eg. He means to come to Harmatia to see the assessments. He must be in the mind to take an apprentice."

"It would do you well to see him."

"He also says he's been waiting on a letter from his master, Lord Farthing. Last I heard, the old man wasn't very well. I may pay him a visit and see how his recovery is going."

"I am sure he'd appreciate that," Heather said distractedly, her eyes once more on the front door.

Zachary examined her. "What is it?" he asked. "You can't stop staring at the door. It's the brat, isn't it?"

Heather frowned, tearing her eyes from the door and back to him. "Master Daniel went to the Southern Quarters this morning. He ought to have been back by now."

Zachary rolled his eyes. "Mothering Prospan, woman—you could fret for Harmatia. It's the Southern Quarters, not the slums. He'll be fine."

Heather's mouth tightened, and she curtsied again. "As you say," she said stiffly. "Will that be all, my lord?"

"Oh don't give me that, Heather," Zachary groaned. "Why do you even occupy yourself with him? You couldn't stand Isolde."

"For what she did, I had cause to," Heather said. "However, I am able to separate the sins of a mother from her son. Besides which, Daniel is no mere brother to you, he is—"

"Heather, you know you can always be open with me," Zachary stood abruptly, his chair scraping on the stone, "but please, don't talk about that."

Heather dropped her gaze down to a corner of the room. "Try to remember what it was like, Arlen—to be alone in this capital. To be friendless. How daunting that was. How secluded you were."

"I was eight. He's nineteen. Old enough to make his own friends," Zachary dismissed. "But if you're really worried, I'll go and find him."

Heather sighed in relief. She opened her mouth to say something but the front door burst open, interrupting them. Marcel strode in, looking dishevelled, as if he'd barely had time to dress.

Zachary jumped at the abrupt entry. His second in command wasted no time announcing the purpose of his arrival.

"Trouble."

Zachary hurried over. "Where?"

"The Southern Quarters. Emeric has gone ahead. A group of alchemists have gathered a mob—they mean to burn the Merle

293

house to the ground."

The colour drained from Zachary's face. In an instant, he was back there again, standing in the doorway of the Merles' home, with all its comforts and warmth. To think of it burnt away and gone forever was too final—like a promise that nothing could ever be well again.

"Daniel!" Heather gasped, and Zachary bolted to the door, Marcel close behind. They sprinted out into the city, Zachary dragging in the stars' power to keep his fatigue at bay as they dodged through crowds in the heaving streets.

"Out of the way!" Zachary shouted ahead. "Move! *MOVE!*" He gesticulated wildly, waving his arms as people parted.

They broke into the Southern Quarter, and Zachary skidded around onto the Merles' street just in time to see Emeric forcefully throwing an alchemist back, extinguishing his torch with wave of his hand.

"If you think I'm going to let you anywhere near this house, you're out of your mind!" Emeric's voice was hoarse, but he forced it out nonetheless. He didn't look well at all, barely recovered from his sickness, face haggard and eyes deeply lined.

"This is going to end badly," Zachary murmured, as Marcel dove past him, forcing his way through the crowd to his apprentice's side. Zachary made to follow, and then to his horror caught sight of Daniel stood within the inner circle of the mob, trapped in a ring of shouting people. The boy looked petrified. "Oh Hexias give me strength—damn it Daniel!"

Zachary pushed his way through the shifting bodies, using his advantageous height to keep watch over the fight. Between the mob and the rabble, the air was full of tension. All it would take was one building, and the entire Southern Quarter stood the risk of going up in flames. If this wasn't resolved soon, the residents of the Southern Quarter would clamour together to protect their homes, and there would be a riot.

Zachary liked to think that was the only thing fuelling

Emeric's rage but he knew better. There was a territorial and personal aspect to this anger.

Emeric threw himself at the leading alchemist as the man once more tried to advance with his torch. "Get back!"

"Are you some faerie-sympathiser, guarding this house? These are tainted stones!" The Kathrak with the torch gestured. "We will cleanse this city of its treacherous mark and we will burn you with it if you don't step aside!"

"You can try!" Emeric spat. "You have one last chance to stand down."

The alchemist shoved Emeric back, almost sending him to the floor. Emeric stumbled a few steps, but remained upright.

He's still unsteady, Zachary thought, his teeth gritted so hard his head throbbed. *Don't start a fight, Emeric.*

But it was useless. Even if Zachary had shouted the command, there was a set expression on Emeric's face. Zachary's unease came back to him in waves. Marcel's apprentice, for all his doey eyes, curled hair and dimples, was a terrible force to be reckoned with. The only thing that stood between Emeric and all out destruction was his sense of morality. In that moment, everything was clouded by anger.

Unless the alchemists took heed of what their instincts ought to have been screaming at them, the entire affair was going to end in blood.

"I said, get out of the way!" The alchemist advanced on Emeric, who rolled his shoulders.

"Don't challenge me," Emeric growled and the alchemist laughed, and then did something profoundly stupid.

Summoning a crude ball of air up, he blasted it at Emeric. Zachary watched, expecting the Magi to shield himself. Emeric did nothing of the sort. Instead he launched himself into the air, making the earth jut up beneath him to give him height. He spun up above the attack, and Zachary saw the crackle of magic—the only hint of what was about to happen.

Emeric landed on all fours, not a man, but a large, feline beast—bigger than any lion, and with teeth made to rip and gorge. The alchemists stopped mid-laugh and froze, their faces going slack. Zachary knew that expression—that cold horror men felt when faced with something so impossibly wild, and raw, and strong that their minds simply went blank. And then Emeric raised his head and roared.

"N-NIGHT PATROL!" The screams broke out through the crowd and Zachary's heart sank. Emeric charged the alchemists, who broke from their stupor with shrieks, and made to scrabble away. All bravado was gone. What their instincts had failed to tell them was now plain to see. Emeric could kill them all—and he had every intention of doing so.

As Emeric went to tear down one of the alchemists, something crashed into him mid-pounce. Marcel, now in the form of a large, lupine creature with a pelt of grey-black fur, grabbed Emeric's throat between his jaws and pinned him down, trying to calm him.

Emeric roared again, so lost now to his bestial nature, he didn't recognise Marcel as they tumbled and scrabbled. The crowd scattered as Emeric finally managed to tear free, swiping at Marcel with perilous claws. Marcel dodged and once more seized Emeric by the throat—the only effective way of holding him down.

Emeric thrashed against Marcel's teeth, blood dribbling over his fur as they struggled and clawed at each other. Marcel's shoulders rippled. The blood was exciting the animal instinct within him. Zachary knew his second in command would never hurt Emeric on purpose, just as Emeric would never hurt Marcel, but they were no longer in the right state of mind. If the pair didn't calm down, without an authority figure to bring them back to their faculties, they might very well tear each other apart.

Marcel tumbled back with a growl of pain as Emeric swept at him again, his long claws digging through the heavy pelt. Marcel retreated, Emeric snapping at him threateningly before looking sharply around to where Daniel was still pressed up against the wall. Zachary cursed—why hadn't the boy run when the crowd split?

Daniel shrank back against the stone and Emeric roared, daring the boy to move. Marcel circled around, looking between the two. Zachary watched, his breath still, waiting to see whether his brother would be foolish enough to try and flee. A running target would be too tempting to ignore.

Emeric roared again and Daniel's terror got the better of him. He bolted to the side.

"No, idiot!" Zachary cried.

Marcel and Emeric moved simultaneously, Emeric lunging forward just as Marcel interceded, throwing himself at his apprentice. Emeric's claws caught Daniel's arm, just as Marcel collided with him, sending the pair tumbling to the side. Daniel lurched back and toppled to the ground with a cry of pain.

The heavy scent of blood was thick in the air. Emeric tried to rise but Marcel clamped his jaw around the back of Emeric's neck, driving him down. Emeric tossed his head with a yowl and, rolling, managed to wriggle free of the careful grip.

"Hathely!" Zachary cried in warning, but there was nothing to be done.

With a powerful kick, Marcel was sent flying into the wall. He hit it hard and crumpled to the ground, shedding his Night Patrol form with a shudder. There was nothing Marcel could do to get Emeric back under control.

It was time for Zachary to step in.

Emeric turned on Daniel. Anything human was now lost to his carnal rage. Zachary thrust himself forward, dragging in as much power as he could. The transformation was never easy—it had been known to make grown men scream—but over time the body grew to anticipate it. For Zachary, who'd transformed every night for almost two years, changing his skin was as easy as pulling on his clothes.

The first sensation was the crackle of magic, so much it felt like the skin was inflating. And then the clothes around him began to fuse with his skin, reacting to the magic in the same way he did, and becoming a part of him. Then his bones shifted, his heart doubled in size and his eyes grew, much too large for his skull until it felt like his sockets might crack.

His wings burst out from his back triumphantly, as if they'd been trapped beneath his shoulders all this time. The world came alive with a magnitude of sounds and smells, the sunlight too bright for his sensitive vision. He felt light, agile, sleek as a snake, but with the power of a dragon.

He beat his vast, black wings and was up in the air before, as quickly as a diving falcon, he drove himself between his brother and Emeric. Daniel gave a short scream of surprise as Zachary landed above him, curling a protective tail around the boy, his left wing hanging over Daniel's head. Zachary bent his head forward and emitted a bone-shattering roar.

The sound ricocheted through Emeric, and he stopped dead, as if he'd struck a wall.

"FOLD!" Zachary's voice boomed, louder than life. "ENOUGH!"

The feline bowed low in submission, prostrating itself, and with Emeric's fear came his sensibilities. With a gasp, he tore away his Night Patrol form and sat, a human once more, the colour draining from his face.

"E-Etheus," Daniel stuttered, as Zachary straightened, also releasing his Night Patrol form. "Etheus blind me."

"There's no need for that." Zachary marched to Emeric's side, Marcel forcing himself up to his feet. Both men were wounded from the fight, but the majority of their injuries were already half-healed, cuts to the chest and neck bleeding sluggishly. Marcel was limping.

"Zach—" Emeric gasped, beginning to shake. He clamped

both hands to his mouth. "Zachary."

"Calm—no one died," Zachary said.

Marcel came to Emeric's side, kneeling down to examine his wounds. Zachary gave his second in command a one-over to make sure he wasn't hurt. Emeric's blood still shone on Marcel's teeth. He spat in the street.

Zachary inhaled deeply, stealing himself, and turned on the alchemists, who were all peering out from around the houses. It always amazed Zachary how fleeing crowds managed to start wandering back toward the source of danger when they realised they weren't being chased.

"You, alchemists!" he marched toward them. "Do you have any idea what you almost did? One burning house could have reduced this entire sector to ashes! Countless lives could have been lost! Did you think about that, before you whipped yourself into this frenzy?"

The alchemists balked away from him. "T-the traitor—"

"*Is dead*—you immeasurable idiots!" Zachary bellowed. "And burning a home he has not set foot in for over a decade will not, magically, make him deader."

The alchemists stammered, trying to shift the blame. "The—the Night Patrol—"

"You could have compromised the investigation into the Merle family's disappearance! You could have set the city on fire! My subordinate was within his *right* to tear you to pieces. That he didn't was under my good graces. Count yourselves fortunate, for your punishment, had you succeeded in this foolery, would have been something much more memorable." Zachary thrust his hand up and pointed toward the castle. "Return to your homes and pray to Athea that the King does not hear of this, or else you may yet meet an unfavourable end. Go!" he ordered and the alchemists fled gladly, shouting to each other in Kathreki as they went.

Silence followed them, and Zachary became aware of the

Southern residents, who'd crept forward, like shy sparrows, peering out at them. An angry, suspicious tension clung to the air. As Magi they might have been accepted, but the Night Patrol were as welcome as the alchemists had been.

Zachary maintained his airs, avoiding the spectators' accusatory eyes. "I apologise for the disturbance to you all. This household, and sector, are protected. You need not fear this again. If there have been any damages, please send word to the castle. I will see to it you're fully reimbursed."

He turned quickly on his heel and strode toward Daniel. He took the boy by the arm, casting his eye down his injury. Daniel was fortunate to have turned his hand inward during the attack. The cut ran shallowly along the forearm rather than the wrist. Daniel clenched the wound tightly, blood seeping between his fingers. There was a grey undertone to his dark skin and his eyes were wide and watery. Zachary tore away the hem of his chemise and, taking the injured arm, he began to wrap it tightly. Daniel gave a yelp of surprise and pain. Zachary shushed him.

"Come." He tugged the boy after him, Marcel and Emeric close behind. "We need to go—come. Don't snivel Daniel—come on."

They quickly made their way back up toward the castle, Emeric's front still stained with blood, though the wounds on his throat and collar were superficial and the skin had already fused. It would be fully healed by the next morning—even expelled, the quantity of magic used to transform would have an effect on the body for several hours to come.

By the time they made it to the house, Zachary was all but dragging Daniel after him, the boy tripping over his own feet.

"Heather," Zachary shouted, as he kicked open the door. "Get the physician, now!"

Heather came running out from the kitchen, took one look at the bloodied set of them, and ran straight for the servant's stairway which connected the household to the rest of the castle.

Zachary pulled his brother into the library, Emeric and Marcel following stiffly. Marcel was still bleeding from a wound to his leg, just below the knee. Emeric must have sunk his teeth in deeply to make such a wound through the Night Patrol armour.

"I'm so sorry," Emeric whispered over and over as he helped Marcel into a seat. Marcel's eyes were fixed on the scratches on Emeric's neck.

Zachary turned his attention back to his brother, taking a hold of his wrist and unwrapping the makeshift bindings to see the damage. "What were you doing down there? Hm?" Zachary said, trying to engage Daniel and keep his mind focused. "Answer me, brat—did you go with the alchemists?"

"N-no...I went to...I w-went to find a tailor...I needed a new...new shirt."

"Why couldn't you have called for a tailor from the upper quarter?"

"...S'pensive," Daniel slurred, his gaze set over Zachary's shoulder to where Emeric was kneeling in front of Marcel, applying pressure to his wound. "What was that?" he asked softly. "He turned into..."

"Night Patrol," Zachary replied, his voice barely over a murmur.

"So you really...you really lead them?"

"Is it that much of a surprise?" Zachary looked up just as a servant came in. She carried a bowl of water and clean bandages, along with a bottle of ointment and wine. "Good, put it there. Thank you, Ruth." Zachary gestured to the table, and taking the ointment, he stretched out Daniel's arm and poured it liberally onto the wound. Daniel hissed. "Don't be pathetic." Zachary passed the bottle over to Emeric, and taking a fresh bandage, began to wrap his brother's wrist. It would stem the bleeding until the physician arrived.

"He almost killed me," Daniel whispered.

"You shouldn't have got in the way." Zachary poured out a

glass of wine and pressed it into his brother's hands. "Drink—no, not all at once, you imbecile." He reached out and pulled the glass down from Daniel's lips. "Steady sips. There, that's it. The physician will be here soon. Once he's seen to you, you're to go and lie down. You won't be going into class today."

"Why?" Daniel still seemed distant.

"You faced a member of the Night Patrol. When that really occurs to you, I'd rather you didn't have an audience."

"But I—"

"Oh Healing Septus, Daniel," Zachary barked. "Rest. Your work shouldn't come before your health." He paused, and added more softly, "And don't think wrongly of Fold. It wasn't a personal attack. You were merely in the wrong place."

"Is he...is he safe?"

Zachary and Daniel both looked across to where Emeric had now dropped his head on Marcel's knee, his breath shallow and stuttered. He looked very unwell. Marcel leant forward, speaking to him in soft, stern tones.

"He's probably more frightened by what happened then you are," Zachary muttered, just as the door opened abruptly. "The physician, at la—" Zachary cut himself off as member of the Royal Guard announced himself.

"The King demands an audience with you," the guard stated, to almost no one in particular. Emeric made to rise, but Zachary pointed strictly at him.

"Stay here," he snapped, stepping forward.

"Zachary," Emeric shook his head, standing abruptly, "Arlen, no. This is my fault."

"Stay exactly where you are. You're not to leave this room until the physician has seen to you. I will deal with this."

"I could have *killed* someone! I almost...your *brother!* You can't take the blame for this, I won't allow it."

"Are you giving me orders?" Zachary asked coolly and Emeric grew compliant, his face falling. "So far as I recall, I am your captain and you will do as I say, or Malak, so help me, I will have you whipped for insubordination. Are we clear?"

Emeric opened and closed his mouth in silent complaint and then nodded, defeated.

"Good. You may rest here as long as you like. I will be back when I can." He nodded stiffly to them all, and swept out of the room after the guard, passing the physician as he went by.

CHAPTER
29

"I regret this decision." Joshua dragged his feet, his body heavy with exhaustion.

Fae laughed, resting an affectionate hand on his back. "Your aches and pains mark another good day of training."

"No, I think Korrick is trying to kill me," Joshua said, still a little breathless. They were walking back together from the training grounds. The training was completed for the morning, and would recommence again later in the afternoon. During this pause, Joshua would eat and then continue his lessons with Rufus on politics, finance, kingship and statecraft. Compared to the training, it was usually less than riveting work, but important nonetheless.

"I warned you it wouldn't be easy. Nothing of worth ever is." Fae pulled him into her side, putting her arm around his shoulders as they walked, her loose hair tickling his nose. Joshua giggled.

Despite how difficult the training was, Joshua had enjoyed every moment. Korrick wasted no time, working the class hard and efficiently, and already Joshua could see improvements in his technique. It wasn't only the sword and bow they were taught however. They learned to navigate the terrain, to be able to move swiftly and soundlessly, and to fight with their bare hands and bodies. Korrick also trained them in the mind. As they exercised, he would conduct lessons, recounting battles, famed strategies, and forgotten wars, until Joshua's head was spinning. It might have been too much, but Joshua wasn't forced to bear it alone.

His training had reconnected him with Kael, and he'd been introduced to several of Kael's cousins too, with whom they shared a class. All of them, Joshua had discovered, were actually much younger than him, between seven and nine, though they looked deceptively older. Cat Sidhe children, Fae had later explained, grew up quicker than humans.

There were approximately seven of them all together in the class, but Kael was by far the friendliest to Joshua. Most of her cousins seemed to hold reservations about him and his inclusion in their training. Kael had no such snobbery. She seemed glad to spend time with Joshua. The pair already made quite a formidable team, and amidst all the hard work, pain and exhaustion, there was also much laughter and chatter. Joshua couldn't recall a time he'd been so happy. He couldn't recall a time when he'd been able to have more than fleeting friends.

"Boyd," Fae called, as they cleared a section of trees to find the physician hunched down, examining the foliage. He had a basket on his arm and was picking through the grass and flowers.

"Good afternoon," Fae said. "And Rufus," she added with surprise, as beyond Boyd they spotted the Magi, sat back against a tree, reading, a similar basket of herbs abandoned at his side.

"Joshua, Fae," Boyd greeted. Rufus gave a vague wave, never looking up from his book. "Done with training, are you? Well how was it today? I can give you something for any muscle pain, if you like?"

"Boyd, I'm fine." Joshua smiled. "Best thing for an aching body is a hot bath, and then to start back up again."

"Gah, you've truly indoctrinated him, haven't you?" Boyd

grumbled at Fae, who beamed.

"What are the pair of you doing?" she asked, eyeing Boyd's basket.

"Well some of my reserves were running low, so I thought I'd come out to refill them. Which would be much quicker if *somebody* was actually doing their part." Boyd raised his voice, glancing over at Rufus.

"I said I'd join you outside. Not that I'd help," Rufus replied, not tearing his eyes from the page. He was insufferable when he was reading—it was clear the rest of the world was disturbing him.

"D'you see this? He comes in, disturbs me in my quarters, uses up all my medicines, and then offers nothing in return," Boyd lamented. "Fae, your Magi is taking liberties with me."

"He's a guest. He's allowed to," Fae said.

"Is that hemlock?" Joshua asked, looking into the basket. "I thought these were herbs for medicine? Isn't hemlock fatally poisonous?"

"Oh, it almost always is." Boyd nodded. In the background, without looking up, Rufus reached over to the basket at his side, took a fistful of the plant and pretended to eat it. Joshua stifled a laugh. Fae spotted it too.

"*Rufus*," she berated, and Rufus ducked his head behind his book and continued to read. Fae watched him, and Joshua sensed the stab of worry pass through her—joke or not, Rufus's actions were unsettling. In the past week, as Joshua had spent more and more time training, Rufus had retreated further into himself. He spent the majority of his time either in Boyd's quarters, his own room, or hidden somewhere in the library. Joshua hadn't seen him speak with anyone else, nor seen him eat more than a few mouthfuls at any meal. And he hadn't seen Rufus produce even a spark of magic. That, more than anything, concerned him.

Magic was to Rufus what paint was to a painter, and only a great unhappiness could prise the two from each other. A great unhappiness that Rufus, as always, seemed unwilling to unburden himself of.

"Come along, Joshua—let's get you washed up and fed." Fae brought Joshua out of his thoughts.

"I think I'll walk back with you, if I might—empty the baskets," Boyd offered. "Rufus, will you come with us?"

Rufus gave a vague grunt, turning another page.

"Well fine, suit yourself. I'm happy to be clear of you anyway. He's been grumpy all morning," Boyd said, his voice forcefully playful. "Won't make polite conversation, or eye-contact, or even greet me as I come and go."

"Good-*day*, Boyd," Rufus said pointedly and Boyd made a high-pitched noise of exasperation.

"D'you see this unpleasantness? D'you see what I have to contend with?"

"Just ignore him." Fae passed by, knocking Rufus's arm with her knee and causing him to drop his book. She smiled at him and, even in his morose mood, Rufus's lips twitched in response as he gathered up his book. Boyd walked past with his nose in the air, and Joshua followed, kicking Rufus in the hip.

"Ow!"

"Don't be horrible," Joshua hissed.

"I'll be whatever I damn well please." Rufus scowled. "I don't interrupt your training, stop interrupting my reading. I'm only out here because you ordered me to be more sociable."

"Try talking," Joshua said. Rufus's moods didn't usually extend beyond a day, but he'd maintained this one for near a week now and Joshua was running out of patience.

"I don't want to." Rufus returned to his book. Joshua knew he'd already read the page three times over and was only pretending to be engrossed in order to avoid the conversation. The Prince growled.

"Insufferable." He stomped after Fae, who'd stopped at the bottom of the path and was ushering him along. He broke into a half-run and collided with her side, her arm wrapping itself firmly around his shoulders as they set off again, Boyd trotting after them.

"It looks like you have been out in the sun too long, physician Dacey," Fae said lightly. Joshua had noticed it too—Boyd's nose, ears and cheeks were all singed brightly. "He so rarely steps out of his quarters—he's built no resilience to the sun."

"She's right—you're very red."

"Well it's not my fault," Boyd said, indignantly. "Honestly, this weather has been absolutely hostile, turning so suddenly. Here I thought I'd get a few more days of spring before summer started creeping in."

Joshua grew still. "Summer?" He frowned. "It can't be, already?"

"We have a few weeks yet but the season certainly seems to have arrived early." Fae peered up at sky. It was a very vibrant blue that afternoon, and streaked with long, delicate clouds, that looked like lines of uncoiled cotton.

"What month is it?"

"Month? Why, it's the...Let's see now." Boyd counted. "We've gone through a full moon-phase since the first day of spring."

"It's the month of Prospan?" Joshua jolted. "Already?"

"Heavens help us, is there nothing you Harmatians won't name after your gods? It must make everything awfully confusing," Boyd jibed, but Joshua wasn't listening.

"How many days has it been? Since the start of the month?"

"Eight—no, nine days," Fae said. "Another six and we're midway through spring."

"So tomorrow will be the tenth day of Prospan?"

"Well, logically, one would assume, yes." Boyd pulled a face. "Is that significant somehow?"

Joshua pursed his lips. "There are calendars in the library, aren't there? Rufus would've known."

"I think so. Why? What's so important about it?" Fae asked.

308

"Etheus blind me, he almost slipped it by. I could have missed it entirely." Joshua gritted his teeth, fiercely determined. "Fae, Boyd, I'm going to need your help with something, and we'd best get planning now."

This time when his sadistic alter-ego subconscious came to him, it did so in a new form. Howell dropped down beside Rufus, who snapped his book shut irritably.

"Conjurin' me up even in the daytime." Howell's accent was thick, just like Rufus remembered, a full Corhlam drawl. "Rufus, you must be gettin' desperate."

"Go away," Rufus hissed.

"I would, but you keep drawin' me back, in one shape or another."

"I didn't ask you here."

"Ach—we both know that's not true." Howell tipped forward and plucked a nearby daisy, putting the end of the stem between his teeth. "And for all your complainin', you're as glad to see my face as I'd be to see yours. Least that's what you 'ope."

"If you're going to torment me, do it with a different person," Rufus growled.

"I don't decide 'ow you see me. You dictate that."

"I don't want to see, Howell."

"*Dictate*. Never said you *chose* to, Love. So, why then? What's brought this lover to the forefront of your mind? You need to ask yourself these questions, else I start appearin' in the day, like now."

Rufus pushed himself to his feet and stalked away. Howell strolled leisurely after. He was a shorter than Rufus, with tan skin, long hair the colour of dark ale and a song always on his lips. Even as they walked, he began to hum, taking the daisy from his mouth and plucking the petals off one by one.

"My Love's got the sky, in bonny blue eyes, a pocket of wit and mind of fire. And still fresh as lily, he stains my breast plate, with wayward promises to keep my heart safe," Howell sang.

Rufus relented in his stride, stopping by a group of flowering hawthorn trees. He bowed his head. "That's not fair."

"What's that?" Howell asked innocently.

"That song." Rufus closed his eyes. He was drawn back into distant memories, to a time when the possibility of a life beyond his care for Joshua had seemed feasible. A future born from tiny, insignificant moments of love. Rufus recalled it all—the way Howell's hair smelled when he'd been out on a voyage; how his voice would carry through the house from outside as he worked, singing with the birds; how sometimes Howell would laugh so hard, tears would spring to his eyes and make them shine like horse-chestnuts. Rufus hadn't loved him straight away, but with each passing day, something had stirred within him, and Rufus knew they could be happy together. It wasn't like Mielane, who'd captivated his every waking and sleeping hour, but it had been good and honest, and Rufus had been ready for it.

"If only you were as ready for DuGilles and his alchemists," Howell spoke Rufus's thoughts. Rufus turned back to him, his hand automatically covering the spot on his stomach where the brand was burnt into his flesh.

"Why are you here as Howell?"

"I think you know," Howell said.

Rufus combed his fingers through his hair, sniffing. "You want me to tell Fae. Tell her what happened."

"Aye, I do."

"And what would that serve other than to distance me even more from her?" Rufus took off again, his feet guiding him toward the ravine where Korrick had tested Joshua. Howell meandered after him, picking another flower, his expression peaceful.

"You 'onestly think that what DuGilles did to you drove me away?"

"You're not Howell," Rufus said fiercely. "Howell is probably hauled in a tavern somewhere in Killian, smuggling another shipment of Sverrin's copper out to Réne, and guzzling his fifth tankard with a better man than me sat opposite him."

"Paint your fine details if you will, but I'd not be 'ere arguin' with you, if a part of you weren't privy to the pissin' truth—that you came 'ome to me, mauled and 'alf-mad, but it weren't your scars that drove me away."

Rufus reached the ravine and stopped at its edge, peering over into the turbulent water below. He closed his eyes, vertigo making his head spin as he tipped, enjoying the freedom of the potential fall. Opening his eyes, he saw a black kite circling up in the sky, dipping in and out of the air as agile as a fish.

"What we decided was mutual."

"Aye, because I wasn't fool enough to fight a decision you'd already made. Not for a man who loved me less than I loved 'im."

"Not this again." Rufus took Howell by the lapels. "It's not true. Our feelings, my feelings, they were different, but not less. I…" Rufus released him. "I cared for him very deeply."

"But not enough to share your burden."

"How could I? Mine wasn't a life to be shared. They'd have caught him too, they'd have killed him or worse." Rufus pulled the ring from around the chain on his neck. "I've caused the death of one lover already—I didn't need to add him to the list."

"Aye, very noble." Howell didn't raise himself to Rufus's dramatics, sidling past him and sitting down on the edge of the ravine.

"What's that supposed to mean?"

"Ach, s'nothin'." Howell pulled out a hipflask and took a swig. "Just wonderin' 'ow you plan to use the same excuse on Fae."

Rufus had no answer for that, and Howell offered him the hipflask. Although Rufus knew it wasn't real, he accepted and took a swig. The brandy slipped down his throat like it had the day he and Howell had parted ways. It had been an awkward exchange. Rufus had struggled to meet his lover's eye, and sensing his discomfort, Howell had done what he did best—made a joke of Rufus's flittering nature, offered him a drink and sang a song.

"My Love's got the sky, in bonny blue eyes,
A pocket of wit and mind of fire.
And still fresh as lily, he stains my breast plate,
With his wayward promises to keep my heart safe

My lover is turned, and colder than bone,
But I'll weep for him sweetness, at the turn of the stone.

A warrior am I, who knows my fate yet
The crimson river where I'll be laid to rest.
To war is my call, my sword is my pride
But I ne'er can forget, my lover's blue eyes.

My lover is far, and I, long from home,
But I'll weep for him sweetness, at the turn of the stone.

My lover is gone, and I to my death,
But I'll weep for him sweetness, 'til my final breath."

"I'd never heard that song before or since," Rufus recalled. "He wrote it on the spot, I think. He always promised to write me a song…It shouldn't have been that one."

"Hmm," Howell hummed in agreement, reclaiming his brandy. "We punish those who break our 'earts in the softest ways."

Rufus came and sat beside him. "Better to break his heart than kill him."

"You think that's 'onestly what it'd come to?"

Rufus turned his hands over. "If you're to be believed, and Morrigan is right…then I'm going to kill a lot of people."

"Have you submitted to that now?"

"I don't want to be. But my hands are already bloodstained."
Rufus chucked sadly. "What waters could clean that away now?"

"Athea if I know, you morose bastard." Howell clapped him on the back and stood. "But the Rufus I knew, 'e wouldn't give up scrubbin' all the same. And if not for me, or you, then for your lad, and the next lover you invite into more than just your bed."

Rufus laughed. "I don't think I have to worry about another lover—" He turned to Howell, but the man had disappeared, and Rufus was alone. "…Howell?" he called faintly. His voice echoed faintly, through the empty ravine.

～⁕～

"You caught him?" Embarr Reagon tried to keep the surprise from his voice as he straddled the young Lieutenant beneath him. "Varyn the Hunter?"

"I did," the Lieutenant replied, the scar down his face pale in the candle light. He caressed Embarr's thighs.

Embarr forced a loving smile easily onto his face, choosing his words carefully. "I heard he was as fierce as a dragon—how did you bring him to justice?"

The Gancanagh stroked his victim's chest. The Lieutenant coughed—a painful sound. He wouldn't last much longer— Embarr had been feeding on him for some time now, using him to spy on the Kathrak court. The Gancanagh didn't take any pleasure killing the man in this way, but he couldn't move on until the Lieutenant was dead. The less people who knew Embarr was in the castle, the longer he would be able to operate before he was discovered.

"There was nothing fierce about the Hunter," the Lieutenant spat.

"No?"

"No. I followed him for days on horseback, chased him down—I was ready for a fight," the Lieutenant said. "But he just surrendered. Made up some cock-and-bull story about being hunted by a dragon. Kept saying we couldn't bring him to the capital, because it was too dangerous...Well he's rotting in the dungeons now."

This news worried Embarr. He knew Varyn—the Hunter wasn't easy prey. That the Lieutenant and his meagre soldiers had succeeded in bringing him down could only mean the worse. The curse was starting to take effect. Embarr tried to keep the concern from his face.

"And what is to be his sentence? As your quarry, surely you will be honoured with claiming his head?"

The Lieutenant coughed again. "No, my beloved," he said. "The King wants to sell him back to the Shin, if the Hunter lasts that long. We cannot get a price until the snow has cleared—the mountains are impenetrable."

Embarr repressed his grimace. Varyn had spent years a slave to the Shin and had sacrificed a great deal in order to buy his freedom. Embarr wouldn't let him be returned to those tyrants, not now.

"What did you mean—if he lasts that long? Is the Hunter unwell?"

The Lieutenant's face soured. "Who knows? They say he does nothing but writhe in pain and cry out like he has poison in his belly...This so called great Hunter."

Embarr nodded, and the Lieutenant coughed again. Embarr leant over to the table, and picked up the tankard that was placed there. He pressed it into the Lieutenant's hand.

"Drink, my darling," he said sweetly. *Drink, and let me think a moment.*

The Lieutenant did as instructed, and Embarr settled back, trying to decide how best to proceed. Isaac Thornton was already on his way to Sigel'eg. Embarr would have to catch him on his arrival and convey the news in secret. Isaac, with his authority as a Magi, might have the power to assist Varyn where Embarr couldn't.

"I feel wretched," the Lieutenant mumbled, finishing his drink. Embarr leant down and kissed him.

"Yes, I can only imagine. You shall not last another week with me."

The Lieutenant only smiled, the words falling on deaf ears, disguised by their sweet tone.

Let him hear what he wants, Embarr thought, *it will be his only comfort now.*

CHAPTER 30

When Zachary arrived in the throne room, it was all but empty. Sverrin was lounged in his throne in the company of an unfamiliar dark-haired man, who stood below him, between a set of guards. Zachary, unsure of what to do, stood silently in the doorway until his King looked up. Sverrin smiled broadly.

"Zachary," he welcomed. "There you are! I am sorry to have disturbed you, I imagine you were still abed. I need your assistance with something. I am dealing with a sensitive matter and need a translator."

Zachary was so taken aback by Sverrin's warm tone that he simply stood for a moment, blinking stupidly. "A translator?"

"Yes." Sverrin gestured down to the man before him.

He was a strong, ruggedly handsome sort, with powerful hands and an amicable air. As Zachary examined him, the prisoner looked back and gave him an inane, cheerful smile.

"This man is from Corhlam—your own county. We picked him up in one of the mining villages, but he seems to only speak Althion. As the matter of our conversation is particular, and you are the only trustworthy man I know who can speak the tongue, I would like you to mediate for me."

Zachary fumbled with his words. He'd gathered himself on the walk down, preparing to defend Emeric's actions in the Southern Quarters. It hadn't occurred to him that his summons might have been for something entirely unrelated.

"I will endeavour to do my best, Your Majesty." Zachary bowed, and greeted the Corlavite, who smiled widely, glad to hear his own language. Somehow, his enthusiastic expression made Zachary feel more at ease. There was a sense about the man, as if he was happy living by life's simplest pleasures.

"Ask him if he knows why he's here," Sverrin bid, and Zachary obeyed.

"My a with balyow y veuredh." The Corlavite pointed a thumb at himself. "Lader vyth ny'm tremenas," he said proudly.

"He guards your mines, Your Majesty." Zachary's smile widened. "He claims no thief has ever gotten passed him."

"That is commendable, and I thank him for his service," Sverrin said. "I am afraid, however," Sverrin continued, and Zachary grew cold, "that his summons was on more unfortunate business."

The Corlavite continued to smile simply. Sverrin had maintained a cordial tone, giving no indication that the air had shifted. He leant forward in his throne.

"You see, there have been reports that this 'faithful' man has been heard spreading rebellious ideals. Ask him if this is true."

Zachary licked his lips, his mouth dry, and obeyed. He reworded the question more politely, asking if the man was conscious of rumours about him raising upheaval.

"My a flows pan evav, mes heb bodh a wul drog," the Corlavite said with a raucous laugh, like he was sharing a joke. His eyes were a bright and shining brown, but Zachary noticed a flicker of something beneath them.

"He says that he's prone to rambling after a few drinks, but I don't think there's any malicious intent behind it," Zachary said. "He seems a simple man."

"Ask him what he thinks of his King?"

Zachary did, and the Corlavite got onto one knee. "Lel vydhav pup-prys dhe Vyghtern a gar y bobel."

I will always be loyal to a King who loves his people.

Zachary narrowed his eyes at the wording of this statement. "He says that he will always be loyal to you, Your Majesty, for the love you have for your people," Zachary reiterated, and the Corlavite looked up and caught his eye. It was brief, but Zachary realised the Corlavite had caught the careful rewording of his translation. And if that were so, the man probably understood everything.

This is a façade, Zachary was suddenly sure. *He understands exactly what's happening and what's being said.*

"Nobly spoken," Sverrin said. "But anyone can speak noble words. Ask him what his thoughts on the traitor are. It is my understanding that Rufus Merle's desertion made him somewhat of a figure head for rebellious ideals. Oh, and Zachary—be sympathetic with him. Make him feel he has nothing to hide."

Zachary fought the urge to shudder. He locked eyes with the Corlavite. "A wodhes'ta kewsel Nowydtavas?" he asked. Not Sverrin's question, but his own.

The Corlavite gave him a shallow nod. Zachary almost groaned—so the man *could* speak Nowydtavas, the Common Tongue. This was just a pretence to play innocent. And it was *good* pretence. Even as Zachary asked the Corlavite whether he understood just how much danger he was in, the man simply gave a nod, and a wide smile, compromising nothing with his expression. He looked utterly harmless.

Why am I disguising the truth? Zachary demanded himself. *Why haven't I told Sverrin that this man is a liar?*

Zachary turned the question on the Corlavite, begging for an excuse. The Corlavite was one of his people, and strange as it was, the Magi wanted to protect him.

Give me a reason, Zachary thought. *Give me a reason not to*

318

sell you out.

The Corlavite stared deeply into Zachary's eyes. "Yn despit dhe'th trayturi, Rufus a gewsi gans revrons ahanas."

Zachary went cold. *Because despite your betrayal, Rufus spoke highly of you.*

"What did he say?" Sverrin voice rose. "I heard the traitor's name."

Zachary swallowed. "He said that he met Merle once, and that…that Merle spoke of me." He tried to stick to as much of the truth as he could.

"Ask him where? When? Did he offer the traitor shelter?" Sverrin spoke quickly. "Does he know where the traitor's parents have gone? Whether they're part of the rebellion?"

Zachary faithfully relayed the question, keen for his own answers. How had the Corlavite known Rufus? When had they been together? What had befallen them?

The Corlavite spoke earnestly with Zachary. Yes, he'd known Rufus for many years. They'd been lovers and had lived together in a small mining village in Corhlam. There, they'd been happy, until the alchemists had started their hunt, and Rufus had been forced to flee. The Corlavite had travelled with him into Bethean, but as the danger mounted, they'd eventually parted ways under Rufus's insistence. The Corlavite never saw Rufus again, and had no knowledge of the rest of the Merle family. The 'treacherous words' the Corlavite had been arrested for saying, had been words of mourning, upon the discovery of Rufus's death.

Zachary listened weakly, imaging it all too well. Somehow, throughout his story, the Corlavite maintained his innocent expression, never wavering in his smile.

"What did he say?" Sverrin asked impatiently.

Zachary collected his thoughts, weighing his options. The smartest thing would be to sell the Corlavite out. Such a show of loyalty on Zachary's part would please Sverrin, and no doubt endear Zachary further to him, smoothing over any previous unpleasantness. Zachary had a great deal to gain from being truthful, and very little incentive to protect the Corlavite, of whom he knew nothing. And yet...

"He says that he met Merle on the road. They shared shelter in a stable for the night and then parted ways. It was ten years ago, but he recalls it well. He says that it was difficult to learn that Merle was a traitor, as they shared bread and Merle was kind to him. He knows nothing beyond that, about any rebellion or the Merle family." Zachary clasped his hands behind his back, standing stiff. "Any sympathetic words he might have said in Merle's defence were called back from a distant impression. He felt betrayed to have such a kindly memory tainted by the reality of who Merle was."

"I see." Sverrin settled back in his throne. "Do you believe him, Zachary?"

"I do." Zachary turned back to his King, who sighed, and gave a forgiving nod.

"In which case, he will be allowed to serve a minimal sentence," Sverrin said. "Guards, take him down to the paupers' dungeon, and call the physician to come and remove his tongue. Better to take it out, before he accidentally betrays himself again."

Sverrin gazed down at the Corlavite, who bowed his head, maintaining his stupid smile. Zachary stood in awe of the man, capable of maintain his façade even in the face of this sentence. A man was free in death—he could curse or praise himself to his own grave and be a martyr for it, but a silenced man was a captured man and Sverrin knew that.

As the guards accompanied the Corlavite away, Zachary couldn't help but call out. "Pyth yw dha hanow?"

The man looked back at him, and for the first time, a trace of sadness came into his expression. "Howell. Ow hanow yw Howell," he said and then left the room in silence.

"What did you ask him?" Sverrin asked.

"His name. I thought it was only right to hear it, before he lost the ability to say."

Sverrin laughed. "I marvel at how sentimental you are sometimes."

"Harmatia would be a very different place were I not," Zachary rasped, his throat dry.

Sverrin laughed again. "Yes, it would. DuGilles!" he called loudly.

Zachary jumped and turned sharply to find the Kathrak stood in the corner close to the servants' door. Zachary couldn't be sure how long he'd been lurking there, but the Magi got the uncomfortable impression it was longer than he'd have liked.

"Your Majesty." DuGilles bowed deeply. "Lord Zachary, a pleasure."

"DuGilles," Zachary said evenly. "I didn't know you'd returned to Harmatia. Last I heard, you were leading a raid into Bethean."

"Indeed—we went searching for a rebel encampment in Brexiam, where some of your fabled Knights of the Delphi were said to be hiding. Unfortunately, someone appears to have told them we were coming. They ambushed us in the forest. We barely escaped with our lives," the alchemist said with a grim cheerfulness. Zachary spared him a tight smile. "Your Majesty, I couldn't help but notice that fine specimen you just excused so graciously. I wonder if you might permit me to make use of him?"

Zachary frowned. "Make use of?"

"Yes, DuGilles has been doing some fascinating experiments." Sverrin clapped his hands together. "You think you can do something with the man?"

"I do. I'm short on subjects, and he looks strong and able-bodied. I could make use of him—give him purpose, good work," DuGilles offered sweetly, and from any other person it might not have made Zachary feel so sick. He didn't know what DuGilles proposed, but he was certain it wasn't nearly as pleasant as it sounded.

"Might I enquire as to the nature of these experiments?"

"Your opinion would actually be very valuable," DuGilles said, delighted. "Why don't you walk with me, Lord Zachary? I can show you my research."

"It warms me to see such collaboration between alchemist and Magi," Sverrin said.

Zachary felt like he was trapped between a set of playful cats, making a game of his slow demise.

"Lead the way." He nodded to DuGilles, who did so, looking smug. The pair left the throne room and walked a while, until they reached the chapel. DuGilles crossed the room to the secret door.

Zachary narrowed his eyes. "Where are you taking me?"

"Now, Lord Zachary, don't be coy. You know this castle better than I. You tell me where we're going."

Zachary's mouth drew into a thin line as DuGilles pushed the door, revealing the long, narrow staircase beneath. "The crypts. Where the Delphi is laid."

DuGilles maintained his smug air. "The catacombs of the castle are surprising spacious. There are a lot of abandoned places down in the bowel of this city where no one thinks to go. Places that are haunted by people nobody remembers."

"And that's where you work?"

"What can I say? The ghosts are good company, and they're quiet. Mostly." DuGilles was mocking him, but Zachary chose to focus on the narrow stairs instead. He'd descended into the crypts many times over the years, in aid of Sverrin's survival, but it had never gotten easier. The further below ground he went, the tighter the walls around him became, and the harder he found it to breathe. Zachary suspected there was a reason his Night Patrol form had wings.

"Tell me, Lord Zachary, what do you know about Isnydea?"

"The land of the damned?" Zachary frowned. "It's the fourth province in Kathra, located in the north and west. A mountainous wasteland in which Kathra have exiled their criminals for centuries, leaving them to die in the wild."

"Yes—the infamous Isnys. Those who weren't picked off by dragons, or monsters, fathered a race bred from criminals and the occupants of the mountain—the ancient Elves. Tell me, have you ever met an Isny?"

"Not in person."

"They're a dangerous people. No delicates among them—to be delicate in Insydea is to die. They work like beasts and have thick skin and small hearts. In many ways, I find them inspiring—they come into the world expecting nothing more than to leave it horribly. No illusions of kindness or love, just suffering." DuGilles let Zachary pass in front of him down the stairs.

Zachary felt oddly as if DuGilles might pull a dagger out at any moment and slot it up between his ribs.

"Do you know anything of the Shin, my lord?" DuGilles asked.

"They're the ruling body in Insydea—tyrants who offer damned people protection from monsters and pirates, in exchange for their complete obedience. They guard the borders, controlling who goes in and out, so the Isnys only choice is to join the Shin or be slaves to them."

"Do I detect a hint of disapproval in your voice?" DuGilles chuckled. "You must understand, people born of cruelty and desperation can't be trusted in our civilised world. The Isnys moulded their society because it fitted them—what is unimaginable to us, is necessity for them. They created the Shin, because people like that need to be ruled with fear. Fear is understood in all languages."

"So is kindness." Zachary kept his eyes ahead, his face blank. "Can I ask the purpose of all these questions?"

They stepped out into the vast chamber at the mouth of the crypt, where Jionathan of the Delphi lay in perpetual paralysis, bathed in the ethereal, blue and green light of the faerie lantern.

"This way, my lord." DuGilles led Zachary down a tunnel that veered off from the chamber.

Zachary felt his body tense as he forced himself after the Kathrak.

"I've travelled a great deal in my life," DuGilles told him, "and during my time in a small village on the boarder of Sigel'eg, I had some contact with the Shin. You see, for all their seclusion, the Isny are actually closer to the source of Kathrak power. It's from the Elves that we learnt alchemy, which once upon a time meant more than the elemental magic you so liberally wield here in Harmatia. Alchemy was once a study of the earthly magics, rather than cosmic elements. Alchemists studied the properties of metals and plants—the foundations of medicines and science. As time went on however, 'alchemist' merely came to mean 'a Kathrak who can wield magic', and all the foundation of our knowledge was lost to the Harmatian renovation. True alchemy disappeared from the world, but Isnydea, separated by a menacing boarder and reputation, kept their knowledge. And it was from the Shin I met, that I came to be a *true* alchemist." DuGilles gave a nostalgic sigh. "I learnt many things. They taught me what stone and minerals I could use to block or inhibit the stars' power—oh yes, more than mica, there are others too. They taught potions which could induce visions and sight into other worlds. And finally, they imparted to me a technique to bind a man, body and soul, to my will." DuGilles stopped. "Incredible, isn't it?"

"Impossible," Zachary said. "You can't bind a person to your will. Not entirely."

"A sceptic." DuGilles rubbed his hands together. "What I'm about to show you many change your mind." Coming to an old, stout door, he pushed it open and stepped down into a chamber beyond.

Zachary, who already felt like they'd delved deep enough below ground, wanted nothing more than to turn and march all the way back up to the castle. Were he a braver man, he might have done. Instead he stepped down after DuGilles, suppressing the shivers that went down his arms and legs.

The chamber beyond was cool and dry, lit by torches that sucked the air from the room, making Zachary feel lightheaded. Though there was nothing immediately offensive about the room, its dark corners gave Zachary the impression that there was something evil lurking over the chamber. Having mocked Emeric for his fear of ghosts, Zachary felt more inclined to believe in them down here, in the crypts of the castle. Here it felt like men had been left in the dark to die. It reminded him of the Korrigans' nest, and yet was somehow worse.

"You don't look well, Lord Zachary. Is the dust troubling your lungs?" DuGilles noted, and then gasped, as if mortified. "Or has this tight, dark space brought back terrible memories?"

Zachary looked up at DuGilles sharply.

DuGilles sniffed knowingly. "During my hunt for the traitor, I stopped several times in Corhlam. Your father, Lord Rivalen, was a kind and generous host to a weary man. He told me many things about you."

Zachary rose up to his full height, his body rigid.

"You certainly had a stern upbringing, didn't you? Beneficial, I'd say—look where you are now, a highly esteemed warrior even among the Magi," DuGilles said, absentmindedly. "But one of your father's stories did stick with me in particular, of an unfortunate accident in the dungeons of your own home. How old were you? Seven?" DuGilles baited, eyeing Zachary who refused to speak. Every second he stood in the chamber, it grew more difficult to breathe. DuGilles continued, his eyes unblinking. "Your father told me how you would often explore the old tunnels beneath the fort, without supervision. And how, unfortunately, one day, having been structurally compromised by flooding the previous winter, one of those tunnels collapsed on you."

Zachary's entire ribcage was now suffocating him, bound

up tightly like bone corset. He held his breath, conscious that DuGilles was watching him, waiting to see the panicked judders that were trying to break up through his throat.

"Poor boy." DuGilles shook his head. "You must have been terrified—buried alive and nobody with any idea of where you were. How long were you down there, before your sister discovered you were missing, and called enough men to dig you out?"

Zachary knew he had to answer—he'd been silent too long, and it was only feeding DuGilles's enthusiasm. "A few hours."

"Hours." Again, DuGilles shook his head. "I can't even imagine what that did to you."

"I was seven. I pissed myself, cried when they found me, had nightmares for a few weeks, and then put it behind me," Zachary lied.

"Oh? That's good to know. So often events in childhood can define and govern us as adults." DuGilles didn't believe a word, his smile long and thin.

Zachary resisted the urge to tug at his collar and loosen it. It really was getting impossibly difficult to breathe, and the shadows in the corners seemed to be creeping even closer.

"If you're able then," DuGilles continued, "let's press on—I'd like to show you my experiments. I have a fresh one out this morning."

"A fresh what? Out from where?" Zachary cleared his throat, following DuGilles unwillingly down into the chamber, away from the torchlight. Through the darkness, Zachary spotted a line of cells, which had long been abandoned, circular and carved out of the rock, as if the castle had been built over the ruins of something more ancient and frightening. As they reached the last cell, DuGilles stopped and bid Zachary to take a look inside.

At first, it appeared to be as empty as the others. Then a ragged section of the wall moved and scurried up to the bars. A pair of animalistic eyes, wide and bloodshot, stared up at Zachary.

He jumped back, and choked as he recognised the grubby face peering up at him.

"Lord Farthing?" Zachary dropped onto his knees, peering in at Isaac's master. "Healing Septus, man—what happened to you? You look half-starved..." Zachary trailed off as the man cocked his head to the side, looking blank. Farthing had once been a dignified, if somewhat prudish man, but now there was nothing of that in his dull, empty eyes. "Athea have mercy, what have you done DuGilles?"

"Lord Farthing was found guilty of consorting with rebels a few weeks ago. The King was prepared to have him executed, but I insisted that such a life shouldn't be wasted. Not when there are measures to correct misguided treachery." DuGilles squatted down and, producing a crust of bread from his pocket, fed it through the bars. Farthing leapt on it, and began to tear it apart, ravenous. Zachary pushed himself away from the cage against the opposite wall.

"What have you done?" he repeated.

"Only what the King asked of me. Don't be so stricken, Lord Zachary—his condition now is only temporary. Soon enough, he will be as capable of speech, interaction and life, as he was before. You must remember—I only just let him out."

"Let him out of *where*?" Zachary found it hard not to shout. His head was spinning, panic beginning to pulse through him. His body was now desperate for fresh air, and he wanted nothing more than to be as far away from this evil place as he could.

"I'll show you." DuGilles pointed further down into the claustrophobic chamber, in the opposite direction that Zachary wanted to go.

And yet, numb and fighting back his shivers, Zachary followed DuGilles, unwilling to be alone with Lord Farthing.

"Here." DuGilles stopped and pointed down into deep pit which had been dug out just below him. Zachary could see the stone tiles which had been lifted from the floor now lined the opposite wall, alongside two huge mounds of earth and rock, which had been dug up.

The pit itself was about three strides deep, and contained within it a peculiar structure that Zachary had to squint to make out in the darkness. It was a rectangular box, long and thin, just large enough for a man to lie flat in. Two thin pipes led out from the sides, up into the chamber above. One pipe filtered out into the open air, and the other looped into a strange glass dome, filled with a milky liquid, and set upon a small, unlit furnace. For a brief moment, Zachary thought he was looking at some sort of strange new heating system, and then slowly the truth dawned on him.

"Do you like it?" DuGilles asked with delight. "Constructed out of a mixture of mica and lead, buried under three strides of earth and stone, this box is a sanctuary of sense. Any who go in are cleansed of the frivolities of the world—no sight, no sound, no sense of the stars or world beyond. Coupling that with a potion that can cause temporary anosmia," DuGilles gestured to the glass dome, "and my subjects find themselves in a new womb, ready to be born again. Don't believe me? Climb down—take a closer look."

Zachary only realised he'd stepped away from DuGilles, when his back struck the opposite wall. He pushed himself against it, his legs weak. He couldn't breathe at all. "W-why?"

"Ah, of course," DuGilles slapped his forehead, "I should have explained my process first. You see, there's a belief that when we're born, we emerge innocent of everything. Of course, the star we are born under may dictate some of our behaviour, but we are as a blank canvas—waiting to be painted by experience." DuGilles pretended not to notice how badly Zachary was struggling not to bolt, though Zachary saw his eyes flash with glee. "Now, when a man questions his loyalty, it's usually because something else has corrupted him. That corruption can leave a stain on the canvas. So I fashioned this technique, which offers men the chance to remove everything undesirable on their canvas—to be blank once more and born again. To return to the earth and be truly cleansed. It's a tricky process to be sure—many steps must be taken. First of all, the subject must be run down, brought to a level where he's susceptible to the change. I usually find that pain is most efficient in this, though the nature of the torture will vary with each subject. For some, it's physical, others…" DuGilles eyed Zachary, "psychological. Next, the subject is stripped of anything which ties him to the life he lived—his clothes, his senses, the very gods he believes in. We cut all connection to that outside world. Finally, we remove everything that makes a man human—food, warmth, sight, smell, sound. At first, they struggle, but after a time their mind stops rebelling against the loss of these things, and begins instead to focus on retaining them again. And with that falls away stubbornness, loyalty, a sense of self. And then we can begin rebuilding, and I as the artist may define how this man ought to be. A brand new canvas to paint. Do you see, Lord Zachary? Complete control."

"This is…this is *insane.*"

"It's not a savoury process, true, but the results make up for that entirely," DuGilles said. "That Corlavite the King has granted me…Howell, was his name? He made a silly mistake that might have marked him forever. Now he can be truly loyal again."

Zachary turned away. He'd fainted only once in his adult life, fourteen years ago, when, having suffered a bad wound, he'd made the mistake of getting out of bed too quickly. Now, he could feel a similar lightness of his head and the sudden heaviness of his body. His vision had begun to tunnel. He knew he had to flee. "You can't…you can't do this to an innocent man."

"But that's the point, Lord Zachary—when I'm done, he *will* be innocent. My experiments have been highly successful. Of those who survived the process, I've only ever failed once, and only because his conversion was interrupted. He was broken out of the box after only a week, you see, before he was ready."

"What happened to him?" Zachary's voice had raised two tones, and was threatening to go higher.

"He was a lost cause—I gave up trying to help and killed him. What can I say? Your brothering apprentice was too stained for even me to clean," DuGilles lamented and Zachary choked.

"Merle?" Zachary said weakly, and then covered his mouth as he retched, swallowing down his breakfast.

"I fear the atmosphere down here doesn't agree with you," DuGilles said kindly. "Perhaps it's time for you to go? You must have many things to do."

Zachary, unable to speak, nodded and turned very quickly away. He knew he'd compromised himself, but he doubted even Howell, who'd smiled so inanely during his sentence, would have been able to maintain that same expression in the face of what DuGilles had revealed.

Zachary made it to the stairway of the chamber just as DuGilles bid him one final farewell.

"Lowena dhis."

Zachary's entire body seized. He stood, frozen on the bottom step. "What did you say?"

"Oh, you'll have to forgive my pronunciation. I said good-day to you." DuGilles chuckled. "I like to pick up new languages wherever I travel. My Althion is yet rudimentary," he said cheerfully, "but I think I'm getting there."

Zachary looked back in time to see DuGilles part his lips, baring his teeth in an ugly grin.

CHAPTER
31

Maybe all the rumours were true—the recent ones, at least. Maybe Rufus had been like a wounded animal—vicious, barbaric, half-crazed in his final days. There hadn't been enough of him left to read his expression, so Zachary couldn't know for sure. Perhaps DuGilles had driven Rufus to madness, and then put him down like a rabid dog.

Zachary stood outside Daniel's bedroom, his hands pressed to his lips. He hadn't returned home all day, choosing instead to fetch his horse and ride as far out of the city as he could. A part of him had been tempted to keep riding. It would be easy to flee to the coast, catch a boat to Réne and further from there. To a place where nobody knew him, or could speak to him.

In the end, sensibilities had driven him back to the capital. The first thing he'd done was catch the evening courier and send a reply to Isaac, urging him not to come to Harmatia and to return to his comfortable, secluded life in La'Kalciar.

He then proceeded to find a tavern and drink it dry. He would rather let people see him as a drunkard, making a fool of himself, then let them know that one of the most vicious warriors in Harmatia was afraid.

Finally, stinking and wretched, he returned home and found himself at his brother's door. It was well past midnight, but, after a long hesitation, Zachary knocked. The reply was quick.

"Who is it?"

"May I come in?" Zachary's voice was husky.

"Yes."

Zachary opened the door. Daniel was sat in bed, the covers pulled up his chin, but by the lit candles, and the open books strewn on the bed, it was clear the boy hadn't been sleeping. He eyed Zachary warily. The Magi dragged a chair from the desk, to the side of the bed, and dropped into it with a huff.

"Where in Malak's name have you been?" Daniel asked. "Mrs Benson's been with worried sick."

"I just saw her."

"And Lord Hathely and Fold waited for you for hours."

"And they will get their apologies tomorrow," Zachary sighed and took Daniel's injured arm, examining the bandages. "The physician healed it?"

Daniel nodded.

"Small blessings."

"You reek of alcohol." Daniel wrinkled his nose, reclaiming his arm. "Is that where you've been? Drinking?"

"Me? Drinking? No, no—you must have me mistook for that brother of yours. You know—the one who doesn't give a damn about your opinion."

Daniel scowled, and looked away, selecting a spot on the wall to focus on instead. "As mean as you like to paint yourself, I know you don't hold me in nearly as much contempt as you pretend. You put on that you're cold and detached, but really you care about people. As crass and bad-tempered as you like to be, you proved that today."

Zachary blinked, absorbing these words. "Oh fuck off, Daniel."

Daniel's mouth twitched with a small smile. Zachary crossed his arms, pulling a face. It was the most normal he'd felt all day.

"Daniel, you're my brother," he eventually said. "As annoying as you are, I wasn't going to let Fold kill you."

"Maybe, but you didn't have to come and check on me."

"Who said I'm checking on you?"

"Why else would you be here?"

Zachary sobered. He could hardly tell Daniel the truth—that he was frightened, and felt alone, and conflicted. He tipped his head back against the chair and shook it from side to side, sighing loudly.

"What did the King do?" Daniel asked.

Zachary laughed and closed his eyes. The Southern Quarter—the issue hadn't even risen with Sverrin. Perhaps that would be tomorrow's burden?

"What did the King do?" Daniel repeated.

"Ach—nothing. Would you be quiet?"

"Nothing?" Daniel scoffed. "A group of alchemists tried to burn down the Southern Quarters, the Night Patrol came out in public, and you're saying the King did nothing?"

"I suppose the alchemists kept their tongues about it. So long as nobody complains, the affair doesn't necessitate his attention." Zachary blinked his tired eyes open and tipped his head forward. "His Majesty required my assistance for another, completely unrelated matter. That's all you need to know *and*," he added as Daniel drew in a sharp breath to interrupt, "all I am going say."

Daniel fiddled with his fingers in an unsatisfied silence. The boy was too curious for his own good. Finally, he seemed to relent, and changed the subject. "News is going to spread that you're Night Patrol."

"Oh, enough people already suspected it—my anonymity is no great loss."

"They'll be talking about it at the academy."

"No doubt," Zachary grunted. "Is that going to be a problem for you?"

Daniel raised his head a little, surprised. Zachary picked at his fingers, feigning indifference.

"After all, it's why they beat you, isn't it? Those bullies taking the Warriors' Assessment."

"They see you as an obstacle to overcome," Daniel agreed softly, "so they use me, because apparently being your brother automatically makes us the same...Never mind that I'm an architect."

"Next time," Zachary suggested, "why don't you tell them to come straight to me? If they want a fight, I'll happily oblige."

"They don't want to fight you," Daniel said. "They just want to win."

"Hah!" Zachary barked. "You are smart, aren't you?"

Daniel studied him, looking quickly away to his spot on the wall when Zachary caught his eye. "Can I ask a question?"

"No."

Daniel ignored him. "How old were you?"

"When what?"

"When you first..." Daniel wrinkled his nose, "when you first killed a man."

Zachary's sat up straight, his eyebrows raised. "What kind of question is that?"

Daniel shrugged. "The Night Patrol have a reputation. And you...The way they talk about you at the academy...I just wondered."

"How old do you think?" Zachary asked.

"I don't know." Daniel thought for a moment. "Fifteen?"

"Fifteen?" Zachary choked. "What on earth do you think I was doing at fifteen to be *killing* people?"

"I don't know, you're a warrior," Daniel said grumpily.

Zachary chuckled. "I was a year older than you."

Daniel peered around at him, his eyes a little wide, as if surprised Zachary was actually divulging this information. Zachary was a little surprised himself.

"One of King Thestian's cousins, an Earl from the western

coast, had amassed an army and was planning a full rebellion in an attempt to claim the throne. He overestimated the popularity of his campaign. I was deployed with the army, alongside my master. It was my first battle."

"What happened to the Earl?"

"Oh, he took an arrow to the eye within the first half-hour. His army scattered, and the affair was over by lunch. I killed thirteen men that day."

"You kept count?"

"The loss of a life should always be noted. You have a duty to remember."

"But the Night Patrol killed hundreds of people during the curfew—" Daniel began. Zachary cut him off.

"Hundreds?" he huffed. "Closer to tens, Daniel. In two years we never rose above thirty casualties. Statistically, due to the curfew, the level of murder in the city actually went down by close to fifty-percent."

Daniel stammered, thrown off by this new information. "Even thirty's too many," he persisted. "And the way you killed them... They still talk about it today."

Zachary narrowed his eyes. "Do you know how many people I personally killed during that time?" he asked softly.

Daniel grew still, and shook his head.

"Four. Their names were Jacob Cobb, Matthew Dwight, Emmett Surrey and Borgis Crabben. Cobb was wanted for raping three young girls and was breaking into the house of a fourth victim when he was caught. Dwight murdered his wife and lover in front of their two daughters, and was attempting to flee the city. And Surrey, well Surrey kidnapped five children and was planning to sell them to slavers on the coast, when a couple managed to escape. He chased them down, and was battering one to death when I found him."

Daniel, for the first time, didn't look away. "What about Crabben?" he asked.

Zachary dropped his eyes. "Crabben fell asleep in his workshop and made the mistake of trying to run home, instead of staying there for the night. He was cornered in the square by several of my greener officers. By the time I reached him, he was near death and in incredible pain. I finished him."

"So it was mercy?" Daniel asked, his mouth dipping at one side sceptically.

"It was my orders. Any man found in the streets after the hour of curfew was to be put to death. Arrangements were made that no innocent should have been out. Crabben broke the law."

"What about the children?"

"Excuse me?"

"You said the children escaped, and that Surrey was hunting them. So the children were also out after curfew. Did you kill them?"

Zachary's mouth tightened, and he grew very quiet.

Daniel gave a knowing nod, looking strangely satisfied. "I didn't think so."

"Be quiet." Zachary folded his arms and a silence grew between the two brothers. Zachary closed his eyes, almost dozing in the chair. He heard Daniel inhale, and groaned.

"Can I ask another question?"

"Oh sons of the gods, will you stop?"

"Was Rufus Merle part of the Night Patrol?"

"Athea," Zachary spat, standing sharply from the chair and pacing away. "He's the sore subject of the day. Why would you ask such a question?"

"I'm only curious."

"Well your curiosity is going to get you killed, damn you!" Zachary snapped, and then checked himself.

Daniel withdrew into the bed, and where he might have looked annoyed in the past, there was now an element of fear in his eyes.

Of course he's afraid, Zachary reminded himself. *He saw you transform this morning.*

Zachary exhaled slowly, his hands moving to the back of his neck and messaging the tight muscles. His head was beginning to throb again. "No," he said evenly, "Merle wasn't Night Patrol. I apologise for raising my voice, but I don't want to think about him."

Daniel bowed his head. "It must be difficult," he murmured, "for you and Lord Odin. People talk about Merle all the time, saying stupid things."

Daniel's tone sparked something in Zachary. "You don't believe what they say?" he asked, warily.

"Is any of it true?"

Zachary thought on this. "He certainly kept company with faeries."

"I doubt the faeries had anything to do with his treachery."

"Oh, don't tell me," Zachary forced a laugh, "you're a faerie sympathiser?"

"That's like asking if I'm a *human* sympathiser—there are hundreds of different kinds of faeries. They're all individual. Some want to eat us, true, but others...Others are just likes us," Daniel said. "I mean, Bethean prospers from their alliance with the Seelie Court, don't they? And was it not Unseelie magic that brought our King back to life? It seems a little hypocritical to use something, and then shit on it the next day."

"You're not wrong," Zachary muttered.

"And after all, it was the Delphi who taught us magic to begin with, and they supposedly came from Avalon. But now, all of that's being erased. I tried to find a book which had been recommended to me by the librarian, Francis, and I was told it'd been removed for heretical passages. It seems to me, the shelves of the Great Library have more spaces these days than they were built for."

Zachary closed his eyes again. "I am of a similar mind to you," he admitted, "but it is rapidly being considered an archaic mode of thought."

"I think we could learn a great deal from an alliance with the faeries," Daniel continued, unaware of the danger of his own words. "If they can return a man from the dead, imagine what else they could do? There are stories. Men returned to their youth, barren women with child," Daniel's voice rose with excitement, "spells that reverse a person's sex!"

Zachary peeked his eyes open. "Why on earth would you want to do that?"

Daniel blinked, his fleeting, wistful expression being replaced by something very neutral.

"It was only an example," he said.

Zachary narrowed his eyes.

"The point is," Daniel moved on quickly, "people segregate these ideas like it's all black and white. And they seem unwilling to consider any parameters beyond the 'obvious'—that because all Harmatian and Magi *must* be good, in order to be a traitor, Merle had to be Betheanian and a faerie."

Zachary gave an exasperated groan. "I said I didn't want to talk about him."

"Do you really hate him that much?"

Zachary turned his back on his brother. "No," he confessed, "but I am afraid of what he might do to me."

"Do to you?"

Zachary laughed emptily. "They say the true value of a man can only be measured by the repercussions of his passing. In the growing months, Daniel, you're going to understand exactly how important Rufus Merle was, and exactly why anyone who has ever spoken his name ought to be afraid."

Daniel shivered at the ominous words. "I don't understand."

Zachary hesitated, and then very quickly went to Daniel's side. He leant in, speaking in conspiratorial whispers. "Don't ever let anybody doubt your loyalty. If they do, fight. And if they win…Take your own life."

Daniel's eyes widened. Zachary swallowed.

"It is much better than the alternative."

"I—" Daniel stammered, "I don't think I could."

"Then by Athea, swear to me you will never ask me, or anyone else about Rufus Merle again."

"I swear." Daniel darted his eyes across Zachary's face, leaning away, intimidated by the proximity.

Zachary fell back into his chair, exhausted and suddenly miserable. He groaned softy, his hands once more messaging his sore neck and shoulders.

"Ah, it's almost morning. The tenth day of Prospan. Damn him, Merle really is the sore subject of the day. May Athea have mercy on his soul."

CHAPTER
32

"Rufus."

A sliver of light peeped through the shutters, casting a stripe over the shadowed bed. Rufus stared at it, still as stone, his arms cradling his pillow. He blinked slowly, still shrouded in a thick veil of sleep. Joshua had climbed onto the bed and lay in front of him, fully clothed but soft-eyed, as if he too had only just woken.

"Rufus?" he called again, and Rufus blinked and smiled.

"I'm here. I'm awake."

"Good morning," Joshua said. "Did you sleep well?"

"I think so." Rufus didn't dare raise his voice. In the column of light, dust hung in the air, swirling lazily. "Strange dreams. Confusing."

Joshua nodded, as if he, too, had been privy to them. "Fae says you have to get up."

"Why?" Rufus frowned. "Shouldn't you be training?"

"Not today. We have somewhere to go. It's important. Are you awake, Rufus?"

"Hm." Rufus hadn't realised his eyes had fallen closed again. "Where?"

"South."

"I don't want to," Rufus mumbled. He was normally the first to rise, but exhaustion clung to him now. He was heavy in his bed and unwilling to leave it.

"Rufus." Joshua squirmed closer. "Papa, come back. Please come back."

"I'm not gone." Rufus could feel himself sinking back into his pillow.

"Yes you are."

The words resonated through Rufus's exhausted body. He forced his eyes open, and freeing an arm from beneath his head, he wrapped it around his brother. It didn't seem right to try and reassure him—Joshua was too clever for that.

They lay a while, Rufus focusing on the beam of light, until his tired eyes stopped blurring in and out of focus. Finally, with an exhausted huff that made him sound like an old man, he rolled out of the bed and stumbled to the window.

Pulling the shutters back, he allowed sudden, blinding light to pour through. The sun was barely rising, but the sky was bright and brilliant with the promise of a glorious day. Rufus allowed the daybreak to rouse him and, mustering up all the energy and courage he could, he washed quickly and dressed.

Leaving the room with Joshua, Rufus was surprised to find the castle already bursting with life. Servants bustled about, busy at their chores, and the usual 'wanderers' were strolling down the corridors, some lounging in window seats, reading, while others laughed and chattered gaily with one another, their eyes vacant. Rufus suspected that, like Boyd, these Sidhe didn't see the merit of sleep.

They met Fae and Boyd in the courtyard, stood by a set of fine-looking horses.

"Good morrow," Rufus greeted them. "I don't suppose either of you are going to tell me where we're going?"

"South," Fae replied, and Rufus shook his head. Something about their manner told him they were in a hurry to go—clearly circumstances had conspired which required both Prince and Magi to be gone from the Neve for the day.

Rufus ran his hands through his hair, and gave his fringe a tug. Typical, today of all days.

Fae threw him the reins of a handsome black mare as he approached, and Rufus's gloom was momentarily displaced as he looked at the horse.

"Gracious, she looks just like Moyna." He stroked the mare's nose, the horse nuzzling his palm fondly. The last Rufus had ever seen of his horse was the night he'd left Harmatia with Joshua. The poor mare was probably long dead now, but Fae's attention to detail had brought back a happy memory.

"I know you're a nostalgic sort." Fae smiled slightly, nodding toward Joshua's horse which was a dark, strong looking bay.

Rufus coughed. "Athea have mercy, tell me we're not riding down to the Myrithian forest for a repeat of our last adventure."

"I said nostalgic, not stupid." Fae offered him a leg-up onto his horse, and Rufus mounted, watching with a quiet appreciation as Fae then crossed to a palomino stallion and hopped onto its back, light as air.

"Breakfast," Boyd called, from where he'd mounted his own bay. He threw Rufus an apple, which the Magi fumbled to catch. "For you," the physician added, "not your horse."

Rufus settled back in the saddle, his eyes narrowed. The mare huffed beneath him, and when Boyd wasn't looking, Rufus bit a section out of the apple, and leaning forward, fed it to her.

They set off together in single file, and rode for an hour or more down through a deep mountainous pass that cast them into shadow, high stone walls either side.

"Is anybody going to tell me where we're going?" Rufus eventually asked again. "And Malak, so help me, Boyd," he warned as the physician made to speak, "if you say 'south', I'll set your quarters on fire."

"We're currently headed east, actually," Boyd said smartly.

"Fine," Rufus snipped. "If you wish to be secretive with me, so be it."

"Oh, he doesn't savour the taste of his own character, does he?" Boyd jibed, and Rufus glared.

"Will you, at least, tell me *why* I was ripped from my bed and Joshua from his training?"

"My father is hosting some guests for the day," Fae said, her eyes ahead. "The Mac Gearailt clan—Reilly's family. I thought it prudent to remove you both, lest someone hear the word Magi and lost their composure."

Rufus had suspected something of the sort. Again the group lapsed into silence, continuing on their journey. Joshua pushed on ahead so that he and Fae rode side-by-side. The pair fell into easy conversation, exchanging jokes and stories. Boyd would occasionally throw in his contribution, and Rufus let his horse fall back, disinclined to join their merriment. His mind wandered, his eyes scaling the mountains either side of him. As Joshua giggled and talked, Rufus listened to him with a foreboding sense of detachment. At least he could now be certain Fae would care of the boy. That was all Rufus could have ever asked.

"Rufus, would you hurry up?" Joshua called back to him.

Rufus's thoughts had seeped into his body, and his horse, sensing his lethargy, had slowed her step to a lazy plod.

"Yes, yes," Rufus muttered, kicking the mare on.

"Rufus," Fae said, her voice sharp, "come and join me here."

Rufus, surprised by the request, complied, riding between Boyd and Joshua. He drew up to her side, noticing that the others had slowed, allowing some distance.

"Am I being berated?" Rufus half-joked, and then grew small under Fae's knowing eyes.

"You need to stop," she said plainly. "You're worrying Joshua, and you're worrying Boyd."

Rufus looked away. "I won't force a smile."

"Tell her," a voice instructed, and Rufus jumped and looked

around. Jionat was sat up on an alcove in the cliff above them. He kicked his legs as they rode by. "Tell her, Rufus."

"I can't," Rufus muttered.

"I am not asking you to, Rufus," Fae sighed. "Please don't be so dramatic."

"Tell her," Jionat insisted. "You can trust her."

Rufus shook his head, trying to cast Jionat away. "This gathering—Reilly's family, you said—will they not expect you to be there?"

"It's not a gathering, only a passing visit. They happen fairly frequently, so it's of no consequence. Besides, I am not very popular in the Neve at the moment, so this trip is as much an escape for me as you."

Rufus straightened with concern. "Why are you out of favour?"

"Well," Fae smiled, "I brought one of the Cat Sidhes' most hated enemies into my home, and then called him my friend, Rufus. Or did you think there would be no consequence?"

"I'm sorry," Rufus coughed. "I...I should have realised how my being here would affect you. That was selfish of me."

"It's nothing to worry about. My brothers may not be speaking with me, but they will recover from this apparent betrayal. Korrick's agreeing to train Joshua certainly eased some of the tension, and over time they will come to accept you...And forgive me, I hope."

Rufus turned his eyes to the road. "You really put yourself at risk when you brought us here, didn't you?"

"You would have done the same for me—that's the nature of friendship." Fae gave a mischievous smile. "We're almost there."

"Almost where?"

She ignored him. "Can you gallop?"

Rufus raised an eyebrow. "I've spent the last twelve years on the run, what do you think?"

Fae blinked prettily, and in the next instant, she was gone as, with an effortless nudge, her horse bolted forward through the pass. Rufus whistled after her, the breath torn from his lungs, and then he dug his heels into the mare's side and coaxed her after Fae.

Up ahead he saw flashes of the palomino bounding through the pathway, its white tail flying after it, like a flickering wil-o'-the-wisp guiding Rufus forward. He shouted joyfully, encouraging the mare on. Fae looked back at him, her hair whipping in the wind. He caught the sound of her laughter, free as air, and he wanted to reach it.

They raced after each other, Fae maintaining the lead by a few strides. The horse galloped so effortlessly below him, it was like flight, and for first time in so long, Rufus felt the weight lift from his body.

And then Fae was drawing to halt all too soon, and Rufus, breathless, joined her as the mountain pass opened up to the glorious sight beyond. Rufus, his head light from the ride, dropped his jaw and stared.

He'd seen it from a distance, spotted it on the road or from a hilltop a handful of times, but never before had he gotten close enough to smell the air and hear the crashing of the waves. The sea was infinitely vast and colourful—blues, white and green sparkling like a million jewels, shifting in endless motion. Rufus had only ever imagined such a sight, and it surpassed all of his expectations.

"I never tire of seeing your amazement—it's a source of constant delight," Fae said, and Rufus climbed down from the saddle and stood, staring out.

"Fae," he choked with wonder, "this is…this is…" He gestured dumbly.

"You mentioned in Sarrin one night that you'd never seen the sea for yourself. Joshua confirmed that remained the case, so I thought it was time to introduce you." Fae's expression softened as Rufus drew in a ragged breath, looking back over the water.

Fae had brought him to a rocky edge that jutted out twenty strides above the sea. A narrow, sandy path led down to a wide, spotless beach that looked so undisturbed it was like something from another world. And yet, the pale sand was familiar to Rufus, like he'd walked it before.

What was the significance of the beach? He'd asked himself that during one of his encounters with his subconscious. They'd met in such a place, and Rufus hadn't recalled or understood why it was so important.

It came to him now, like a wonderful childhood memory. Suddenly, Rufus was flooded with excitement.

As a boy, he'd always had an insatiable adoration for the adventurous tales of seafarers and explorers. He'd poured over the books with an imagination so vivid it felt like he was walking with the characters, touching the sand beneath their feet, savouring the cooling lick of the waves, and breathing the salty air. It had inspired his desire to travel, and Rufus had drawn map after map of his neighbouring countries, planning daring expeditions. The idea of the sea had always instilled a renewed sense of life, possibility and adventure. It held a promise that nothing was ever over, or predestined or impossible—that for those who strove against the tide, life could offer something new and astonishing in return.

Rufus didn't know when he'd lost that sense of curiosity and wonder, but somehow, in an instant, Fae had gifted it back to him, and he was speechless. It had been so long since he'd tasted hopefulness, in any form.

"The tenth day of Prospan." Joshua and Boyd appeared behind Fae, the Prince gleeful. "Or did you think I had forgotten your birthday?"

Rufus only stared, the words slow to process. "For me..." he eventually forced out, dumb still from awe. "All this...for me?"

"Of course." Boyd looked equally pleased with himself.

"It wasn't all a lie—several of Reilly's clan are visiting today,"

Fae said innocently. "But they wouldn't have dared touch you." Fae's smile elongated and Rufus fought back the sudden, great urge to burst into tears.

"Papa?" Joshua asked, his brow furrowed in concern. "Are you upset?"

Rufus couldn't speak, so instead he crossed to his brother and pulled him from the horse, into a tight embrace. He rocked the boy from side to side, holding him as close as he could before gently letting him go. And then, feeling as if he were hovering a foot about the ground, Rufus kicked off his shoes and took off toward the edge of the jagged rock.

"Rufus? *Rufus!*" Fae called urgently after him, but he couldn't be stopped. All at once he was a boy of ten again, sprinting along the cliff, his body in a constant state of pre-tumble as he drove his weight forward.

The edge came at him fast, the water crashing below. He could hear Boyd shouting after him now too, but there were no fear in Rufus's heart. He whooped and shouted, his hands in the air like a madman, until there was no ground beneath him and he leapt and dove into the churning water beneath

Even as he fell, he could feel the magic pulsing through him, and even without his command, the water rose up to greet and catch him, pulling him down into the depths. He sank like a stone, plunging, and then scrabbled with his arms and legs, pushing up to the surface. The current heaved around him, sending him tumbling, helpless against the force of the waves. He thrashed, and broke the surface for a quick breath, before another wave drove him down again, spinning him like driftwood. Rufus was powerless, but it exhilarated him, relieving him of all responsibility. As the sea took hold of his body, a hundred hands pulling him in all directions, he felt a relief he hadn't experienced in years. The water seemed to wash away everything, and this time, when he fought his way to the surface and broke through, Rufus was laughing. The salt stung his eyes, making the day a blur of blue and white. He could just see Fae, Joshua and Boyd all peering down at him.

"Are you *out of your mind*?" Boyd screamed, and Rufus laughed, harder than he had in years, the waves crashing against him. "Wait, Fae—FAE!"

Rufus heard a splash close by, and then Fae was swimming in his direction, flicking her wet hair from where it clung to her face.

"Lowly lord." She pushed through the weight of the water toward him. "Take my hand—I think you may be drowning."

Rufus, who could barely keep himself above the water for the force of his laughter, managed to peek his stinging eyes open once more and beam at her, tears streaming down his face. "Yes Fae," he reached for her as she came to his side, "I think I am."

The Knights' ambush of the alchemists had been a success, but after the battle, Brexiam, undiscovered as it was, had fallen into silent chaos. The proximity of the alchemists to their homes had warned them that, though they'd prevented it once, it wouldn't be long before the Kathraks finished licking their wounds and came back again. A bitter acceptance had fallen among the townspeople. They'd taken a few days to pack away their things and bury their dead.

"We could have used the Faucon," Luca murmured absentmindedly, as she packed away was what was left in the kitchen.

"The Faucon? Hah, they're too busy guzzling themselves dizzy these days. Always were unreliable," Ivar grunted, his arms crossed as Luca rolled her eyes. At the table, Nora Merle sat, her face drawn and eyes unseeing. She'd been like that most of the day, but for when she'd fed the children, where she'd forced a weary smile, as false as it was well-meaning. Luca crossed to her aunt, one hand on her hip, the other holding a ladle.

"If my mother could see you now, Aunty Nora, she'd be hysterical. You've not eaten a thing all day—you'll waste away. Please, take something, even a wee bit of stew, for my sake. The journey to Sarrin isn't long, but you'll need your strength."

"Leave her to it, Luca—she won't budge," Ivar yawned.

"Oh, I could just beat you!" Luca turned on him, her expression furious. "Get out. Get out and go be useful! You've stood there all morning, watching me work. Go—your wounds aren't so bad. I can't imagine the children have finished packing, go and help them."

"But I—" Ivar began, but Luca cut him off with a furious swipe of the ladle. "Ow!"

"Go, you useless man!" she ordered, and he fled the room, darting past Torin as he appeared in the doorway. Luca scowled after her lover and then slipped into a chair beside Nora, pouting dramatically. "And to think, you pulled him into this world. You should have left him in his mother's womb a little longer—he might have grown some balls."

Nora cracked her first smile, and Torin joined his wife, putting his arm around her. He kissed her on the temple.

"Nora, talk to me, please."

"I dreamt about Rufus this morning," Nora said softly, her voice small. "And when I woke, I'd forgotten…just for a moment I'd forgotten." She paused, and her eyes filled with tears, her arms tight around her stomach. "A mother's supposed to feel when her baby's gone, she's supposed to *feel* it inside. But I don't feel anything. Maybe if I was his real mother, maybe…maybe…"

Torin seized her at these words and she buried her face into his chest. "Don't you say that, my love," he scolded gently. "Never even think it. You were Rufus's mother as I was his father, and he never thought otherwise. He loved you. Never doubt that."

Nora sobbed and Torin kissed the top of her head, his own eyes watering. Luca stood, brushing her fingers over Torin's shoulder in condolence as she left the room.

At the doorway of the house, she removed her apron, throwing it over the banister and taking up her sword instead. She called up to the children to stay indoors and then left the house.

She walked to the stable, all but empty now with many of the Knights already gone. In the corner of the room, a set of guards stood vigilant. Behind them a figure shifted. His arms were chained behind his back, his legs bound together with rope. A gag had been forced across in his mouth. As Luca approached he looked up at her with tired, red-rimmed eyes. Luca felt no pity. He was an alchemist. They'd taken him prisoner for interrogation, but now his usefulness had run dry.

She dismissed the guards with a flick of her hand. The alchemist's eyes widened ever so lightly as the guards both silently left the stable. From behind, Luca heard footsteps, and Ivar appeared in the doorway, breathless from running after her.

He caught her arm. "What are you doing?"

"Cleaning up," she responded, and she saw the alchemist draw himself up rigid, his breathing uneven.

Ivar hesitated and then released her arm. He didn't have the strength to calm her rage, and Luca almost resented him when he turned away, and left her to her business.

Entering the Kathrak's makeshift cell, Luca did him the courtesy of ungagging him before drawing her sword.

The Kathrak spat the taste of leather from his mouth and sneered at her. "So the Betheanian whores clean up all their men's mess, do they?"

Luca ignored him, crouching down so that their eyes were level. She knew the smell of death well now, and for all the prisoner's sneers, by the sheen of sweat on his brow and the trembling of his body she could see he was afraid. "For a man so scared of death, you're foolishly inviting it."

"Does the bitch expect me to beg? Kill me first, heretic."

"I'm not a heretic."

"Delphi Knights, faerie scum—you're all the same, and soon

we'll wipe you out."

"Says the man on the losing side of the battle…" Luca looked down over the edge of her sword, judging it. She'd sharpened it dutifully after the battle, and it was ready to use again. It looked odd in her small hands, the claymore, but she'd learnt to wield it well.

"We caught the traitor Rufus Merle. We'll catch you too, soon enough."

Luca blinked slowly, turning the sword in her hands.

The Kathrak strained against his bonds. "Tell me, how did it feel? When you heard of his death—your leader? The rebellion's figurehead."

"Rufus wasn't our leader."

"No?" The Kathrak smiled, but his voice shook dangerously as Luca continued to judge her sword. "It won't hurt you then, to hear what we did to his corpse? That we cut it into pieces and put his head on the main gate for display? That we danced and pissed on his body, then strung it up around the city for the scavengers and birds." The Kathrak tittered. "By now, they'll have burnt down his house, and sent everything he ever touched up in flames. Harmatia will forever use the name Merle as an insult and a slur. But no, why would that concern you? He wasn't your leader."

"No." Luca's voice quivered. "He wasn't our leader. He was my first love."

The Kathrak froze.

"He was my friend." Luca's hands tightened around the hilt, and the alchemist drew back as far as he could. "He was my *family*," Luca seethed, her cheeks flaring red, "*and you bastards killed him!*"

The alchemist screamed in the last second as she swung her sword, and with a thud, it passed through his thick neck as easily as a wire through clay. Her blade hit the wall behind him with a crash. The alchemist's head rolled from his shoulders and Luca stood, heaving with anger. She pulled the sword free and stared down at her victim, her face contorted with tears. "I piss on you," she spat, and then turned and left, her dress sprayed with blood.

CHAPTER
33

❧

"Good evening," Rufus said.

Fae looked up from her book. Beside her, the candle flickered. The evening had drawn in quickly during their time at the beach, and so at last they'd returned to the Neve. Fae had washed and changed, then gone to the library, placing herself in Rufus's usual spot beneath the domed glass roof. It wasn't long before Rufus came to join her.

"May I sit with you? I'd like to talk to you about something."

He put his hand on a chair beside her. There was a looseness about him now, his once rigid shoulders low and relaxed. Though he'd clearly washed, the smell of the sea clung to him. It was pleasant.

Fae closed her book. "Please."

Rufus sat, and breathing deeply he clasped his hands together and set his eyes out into darkened library. "I'm not sure where to start." He tipped back his chair, so that it balanced precariously on two legs. "Harmatia," he decided. "In a few months, it'll have been thirteen years since I left. Most of the story, you know—it was a dark time for me. I'd lost my best friend, and I was angry and vengeful. Joshua and I travelled between the homes of

Knights of the Delphi, who housed and hid us." Rufus gave a wry smile. "When my absence, after several months, became too noticeable, the Magi began to send patrols after me. They were merely curious inquisitions—my master was being lenient. After a year, it became apparent I wasn't returning however, and the searches became more serious.

"We lived in various places in Harmatia for another few years, moving frequently. Eventually those searches stopped as well. After no word or sighting, perhaps they presumed me dead. I thought I was safe. We settled in Corhlam, in a small mining village in the south, and I met a Knight there. His name was Howell."

"And you fell in love with him?"

"He fell in love with me." Rufus allowed his chair to drop onto all four legs, "And I...I did. I loved him too. More every day. We lived together peacefully for some time. Then, someone passing through the village happened to recognise me, and the searches began again. Bigger, this time—worse. After eight years of absence, I was most definitely classed as a traitor. Worse than that, it wasn't my brethren searching for me anymore. The King hired alchemists, trained in the hunt. Among them was a man named Brandt DuGilles..."

Something of Rufus's composure seemed to darken. It was an unpleasant sight. They'd had a wonderful day, full of laughter and joy. Rufus hadn't stopped smiling throughout. To see his face turn now made Fae ache, but she didn't interrupt.

"We fled to Bethean, Howell coming with us. I was careful to cover my trail—we always used false names, and I passed Joshua off as my son. Despite this, DuGilles found me. I managed to escape, but it was very close." Rufus reached up to the scar around his eye, stroking it absentmindedly. "I knew then that we were in danger. DuGilles was ruthless, he was clever and he was obsessed with catching me..." Rufus drew off again, his eyes unseeing. Fae knew, inevitably, how the story would end.

"Joshua was eleven years old when they finally succeeded."
Rufus exhaled. "Honestly Fae, I thought they were only going
to drag me back to Harmatia. I planned to beg the King for
forgiveness. I'd tell them that I'd lost myself to my grief, and that
by the time I came to my senses, I was too frightened to step
forward…They all knew me to be a coward—I was certain I
could buy forgiveness.

"But DuGilles didn't take me to Harmatia. He brought me
to a dungeon and he—" Rufus broke off, and ran his hands
aggressively through his hair, gripping his fringe tightly.

"He tortured you," Fae finished for him.

"For days," Rufus said. "Weeks, maybe. I lost count. They…
they did things, Fae. Things I don't want to describe…They found
ways to drain me of power—I never thought it possible. Even my
ability not to burn…They suppressed it, and DuGilles branded
me. Like I belonged to him. They tore everything away from me,
Fae. And then…and then they…" Rufus hid his face in his hands.
The slick smell of sweat and fear was suddenly heavy in the air.

Fae put a hand to Rufus's shoulder. "Rufus, it's alright. You
don't need to say it, if you aren't ready."

"But I do," Rufus moaned. "I have to say it…"

Fae watched, helplessly, her whole chest aching. "You're safe
with me," she said, unable to offer anything else. The gods knew
Fae couldn't say the words for Rufus.

"There was a box," Rufus whispered. "It was a…a lightless,
soundless box, barely long enough to lie in. And they shut me
inside and buried me in it."

Of all the things Fae had expected, that wasn't it. She sat in
horrified silence, Rufus shaking beneath her hands.

"Oh Rufus," she eventually forced out, but there were no
words of comfort. "They buried you *alive*?"

Rufus's hands moved down to where Fae knew the brand was
seared into his flesh, and he held it. "At first, I was calm. After
the endless torture, it was almost a relief. But I couldn't see, or

hear, or feel, or smell anything. They gave me water occasionally through a small pipe, like I was an animal. But it was never enough, and it was always drugged with something that set my mind on fire. I began to lose myself, to go mad—can you imagine being separated from everything that lets you know you're alive? I was hungry, and weak, and sometimes it was so difficult to breathe I'd almost suffocate.

"There was no difference between waking and sleeping. It was just dark...painful...an endless hell. There was no relief. In the end the only thing that kept me alive was this." Rufus lifted the front of his shirt, showing her the brand again. "DuGilles told me I was one of his experiments—his own work of art. In that lightless, soundless hell I clung to the feeling of the brand burning into me, and I let it fuel my rage. I allowed hatred to fester with my wounds." Rufus dropped the shirt again, covering the awful burn. "I don't know how long I was in there before Howell and the other Knights found me. They were able to free me, carry me to safety...I don't remember it. I was very unwell for many weeks. They tended to me, nursed back to health. But my heart...That wasn't so easy to mend. When the alchemists found us again, I killed every single one that got close, and I damned well enjoyed it." Rufus turned away from her, heaving in several sharp, quick breaths, his face hidden in his hand.

Fae took his arm instinctually, trying to anchor him back into the room, away from his memories.

After a few moments, Rufus composed himself and turned back to her. His eyes were glassy, and he spoke very quietly. "I knew, after that day, that I could never be good again. My wrath was too great. My power, my affiliation with Athea—I can rain fire down from the sky, how can I ever be good?"

"Rufus, you know that's now true. You must know." Fae ran her hand up his arm to his neck, her thumb brushing against the stubble on his chin. His skin was warm and her hands were cold, but he moved into her touch ever so slightly. His expression was doubtful, as if he'd just caught her telling a lie.

"You know about Morrigan, don't you?" he asked.

Fae dropped her hand. "You can't blame Joshua for telling me—he was worried."

"I don't blame him. I'm only sorry he had to witness it." Rufus sighed, looking away again. The candle flickered as he reached over to it, running his hand slowly through the flame, deep in thought. "Morrigan wants me to join her, to embrace that growing part of me—to become what I was when I defeated Zachary on the road to Avalon. I have a feeling she's been planning it for some time. Until now I felt it was inevitable that I'd give in to her one day. It's in my nature, this darkness, and it's an ugly side of me, for which I need to atone if I'm ever to redefine my fate." Rufus breathed out heavily. "I've killed, Fae, and it wasn't in self-defence."

"The halfling?" Fae guessed.

Rufus looked up sharply. "Please tell me Joshua doesn't know about that."

"He mentioned something."

Rufus looked away. "I'd hoped he was too delirious to remember."

"Rufus," Fae asked cautiously. "Did...did this halfling rape you?"

Rufus didn't speak for a while. "We made a deal."

"Was it a deal or was it extortion?" Fae said, unconvinced. Rufus hunched his shoulders, looking uneasy.

"He betrayed me," was all Rufus said. "He called the magistrate. And I...I lost myself. I killed him...so horrifically. I was like a man possessed."

"That's exactly what you were." Fae pursed her lips. "Rufus, regardless of whether he deserved it or not, Morrigan is to blame for the halfling's death—not you."

"She wasn't controlling me."

"No, I know she wasn't." Fae leant in. "But even so, she's

powerful and she's poisonous. Joshua saw it—her presence has lingered on you since your first encounter. It was her influence that drove you to the act. It's been her influence feeding your rage and fear all this time. Nothing short of desperation would have led you to it otherwise, I believe that."

"That doesn't excuse it." Rufus tugged at his fringe. "Even if Morrigan affected me, even if I was sick, and driven by fear, I still murdered an unarmed man." He dropped his hands, looking searchingly into Fae's eyes. "But that doesn't mean I'm destined to do it again," he said, with a quiet intensity. "Today, you showed me that. What I've done doesn't have to mark the beginning of my descent into darkness. I touched something unspeakably evil within me—a desire to reap havoc and revenge on the whole world, but I'm still capable of love. I can still forgive. I can still hope." He reached forward and tucked a strand of Fae's hair behind her ear. Fae didn't move a muscle. "I have to believe that I can be good again. That this doesn't all end in blood and fire…" Rufus mouth twitched slightly in small, but earnest smile. "Until now, I was too afraid to trust anybody with this truth—afraid they would confirm what I feared. I pushed Howell away, refused to let anybody else get close. But you know me. Somehow, after a decade, you still *know* me. So if you're willing to fight for a damned man," his voice trembled, "I can't do this alone anymore."

Fae rose and taking him by the back of the head, she pulled him gently toward her, resting his cheek against her stomach. He wrapped his arms around her waist, and she could hear his heart slow at the touch of her fingers, stroking his hair. Fae realised just how much she'd missed him all those years.

"You have endured so much." She leant down and kissed the top of his head. "But now you're here, and I promise you, I will do everything in my power to keep you safe. You're not alone." She released him and stepped back, kneeling down so that he could see the sincerity in her face. "You're not alone," she repeated and Rufus closed his eyes, and dropped his head, resting his forehead against hers.

"Thank you, Fae," he replied, and their voices echoed in the vast library which lay, long forgotten, beyond the tiny spectrum of candle light.

CHAPTER 34

Getting past the guards proved easy enough, not that Béatrice had anticipated trouble. A little gold, a quick distraction, and she was down in the dankest part of the castle, keys in hand, outside the cell.

"DuGilles has yet to claim you. You are very fortunate," she purred to the prisoner inside, who jumped, pushing himself against the back wall. He hadn't heard her approach. Béatrice held up the keys and unlocked the door, stepping back to allow him out. "Be assured, Howell," she said, "I am here to help."

He eyed her distrustfully, not moving. His face was slick with sweat, and there was dried blood still around his mouth.

Béatrice was sympathetic, but not particularly patient. She tapped her foot. "You may remain in the cell if you wish," she turned away, "but unless you come with me in the next minute, I will lock the door again, and leave you to DuGilles. You, I suspect, know just of what he is capable."

Howell hesitated, then strode out. He tried to speak, but without a tongue, his words were mangled and painful.

"My name is Béatrice Hathely," Béatrice said, decoding his grunts. "And non—I am not a Knight of the Delphi." She came forward and unbound the shackles around his wrists. "But I know about the Prince."

Howell grew still. He was much bigger than Béatrice and could easily overpower her, if he chose. Béatrice wasn't deterred. She wasn't frightened of anybody.

"Did you honestly think that all of the Harmatians were happy with their Puppet King?" she tutted, throwing the shackles into the empty cell.

Howell tried to speak again, fighting to make himself understood. Béatrice was able to make out the gist of his question.

"Let us say I have a very informative friend." Béatrice looked past Howell to a shrouded figure who hid in the shadows.

Howell, sensing the other presence, turned rapidly, raising his arms as if ready for a fight.

"Do not look too closely at him," Béatrice warned. "He is a frightfully handsome man, and I sense that is rather your flavour of choice."

The shrouded figure bowed. "Sir Howell," he greeted, "my name is Embarr Reagon, and if you are willing, I shall be escorting you out of this dark city tonight."

Howell froze on the spot, Embarr's luscious tone sinking over them both. The Corlavite uttered something in surprise.

"Yes, he is a Gancanagh," Béatrice said. "And, so too, the personal spy of the Sidhe goddess, Niamh." Béatrice gave Howell a small, consoling pat on the arm. "Do not fret your pretty little head—he will not feed on you unless you ask him nicely."

"My gracious Lady Niamh has heard you have a great gift for weaving songs and tales." Embarr moved a little more out of the shadows, ignore Béatrice's teasing. "She would like to extend a most honourable invitation, and offer you a place as her personal bard, should you be willing."

Howell raised an eyebrow, and then gave a sodden laugh. He pointed to his tongue-less mouth with a shake of his head. For all his bravery in the face of Sverrin's punishment, there was a defeated slump to Howell's shoulders now.

Embarr took another step forward. "Have faith," he said, in an even softer, more soothing voice. "My Lady Niamh rewards those who serve her. Do so honestly, and you will reclaim all that has been lost to you."

Howell stared hard at Embarr's extended hand. When he didn't immediately take it, Béatrice clasped the Corlavite's fingers in her own, knocking his elbow.

"There is nothing for you here. The rebellion will survive without you—you have played your part, and you have done it beautifully. Look now to your new life."

Howell frowned deeply, and then reached across and took the Gancanagh's extended hand. He attempted to say the faerie's name.

"Yes, one in the very same," Embarr said. "Perhaps Rufus Merle spoke of me?"

Howell hung his head, and gave a small nod.

Béatrice turned to where she'd dropped a bundle of clothes and, unravelling it, she passed Howell a cloak and a new chemise to replace the blood spattered one he wore. "You should make yourself presentable. As I understand, Niamh prefers the pretty things in life."

"Where?" Howell managed to say.

"I shall be spiriting you to a harbour on the fair shores of Avalon, where a silver ship will take you straight to the blessed isle of Tír na nÓg," Embarr said. "My Lady Niamh is already expecting you."

Howell nodded in thanks and then turned away to change. Embarr moved back into the shadows, Béatrice watching him curiously. As Howell removed his clothes, she dared to step closer to the Embarr. She liked to push her limitations around him. One day, she hoped to overcome his lustful toxicity entirely, but for now she could tolerate it.

"You must be well fed, to be able to transport yourself and

another over such a distance."

"I am deep within the Kathrak court—they are not short of easy prey." Embarr didn't look her in the face, but Béatrice knew this was out of a respect for her, rather than indifference. He sniffed. "They caught him, you know."

"Who?" Béatrice feigned ignorance.

"Béatrice," Embarr sounded serious, a rarity onto itself. "He's dying. Isaac arrived in Sigel'eg today and is doing everything in his meagre power to free him, but you and I both know Varyn is not going last much longer."

Béatrice kept her expression the same, blinking prettily. Her emotions wouldn't serve her in this instance, so she pushed them away. "What do you expect me to do?"

"You should at least come and see him."

"And why would I do that? The journey to Sigel'eg is long and tiresome, and if you tried to spirit me away, they would take my sudden disappearance as kidnapping or treachery. I am not inclined to either."

"You have caused this," Embarr said simply. "It is not my place to judge you on that…But if you insist on killing him, Béatrice, you should look him in the face while you do it." Embarr examined his bluish hands, turning them over.

"I did," Béatrice dismissed. "The day I laid the curse on him—I said it directly to him. Looked him straight in the eye."

Embarr laughed brusquely, causing both Howell and Béatrice to jump, though she suppressed the lightning bolt of pleasure it sent down her spine to the pit of her stomach.

"Of course you did," Embarr purred, "and even despite that, he still loves you."

"How does that concern me?"

Embarr made a soft, strangely endearing clucking sound. "At the very least, do you not think you owe it to him to tell him that he has a daughter?"

Béatrice was quiet. In the castle above her, her sweet Morelle would be fast asleep now, in the keep of her disgruntled Uncle Marcel. The thought of Varyn's daughter—*their* daughter— made Béatrice take pause and stirred unwanted feelings through her.

Embarr knew he'd struck a chord, but Béatrice maintained her air of indifference.

"I will think on it," she said.

"I will see you in Sigel'eg." The corner of Embarr's smile was just visible from beneath his hood. "Sir Howell, are you ready to flee from this terrible nest?"

Howell nodded.

"Then we shall. Béatrice, be well," Embarr said, and stepping forward he clasped Howell in a tight embrace.

"Best of luck," Béatrice said, and Howell managed to smile before an explosion of air informed Béatrice that they were gone. She covered her eyes to avoid the dust, and then stood in the empty dungeon as it settled. Alone, she allowed some of her vivacity to fade, her expression turning to something much more resemblant of her brother Marcel's.

How she would make her excuses to go to Sigel'eg she wasn't yet sure, but Béatrice was confident an idea would come to her by dawn.

～➳～

"Didn't I tell you not sex my body while I was shut-eyed?" Aeron demanded furiously, looking down at Emerald, who was curled, half-naked, around him.

"You lie in my bed, you become my pillow," was her easy reply. "Besides—you were startin' to smell. Thought I'd get one last night in, before I tossed you out."

"Bone-rapist," Aeron grumbled, stretching his stiff limbs. Few humans could claim to know the ache of rigor mortis, but Aeron was increasingly accustomed to it.

Emerald stroked a hand down his chest. "You aren't so different animated."

364

"Now you're just puttin' salt on the slug." Aeron closed his eyes. He was exhausted. He'd been trained from a young age to withstand great tortures, but Nicnivin was difficult to please. For the information she gave, she'd demanded immediate payment in a form that was unbefitting of her choice of currency.

"Did she drain you?" Emerald asked, rolling so that she was atop Aeron. Even though no physical bones in his body had been broken, he felt as if his pelvis was shattered, and hips cracked in two.

"Rah." Aeron tried to push Emerald off, but was unable to lift his arms off the bed.

"Better've been worth the price."

"It wasn't a pit." Aeron coughed. "I sexed out what I needed. Merle is up on the spattered peaks of the Neve, still pulsin'. For now."

"Ooh," Emerald said, almost sounding impressed. "That's a trek and a half." She poked Aeron hard in the stomach. His body was rejecting his shattered soul, and every sensation was painful beyond belief. "I can't imagine you'll be makin' it any time soon."

"I'll recover, and when I do..." Aeron paused and took a long sniff of the air. "Did I golden arc my flowers down south?"

"What?" Emerald sat up and Aeron looked down.

"Did I piss myself?"

"Oh. Yes. Several times."

"Piss-pox and plagues." The assassin allowed his head to fall back against the pillow. "The lashes I take for that whoopsie-basher...I'm lickin' to give him a good skull-thrust for this."

"I thought the Unseelie Queen tired you out." Emerald retook her position at his side, unmindful of how painful her extra weight was. "But I suppose it's anythin' that screams and fights back with you, isn't it?"

"At least mine pulses."

"Mine don't complain."

"Mine can brain what I'm doing to them."

"Mine don't leave a mess."

"I don't leave a mess." Aeron looked down at her, his brow lowered.

"Hah! Says the man who's been pissin' blood on himself like a nervous dog for days now." She patted his stomach. "There, there—I changed the baby, don't cry."

"Baby's kidneys feel like they're leechin' his spine," was the gargled response. "I've been dead too long—Nicnivin was thorough. I need to recover."

"Want me to send a message to Lemra?"

"Rah." Aeron coughed again, the taste metallic. "Tell'em Merle's still twitchin' and that I'll get to him and the boy quick enough."

"S'no rush—the alchemists aren't huntin' him anymore. The world thinks he's dead," Emerald said. "Your work's as good as done."

"I couldn't give a head-screw 'bout the alchemists—bunch of unplucked griffons swingin' wooden swords. It's Morrigan who's playing the lute now."

"You honestly think Nicnivin is just plannin' to let Morrigan do what she wants?"

"Nicnivin will sit, spread on her throne without a lip-bite, for a thousand beats if she gets her way, and Morrigan knows all about Embarrette being Niamh's little spy. It's not a power struggle—it'll be a clean exchange." Aeron tried to twitch his fingers, checking that none of his appendages had become paralysed in his absence. "This is danker than we thought. If Merle succumbs to Morrigan's lust, we're *all* through." Aeron closed his eyes and gave a lazy sigh. "And on that note, sew your mouth. I'm blinkin' off."

"Baby still smells."

"Baby'll throttle you in a minute."

"Baby's welcome to try." Emerald kissed his brow. "Sleep."

Aeron grunted and drifted into a satisfyingly sexless slumber.

CHAPTER
35

"Rufus." Fae tapped the top of his book, tipping it down so she could see his face. "It's time."

"Alright." Rufus nodded, snapping his book shut and standing with a great air of authority. "Sweet Athea—*what's that?*" he gasped, pointing over Fae's shoulder. Fae looked around, and Rufus darted away, fleeing for the door.

Quick as a lightening, Fae hooked two fingers into his collar and dragged him back. "Try to think of them as my parents rather than the Lord and Lady of the Neve," she suggested as he whimpered, trying to wriggle free.

"Fae," Rufus ceased his struggling, "the first time I met you, you single-handedly faced off a group of vicious bandits and then tried to throttle me to death. I beseech you—consider carefully the wholeheartedly remarkable and petrifying impression you have left on me, and then multiply it by two, and you'll have some idea how I feel about meeting your parents."

Fae laughed and pulled him along, looping her arm through his. "You have faced Korrick and Reilly. My parents actually welcomed you into the Neve. You have nothing to fear from them."

"I always fear the people I respect. It's why I'm terrified of you."

Fae snorted. "Your flattery won't get you out of this, my lowly lord."

"I had to try."

They walked together down the corridor, arm in arm, and Fae could feel by the sureness of his grip that Rufus was glad she was with him. Kathel by reputation was intimidating enough among both Seelie and Unseelie Courts, but to a Magi, the prospect of an audience must have been terrifying.

As they walked, Fae felt a tingle down the back of her neck. She looked over her shoulder to spot her younger brother Eadoin watching them from a long way down the hall. Fae met his gaze, and he narrowed his eyes and sneered with disgust, turning and marching away.

Fae sighed.

"One of your brothers?"

"Eadoin—yes. He and his twin Arton were once very close to me."

"They still resent you for bringing me here?" Rufus asked softly, and Fae tried to appear nonchalant. As willing as she was to bear the consequence of her actions, she'd grown tired of the cold reception from everyone in the Neve. Should Rufus's meeting with her parents go well, Fae hoped that her brothers would start to veer more toward the opinion of their father and mother, than Reilly, who'd done everything in his power to stir trouble.

"They don't know you." Fae squeezed Rufus's hand. "And perhaps they have forgotten me a little."

Fae led Rufus down into one of the inner gardens. It was a quiet little sanctuary away from the training grounds, where a large fountain bubbled, and an array of flowers had begun to push through, attracting bees and butterflies.

There, her mother and father sat together on a marble bench, hand in hand, their shoulders lightly touching. Rufus faulted in his step, and Fae saw his eyes dart over the pair, analysing them.

Her parents had done Rufus the courtesy of not carrying any weapons with them. Indeed, neither were even wearing armour, dressed comfortably instead, her father in a tunic, and her mother in a long white dress. Fae was surprised to see that her mother's long, pale hair had even been released from its usual plait, and was curled slightly, cascading down her back and shoulders. Both parents were smiling.

They weren't alone either—Kael and Joshua were with them already, deep in conversation. Kathel looked up as they approached, his green eyes sparkling.

"Ah—my eldest daughter and our honoured Magi guest." He ushered them forward, and Fae felt oddly relieved at his warm reception. "Allow me to introduce my wife, Saraid."

Rufus bowed deeply. "It's an honour to make your acquaintance."

"It is we who are honoured." Saraid bowed her own head, and Fae watched for her mother's reaction. Kathel might have approved of Rufus, but Saraid's opinion almost mattered more. Saraid smiled, but there was a quiet reservation in her eyes. "My daughter has spoken very highly of you."

"I can't imagine why." Rufus gave Fae a sidelong glance, and Fae realised that she'd grown as still as him. It hadn't occurred to her that she might be as nervous about the introduction as Rufus was.

"Rufus." Joshua bounced up, his face bright. "You remember Kael, don't you?"

"Ah yes—the renegade from the tree. How do you do, Kael? You've been taking care of my brother, I hear. You have my thanks." Rufus lowered himself to his knees so that he was at eye-level with Kael. Kael eyed him shyly, and then came forward and accepted his hand, shaking it. Fae spotted her mother give a slim smile of approval, and felt a flare of triumph.

"You look just like your sister," Rufus noted to Kael, who flashed a big smile up at Fae, pleased by the comment.

"One day, I'll be even better than her," she announced. Fae scoffed as Rufus peered around, his eyebrows raised.

"You have a rival."

"Don't I know it?" Fae seized Kael and pulled the girl onto her lap. Kael giggled and then settled against Fae, though at eight years old, and near Joshua's size, she was really getting far too big. Sometimes Fae wished that Cat Sidhe children didn't grow so fast.

"I must say, Lord Merle—" Kathel began, but was interrupted.

"Rufus, please," Rufus implored, taking a seat beside Fae, Joshua coming to sit on his other side. "I'm far from being a lord here."

"Rufus," Kathel corrected. He'd always liked humble men. "You seem much recovered. Both you, and the Prince."

"Your hospitality has ensured a speedy recovery." Rufus bowed his head again, and Fae chuckled to herself. He was going to get a stiff neck.

"I doubt that's the key to it," Kathel dismissed. "You are a resilient man, by all accounts. Combining that with the skills of the Physician Dacey, and my daughter's controversial methods of comfort, you look much better than when I last saw you." Kathel fought back a smile. "Raving like a madman."

"Yes," Rufus laughed nervously. "I apologise for that."

"No need," Kathel chuckled. "My days as a soldier have long passed, and I have spent the last century on this mountain top, very happily with my wife." He patted Saraid's knee. "That being said, when you live as long as we do, life can get fairly repetitive. Your arrival caused something of an unexpected stir, and I confess to being quite excited by what may follow."

"Rufus causes a stir wherever he goes," Joshua said proudly.

"Don't say that, you'll make them think I'm a trouble-maker," Rufus begged playfully.

"You are a trouble-maker." Fae shrugged and Rufus gave her a helpless look. Fae laughed at his expression, and then quickly caught herself as she became aware that both of her parents were watching her carefully. She'd been so focused on seeing their reactions to Rufus, she'd forgotten that she, too, would be watched.

"There are many stories about you, Rufus," Saraid said. "We've heard tales throughout the land of a man imbued with extraordinary powers."

"Yes, I've heard them too," Rufus said. "A lot of nonsense for the most part—that I can control the weather, eat men alive, and that I'm a necromancer who bathes in the blood of children," he said dramatically, giving Joshua and Kael a ghoulish look and making them giggle.

"I have a question for you." Saraid sat forward, and Fae felt her heart grow still. Her mother's blue eyes were intense and focused, as any interrogator. "Tell me, why are you trying to change the world?"

Rufus blinked, taken aback. "I'm not sure that I am."

"But you are," Saraid insisted, her tone firm. Her expression was serious. "Harmatia brought their Prince back from the dead and crowned him, and now you are the figurehead of a revolution that will affect the whole continent."

Rufus frowned deeply. "It's Harmatian politics."

"Harmatia is entangled with Bethean and Kathra, who are in turn nations tied to Avalon and countries over the sea. Your revolution will cause ripples throughout all."

Rufus didn't speak a while, pondering. He exchanged a look with Joshua before finally replying, "You're right. Our actions will have a great effect beyond Harmatia, and I have no way of knowing what the full repercussions of that could be. All I know is that we are fighting for the freedom of our people, and can only do what we believe to be right."

Saraid settled back, seemingly unimpressed by his response.

"That is an arrogant game."

"It's a human game," Rufus replied. "We have a saying in the Magi: brothers fight, we even kill, but against a common foe, we will unite. I believe that of the people of Harmatia, and of Bethean and Kathra."

"Then who is your common foe?"

"Tyranny." Rufus exchanged another look with Joshua who nodded his head in agreement.

Saraid clasped her hands together. "Then your war is idealistic?"

"Idealistic implies that it's unattainable, and perhaps if we consider it wholly, it may appear so." Rufus held her gaze steadily. "All I know, is that the foundation of Harmatia was built on an alliance between the Delphi and Harmatians. King Thestian married Éliane of the Delphi to unify the two families once and for all. Joshua is the final product of that—the son of the founding families, and the rightful heir."

"So it is lineage that makes your cause right?"

"No, but lineage gives it power." Rufus shrugged. "What makes our cause right is that a dead man is ruling Harmatia, and he's doing it badly."

Fae snorted, and Saraid's eyes snapped to her daughter. Fae disguised the sound, looking away innocently.

"And you think this boy will do better?" Saraid gestured to Joshua, her voice now more curious than accusatory.

"Saraid," Kathel appealed, "is this interrogation really necessary?"

"I am curious," Saraid said. "I want to know what manner of people my daughters have befriended. I have met revolutionaries before. I want to know what they think marks *them* as any different."

"I'll be a better ruler than my brother, Sverrin," Joshua spoke up, his voice quiet but firm, "because I am willing to be challenged. Sverrin doesn't realise the damage he causes, because

372

he hides behind a wall of courtiers who justify his tyranny, and punishes those who disagree with him. His trade restrictions, his suffocating tax have left the poorest of my people with nothing—no money, or food, or hope. They're starving, but if Sverrin can't see them, why should he believe or care about their suffering?" Joshua dropped his gaze, and in an instant he looked more like Jionat than Fae had ever seen. There was something sad in Joshua's wisdom. "If there's anything my brothers have taught me, it's that the greatness of a ruler is not measured in the ability to swing a sword, but in the ability to seek truth, and heed the advice of others. It is good to be decisive, but it is better still be decisive and informed.

"I'm only a boy, I know, and I'm not ready to rule yet, but my life has been devoted to learning how. I know it won't be easy, but we—together—have to try and be better than our forefathers, otherwise how can we hope for anything to ever change?" Joshua looked up at Rufus, and his brother's expression was filled with a fierce pride.

Fae felt it too, welling up inside of her—she couldn't speak for the King of Harmatia, or Éliane of the Delphi, but she knew that Jionat would have been immensely proud of Joshua for his wise words.

"Well, Saraid?" Kathel smiled, looking at his wife.

Saraid settled back onto the bench, apparently satisfied. "I think I understand why Fae is so taken by you both," she decreed. "You have raised a profound little boy, Rufus."

"I can take no credit for that." Rufus ruffled Joshua's hair, the Prince batting away his hand.

"I rather think you can," Saraid smiled knowingly, "for the son will echo the philosophy of the father."

"And also the ambition," Kathel put in, "which is good—young people *should* be ambitious. We should never settle just for what we are—it is life's meaning to strive for better." Kathel looked past Rufus to Fae, who squirmed at the unspoken implication of his words. Rufus caught the exchange, and Fae saw him frown deeply.

"Father," Kael interrupted them, "Korrick will be expecting us back. He's going to teach us how to kill a man with our bare hands today."

"Well," Rufus said tightly, Joshua jumping to his feet, "we wouldn't want to get into the way of that…"

"Go on then," Saraid leant forward to kiss her youngest daughter as she ran past, "and see to it Korrick does not work you too hard, or else I will have words with him. He is not yet too old to be scolded by his mother."

Kael giggled, waiting for Joshua, who bowed respectfully to Kathel and Saraid before running after his friend. As the children disappeared, Kathel and Saraid also rose.

"Thank you for meeting us, Rufus," Kathel said. "This has been an informative discussion—I should be glad to continue it some time."

"If I might," Rufus also stood, his hands twisted nervously into his chemise. "I owe you a debt of gratitude, and I owe one, even greater, to your daughter." He swallowed as Fae also stood slowly. "She saved my life, in more ways than one. I know that my presence here has caused her some difficulties in the Neve—"

"Rufus, you don't—" Fae tried to interject, but Rufus continued.

"I'm conscious of it. When we first met, your daughter had no reason to trust me, and yet she's now the greatest of my friends. Her sacrifice, her nobility," again, Rufus caught her eye, and smiled softly, "her abundance of kindness…Without her, I don't want to know who I would've been. She's an inspiration to me, and I can only imagine how immeasurably proud you must be of her."

Saraid and Kathel both grew very still, as taken back by this declaration as Fae. Then, the pair gave each other a knowing look.

"Yes, we are." Kathel reached over and squeezed Fae's hand,

his bright green eyes sparkling. He winked at her, and then he and Saraid both bowed their goodbyes, and moved off, hand in hand.

Rufus waited until they were gone before sinking back onto the bench with a ragged huff.

Fae flopped down beside him. "You didn't have to say that," she muttered, her face flushed. "...Thank you."

Rufus gazed off into the garden. "Our relationships with our parents can be complicated. Sometimes they can have ideas about what's right for you and who you ought to be, without consulting you about it first."

Fae gave a shaky laugh. "Yes, that's a good summary of it."

"If it in any way comforts you," Rufus kept his attention focused on the other side of the garden, "I think the person you are is more impressive than anything they might have conceived."

"You don't know what they conceived."

"I don't need to," Rufus said. "I know *you*."

It had taken some argument and a few bribes before Isaac was allowed into the dungeons to see him, but with Embarr Reagon's assistance, they'd managed between them. What greeted the young Magi was worse than he'd imagined.

Isaac had known Varyn for well over seventeen years. They were the firmest of friends despite their differences, and the sight of the Hunter slumped against the dungeon walls, soiled and half-starved, was almost too much to bear. The servants said Varyn hadn't eaten or drunk anything for days, and he was slowly wasting away. Isaac knelt at his side, unmindful of the filth, and held a cup to his friend's lips.

"Come. Drink something, my friend," he begged. He tipped the wooden goblet against Varyn's mouth, cool water dribbling down the sides of his slacked face. "You need to regain your strength, you're not well."

Isaac clamped the Hunter's chin between his fingers and forced the water into Varyn's mouth in small, considerate sips. Varyn choked and spluttered, his head rocking backward as he was released. Isaac propped him gently against the wall again, scanning his face desperately. Finally, unable to bear the silence, Isaac seized the dried bread left for Varyn that morning.

"You haven't eaten. Is it too hard? I can soften if you like, I can chew it for you—please, Varyn, tell me what you need."

Varyn shifted and groaned.

"Varyn? Varyn, what? What is it?" Isaac leant in as the Hunter exhaled, shuddering with the effort. "What? What are you trying to say?" Isaac whispered. He put his ear to Varyn's mouth and strained to hear the words. Unable to discern anything from the muffled breaths and pants, he drew back and concentrated on Varyn's lips, trying to distinguish their twitches into a coherent movement. The rasping continued, singular and painful.

Isaac drew back with dismay. A cold sweat erupted down his body as Varyn's head, once more unsupported, dropped forward again. Isaac stared at him, his own breathing stifled. He couldn't make out words through the breathy gasps, not because they were unintelligible, but because Varyn wasn't trying to speak.

He was screaming.

CHAPTER
36

~⚮~

"Is this really necessary, Arlen?" Belphegore exhaled wearily, as Zachary drew his blade.

"Yes. Draw." Zachary moved into a fighting stance, his left hand behind his back, sword extended.

"You have bested me three times already. I sense the outcome of this next match is already fairly conclusive." Belphegore complied all the same, raising his sword.

"Nothing is certain." Zachary lunged forward, striking at his master's chest. Belphegore parried the blow, their weapons meeting with a familiar clash. But even as Belphegore fought, there was no enthusiasm, and after a brief exchange, Zachary was able to move around and slide his steel below his master's guard.

"Another victory," Belphegore congratulated.

"You let me win," Zachary said.

"Arlen," Belphegore chuckled, "your skills with the sword have long outmatched mine. By the might of Penthar, you defeated the Royal Master-at-Arms when you were only twenty."

"That was an accident," Zachary muttered, throwing the training sword to the side with a grunt. "And did you never duel with your master, even when you surpassed him?"

Belphegore paused, and something strange flickered over his expression. "Only once," he said, mysteriously. Zachary should have known better than to expect a real response.

Belphegore very rarely spoke about his master, Horatio of the Delphi. Once, Zachary had asked what Horatio had been like. Belphegore hadn't been particularly forthcoming, rattling off a list of facts about how Horatio had built the Great Library, and founded the first Magi academy. When Zachary asked after his character, Belphegore had grown quiet and then simply said:

"It was the way, back then, to apprentice us as children. The Magi were not only masters in teaching, but in life. I did his bidding, day and night, for years, and in exchange I learnt everything I needed to surpass him."

Zachary had never raised the subject again. Needless to say, he'd sensed the relationship hadn't been a good one.

"I cannot think what has put you in such an aggressive mood." Belphegore took a towel from the table nearby and wiped his face.

"I only wanted to train—my sword has been neglected," Zachary muttered.

Belphegore raised an eyebrow, catching the lie. The day Zachary neglected his sword was the day he neglected to breathe. "I do sometimes wish," he said, with a sigh, "that you would be more forthcoming with me. I cannot read your mind, Arlen, but something is clearly troubling you."

Zachary wiped his face with a towel. A part of him had been desperate to tell Belphegore about DuGilles's experiments. Another part had been too terrified by the possibility that Belphegore already knew. Either way, Zachary kept his peace, bound by the unspoken threat. He turned his back on his master.

"It's almost noon, I must go."

"You have a duty?"

"Not for another hour. I am accompanying Béatrice to Helena's Fort. She is going to Sigel'eg to see King Bozidar."

"I have not heard anything about this." Belphegore frowned.

"Sverrin has been talking of finding a Kathrak wife. Béatrice suggested going as his envoy to scout for plausible candidates..." Zachary trailed off. "Apparently."

Belphegore narrowed his eyes. "You think she may her own objective?"

"I think Béatrice always has her own objective," Zachary admitted, shrugging. "But it doesn't matter. I am merely her guard for the first leg of the journey. Before I left, however, I felt it prudent to meet with my men."

"The Night Patrol?" Belphegore lowered his voice. Zachary could have told him not to bother with the secrecy—after the incident in the Southern Quarters, everyone in the capital knew who and what he was.

"There were a few matters I wanted to discuss with them, before I left," Zachary said.

"Of what nature?"

"Oh, the mundane."

"You are being very secretive, Arlen."

"It's become the general theme in the city." Zachary reached across the table and poured himself a glass of water from the earthenware jug.

Belphegore watched him steadily.

"What would you do?" Zachary eventually asked, putting down the glass. "In my position?"

"What exactly *is* your position?" Belphegore folded his arms.

Zachary shook off the question, unwilling to divulge any more.

"Arlen," his master began carefully, "do you owe money to somebody?"

"Excuse me?"

"I recognise that expression—men who have played one too many hands at the card table and found their pockets to be shallower than they anticipated."

Zachary laughed. "Yes, I suppose I have, in a manner of speaking."

He'd brought a man back from the dead—if that wasn't a dangerous wager against the gods, Zachary didn't know what to call it.

"If you require financial aid from me, I can lend." Belphegore frowned. "Though I never pictured you as a gambling man."

"And yet you're so quick to assume..." Zachary grinned tightly. "No, I am possessed of more riches than sense. It's not the card table that I lost my fortune to—at least not the literal one." He leant back against the table.

"That tiredness you spoke of before," Belphegore said, and Zachary winced, drawn back to the rooftop and their discussion. "Does it persist?"

"I am getting too old to go to bed at sunrise."

"Perhaps you should speak with the head of the Healing sector?"

"Edwin's apprentice? No."

"Arlen," Belphegore tsked.

"I don't like him, and I don't trust him," Zachary snubbed. "By the by, I need to be off. Thank you for the training, Master." He bowed, and then, seizing his robe, threw it over his shoulders and left before Belphegore could object.

Exiting the castle, he took off toward the Magi academy and was so deep in thought that, as he turned a corner, he almost collided with Daniel coming the other way.

"Damn it, Daniel," Zachary barked, and his little brother jumped back, surprised.

"Arlen."

It was the first time Zachary had ever heard the boy call him by name. What was more, he was smiling—something Zachary had never seen at all.

"I was looking for you." Daniel beamed. "Our father has replied." He held up the letter, Zachary's stomach plummeting.

"What does Rivalen say?" he asked wearily. "And summarise—I have somewhere to be."

"He's agreed to let my mother visit," Daniel said brightly.

Zachary slumped. "Of course he did."

Daniel deflated, frowning. "You suggested it," he reminded defensively. "Insisted, in fact."

"Because I thought he would deny me," Zachary grunted.

"I don't understand." All of the glow in Daniel's cheeks seeped away, and Zachary was almost sorry to have chased it off. "You don't want my mother to visit, so you agreed to it under the assumption our father would refuse?"

"Oh, good, you understand. Small blessings." Zachary pushed past his brother. "Summon your mother then. If I revoke the invitation now, Rivalen will only take it as his victory. Better I see this through."

"What *are* you talking about?" Daniel demanded, his smile now gone.

"I am leaving Harmatia." Zachary stalked away, waving behind him. "Tell Mrs Benson I may be some time. Goodbye forever, Daniel."

"Wait, Arlen—what?" Daniel shouted after him as Zachary dodged all responsibility and stepped into the academy. His mood was now even worse. He felt appalling enough without having to face Isolde for the first time in twenty years, but there was no point worrying about that now. He would just have to take it in his stride, cursing loudly as he went.

Lord Rothschild, ever eager to please, was the first to greet Zachary as he stepped into the meeting room. Zachary gave him a cheerless nod and looked around. He was the last to arrive.

Emeric sat in the corner, still bandaged, with Marcel, who was for once without his pipe. The pair looked utterly forlorn, and as tired as Zachary felt. In fact, the energy of the whole room was sombre, the men now watching him with tense expressions, a hush falling over them.

Zachary cleared his throat. "My friends," he began, "it is with regret that I come today to inform you, that as of now I will be stepping down from my duties as captain of the Night Patrol." He clasped his hands and looked down to his feet, trying to keep a straight face at the sounds of inhalation. "I have done everything in my power to delay this, but I am afraid that the yearning within me is too strong. I will shortly be retiring to the Myrithian forest to follow my brother's example, and become a half-blind, one-legged necromancer."

There was pause and in the corner, Marcel settled back into his seat with a quiet huff. A small spatter of laughter spread through the room. Zachary continued, his expression serious.

"In my absence, my housekeeper Heather Benson will fulfil my role as captain. She's near enough seventy, but energetic for her age so I am sure she will do nicely."

This earned a few more laughs, and the mood relaxed.

Zachary folded his arms, sniffing. "In other news, Merle's headless corpse is somehow still causing concern among our Kathrak guests, so be warned—they may try to set something on-fire. For some reason it puts them at ease."

The laughter was louder this time, and Zachary shrugged, ignoring Emeric's wince. He knew his subordinate thought it too early to joke in good humour about Rufus, but Zachary couldn't afford to mourn.

"To prevent further panic, the King, in his wisdom, has taken special precautions to ensure that Merle's body is inaccessible in its complete form—just in-case he tries to reanimate himself. Incidentally," Zachary mused, "has anyone figured out what exactly they've been serving at the banquet these last few nights?"

The laughter this time was genuine, and again Zachary shrugged, as if oblivious to what he'd just implied. He caught Emeric's eye, and his friend looked away, gritting his teeth. He was upset, but the general unease had been expelled from the room, granting Zachary the chance to turn to graver matters.

"Regardless, gentlemen, I didn't call you here to amuse you. So, before any of you get ambitions toward my station, allow me to assure you it is not yet vacated. Now, you will, no doubt, have already heard about the incident in the Southern Quarters."

There was a quiet murmur of agreement, a few shooting glances in Emeric's direction. Zachary didn't allow the silence to hold long.

"Fold protected the city from a group of alchemists who threatened to burn it down. These men have been punished, but at the cost of mine, Hathely's and Fold's privacy. We are named Night Patrol now, but the rest of you may be reassured in your anonymity, should you choose to keep it. That's now your decision—the time of secrecy is over. I won't enforce it anymore."

The Night Patrol looked amongst one another. For some, the burden of the truth had been grave, whilst others wanted nothing more than to keep their involvement in the shadows. Zachary respected them either way.

"Oh, try not to look so sullen, my friends—nothing screams suspicious more than a sullen face. Here in Harmatia, the King ensures we are happy, and he has ways of making us happy if we are not. And that is what I mean to speak to you about, in light of certain events." Zachary heaved a sigh and leant back against the door, blocking it. "You know I handpicked each of you. Your skills, your courage, your character—these are all aspects that I marked before I brought you into the fold. I should hope that, even if you agreed to my terms as nothing more than a formality, you have some sense of loyalty to me and, more importantly, that you have come to appreciate the loyalty I have to all of you.

"I won't decorate the truth. We are soldiers, I am your captain, and at my whim I could have you face an army of considerable force and be slaughtered. In the event that we are faced with such odds, however, I would rather be at your sides and die fighting with you. I hope you all know me to be that kind of man." Zachary saw several of the men nod—they knew their captain would never abandon them, and Zachary felt a fierce sense of pride in their trust. "Good. I am glad." He closed his eyes and breathed deeply. "Because should a day arise when something changes and gives you reason to question my words today—and such a day *will* come, it is a fate carved into my back—then I hope you know that you have no obligation to me. If my loyalty wanes or stands compromised, then so should yours."

At the look of confusion on their faces, Zachary pushed himself away from the door, trying to offer comfort where none could truthfully be given.

"Don't let your minds expand on that thought, gentlemen," he advised. "It is merely speculation for the future, and the future may be a long time from now. But before you meet it—*if* you meet it—I thought it only fair to warn you."

The quiet that rung after his words was phenomenal. Never had Zachary known a group of men to stand so still, and he wasn't sure what had shocked them more—a warning of his own, inevitable betrayal, or the confusion that came with this confession. A part of Zachary wished he'd never spoken at all, but his men deserved some warning. If he became DuGilles's puppet, as the Kathrak claimed he could make him, Zachary wanted his men to recognise it.

For now, he would rather they put his words down to drunken blather than take them to heart. "Enough now," he announced, "I have said all I needed to, and perhaps a little too much. Let it be known I am not conspiring here—if any man is an agent of the King, he can report only good things. See how we prepare for a war before it's even been declared—what organised creatures we are." Zachary forced a laugh, which was reciprocated uneasily. "Go—away with all of you. Should some incident occur in the next few days during my absence, fall to Hathely for his command. Good-day to you all, and I shall see you, Malak willing, in a few days."

"He's going to die, isn't he?" Isaac murmured disparagingly into his hands. He'd been sat, almost unmoving at Varyn's bedside for the best part of the day.

From his shadowy corner in the room, Embarr leant forward. "Are you not supposed to be the optimist of our merry circle, Isaac?"

Isaac huffed a bitter laugh. "There's a limit even to my optimism."

It had taken much debate and a no short amount of bribery, but Isaac had finally succeeded in having Varyn moved from the dungeons to a bedchamber. Prisoner, Varyn may have been, but he was no use to anybody dead, and Isaac had insisted that if the Hunter remained a day longer in the cold, dank cell, he wouldn't live to see the night out. Even so, the luxury of a proper bed and medicinal care had done little to improve Varyn's condition. Isaac was at his wit's end.

"Take courage, my friend," Embarr tried to ease. "I have had word from Béatrice—she travels today."

This didn't improve Isaac's mood in the slightest. He dropped his hands and glared at Embarr. "Why would I take courage from that? It was her curse that did this. She's *killing* him!"

"You and I both know it's a great deal more complicated than that," Embarr said, his voice distant. "She loves him."

Isaac laughed bitterly. "But does she love him enough?"

"Time will tell." Embarr shrugged, his black eyes cast over Varyn. "Her habit is to take pause at Helena's Fort, before crossing into Kathra. My wager is that she will be with us before the week is out."

"Does he have that long?" Isaac turned back to Varyn, concentrating on the unsteady rise and fall of Varyn's chest.

"Dragons," Embarr suddenly said.

"Pardon?"

"He said he was being hunted by a dragon. Do you have any idea what he meant by that, Isaac? Because Varyn has never been one for fanciful exclamations, but that one certainly borders close."

Isaac actually laughed. "He told me about it long that—that a dragon from the Sickle Mountains was hunting him and that's why he couldn't stay in one place too long. I used to think it was just an excuse for his rambling nature, but…it's as you say—it's not in his character. He really believed it, trained every day in preparation. He told me he would either defeat the dragon, or die by it."

Embarr looked over Isaac's shoulder out of the window. "I see no dragons here."

"No," Isaac agreed. "Perhaps Varyn was wrong. The dragon isn't from the Sickle—she's from Harmatia, and she takes a human form."

"Now, Isaac," Embarr pretended to gasp, "I am frankly shocked you would even speak of Béatrice in that way. It's very unlike you. I know—your optimistic heart has been solemn for too long. Come and lay your head upon my breast a while, I will sooth your troubles away."

"I've seen what you do to the men who 'lay their heads upon your breast', so if you don't mind, I'll respectfully decline."

"You wound me, but I will forgive you that." Embarr fanned himself woefully.

"I heard that your Lieutenant's dying. They're calling it consumption. Shouldn't you be at his bedside in his final hours?"

"Only if you want him to die quicker." Embarr waved his hand. "By the by, the room is full of people. I can only function within this court if I prey on its individuals. A paragon of sensuality I may be, but my allure will not work against a mob."

"Isn't it dangerous for you to be here?"

"Hardly. Nobody wants to come in and see Varyn. They are all too afraid of him," Embarr said. "But if I mean to be any use to anybody, I have to find a new victim. I want to go deeper into the court. Find someone with more influence, more power.

Unfortunately, the higher I go, the more guarded they become, and the harder it is to slip my way in."

"I might have the man for you," Isaac said. "There's a General who's quite close to Bozidar—his brother in law."

"Consider me intrigued. Tell me more—what can I expect?"

"He's corrupt, boastful and lecherous, and they say his sexual tastes are...indecent."

"All the qualities I look for in a man." Embarr clapped a hand to his chest, as if swooning. "I thank you Isaac. I shall pay this General a little visit tonight, and see if I cannot establish myself more permanently in his chambers."

Isaac laughed faintly. "At least one of us is amusing ourselves in this damned castle." He looked mournfully back at Varyn, and Embarr grew sombre.

"Isaac," he said softly, "you understand that it would be easier for Varyn if he died."

Isaac groaned, hunching around himself a little tighter. "Don't say that."

"Death is better than the alternative. The King plans to sell him to the Shin."

"They can't banish him back, he hasn't committed any crime!" Isaac cried. "He *saved* that lord's family. He wouldn't have killed him unless he had too. Varyn doesn't murder innocents. But if the Shin get hold of him again, he'll..." he couldn't finish.

"In reality," Embarr muttered, "Varyn's crime is that he has the strength and power of a small army. That makes him valuable."

"He's a human being," Isaac snapped his head up, "not some bundle of silks to be sold. Bozidar doesn't understand Varyn's worth. He's saved hundreds of lives in the last twenty years...But in the hands of the Shin, he could kill thousands." Isaac wilted. "Varyn would rather die than return to that life, I know...but all the same, I have to hope that there's an alternative."

"Isaac Thornton!" Embarr gasped, and Isaac jumped, looking around. Embarr was staring directly at Isaac, his black eyes wide and mouth split into a large smile. "You have just given me the spark of a brilliant idea!"

Isaac stared. "I have?"

"You have! That alternative you wish so desperately for—I may have it!" Embarr stood, speaking rapidly. "If I can get my hooks into that General you spoke of, than I may be able to save Varyn from the Shin."

"Do you think your influence will really be enough to cheat King Bozidar out of that much gold?"

"There is something that Bozidar loves more than gold." Embarr was pacing, his bluish skin catching the fire-light, giving it a translucent quality. "War."

"You think there will be one?"

"All the stars are aligning, and the cards are falling prettily on the table. The Knights of the Delphi have their Prince, and they are angered by the death of Rufus Merle. I cannot imagine it will be long before they ride against Harmatia, and Bethean will follow."

"How does that help us?"

"Because it will be all too sweet an opportunity for Bozidar to miss. By the laws of their alliance, Bozidar would send reinforcements to his grandson Sverrin. Should the war go in their favour, Bozidar could pillage Bethean to his heart's content. But should the power tip against Harmatia, Bozidar would take the opportunity to seize control of it instead—something he has been craving since he sent his daughter off to marry Thestian." Embarr stopped his pacing and clapped his hands together. "Bethean and Harmatia are worth more gold than Varyn."

"But how does Varyn come into it?" Isaac asked.

"Simple. I could have it whispered into the King's ear what an asset Varyn would be in his conquest. There are two things which stand in Bozidar's way. Harmatia have their Night Patrol, and the Faerie alliance with Bethean means that they had the aid of the Seelie Court. But Varyn has fought monsters for years—they are his speciality. Put him at the head of an Isny army and he could be unstoppable."

"Octania's spark—that may just work! But..." Isaac shook his head. "Varyn won't want anything to do with it."

"Varyn may not live the night out," Embarr said. "Should he somehow survive this trial, he would like the Shin even less. I am sorry, my friend, but unpleasant situations call for unpleasant solutions. I cannot simply whisk him away, as I have done with others. He is too notorious, and I could never convince him to stay away from Kathra. So he must earn his own freedom."

Isaac frowned. "If he was enlisted in the army, he'll be riding against the Knights of the Delphi, and the Seelie Court..."

"Most likely, yes."

Isaac laughed humourlessly. "Then whose side are you on, Embarr?"

"Where I have always been," Embarr said. "On the side of my friends."

CHAPTER
37

"Are you measuring me up for a portrait?" Zachary asked dully, not bothering to look up from his book.

Marcel didn't reply, continuing his strict vigil. Zachary snapped the book closed. He felt queasy under Marcel's gaze. All the other Night Patrol had long since left, including Emeric who hadn't bothered to bid Zachary farewell. Marcel might have stayed behind to see his sister safely off, but by his intent stare, Zachary suspected there was another, more prominent reason.

"Oh, what?" he eventually demanded. "What do you want me to say? That I am sorry for rambling like a drunkard? That what I said made no sense? That today is my last day on earth? What do you want me to say, Hathely?"

"Are you demented?" Marcel responded, and Zachary threw back his head with a hard laugh, his eyes squeezed shut. For a horrifying moment, he thought he might cry. He dropped his face into his hands and took several long, shuddering breaths. It felt like so long since he'd slept.

Marcel touched his shoulder. He'd seen Zachary through many emotions—rage, joy, absolute despair, but he'd never witnessed this particular brand of fear. He pried Zachary's hands away and looked him hard in the eye. "What are you doing?" he asked in a hard whisper. "You are our captain—pull yourself together."

Again, Zachary wanted to laugh, but a quick look from Marcel told him it wouldn't be wise. His second in command had gone from his usual monotone to very serious, his golden eyes narrowed.

"Arlen?"

"Marcel," Zachary's voice cracked a little, "you're my second in command—Athea, you're my closest friend. Can't you see what's happening? I am not losing control—that would imply I had any. Gods man, you see *everything* in this city." He seized his friend and drew him closer, pressing his forehead almost feverishly to Marcel's, as if willing the information to cross telepathically. "Can't you see this?"

Marcel grew rigid at this uncharacteristic contact. Slowly he pushed himself away, and Zachary dropped his head. Marcel knelt down, careful to keep a small distance between them.

"You are not well," he said.

"That's an understatement," Zachary spat bitterly, and at Marcel's perplexed expression, heaved a sigh. "Hathely, I am terrified. And I wish I could tell you what I know, but I can't involve you." He closed his eyes. "Before being my friend, I sometimes have to allow you to be my subordinate. If I am compromised, your head must be clear."

Marcel's frown remained. It must have been difficult for him—he usually knew everybody's secrets before they did. To be kept in the dark now, about an affair so close to him, must have been a great frustration.

This is stupid, Zachary thought. *He'll be safer knowing. He'll be able to prepare.*

Safer? Zachary's more sensible side spoke out. *No. If he knew, he'd try to help. He'd get involved. I can't put him at risk just for the satisfaction of sharing my fear.*

Marcel seemed to be in tune with his mental debate and, not for the first time, Zachary wondered whether the Hathelys—for Béatrice was also notoriously good at weaning out secrets—might not have some ability to read minds.

"I think now," Marcel spoke slowly, "you are in need of a friend before a soldier. You may permit yourself that."

"Not today." Zachary gave a strained grin. "One of us needs to sleep at night."

Marcel growled deeply. He picked himself up and moved away, pulling out his pipe. "Incroyable," he muttered in Réneian.

Zachary could hear an odd note of disappointment in his friend's voice. His resolution began to stumble, like a child trying to appease an older sibling. "Have you seen Lord Farthing these days?"

Marcel paused in preparing his pipe. "Isaac Thornton's master?"

"Have you noticed how…strange, he's been?"

"He was almost fatally sick," Marcel said, echoing the lie that had been passed on through the court. "Why?"

Zachary thought on the man. He'd known Lord Farthing only fleetingly through Isaac, but there had always been a mutual respect. Now, whenever Zachary saw him, he was cast back to that encounter in the crypts—Lord Farthing, starved of light and sensation, staring with hungry, empty eyes. Even now, something of his eyes seemed to still be searching for the light. Something of his eyes resembled Sverrin's.

"Arlen," Marcel asked softly, "are you taken with what he had?"

"What?" Zachary momentarily forgot the lie. "Oh Healing Septus, no. I am in perfect health." He watched Marcel's expression grow tight with frustration. "Peace, my friend—truly, I am well. Only tired. Very, very tired."

At the very least, Marcel seemed to believe that, though the answer clearly hadn't satisfied him.

Zachary, feeling himself close to succumbing, steered the

conversation. Marcel wanted to know what was wrong, and at the very least, Zachary could answer one aspect of that.

"You remember Daniel?"

"Your brother."

"Yes." Zachary looked up at the ceiling. "He invited his mother to come and stay in the house."

"Isolde?"

"Yes," Zachary huffed. "May I sleep at yours?"

"No," Marcel answered flatly.

"Hah. Some sanctuary you are." Zachary chuckled, and then grew quiet. "Hathely, I can trust you, can't I?"

"Always."

The word, said with such fierce sincerity, filled Zachary with great calm. The world stood in disorder—dead men alive, good men dead, friends as traitors and the living buried in stone coffins, but there remained one constant in Marcel's assurance. One thing on which Zachary could absolutely rely. He stood abruptly.

"I am going to die, Hathely," he announced. "I don't know when, but it is not a distant fate. Don't talk," he said as Marcel made to interrupt. "Listen. Don't argue with me. I am going to die. This is now a fact. But before I do, I need your assurance. My men, *our* men, require guidance. Promise me that you will—"

"No," Marcel cut in plainly, and putting his pipe in his mouth he turned away.

"Hathely—"

"No," Marcel repeated. "I will not lead them."

"Damn you, there's no one else to succeed me!"

"Train someone."

"That could take years!"

"Then do not die," Marcel said flippantly.

Zachary groaned. "Oh, you're so incredibly difficult sometimes."

Marcel didn't justify that with a response, giving Zachary a pointed look just as the door opened. Béatrice flounced in.

"My darling cousin told me I would find you here." She beamed at them both, clad in a black and crimson gown, embedded with garnets to match her eyes. "Come Arlen, the carriage is ready and the road awaits."

Zachary had almost forgotten his duty. He bowed. "Of course. I am ready to leave at your leisure."

Béatrice looked between the pair, like a mother who'd come across her children squabbling. "Ça alors, the pair of you look utterly morose. Have I interrupted something?"

"No," Zachary assured. "You brother is simply unforgivably lazy."

"This we know." Béatrice leant forward and pinched Marcel's cheek, as if he were still a baby. He scowled, but didn't bat her away. "Mon p'tit bébé paresseux," she goaded.

"Tais-toi," he shushed her.

"Maman?" From the door a tiny figure appeared. Béatrice turned with a smile and held out her hand.

"Morelle," she invited, summoning her daughter to her. The young girl approached, looking between her uncle and Zachary with a carefree curiosity. She curtsied to the latter.

"Good evening, my lord."

Zachary inclined his head with a smile. He knew very little about Marcel's niece, but that she was a legitimised bastard from one of Béatrice's love affairs, and that she'd inherited all of her mother's grace and beauty, with the same dark hair, Réneian complexion, and curved features. Her eyes, however, must have come from her father, for they were almost black, and hinted to a lineage that should have brought shame down on her. In fact, Morelle's entire conception should have ruined Béatrice's reputation in civil society forever, but the woman was clever. She'd formed a quick alliance with Sverrin during the early months of her pregnancy, and then had stopped all slander by merely giving no room for it. Where others might have retreated to the country in quiet shame, Béatrice had flaunted her pregnancy with boastful pride, as any married woman might. The lords and ladies of the court, bewitched by her charm and charisma, had fallen into step with her whims, and Morelle was born already adored and recognised as a legitimate daughter of the court.

It was the single greatest manipulation Zachary had ever seen, and it made him more wary of the woman than ever. Béatrice could talk the noose away from around her neck, her silver tongue was so smart.

"Ma chérie," Béatrice clasped her daughter's face gently. She tipped it down and planted a kiss on top of Morelle's head. "Il faut que je m'en aille. Your uncles Marcel and Emeric will take care of you until I am home."

Morelle took her mother's wrists. "Maman," her vowels were warm and lightly accented, like her mother, "in your heart, you will know what to do."

Béatrice laughed softly. "Ah, ma belle, I have known what I was going to do all along."

Morelle wasn't deterred, "But in your heart," she repeated, "you will know what to do *now*."

An almost invisible stiffness came over Béatrice, and she smiled and traced her fingers down Morelle's cheek, mapping her face. "Je l'espère."

Zachary watched the display with interest. It was as he and Belphegore had thought— Béatrice was going to Sigel'eg for her own reasons.

"Shall we?" Zachary gestured and Béatrice made to follow him, giving her daughter one last kiss goodbye.

As Béatrice passed him however, quick as lightening, Marcel seized her elbow. Béatrice faltered and the two siblings shared a meaningful stare, as if speaking internally.

It was times like this that Marcel and Béatrice, who couldn't have been more contrary people in features and manner, shared a resemblance with one another so striking they might have been twins. For all their superficial dissimilarities, Zachary knew they couldn't be more alike.

"Petit frère, joie du mon cœur," Béatrice said, teasing him sweetly.

"Grande sœur, le mal de ma vie," Marcel replied dutifully and Zachary, for all the non-existent Réneian he knew, understood these two common phrases passed between the siblings. Little brother, the joy of my heart. Big sister, the bane of my existence.

Marcel released Béatrice, and there was a heavy tension between them. Whatever Béatrice's purpose was in Kathra, Marcel wasn't enamoured with it. This only served to pique Zachary's curiosity even more. Béatrice had many instantaneous and peculiar fancies, which her brother was accustomed to accommodating, so Zachary couldn't conceive what she was doing now to earn Marcel's disapproval.

Béatrice came to the door, Zachary holding it open.

"She'll be safe," he reassured Marcel, knowing his second would never ask out loud. Marcel inclined his head in thanks and Zachary left, following Béatrice out into the waiting carriage.

As they departed, Morelle strode out into the middle of the street alone, and watched her mother leave, her wilful eyes as black as coal.

CHAPTER 38

"What is it like to kill a man, Arlen?" Béatrice broke the silence. Zachary turned his head, surprised. She was staring at him in the gloom, and as the lantern outside swung, the light caught her eyes, making them burn a sudden cherry red. He felt his skin crawl at the intensity of her gaze.

"It depends," he replied. "For some, it is abhorrent, for others mundane."

Béatrice considered this. "My hands feel very weighted."

Zachary frowned. "I don't understand."

"I have never killed a man before." Béatrice turned and looked out of the window. "I always wagered that I could, should I need to…But as of yet, the feeling is unknown to me."

Zachary blinked, incredulous. "Why exactly are you going to Kathra?"

"To enquire after a suitable bride for the King."

"And how does that concern killing a man?"

"It does not," Béatrice dismissed, and then looked down to her hands. "But to have another's life in your hands—that power must be euphoric, and then quite maddening. A drug that threatens to leave a bitter stain. Hatred and love are not such different things, you know, Arlen."

"I won't even pretend to understand what you're talking about, woman. Why can't you speak plainly, like Hathely?"

"I am not sure how I can be plainer. Is it not dizzying to have, within your grasp, the life of a man who has wronged you? Is justice not so dangerously pleasing?"

"What you're describing sounds more like revenge," Zachary grunted. "It has a similar flavour, granted, but a contrary aftertaste. A man can forget himself in the pursuit of revenge."

"And does a woman?"

"I can't answer that."

"A pity." Béatrice examined her nails, the carriage rocking from the force of the wind outside. Zachary didn't envy the driver. "You are the most learned man I know on the subject."

"That wasn't a compliment, was it?"

"I suppose whether you take it as one is more a testament to your character than mine." Béatrice steepled her fingers. "You struggle with it, do you not? Clarity."

"I assure you, clarity is exactly what I want from you right now."

"No, you misunderstand."

"Oh, what a surprise." Zachary rolled his eyes and Béatrice gave him an impatient huff. "Sorry, but I am not the one speaking in riddles."

"From all accounts, that was precisely what you were doing with your men. Or do you suppose that my darling Emeric did not recount the entire meeting to me the moment I caught him sulking?"

"Traitor."

"Only for love of you." Béatrice's eyes flashed crimson as they caught the light again. "You have seen it, have you not?"

Something of the way she said those words sent anxious tingles up Zachary's spine. "Excuse me?"

"I have spent many years travelling Kathra. I have met Isnys.

I know what happens in Isnydea behind their boarders." She paused. "And I know the kind of man Brandt DuGilles is, and just of what he is capable. I suspected that you might be struggling with the truth yourself, but your words to Emeric and Marcel today confirmed it. You have seen it."

Zachary could scarcely breathe. The words felt conspiratorial and he almost didn't dare voice them, in case somehow DuGilles could hear. "Yes."

"So it is true—DuGilles is continuing his sick work in the heart of the capital."

"Yes." Zachary swallowed. "He told me he'd learnt alchemy from the Shin, that they taught him how to do those…things. But how did you—"

"Know?" Béatrice tossed her head. "Because DuGilles has not merely done dealings with the Shin—he *is* one."

"That's impossible."

"The Shin do not share their techniques—they are as greedy with them as the Magi. I have known what DuGilles was all along, Arlen." Her voice became very soft. "You made the right decision in keeping Emeric and Marcel out of it, and for their safety I must insist you continue to do so."

"Is that a threat?"

"I think you have had enough of those already, my dear." Béatrice turned absently back to the world outside. Zachary felt icy.

"You still haven't told me exactly what you mean to do in Sigel'eg."

"Your persistence and curiosity is no doubt what got you into this mess." Béatrice breathed on the glass. "Very well. I shall tell you a story to pacify you, if it will please you?"

"Do I have a choice?"

Béatrice ignored him, clearing her throat. When she spoke, it was in a sing-song voice, as if she were reading from a children's book.

"Once, long ago, there lived a young girl who found herself to be wanting in life. Not for gold, or silver, but for adventure. The people around her were predictable you see—boring and without wit, and she craved more from her life than her dull routine."

"Oh Béatrice, are we such sour company?"

"I do not claim her, she is merely a girl of a fictional nature. Now do not interrupt," Béatrice shushed him. "One day, the young girl was visiting her family in Helena's Fort."

"Oh, so she's a Hathely too? What a coincidence." Zachary whistled, and then grew still under Béatrice impatient, penetrating gaze. "Sorry."

Béatrice huffed through her nose, and continued. "It was while she was there that she encountered a man out on the moors. He was older than her, and wild and, as she discovered, a Hunter indebted to the Shin. She fell madly in love with him, and he with her, and they agreed to elope just as soon as he was released from his debt."

This, Zachary hadn't expected. He sat up a little straighter, watching Béatrice who was now looking out of the rain-spattered window. Her voice became soft and mellow, losing its dramatic flair.

"Time passed, and she waited for him dutifully, thinking on him every day. Finally, she received word from him—his debt was almost repaid. One final job, and he would be free of the Shin at last, and could come for her. Her heart swelled at the prospect, and she waited keenly, barely able to sleep or think for her excitement."

Béatrice didn't vary her tone, though Zachary saw something akin to a smile creep into the corners of her mouth. For a second it was a little mischievous, then cold, and then as quickly as it had come, it was gone. Béatrice inhaled, and waved her hand, as if with an air of indifference.

"But weeks past, and he did not come. Her hope began to dwindle, and then at last she received word of him. Unhappy words. Her lover, you see, had been killed by his apprentice, who had absconded with the gold they gathered and used it to buy his own freedom instead. And like that, all of her hopes and dreams were gone."

Zachary shivered slightly, trying to read Béatrice's expression and discern where the tale was leading. She gave nothing away, perfectly collected and calm.

"The woman—for she was a woman by then—knew no greater pain or fury, but time had taught her patience, and so she plotted. She followed the apprentice, now a Hunter himself on his exploits, careful to gather as much information as she could. When she had learnt everything she might, she lured him, using her influence, to a small port town in Réne. And there, she sought her revenge by playing a cruel trick."

Béatrice trailed off, humming quietly to herself, as if she wasn't sure how the rest of the story went. Zachary leant in.

"What happened?"

Béatrice looked briefly away from the window toward him, and once more he saw that same mischief in the corners of her mouth, twisted ever so slightly like a malicious cat.

"Everything went according to her plan, and then altogether did not."

"How so?"

"How so?" Béatrice looked back out of the window, propping her chin in her hand. "One does not obsess over a man for years, without growing curious of him. She allowed herself to get close, if for nothing more than to satisfy her interest. This Hunter, as it turned out, was not at all as she had imagined. Feelings stirred with her—truths came out. The villain she had created in her mind was fictitious. And yet, his crime existed."

Béatrice drummed her fingers lightly on her cheek, her forehead pressed against the window, as if she were bored. The story continued.

"Her punishment for him was fitting. He had deprived her of

401

her lover, had left her with years of uncertainty and anguish. She wished to treat him in kind. So she discovered a magical creature with great power, tricked him into hunting it for her, and then used it to curse him. He had caused her fifteen years of pain, so she gave him the same amount of time to suffer and redeem himself before his heart stopped. Fifteen years of debt—his life in her hands. But…" Béatrice paused, and brushed a stray curl of greying hair out of her eyes. "But the curse entangled them both, and they found themselves allied again and again. He fell in love her, and gave her a child that she never told him about. And yet, in all that time, he never asked once for forgiveness, and so it never occurred to her to give it. C'est triste, n'est pas?"

Zachary was barely breathing, sitting as still as possible so as not to miss a word Béatrice said. Over the years, she'd told him many stories, but none like this. None with such a forced neutrality that was almost worthy of Marcel it was so indifferent. He waited for her to continue, but she'd become occupied with her reflection, fixing her hair.

"What happened to them?" Zachary eventually lost his patience, and Béatrice peered around, as if she'd forgotten he was there. She raised her eyebrows, apparently amused by his curiosity.

"Well, by the time she realised she loved him, the die had been cast. Her curse was irreversible, and lay as much upon her as it did on him. And so she put on a resilient face and pretended it was all her decision, because she could not bear the hope of loving again, only to be separated. Better his death be justice for a man she could barely remember, than a terrible mistake she could never reverse." Béatrice exhaled, and then chuckled, returning to her vigil at the window. "It is strange…now that I think on it, it is not so dissimilar to a tale that you might have told Arlen. People make terrible decisions for love."

Zachary stared at her, his mouth slack. "I don't know whether you're teasing me or not," he eventually admitted, and Béatrice didn't look back at him, reaching over and patting his knee.

"There, there, it is but a story," she comforted sadly. "Like all dead people become."

They were in the middle of duelling when the first wave of dizzy anxiety struck Joshua. It was just after sunrise, and Korrick had been putting their acquired skills to the test. The students had been broken into pairs and commanded to duel.

For the first time, Joshua actually seemed to have the upper hand. Kael was naturally quicker and stronger than him, but she had a tendency to be repetitive in her fighting patterns, allowing Joshua to predict her strikes and work around them. Joshua had just begun to feel triumphant when the sudden, unbidden panic settled over him and, in his distraction, Kael floored him.

He lay on the ground, winded and gasping for air, the fall only partially responsible for knocking the breath out of him. Terror crawled along his skin, his vision swimming. It was so sudden he hadn't time to prepare for it. His visions usually gave him some forewarning—a burst of colours or a gathering headache. This was different. It was urgent, frightened.

When the Prince didn't immediately swing himself back up to his feet, as usual, Kael put down her sword.

"Joshua?" She squatted down as the Prince began to shake. He could see flames, flames and uproar, though it was all unclear, his sight flittering between reality and vision.

A dark shadow came over them and Korrick appeared, looking down. He scanned Joshua for injury, and when he didn't immediately see one, growled and dragged the Prince upright.

"You ask me to train you. I agree to train you. And yet you do not train," he began, and then caught Joshua as the boy's legs gave way. "Get up."

Joshua felt sluggish, turning his head. Out, in the centre of a ring of charred earth, he saw Varyn standing, a great, double-handed sword raised in his hand.

"Varyn?" Joshua slurred, trying to free himself of Korrick's grip and move toward the Hunter.

"Joshua." Korrick shook him.

"He's bleeding," Joshua whimpered. Varyn's clothes were in tatters, and there was blood across his chest and legs. Smoke rose from his skin, which was stained black. His eyes didn't even reflect the light. The Hunter dropped to his knees, exhausted, the sky darkening above him. "No, no," Joshua moaned. "No, get up. Varyn, get up!"

"Boy, listen to me." Korrick shook him again. "Joshua?"

Joshua pushed that reality away, allowing himself to be submerged in the fiery vision. He was needed there more.

Varyn, for the first time, saw him and raised his head. "You shouldn't be here."

"You're hurt." Joshua ambled toward him, his legs woolly. Up close he could see shackles on Varyn's wrists and ankles, though he couldn't see where the chains ended.

"It's close now." Varyn grimaced, but didn't rise to his feet.

"What is?"

"The end." Varyn planted his sword into the ground and pushed himself up. Something large swooped above them, and Joshua threw himself down and out of the way on instinct.

"Athea!" Joshua gasped, turning on his back in time to see the tail of a colossal black dragon whip through the air behind it.

"It found me," Varyn said.

"Where are we?"

"Sigel'eg. They brought me to Sigel'eg."

Sigel'eg? The world around Joshua was nothing but ash and fire—there was no city to speak of. Empty shells of great buildings loomed around them, husks of black brick stained with fire and smoke. Varyn seemed to be fairing no better, barely standing and resting heavily on his sword.

"You have to fight," Joshua said urgently. "You have to kill it!"

404

"That is not the end he means." A woman spoke and Joshua twisted, shocked to see a finely clad lady among the wreckage. She looked out of place, her skirts immaculate, her greying hair styled, the jewels on her throat still shining. Joshua almost got the impression that she was the dragon, transformed to trick them, but as he looked closer he realised that her wrists, too, were bound in shackles, and that it was she Varyn was chained to.

Varyn stared at her. "Béatrice." Her name came out as a soft grumble, low and intense.

Béatrice stepped out among the rubble, and as she did, a strange energy began to gather in the air around them. The heavy chains glowed bright red, like they were burning, but neither seemed to notice.

"He and I are bound." Béatrice circled Joshua, the hem of her dress whispering over the ground. "How have you come to be here?"

"Does it matter?" Joshua gestured to the city around him. "We need to do something, before everything burns. People are going to die!"

"I know who you are." Béatrice gently lowered herself to his height, her skirt spilling out around her like a pool of silk. "You are the Delphi Prince." She breathed out slowly, her maroon eyes lighting up with excitement. "For all my meddling, I did not know if I would ever get the chance to meet you. And yet here you are. So beautiful." She touched his face. "So young," she said with disapproval. "You have many battles ahead of you, little Prince. This," she gestured all around her, "is not one of them."

And then, with a light hand, she pushed him away. Joshua scrabbled to stay upright, reaching out.

"No!" he screamed, the world falling away from him. "NO!"

"Joshua?"

Joshua opened his eyes with a jolt. His head was resting in Rufus's lap. Korrick stood nearby, watching with a grim expression. Rufus moped Joshua's forehead gently with a damp cloth.

"It's alright, come back to me now."

Joshua nodded. His chest was on fire.

Rufus kept his voice low and calm. "What did you see?"

"Fire," Joshua croaked. His mouth felt strange, as if he'd entered a body that wasn't his own. "Sigel'eg is burning."

"What is he talking about?" Korrick's expression was severe, but he didn't seem angry.

"Dragon." Joshua's eyes fluttered. He felt exhausted, like he'd run all the way there and back. "A dragon is attacking Sigel'eg. It's burning the city to the ground. It's after Varyn," Joshua moaned. "Varyn has to fight it. Please fight. Or everybody's going to die." His vision began to tunnel, black spots dancing in his peripheral. "Everybody's going to die," he repeated, and fell unconscious.

CHAPTER
39

It came upon the city very suddenly. The watchers barely had time to ring the alarm before the dragon ripped the bell-tower from the wall and sent it crashing down into the street below.

It had been a bright afternoon, but as the monster unleashed its fiery breath, the sky had darkened into a red and black inferno. They'd not seen the day-light since.

Of course, a city built in a country of dragons, rare as they were, had taken some precautions. The buildings were designed to withstand a bestial siege, though it had been near a century since any such creature had descended from the mountains and attacked. Some people even believed that dragons were long extinct.

"We won't hold much longer!" Isaac bellowed, turning furiously to the line of Kathrak soldiers behind him. The Generals and their Lieutenants had gone to hide within the castle walls, letting Isaac take charge of their frightened men. The Magi was the only one brave enough to do it. He pointed to the columns of fire, rising out of the lower town, obstructing the sky and silhouetting the humongous beast that soared through it. "In another two days everything will be gone!"

"It's already destroyed all of our defences," a Kathrak soldier wailed helplessly. The dragon had removed all of the siege weaponry on the battlements. The monster was clever and methodical, and the soldiers had no training against it.

"Not all of them." Isaac whirled around. "You have one thing left—the prisoner it seeks. You *have* to release him! Release Varyn!"

"And then what?" Béatrice stepped out onto the battlement. Even in the midst of fire and death, she managed to look elegant. Isaac was half-tempted to shake her until the jewels flew off her ears and neck. Did nothing frighten the woman? Was there no pain or anguish that could stammer her velvet voice? Isaac had always admired her, but in that moment, he hated her too.

"The dragon's after his blood. Damn me for not believing him, but Varyn said this would happen. It won't stop until it has him."

"How very unlike you, Isaac." Béatrice stepped over a gap in the stone, where an entire section of the battlement had crumbled away. "To hear you propose sacrificing your friend to quail the dragon's rage."

Isaac grimaced. "I don't mean for Varyn to be taken by it. He's the only one who can *fight* it."

"How?" Béatrice looked out over the burning city. There might have been regret in her gaze, but Isaac couldn't say for sure. "He will be dead before sunrise."

"But not like this!" another voice cried, and both turned to see Embarr, stood in the doorway of the battlement, his handsome face smeared already with soot and sweat.

"Embarr?" Isaac gasped. The Gancanagh wasn't supposed to be out of his new General's chambers. With this black eyes and alluring toxicity, he stood out all too much to be walking idly about on the battlements. All it would take was for someone to recognise him for what he was, and his work as a spy would be exposed. "Embarr, you shouldn't be here—get back inside," Isaac whispered urgently. The Gancanagh, Isaac knew, was vulnerable to smoke and fire, and looked decidedly unwell, leaning heavily against the wall. Still, he forced himself forward, his mouth hidden in the crook of his elbow.

"Béatrice," Embarr called in a hoarse voice. "I swore I would not take sides, but I cannot abide this any longer. You have to break these chains."

Embarr stepped to the side. From behind him, a set of guards came, carrying the huge form of Varyn between them. Isaac stared hard into the face of the Hunter, and tried to find anything of the man he knew in there. Even Béatrice, with all her fortitude, stilled at the sight of Varyn.

"This man is supposed to be locked in his chamber," one of the Kathrak soldiers objected, but nobody heeded him. Béatrice took an uncertain step toward Varyn, who was laid unceremoniously on the floor. Isaac couldn't even see if the Hunter was still breathing.

"It would seem, Embarr, that you have done a fine job of removing his chains yourself." Béatrice gestured to the Hunter's wrists, rubbed raw from shackles, but now bare. "Or do you mean the chains of this curse?"

Embarr, usually so playful, looked like he meant to slap Béatrice around the face, his hand raised. The smoke and fire had brought out the worst in the Gancanagh, and he wasted no time with pretty words. "I mean the chains that hold you to Cyryl! That bind you to this ludicrous punishment."

"Varyn murdered Cyryl. Do you expect me to choose him still?"

"Yes, you foolish woman!" Embarr bellowed, and the dragon roared in the distance, a flash of flames casting its shadow against the murk and smoke. "Because you *love* him. And he loves you. And you cannot break those feelings through sheer force of will, however strong you are! I should know—I have tried!"

Béatrice came as close to flinching as Isaac had ever seen. "What would you have me do?"

"You cannot see it, can you?" Embarr almost laughed, looking slightly manic, his eyes wide. "I have stood by for months, waiting for you to piece it together. The curse was meant to *teach* you. That's what curses are—*lessons!* You had the ability to break it all along, *both* of you did, but you were so tethered by the death that bound you, neither of you ever dared try."

Béatrice closed her eyes. Her porcelain mask was breaking. For as long as Isaac had known her, she'd worn it but at last the cracks were giving way.

"I do not understand," she lied, unconvincingly, her voice uneven. She was afraid. Afraid to hope.

"Let go of your resentment, your fear and your anger. Embrace what you have been given. Admit that you forgave him long ago." Embarr broke out into coughs, his arm raised around his head if he were trying to shield himself from the invasive heat. He collapsed a little more against the wall, breathing hard. "Must a whole city burn for your broken heart? At least, if you mean for him to die, let him do so on his own two feet!"

Béatrice stared down at Varyn, and drew her hand across her eyes where tears had sprung, perhaps for the first time in thirty years. "Yes," she agreed, soft as snow. "Yes." She knelt down, stroking Varyn's face as she cried. "I can do that."

She pressed her lips against his.

The dragon rose up from beneath them with a terrible shriek. Isaac spun on the spot, his sword raised. "LOOK OUT!"

Varyn opened his eyes with a start.

～☙～

"You want me to send an army to Kathra?" Sverrin drawled, a disbelieving smile on his face. Zachary looked helplessly across to Belphegore, who gave a small shake of his head.

The news of the dragon attack had followed Zachary's return by a few days, and had sent the capital in Harmatia into a flurry of whispers.

Marcel was beside himself. It took all of Zachary and Emeric's persuasion to stop the man charging off to Sigel'eg, in rescue of his sister. Such a venture would be suicide, though if Marcel had insisted, both friends would have followed him to death.

"I should not have let her go," Marcel had muttered repeatedly, to which Emeric and Zachary had reminded him that there was no power in all of Mag Mell that could stop Béatrice Hathely doing what she wanted. In the end, despite his worry, Marcel had conceded that the sensible thing was to remain in Harmatia.

"You can ask," Zachary had invited him, as Marcel's options dwindled. *"Ask me."*

"Speak with the King. Please. Implore him to send an army to Sigel'eg," Marcel had said with difficulty, his voice hesitant, knowing his captain wouldn't refuse him, despite the weight of his appeal. It was difficult enough for Zachary to address Sverrin these days, let alone offer political advice or ask favours. Even so, Zachary had agreed, and with Belphegore beside him, had begged an audience with the King to make their plea.

Sverrin didn't welcome it. "What exactly would a Harmatian army do against a *dragon*? Kathra have forces especially designed for this sort of attack, don't they, Mother?"

At his side, the King's mother sat, her face pale and drawn. The years had long ago sapped the colour from her hair, but it was the first time Zachary really saw how old she'd become. Her bronze eyes were wide and helpless—Sigel'eg was her home, the kingdom of her father, and it was burning. "Yes, Your Majesty."

Zachary couldn't believe his ears. He'd never heard Reine sound so defeated. Clearly there had been an exchange already on the subject, and Sverrin hadn't spoken kindly.

"There—Kathra will be fine." Sverrin bit into a ripe plum, which he'd been tossing idly between his hands. The sticky juice ran down the side of his lips like blood and for some reason it turned Zachary's stomach.

You used to gorge men alive, and savour the flavour in Sverrin's name, he reminded himself, and only felt sicker.

"I know why *you're* here." Sverrin pointed a finger at Zachary, smiling like he'd caught a boy in the middle of a wrong-doing. He slouched back in his throne, taking another bite of the plum. "But Marcel Hathely isn't to leave the city, do you understand? *None* of the Night Patrol are. There's nothing you can do—Béatrice will have to depend on my grandfather's defences. Though," he mused, waggling his finger as if Zachary, in his mortified silence, had given him an idea. "If Sigel'eg *is* destroyed—and we must all consider that possibility—it would leave Harmatia in a terrible position, politically."

"It is as you say Your Majesty," Belphegore said. "Therefore I implore you to reconsider. Send an army to aid Sigel'eg in its hour of need. As allies, it is our duty."

"Allies," Sverrin chuckled, throwing the pit of the plum over his shoulder, down behind the back of the throne. "Allies only in fortune. There are no benefits to sending aid at this time— Kathra will see to the dragon themselves, I promise you. In the meantime, I must pursue my search for a wife elsewhere."

Reine grimaced, appalled. "Sverrin, you cannot mean…"

"I hear the Princess of Bethean is quite a beauty. Aurora is her name, I think."

"You—You cannot—" Reine gabbled, aghast, her mouth opening and closing.

"I can, and I will," Sverrin snapped. "If it pleases me. Bethean may be a den of drunkards and faerie-lovers, but it's not without its wealth. Strengthening our alliance with marriage would give me leave to send forces undisturbed into Bethean, and wipe out what remains of the Knights of the Delphi, once and for all. Something you never managed to do," he reminded spitefully, and Reine withdrew soundlessly. "I can always take a Kathrak Princess as a second wife, when they recover from their affairs, but in this unstable time, I must look to my kingdom and its needs."

"That is indeed wise, Your Majesty." Belphegore bowed and Sverrin hummed, pleased with his idea.

"I want it arranged," he decreed. "Send an invitation to the Princess. She is of marrying age, is she not? Perhaps even beyond. I am sure King Markus would be thrilled at such an offer."

King Markus, Zachary suspected, would sooner marry his daughter to a pig-farmer, but Zachary kept that to himself.

"It will be done." Belphegore bowed again, and Zachary was close to furious. If Reine wouldn't speak, Belphegore was the only one with the political power to stand up to Sverrin. Harmatia didn't require a sycophant in this hour—it required someone who would challenge the King.

Zachary reeled in his anger. He had no right to judge. He'd kept silent throughout, tethered by his own fear. His true anger was at himself.

"Excellent, and Lord Zachary," Sverrin sat forward, "I stress again—keep your men in check. None of the Night Patrol are to step out of this city without my direct permission. Are we clear?"

Zachary nodded, unwilling to betray his anger. Both Magi bowed and left as quickly as they could. Only when they'd cleared the throne room did Zachary turn to his master.

"What do we do?"

"As the King requests."

"Béatrice is in Sigel'eg, Thornton too! Hundreds of lives—women and children are in peril and you want to arrange a marriage proposal?" Zachary saw white.

Belphegore stopped short and looked Zachary firmly in the eye, affronted. He raised himself up to his full height. "What would you have me do?" he demanded softly. "The King has only a waning respect for me now. It was not *I* who was designed to be his advisor and companion—that was a legacy meant for you."

Zachary didn't reply. It had been a long time since his word had held any gravity with Sverrin, though he knew it had always been his duty to be the King's friend. "My only legacy is to do as

I am told. But you…you could still save Sigel'eg."

"That, I should like to know how." Belphegore started to walk again, Zachary striding behind him.

"You're a Child of Aramathea, aren't you? You're Notameer's vessel. You could call on the power of the heavens and destroy the dragon."

Belphegore chuckled darkly. "The magnitude of your faith in me is a little alarming, Arlen."

"I saw what Merle was capable of. You're the same as him."

"I am not the same. Rufus was a vessel of Athea. The fire lived within him—it was born of his emotion and rage. That is Athea's nature, after all. But Notameer…Notameer's power comes from peace and serenity." Belphegore looked down at his hands, with a rueful smile. "I have not known those virtues in a long time."

Zachary blinked, and shook his head. "Even so, you're the strongest Magi in Harmatia. In all of *Mag Mell*. It was you who taught me how to transform into the Night Patrol form. You could still fight—*win*—against that dragon, Child of Aramathea or not."

"I am as bound by the King's wishes as you are, Arlen. He would never permit me to go."

"Permit you? You're the leader of the Magi!"

"Stop." Belphegore whirled around and Zachary flinched back. His master didn't seem to notice. "Whatever grand authority you think I have, it is in your head. You ask things of me that I cannot give. Just as Reine asked them of me. Do you think I obey these orders with a light heart? That I forsake the city of the woman I—" He cut himself off, but Zachary knew what he meant to say.

Zachary had always known about the affair between Reine DuBlanche and his master. As close as Belphegore had been to King Thestian—the truest of friends—he'd never approved of Thestian putting Reine to the side for Éliane. The royal marriage had been arranged, and was civil enough, though never passionate. Thestian had been plain in his feelings—he'd respected Reine, but he'd loved Éliane.

It had seemed unfair that the King might marry for love *and* politics, whilst Reine was left jealous, used only for the wealth she brought with her, her own feelings disregarded. Zachary had once heard her say to Belphegore that she would have married him one hundred times over before Thestian, had she been able to.

Perhaps the whole of Harmatia would have benefitted from that match, but it was too late to linger on that possibility. That Reine and Belphegore had never been able to publicise their feelings, even after Thestian's death, was all to ensure no suspicion fell on Sverrin's heritage. After all, it was easy enough to forget the likeness between King and Prince when scandal reared its ugly head.

"The King has made his will known and I must honour it. That is all I can do now." Belphegore stalked a few more steps and then stopped.

They were stood between the academy and the forum. Out beyond, Zachary could see people gathered around a sad looking market, selling meagre things. During Thestian's reign, that marketplace would have been filled. Now the stalls barely occupied a quarter of the space. Businesses and families had left the capital by the dozen over the last few years, unable to afford the city tax. Zachary wondered how he'd never noticed how much their capital had shrunk.

"Look at that," Belphegore said with despair. "Harmatia is crumbling, and I perpetrated it. I betrayed Thestian, stood idle as his infant son was murdered, and Prince Jionathan forced to sacrifice himself. Even after everything I did, the sins I committed, nothing has changed. The Magi were supposed to be a source of inspiration to these people, but we are, as we have always been, the hand of tyranny. Tell me, Arlen—is this the Harmatia you fought for?"

Zachary stood, petrified to the spot. A hot, sick feeling rose up into his face. How was he supposed to respond? Belphegore already knew the answer—knew the uncertainties that wriggled in Zachary's stomach. Did his master truly expect Zachary to say it all out loud? To confess that with each strike of doubt and regret, Zachary had already betrayed Sverrin a dozen times in his heart?

Wasn't it enough that Sverrin could already see the fear in Zachary's eyes, and that DuGilles had accounts of his dishonesty? Why must Belphegore too demand Zachary to admit it? To speak the words that resonated louder within him each day.

Zachary could suddenly hear Emeric's voice, echoing in the back of his mind.

"We should have never brought Sverrin back."

Zachary recoiled from Belphegore with a gasp, betrayed in an instant. Belphegore stared at him, stunned by the sharp movement. "Arlen?"

"Why would you ask such a question?" Zachary felt like someone had thrown a pillow over his face and was holding it down. "Do you want me dead?"

Belphegore shook his head, baffled. "Arlen, what are you talking about?"

"You can't rush the inevitable," Zachary clamoured. If he said the words out loud there would be no returning from it. The last, lingering illusion would be severed. Zachary would be breaking the lie he'd woven himself into, and there would be nothing left to protect him. Nothing left to stop DuGilles.

Belphegore wouldn't even risk disobeying Sverrin to save one hundred people in Sigel'eg. Zachary could hardly expect his master to protect him against Sverrin and DuGilles when the time came. Perhaps Belphegore already knew all about it. Perhaps this was all a trap.

"You can't do this to me! Do you resent me so much for being the one who lived, instead of Merle? Is he so much your favourite you can't settle for anything less?"

Belphegore's face grew red with anger, his pale eyes bulging. "Arlen, I suggest you be quiet."

"You owe me this, at least!" Zachary cried. "At least one ounce of love! Don't remove my blindfold now, there's no way for me to go back." He was almost hysterical, his heart pounding in his ears. A cold sweat had broken out all over his body. "Praise Harmatia—it is a city of gold and light. Praise it until it crumbles to dust."

"Arlen, stop!" Belphegore roared, and out and around the grounds, people turned to look at them. Belphegore quickly calmed himself, Zachary putting several strides between them and flopping back against the wall. "How dare you question my love for you?" Belphegore continued in a soft voice. "How dare you use Rufus's name in such a way? You are my apprentice. Have I failed you so badly that you think I do not still honour that?"

"I think that very soon, any semblance of me that you're proud of will be gone. And you'll never hear my voice again, or see my eyes, or know me. My only request is that you don't hurry that process."

"Arlen, what *are* you talking about?"

"You really don't know, do you?" Zachary pushed himself away from the wall. "Would you do anything if you did?" He shook his head before Belphegore could answer, drawing in a ragged breath. "It doesn't matter. You'd better go—the King isn't a patient man. I will lead an envoy to Bethean if that's your wish, but spare me the politics. From here, I only want to live in peace."

Belphegore called after him, but Zachary stalked away, unwilling to expose any more of himself. Their display had been too public—Zachary would have to control himself before rumours began to fly that he was running mad. If he maintained his behaviour, they would confine him to his chambers, and the physicians would start clucking around him, throwing about their remedies. And then DuGilles would arrive, with his magical cure.

Zachary made it home without incident, people quickly moving out of his path, wary of his dark expression. There was one good thing to be said about having severe features—they were an excellent deterrent when Zachary wanted to be alone.

He threw open the doors and almost collided with woman on the other side. Zachary corrected himself, made to apologise and then, for the second time in so many minutes, grew very still.

Isolde stared back at him, her own eyes wide. Amidst the chaos of the dragon attack, Zachary had forgotten that Daniel had invited her, and now here she was, like something out of a nightmare.

She'd changed over the last nineteen years. Her face was still as lovely as the day he'd met her, but it seemed drained of something, somehow. Where once she'd toiled in the kitchen and around the house as a servant, she was now well-dressed and pampered. And yet, she looked as if she hadn't slept a full night in ten years. There were no lines of laughter around her eyes and mouth, where Zachary had expected them to form. Her dark eyes were dull, and her full lips somehow seemed thinner, though that was perhaps because she was pursing her mouth.

Neither of them spoke as they studied each other in stunned silence. Daniel came in from the dining hall and stopping short. The boy had no idea of the history that lay between them, and as the silence stretched, it grew heavier. Finally, Isolde seemed to remember herself.

"Milord." She curtsied deeply, tearing her eyes away from Zachary.

"Isolde," he forced back stiffly, and then, feeling his duty as host done, he pushed past her and made his way up to his bedroom. Only when the door was closed and locked, did he allow himself to slide to the floor, helpless.

CHAPTER
40

"Korrick has returned from the border—it's as Joshua says," Fae said, throwing open Boyd's doors and stepping into the physician's chambers. Inside, Boyd, Rufus and Joshua were gathered waiting for news. The Prince looked up from where he was resting, exhausted, in Rufus's arms.

Since the first vision of the dragon attack, they'd come again in waves. Korrick had excused Joshua from training, and had departed solemnly for Bethean to confirm whether the visions were true. The Prince had spent most of the days since out of sunlight, flittering between consciousness under Boyd's care.

Never before had his visions come so strongly and with such force. Yet, try as Joshua might to connect with Varyn again, he'd been unable since the woman named Béatrice had pushed him out of the dream.

"Sigel'eg is under attack from the largest dragon in written history."

"Is the city lost?" Boyd chewed his thumb, glancing nervously at Joshua, who closed his eyes.

"It's uncertain. The dragon has already caused considerable damage however, and the armies of Kathra have not been able to bring it down. The death toll continues to rise." Fae sat on the bed where Joshua was laid, cradled in his brother's lap. He felt her hand brush his arm in quiet comfort.

"How is he?" she asked Rufus.

"The visions are getting stronger. Whatever is drawing him to Sigel'eg must be very important."

"Have you seen any of it?" Fae asked.

"Flashes," Rufus admitted. "Sometimes when I'm near him, I share the burden. But I've never seen them come so frequently and so strong."

"Varyn," Joshua moaned. "He's...Varyn is..." he drew off and slumped. "He needs to live."

"Who is Varyn?" Boyd asked softly, as if Joshua might not hear him if he spoke low enough.

"I don't know, but he's clearly someone significant to our future." Rufus kissed the crown of Joshua's head. "Did Korrick bring any more news, Fae?"

"Rumours are spreading in Bethean that Harmatia has not yet sent aid. Many believe they don't intend to."

"So Sverrin is content to watch Sigel'eg burn?" Rufus cursed. "Those poor people."

"King Markus is sending relief and aid for the villages around Sigel'eg that can be reached, but the situation is dire." Fae wrapped her fingers around Joshua's, and he could feel her fear strumming through her. She was worried about him, worried what the continuous destruction would do for his visions. Joshua pushed himself up.

"I need to see," he said weakly. "I need to reach Varyn."

"What you need is to rest." Boyd moved around from his desk. "These visions are putting your body under extreme stress. You shouldn't encourage them."

"The visions won't stop until it's over. And if my visions won't show me what I need, then I have to get my own answers." Joshua pushed himself up and away from Rufus, and struggled down onto the floor. He wobbled dangerously but steadied himself, stumbling slowly across to Boyd's shelves. Fae stayed close behind him, shadowing Joshua in-case he fell. "I need an opiate. Some colour-leaf seeds, or poppy maybe."

Rufus inhaled sharply. "You mean to reach Varyn as you did me?" he realised, and Joshua nodded. "Will it work? Our ability is usually limited within the Delphi."

"What exactly is he trying to do?" Boyd demanded.

"We have a certain skill," Rufus explained, "of finding each other. I used it often to track Jionat when he ran away, and Éliane used it to find us in Sarrin after the munity. It allows us to sense each other's presence, and follow the shadow of their journey until we find them."

"And what exactly does that have to do with opiates?" Boyd was rapidly losing his temper, snatching a bottle of dried herbs from Joshua's hands as he examined it.

"When DuGilles took Rufus," Joshua said calmly, "I couldn't follow his trail. I had visions, but couldn't see where they were keeping him. Finally, Howell found a book that said certain medicinal herbs could be used to direct powers like mine. If I couldn't follow Rufus physically, I could do it mentally. I took some opiates, and was able to project myself to Rufus's location. I want to try the same for Varyn—if I could speak with him, if I could just see what's happening—"

"That is absolute madness!" Boyd gabbled.

"Joshua," Fae said, "are you even sure it would work? Varyn is not of your blood."

"No, but we're connected. I've spoken with him before, in dreams. Somehow, he and I are tied. Fae, please—if I don't do this, I think these visions are going to kill me," Joshua admitted, his legs shaking.

Fae exchanged a dismayed look with Boyd, and then turned to Rufus, who gave a solemn nod.

"I don't like the risk, but I fear the alternative would be worse.

Let's try."

Joshua almost sank to the floor with relief. His brother came and fetched him from the shelves, bringing him back to the bed. He was laid down gently, while Boyd mixed a concoction, muttering angrily as he did.

Rufus helped Joshua drink it down, resuming his position behind the boy, so that Joshua could rest against his chest.

As Joshua swallowed the bitter potion, he was seized with a sudden fear. "Don't let go of me," he begged Rufus. "I don't want to go alone."

"I've got you, I promise."

The drugs worked quickly, to Boyd's credit, and they didn't bring with them the rush of nausea that Joshua had suffered last time.

As his mind grew lax, he felt himself begin to drift from the room. It was the first moment of relief he'd had since the visions had started and he was tempted to simply float in the in between state and rest. But Joshua knew he didn't have time. The effects of the drug wouldn't last for long—he had to find Varyn.

The Prince forced himself to focus, casting his mind out to the Hunter, searching desperately for any sense of him. Everything felt clouded, but Joshua pushed himself further, wading through the haze. There had to be something he could use, the tail end of a memory he could grip onto—anything to drag himself toward Varyn...

Something moved through the mist ahead. Joshua jolted, surprised. It was a young girl, around his age, with dark hair and deep black eyes. She stood in the swirling darkness, and extended her hand toward him.

"Par ici," she said.

"What?" Joshua blinked, and she grabbed his hand.

There was a rushing sound. The girl disappeared, swallowed up in the darkness, and Joshua was dragged forward. A strange mix of noises and sensations flooded over him, like he was being pierced with needles, dangled upside down and twisted all at once. And then the smell of smoke filled his nostrils and he coughed hard, the world clearing around him.

A pair of blazing yellow eyes stared hard into his, and Joshua grew still, petrified, as he looked directly into the face of the black-scaled dragon.

It was crouched barely a few strides from him, neck elongated, head resting on the ground. Fire curled from its nostrils, which were bleeding—someone had slashed it across the snout.

Fear, anger and confusion descended over Joshua, like a heavy fall of snow. It took him a moment to realise that the emotions weren't his own. He choked and gasped, and the dragon seemed to whine, its voice reverberating through the stone.

Joshua looked up and around, and saw the reason for its discomfort. Dragons were creatures of the air, but this one had been lured down into the streets of Sigel'eg. It had squeezed its vast body between the buildings in pursuit of its prey, and now it couldn't spread its wings or move.

Somehow, it had allowed itself to be trapped in a way that no intelligent creature should have. Joshua, terrified as he was, found himself extending his hand, and tremulously he rested it against the monster's torn snout. As he looked, he realised that the hand wasn't his own.

"This your power, Joshua? To look into the hearts of others?" Varyn's voice came from his mouth. No—it was the other way around, it was Varyn's mouth, his body. Joshua had slipped into the Hunter's mind, the two suddenly unified. He could feel everything that Varyn did, just as Varyn could feel him. Their minds collided, and mixed.

The waves of intelligible emotion shifted into a concise line as Varyn's fingers stroked the Dragon's snout. Joshua felt himself fading, disintegrating into Varyn. All at once he was the Hunter, and he knew things, his head pooling with memories and sensations *that weren't his own*

This wasn't the first dragon he'd killed. That had been when he was eight years old. The dragon too had been nothing but a baby, hunting on its own for the first time, barely bigger than the house it attacked. Varyn's house—no, not Varyn, his name had been Marek then. That was what all the little boys from Mont'aria were called, until they earned their names.

His father was a blacksmith, whose fine work had earned him general favour in the community, and with the Shin, allowing them a comfortable life. They could afford a meal a day—two sometimes on occasions, and had a house that had two rooms. His mother had been a descendent of one of the Elves—a Fomorii, as they called themselves. Black-eyed, beautiful, impossibly strong.

Her strength didn't save her however, when the dragon ripped through the thatched roof of their home, and doused the room below in flames. She was dead before she had the chance to fight, and Marek's father burnt so badly he could do nothing more than scream until the young dragon ate him.

Feasting on its quarry, the monster hadn't noticed Marek sneaking over to it, his father's knife in his hand. The foolish creature hadn't learnt to be wary—had not yet met an adversary worthy of it. Marek got it in the eye, and then in the other, and in the snout, and everywhere he could reach. The dragon's scales, not yet fully developed, would have still been a hard armour to break through for another man—but Marek had inherited his mother's strength.

Marek remembered little of the fight. He knew only the white blankness of a hunter fighting for his life. No fear, no sadness really—not yet, at least. Only determination, his focus entirely on the task at hand, until the baby dragon was dead, and Marek collapsed beneath it, bleeding and half-dead himself.

What happened next, the herb-witches described as a blood-binding. The dragon's blood had flowed over him, into his wounds and mouth. It would have killed a normal man, toxic and poisonous as it were, but Marek had a drop of Fomorii blood in him—a tiny shred of ancient magic that bound itself with the invading blood.

The Shin found him like this, screaming and writhing, and their alchemists took him in for observation, keen to see what the result of this strange mutation would be.

It changed him, snapping and resetting his bones, his muscles and organ-tissue disintegrating away to be replaced with something even stronger, and more resilient. His senses improved to the point where no mortal mind could withstand the wealth of information it was constantly receiving. Marek was a wild thing, confined to a human body. The Shin used that to their advantage. He was their monster, until he broke free, taking his own name—Varyn.

Joshua could feel the difference now. The Hunter's heart felt three times bigger. His lungs were deeper, his liver stronger. His bones felt light and flexible, capable of withstanding shock and force. And his senses—gods, that was the worst. Joshua could see everything, sound clamping around him like a headache, each frail sensation magnified.

Gently, he felt Varyn reach for him, deep within his own mind, and it was as if the Hunter had covered his ears and eyes, muffling the pulsing world.

"You get used to it," Varyn said. "You learn to control it."

Joshua could have wept, he was so relieved. He allowed himself to settle back, a passenger in Varyn's mind, and watched as the Hunter turned his attention back to the dragon.

She'd hunted him because of the blood that ran through his veins. The blood of her own spawn, which had flown out from the nest one day, and never returned. She was as confused as Varyn by this strange mutation—able to smell her child in his blood, and yet faced with a human.

That was how Varyn had tricked her onto the ground. It was how he'd managed to persuade her to come down among the buildings, where she was at a disadvantage. Her loss had fuelled her fury, and she'd allowed herself to be grounded. From there, it had almost been easy. First, Varyn had slipped his sword into the base of her jaw and pierced the swollen air-pouch, puncturing the gland that dispersed the igniting oil. When she'd tried to douse him in flames, the fire had rolled out over her tongue instead and petered out. Next, Varyn had gone for her legs, piercing the weak joints in the pit and cutting the ligaments, so that she couldn't stand or fight. Robbed of movement and breath, the dragon crumpled, defeated.

Varyn didn't remove his hand from her snout. He'd trained every day in preparation for this fight, had learnt about the dragon's weaknesses—discovered where she was vulnerable and how best to bring her down, But he'd never actually expected to defeat her.

He ran his hand up to the centre of her forehead, patting it. The dragon gave a forlorn wail, and Varyn moved around her slowly as she slumped. He stopped at the base of the skull, where the spine began.

No human was capable of wielding a weapon with enough strength to break through dragon scales, but Varyn had never been limited by the same weaknesses as others. He raised his sword, positioning it against the weak point and then, without sentiment, drove it hard through the bottom of the skull, up into the dragon's brain.

The dragon grew still at last. Varyn drew out his blade, and then turned and sat, resting against her head.

"I'm so sorry," was all Joshua could manage. He hadn't anticipated learning so much, he hadn't anticipated joining with Varyn and stealing the tragedies of his life. Despite this invasion, and the aches of the fight, Varyn seemed happy.

The Hunter breathed deeply, head tipped back against the dragon and laughed. "I have a daughter," he said. Béatrice had kissed him and whispered it in his ear. A daughter. Their daughter. No such thing should have been possible—the mutation should have neutered Varyn for good, but Béatrice wouldn't have lied. "I have a daughter..." he repeated, with wonder.

The last restraints that had bound Varyn came loose, and with them Joshua felt himself grow lighter. He slipped back to his own body, content at last.

The battle was over.

"Piss-pox and plagues—has the world gone to shit?" Aeron growled, head resting in one hand, a tankard of ale nurtured in the other. Emerald gave him a look of contemplative glee and turned back to the counter, filling a glass for herself.

"What's wrong with the baby now?" she asked, and Aeron grumbled.

"What d'you think? Brain-thumpin' me with news like that. It hardly takes a rack, does it? Sigel'eg has barely stopped humpin' its reaper, Harmatia pisses into the southern wind and Bethean decides to call it a fountain? What the livin' piss is Kingship Markus thinkin'? This is all goin' to end in gut-tears. What's he goin' to say to the populous when that Puppet-King rapes his daughter? 'Well, bugger me with bells for the inevitable betrayal of a shine-grabber, but I've whored your heir to Harmatia!' Piss off."

"I love it when you're angry—you talk less and less sense." Emerald took a long drink.

Aeron grumbled to himself and did the same. He took a swig from his tankard and choked almost immediately, spitting his mouthful back in. "The hell's this?" he demanded.

"Found it in the cellar."

"It tastes like fermented rat-balls."

"I found it in the cellar." Emerald repeated and Aeron glanced suspiciously into the drink, shrugged and took another gulp.

"I'm tongueless anyhow," he reasoned. "Or will be."

"The baby talks a lot for being tongueless," Emerald said sweetly. Aeron sneered in response.

"Baby's pocketless and glazed eyed for Cal, who's fire-eatin' Lemra like there's no authority to sharp. He's pissin' a brawl and I'm festerin' here like a sodomite in a woman's bath."

"Aw, sweetness—aren't you such a victim." Emerald battered her eyelashes and Aeron downed his drink, returning to the matter at hand.

"So Markus has actually agreed to let 'ti Aurora tap dance herself to a whore-ary?"

"She decided, actually. Said she wanted to go to Harmatia and hear what the Puppet King had to offer. It's been tense 'tween Kathra and Bethean. Should Harmatia align with us, it could make for a pretty treaty."

"Or a drawbridge to hell."

"More likely. She said she'd go though, so she's gone." Emerald seemed to sober, "I can't see that Aurora'll be much taken with the Puppet-King. But if she is, and this turns sour," Emerald flicked his nose, "it'll be your fault."

Aeron snatched her hand and pulled her arm taut, threatening to break her fingers. She didn't flinch. "How's it *my* fault?"

"Because you clearly can't get a job done."

"It was your mothers that salivated Sverrin DuBlanche back to life, not my game. Torin gave me my orders, and I stabbed him dead. Dead's where he should've stayed." Aeron's eyes burnt their reaper-black.

"I was talkin' about Rufus Merle." Emerald snatched her hand back. "You've finally stopped pissin' blood and pel-thrustin' everythin' like a dog in heat. Don't you think it's time you get to the Neve?"

Aeron's mouth twitched. "Pel-thrustin'?" he raised an eyebrow, drawing another smile out of Emerald. "That's Lemra'n slang, my dove."

"Clearly you've been here too long, my bed-wettin' falcon."

Aeron stood. It had taken some days to regain his ability to walk, but his strength was almost all returned to him now.

The journey to the Neve would be a long one, but with this new development, Aeron could no longer delay it.

"Looks like the hunt continues." He reached out and touched one of the flowers Emerald had set in the middle of the table. At his touch, it withered and died, the life seeping into his fingers like a sip of sweet wine. Aeron flexed his hand. "I knew this was goin' to end in blood."

CHAPTER 41

"He's quite resilient, for a human," Korrick observed softly. A few strides from them the children were training, Joshua battling Kael and one of his other class-mates simultaneously. "I did not expect him back on his feet so quickly."

"He's determined and strong-willed," Rufus said with pride, though his chest was still flittering with worry. It had only been a few days since Joshua's visions of Sigel'eg had ended, and already the Prince was insisting he return to his training. Korrick had agreed, but was surveying Joshua carefully, looking out for any more signs of trouble. Rufus had come to understand over the last week that, as stern and brisk as Korrick was, he truly cared for the welfare of his students.

"Kael," Korrick shouted, his hands clasped behind his back, "raise your guard or lose your life."

From the duel, Kael obeyed, moving in to strike Joshua. He parried expertly.

"Your Prince learns quickly," Korrick said. "He is already besting my kin. In another few weeks he may be outmatching the whole class."

"He has more of an incentive than they do, and experience that they lack." Rufus ran his hand up through his hair. "He also finds you to be an excellent instructor."

Korrick wasn't taken by the praise. "Do not think to give me false acclaim—Kael, I said bring that guard up!—I am well aware of how your Prince feels about me."

"Oh, he doesn't like you—I'm not sure anyone in the Neve actually does," Rufus agreed. "But Joshua respects you, and he wants your approval."

Korrick didn't move, but Rufus saw a spark of amusement in his stern green eyes. "And what is it you want, Magi?"

"For him never to have to use these skills," Rufus admitted wistfully, giving Joshua a half-wave. The boy reciprocated it before returning quickly to his fight, his face pinched with concentration. Rufus marvelled at how, already, he could see an element of Fae in the way Joshua fought. The Prince would one day become a very formidable foe. "I will leave you to it, Lord Korrick."

"Magi," Korrick called after him as Rufus walked away, "you have been our guest some time now, but do not grow comfortable yet. You are still the enemy of many and you should not be walking these grounds unattended."

"I'll go straight to the library," Rufus promised.

"I doubt that." Korrick gestured sharply at his students. "Kael—if you cannot wield your sword properly, then I will take it from you. *Raise your guard!*"

Rufus, mildly perplexed, left the training grounds and wandered back toward the castle. It occurred to him how alone he was, and he realised that he hadn't seen his subconscious since he'd told Fae about his ordeals. The bad dreams had also stopped again, and though Rufus didn't dare hope this mental silence was permanent, he enjoyed it while it lasted.

Turning up along the path, Rufus hummed softly, cheerful in the fine weather. As he came toward the courtyard, however, he spotted something in one of the banks below. Immediately he faltered.

Reilly Mac Gearailt was stood barely twenty strides down from him, entwined with one of the fair-haired wanderers, kissing her with abandon.

Rufus couldn't move. He felt as if someone was squeezing his throat. His surprise quickly turning to anger. Fae had shared very little about her relationship with Reilly, but something about her conduct toward him had set Rufus's teeth on edge.

Looking down at Reilly now, it was all Rufus could do to contain himself. It was none of his business if Reilly was having an affair, but to do it so brazenly, without any consideration, was an affront to Fae. And that was unforgivable.

Rufus found himself skidding down the bank, his face red. "What in *Athea's* name are you doing?"

Reilly broke the kiss, and looked leisurely over his shoulder. He'd known Rufus was there all along, but had continued the display regardless. On instinct, Rufus began to gather magic to him.

"This is none of your concern, Magi," Reilly dismissed.

"Have you no shame? No sense of propriety?" Rufus opened and closed his hands, trying to even the anger that boiled through him. His skin was growing hotter each minute. "You would do this, out in the open? You would demean your wife in her own home?"

"My dear," Reilly addressed the beautiful wanderer who still had her arms draped around his neck, her body pressed against his, "perhaps you should be on your way. I must clearly educate this human."

The wanderer flicked her eyes over to Rufus, smiled inanely and then sidled gracefully away, skipping up the bank toward the house. Reilly advanced on Rufus with a smile that only enraged him more.

"I think," Reilly said slowly, "you ought to remember your place."

"And I think you ought to remember yours. These are Lord Kathel and Lady Saraid's lands, and I doubt they would think much of your actions."

"Perhaps not," Reilly shrugged, "but they would forgive a man for straying. It's not my fault my wife cannot satisfy me."

"You sicken me," Rufus spat. "You think you can treat her like this? Belittle her, shame her, ostracise her from her own family?"

"What are you going to do?" Reilly was unperturbed by Rufus's words. "She is my wife and I can do with her as I please, be that play false, or send her away, or strike her when she does not obey me."

It was too much. Rufus lost himself to his rage. In an instant he recalled Fae's broken cheekbone, and he knew precisely what had happened.

He threw the first, clumsy punch before he knew it. Reilly could have easily parried, but instead he allowed Rufus's hand to connect with his cheek. It was like punching a tree, and had about the same result.

Reilly, eyebrows raised, planted his hand firmly into Rufus's chest and threw him back with enough force to make his ribs rattle. The Magi hit into the ground with yelp of pain.

"Are you trying to *kill me*, Magi?" Reilly shouted.

Rufus blinked, his eyes watering. "You bastard..." he wheezed, just as a set of identical Cat Sidhe appeared at the top of the knoll.

"Commander Mac Gearailt, we heard a commotion," the first said.

Is everything alright?" The second narrowed his eyes. Rufus recognised them as Fae's twin brothers—Arton and Eadoin.

"The Magi attacked me," Reilly sneered, and both twins looked down at Rufus with terrifying eyes, drawing their weapons.

Etheus blind me. This was a trap. Rufus groaned, trying to roll to his feet. Reilly had purposefully goaded him into attacking.

Rufus's protection as a guest was forfeited if he turned on his hosts, and Reilly was going to make the most of that pathetic punch.

Korrick knew about this. He must have. Damn it, how can I be so stupid?

Rufus managed to scrabble upright, his ribs screaming in protest. Boyd was going to be very unhappy with him. "It's not what it seems," Rufus said, but both Arton and Eadoin descended down the bank, their swords out. Rufus raised his hands in surrender, but at the sight of it, the twins jumped back, as if they expected Rufus to throw out a wall of flame. "No, no!" Rufus said quickly, "I'm not going to hurt you. I'm unarmed, see?"

"A Magi is never unarmed." Reilly kept his voice low, but Rufus could see the smugness in his eyes.

"Please." Rufus looked between the twins. He had no desire to hurt either of them. "Please, you must understand, it was only a punch. He was kissing another woman!"

But the twins wouldn't be so easily deterred form their commander, their eyes never leaving Rufus.

"I was defending your sister's honour."

"Our sister has no honour," Arton growled.

"She brought a Magi into our home," Eadoin said.

"She loves you. She loves all of you." Rufus tried to push himself back. "Damn you, can't you see you're being manipulated?" Rufus pointed at Reilly. "He's using you to punish Fae. He's twisting your minds. I'm not the villain here!"

"I was suspicious of your intentions when you arrived," Reilly snarled, "but to honour my lord, I tolerated your presence. And in exchange, you throw about slander and attack me unprovoked."

"You're inexcusable," Rufus spat. "You'd have me defend myself against Fae's brothers? That's your hope, isn't it? That I'll fight them, and hurt them—even kill them, all so you can be right in your judgement. All so you can shame Fae and segregate her even more from those she loves. I won't do it!"

"Stand, Magi." Arton thrust his sword toward Rufus, and it took all of Rufus's self-control not to retaliate. His nerves jumped down his body, magic sweeping through his blood.

"You will fight us." Eadoin's sword joined his brother's.

"No." Rufus closed his eyes. "If you think I've done wrong, then kill me. I refuse to raise a hand to either of you."

"Stand, Magi!"

"No."

"Stand!"

"NO!" Rufus twisted his hands into the grass, shaking. He'd faced death many times, but this was different.

He'd only just been with Joshua. What would the boy think when he returned from his training, looked down into the bank and saw Rufus, murdered? Rufus opened his eyes, looking pleadingly between the two brothers. They were angry and confused, but there was no pity for Rufus to exploit.

"Then you will die," both twins said in terrifying unison, and in an instant, Rufus knew he had to defend himself.

Unwilling to play into Reilly's hands, Rufus focused his attention on the swords. He extended his senses, trying to reach into the metal and break it down into useless pieces, as he'd so often done with the exploding apples.

But as his senses found their targets, rather than break the bonds that held the swords together, Rufus felt the sensation deepen. He was conscious of his mind gripping the swords, like a million tiny hands reaching inside of them. And as he jerked his senses, trying to snap the blades into pieces, he instead carried them up and out of the twins' hands, as if he'd somehow reached and grabbed them for himself.

The swords flew up out of the Cat Sidhes' reach and were tossed uselessly to the side. Arton and Eadoin both gaped, opening and closing their empty hands in surprise as Rufus blinked.

He'd just moved those swords with his mind—a level six technique.

"He has disarmed you! He means to *kill* you!" Reilly shouted, but before anyone was given a chance to move, a sudden bolt of pure white light had appeared between Rufus and the twins. Arton and Eadoin were lifted up into the air by the shining force, and tossed to the side after their swords.

Rufus cried out, shielding his eyes from the dazzling newcomer, who shimmered like sunshine on a pool of water. Through the bright rays, Rufus could see hair as pale as ivory, and skin so fair it was almost translucent.

"What," Fae's voice rang out from the light and Rufus balked, "in the name of Danu, is the meaning of this?"

Her voice was terrible. It sounded alien, and echoed like a thousand beings before her. It was the voice of an immortal, and Rufus knew it, for he too had spoken like that once, when he'd become Athea. The power terrified him.

"Fae?" Reilly was as astounded as Rufus to see her, his own eyes shaded against the vibrant light. His amazement quickly turned to anger, the gaping mouth curling into a snarl. "You dare come between us? Your Magi attacked me."

"If Rufus attacked you, you'd be on fire or worse." Fae's entire body shimmered, power pulsing around her. Rufus didn't understand what was going on. He didn't recognise anything of the woman in-front of him, and yet she was Fae in every way.

"He is a Magi, his nature is clear." Reilly gritted his teeth.

"All you have proven in this farce is your own true nature," Fae said. "Get out of my sight, Reilly, before you make an enemy of me."

With a burst of black mist, Reilly changed. His cat form was larger than Fae's, but somehow, he wasn't nearly as imposing. "I am your commander!" he roared. "You think because you are a Chosen that elevates you above me?"

A Chosen, the words resonated through Rufus. Where had he heard them before?

"I think that the truth of what happened here is something

you might heed." Fae stood her ground. The light wrapped around her like hundreds of knives, slicing through the air. "I saw the entire exchange—saw you bait and provoke and the aforementioned 'attack' you are using to justify this. I suggest you retreat before I report your fraudulence and dishonesty to my parents. Commander you may be, but only by appointment. Think carefully before you let your dishonesty strip you of rank."

Reilly grew quiet, his tail flicking. Rufus understood enough about Kathel and Saraid that such an incident, if reported truthfully, wouldn't be welcomed. Reilly had been snagged in his own trap.

"He will betray you." Reilly stood down, transforming back and stepping away. "Mark my words."

"No quicker than you did," Fae said.

Reilly snarled, and retreated, disappearing up the bank. Fae remained as she was, and then the bright light slowly began to ebb away from her. Rufus recalled that he'd seen it before, blurred, and during a great confusion, the day Fae broke through the roof of the Korrigans' nest and rescued them.

As the light disappeared, her hair returned to its natural gold, the hue of her skin growing darker until she was the woman he knew.

Fae didn't stop. She strode across to her brothers and leant down, seizing them both by the ears as if they were children. They yelped as she knocked their heads lightly together.

"I hope the pair of you are suitably embarrassed with yourselves," she said, speaking over them as they made to protest. "Silence!" her voice rang, and they grew meek, eyes wide. "You are a disappointment to our family—I have never been so ashamed to call you kindred."

"You brought a Magi into our home—*you* are the disappointment!" Arton cried and Fae slapped him across the face.

"I said silence!" she bellowed. "You have sulked long enough.

Father welcomed Rufus into the Neve. He's a Delphi and my friend. Now, I love you both more than life, and I have given you time to adjust, but I am growing tired of your continued ignorance. The pair of you will grow up, or I will have Korrick put you into the same class as the children you are behaving as. Do you understand?"

Neither replied, and Fae bristled, straightening up.

"Do you *understand*?" she repeated and both nodded. Fae huffed, putting her hands on her hips. "Good. Then, if you're done letting Reilly use you, I would like my brothers back now."

Arton and Eadoin struggled to keep the dismay from their faces. Fae knelt down and took one in either arm, holding them both. They returned the embrace.

"Sorry," Arton muttered sheepishly.

"We were foolish," Eadoin echoed.

Fae released them and stood, looking pointedly at Rufus, who'd yet to find his feet.

"Are you hurt, Magi?" Arton asked, avoiding Rufus's eyes.

"No," Rufus said, and then winced as he tried to sit forward. "Bruised ribs…but I'll heal."

"Sorry for…We're sorry." Eadoin gestured loosely, before both twins looked up at Fae for her approval. She nodded, and the pair quickly gathered their swords and, with another mumbled apology, departed in the opposite direction to Reilly. Fae crossed to Rufus and gently pulled him upright. Rufus gripped her by the arms.

"Fae…" he said. "What was that? That light when you appeared…"

"Don't worry about it," Fae tried to assure him, but it was too late.

"Did they call you a *Chosen?*" he choked.

Fae winced ever so slightly. "Yes."

"A Chosen." Rufus's hands slipped from her arms and he staggered back. He hit the bank wall and sank down again.

Fae remained stood, her eyes cast down. Rufus couldn't count the emotions that passed through her expression—anger, uncertainty, sadness, irritation.

"What do you know about it?" she eventually asked.

Rufus swallowed. The term had cropped up in one of the books he'd been reading in Fae's library. He could see the page in his mind's eye, clear as if he were holding it in-front of him. He recited it, dumb for his words. "A rare gift found among those with divine ancestry is the ability to safely and completely dispose of one's own mortality. These lucky few are encouraged to live a mortal childhood, and then transcend into a full, immortal form during the peak of adulthood. They are aptly known as 'The Chosen."

Fae looked up at him, her eyes glowing their vivacious green.

"That summarises it, yes," she finally said.

"So that's it?" Rufus tore his hands through his hair, tugging his fringe. A new kind of terror had gripped him as he finally understood. "That's what your parents were referring to? That you should be *ambitious*? They expected you to have *transcended*."

Fae sighed heavily. "We have only had one other Chosen in my family—my eldest brother, Oscar. He shed his mortality on his twentieth birthday, and now lives on the Sidhe islands, among the Tuatha de Danaan. It's a great honour, you know, to have a Chosen child. To have had two—well..." She clenched her left hand in her right. "They're waiting for me to follow Oscar's example."

"Why haven't you?"

"You know why," Fae said tersely. She rang her hands. "What you just saw was a small glimpse of my potential power. I am able to tip the balance between Soul and Mortal. For a short time I can almost entirely transcend. The first time I did it was by accident when I came through the roof of the Korrigans' nest. It took me years to learn to replicate it, but I can do it at will now. If I held the form for more than a few minutes, however, the change would be permanent."

"You can't," Rufus whispered. "You can't change."

Fae looked up at him sharply. "That's not for you to decide."

"You can't! I know you—you could never be like Niamh, capable of kidnapping children. Or those bloody wanderers, parading down the corridor with no purpose or sight beyond their pleasures." Rufus's voice cracked, but he forced himself on. "That's your parents' ambition for you? *That!*"

"You wouldn't understand." Fae didn't rise to his anger, her voice level. "I have an ability within me to surpass anyone who has come before me, to shape the terrain, to build and conquer and create a new world single-handedly. And all it would cost me is my natural death."

"As if you weren't already capable of all that!" Rufus gestured wildly. "Isn't it just an ill-disguised excuse to run away from hardship—to submit to the temptation of having everything, so that you never have to be attached to anything."

"Lose your tone and lower your voice or I am leaving," Fae said softly.

Rufus gulped in several lungful's of air, trying to calm himself. Finally he nodded, his face red. He could feel the blood thundering through him, hard and fast.

"Are you really willing to sacrifice half of yourself to fulfil an expectation you already meet?" He looked desperately up at her from where he was still on his knees. "Do none of them care how much it would change you?"

Fae swallowed, then very slowly she lowered herself to the ground in-front of him.

"Do you remember that night, before we left Sarrin," she said quietly. "I told you the old Sidhe story about the two snakes of humanity—Betrayal and Death?"

Rufus nodded dumbly.

"The story was a lesson, written to separate us from humans— to divide and protect us."

"I remember."

Fae paused. "I savoured my pain when Jionat died. It was terrible, and great, and a reflection of how much I loved him." She stopped again. "Rufus, why would I ever submit to the same powers who would summarise everything I shared with Jionat by his death?" She took Rufus's hand. "I don't want to be immortal. I don't want to lose sight of the value of life. I don't want to grow so afraid of loss that I cut its potential from my life." She cupped his chin with her other hand. "The reason I didn't tell you about being a Chosen, was that I had already made my choice, and I didn't need you to tell me it was the right one." She let her fingers drop and then moved, so she was sat beside him, their shoulders lightly touching.

"I'm sorry," Rufus mumbled. "I jumped to conclusions. I thought you were going to…"

"Leave you behind?" Fae said, and Rufus winced. That was precisely what he'd thought. "Rufus, there has always been an expectation of greatness from me, and I have shied away from it time and time again. I have done things which I am ashamed of, but this wasn't one of them. I *chose* mortality, and I will choose it again every day."

Rufus closed his eyes in wordless relief. Carefully, he dropped his head onto her shoulder. She rested her cheek against his hair, blowing it gently out of her face. He heard the deepness of her breath, his ear against her skin. She smelt sweet, and light, like warm fields at sunset. He turned her wrist over, and without looking, traced the crescent birthmark there.

He hadn't seen it on her, in her white form, and its absence had marked him profoundly. Fae looped her fingers reassuringly between his.

"Why?" she asked softly. "Why did you confront Reilly? You could have been killed."

"He was kissing her…" Rufus stroked his thumb over hers, still getting his breath back.

441

"It has nothing to do with you."

"He was trying to humiliate you. I couldn't forgive that." Rufus exhaled deeply. Fae laughed breathily.

"You are so stupid sometimes…"

"And you're too strong," Rufus sighed. "You bear too much, Fae. Stupid I may have been, but I wasn't wrong."

Fae laughed again, squeezing his hand. "Nobody has ever fought for my honour before," she said softly, and turning her face, she kissed him on the cheek. "Thank you, Rufus."

CHAPTER
42

The dragon was gargantuan. Zachary hovered high up above it, disguised among the clouds as he circled Sigel'eg, trying to find a safe place to land.

News of the dragon's defeat had reached them a few days ago, and he'd flown as soon as he could. A part of Zachary hadn't dared to believe it was true, but there was the dragon, stretched out in the lower part of the city. Already it was being harvested for its rich parts, scales pulled away, teeth removed, flesh and body carved for concoctions and potions. Zachary wouldn't be surprised if some of the hungry citizens hadn't attempted to steal away parts for their dinner. He doubted they'd get very far. Bozidar wouldn't be willing to share in the bounty that had almost destroyed his city.

The story was that it had been killed by an Isny Hunter that Bozidar had been keeping prisoner. Zachary couldn't think how that could possibly be true, but the Hunter, excused of all crimes, now bore the title of 'the Dragon of Sigel'eg', and was being heralded throughout the land. Varyn was his name, or so Zachary had heard.

There was evidence of celebrating in the capital too. Zachary could see streamers and confetti littering the streets. On all accounts it might have been a happy image, were half of the lower town not completely destroyed and the entire city on high guard.

Bozidar had closed off the capital during the repairs, minimising the chance of looting, until order was re-established. Nobody could get in or out without permission.

As a gesture of good will, Sverrin had arranged to send aid in the form of medics, Magi, and food, to help the city reclaim itself. Zachary wasn't among the list of those appointed to go, and thus, had absconded in the night.

The journey, long enough by carriage or horse, was made considerably shorter in flight, though Zachary had been forced to fly cautiously, wary of being spotted in his Night Patrol form. Much smaller as he was, he didn't want to give the residence of Sigel'eg the impression that there was *another* dragon swooping down on their city.

Whilst Zachary had expected some difficulty in getting into the capital, he hadn't anticipated quite this much. The battlements were well guarded, the soldiers patrolling and on lookout, their eyes cast to the sky as much as to the ground. Zachary's black scales allowed him to blend with the night but he wasn't invisible and the guards were being especially vigilant.

After several long minutes, Zachary finally saw a blind spot behind the roof of a tower. Feeling relieved, he flew toward it, landing silently as a ghost. Quickly he transformed back.

He crept to the edge and looked down into the window below him. It was ajar, just wide enough for him to slip through. Carefully, he lowered himself down and dangled over the edge. Shifting across, he eased himself in, stepping out onto a thick rug on the other side.

It was a child's bedroom, or so Zachary guessed by the dolls and toys littered about the place. He crept to the door and peered out into the corridor beyond. It was empty, with a set of winding stairs in the far left, leading down into the rest of the castle.

Zachary followed them, creeping through the darkness.

As he descended, he started to hear more signs of life. People talking, some snoring in the rooms he passed. There were obviously still celebrations, laughter and music rising up from the belly of the castle.

He'd just managed to sneak into the eastern wing of the castle, where the Harmatian envoys were usually kept, when he came face to face with a group of patrolling guards.

For a brief moment nobody moved, Zachary stood suspiciously, all in black, creeping down the corridor. The guards stared at him, waiting for him to move or explain himself. The last thing they wanted to do was attack one of Bozidar's guests, but the longer Zachary kept his silence, the more suspicious he became.

"Gentlemen," Zachary eventually said, bowing his head slightly. The guards all bowed slowly back, and Zachary turned and sprinted in the opposite direction. He heard them shouting out behind him, and grimaced to himself. Had he told them who he was, they would have let him be, but if word got back to Sverrin that Zachary was in Sigel'eg…Zachary shuddered at the mere thought of it.

The guards' heavy footsteps were getting louder behind him, and Zachary flittered quickly down another corridor. He didn't know the castle well, unless he shook his pursuers soon, he was going to get cornered eventually.

Swearing under his breath, Zachary ran toward a window. Throwing it open, he climbed out, dangling himself off the ledge out of sight. No sooner had he done so, than he heard the guards running past.

The things I do for you, Hathely, Zachary thought, counting the scuffled footsteps as he clung to the edge, his feet balanced on the small cracks in the brickwork.

From below him, he heard a sound, and he looked down in time to see Béatrice stick her head out a window and look up at him. "I was starting to wonder when you would arrive." She ushered him closer, and stepped back from the sill.

Zachary huffed a laugh and, agile as a cat, climbed down to her window and swung himself in.

"Ah là là, you would make a terrific assassin, Arlen," Béatrice said as he came into the room, and immediately he crossed to her. A quick examination showed no injuries, and the pair embraced.

"Thank Notameer, you're safe," Zachary exhaled.

Béatrice released him. "Marcel?"

"He's in Harmatia, under watch. He knows nothing about this."

"Good." Béatrice stepped back, revealing she wasn't alone in the room. Behind her, Isaac Thornton had risen from a chair and was beaming.

"Thornton," Zachary greeted with relief.

Isaac had changed very little over the years, though he wore his hair shorter now, and seemed stockier for the cold he lived in, his skin a little ruddy.

"Zachary." Isaac strode forward and, before Zachary could object, dragged him into a bone-crushing hug. "I didn't expect to see you. It's been so long."

"The mountain air seems to have suited you," Zachary wheezed, slapping Isaac on the back. "Let go of me, you bear—I can't breathe."

Isaac laughed, and released him. Zachary noted that his friend's accent had softened, into something more northern. "But how did you get into the city?" he asked. "Did King Sverrin send you?"

"I am here unofficially," Zachary said delicately, straightening his clothes.

"Here, to quench your thirst." Béatrice passed Zachary a goblet and gestured for him to sit. "What news of Harmatia?"

"More of the same." Zachary dropped into a chair, taking a grateful swig of wine. "Sverrin is sending aid to Kathra as we speak—food and supplies."

"Too little, too late." Béatrice kept her voice low. "He should have sent Magi to help immediately."

"We advised it. You know I would have come myself, but—"

"You don't have to explain," Isaac said. "You made the right decision in staying away."

Zachary sighed, kneading his forehead. "I don't know about that." He sat back. "How long until Bozidar lets you leave?"

"Another few weeks, I think." Béatrice paused. "Will you carry a letter for me, Arlen? To my brother?"

"Of course."

She went immediately to the writing desk in the corner of the room, and Zachary closed his eyes, tempted to sleep for a minute.

"You seem tired, my friend." Isaac refilled Zachary's glass generously.

Zachary waved him a thanks and took a long draught, massaging his forehead with his other hand. "No more than we all are. But I must depart soon, if I hope to be back in Harmatia by morning."

"You have business to attend to?" Isaac drew up a chair opposite Zachary, leaning in.

"I don't want to be missed." Zachary smiled tersely, ignoring his friend's worried frown. "I am set to ride with a party in a few days, to meet and accompany the Princess Aurora to the capital."

"So it's true?" Isaac coughed with disbelief. "Sverrin denied Kathra aid, and now he's propositioning Bethean? And King Markus has agreed to it?"

"I was as surprised as you are." Zachary continued to massage his forehead. Lately, he seemed to have a perpetual headache. He watched Béatrice write in silence, and released a shuddering breath. "Thornton," he began softly, "I have a favour to ask of you, but it is no small thing."

"Name it," Isaac said.

Zachary smiled at his friend's easy generosity. "I have a brother," he explained. "Daniel. He's studying at the academy, specialising in architecture. He means to be an ambassador, like you."

Isaac didn't falter, seeing the link quickly. "You want me to take him as my apprentice?"

"What I want is for you to take him away. Back to La'Kalciar, if you can. He's a hard worker, good head on his shoulders. Too curious at times but he'll grow out of it. I want him to be safe in the event that...I want him safe."

Isaac studied Zachary closely. He gave a firm nod. "I look forward to meeting him."

Zachary gave a slim smile of thanks, relief pouring through him. Béatrice returned to the table, slipping him her letter and giving him a firm kiss on the temple. Zachary narrowed his eyes at her.

"If you expect me to pass *that* on to Hathely as well, you're sorely mistaken."

"It was for you." She kissed him again and he rose.

"I should go." Zachary shook Isaac's hand, as his friend also mounted to his feet.

"How do you plan on getting out?" Isaac asked.

"It'll be easier than getting in." Zachary concentrated and began to draw magic sharply into himself. The familiar feeling of the transformation crackled through him, but he quelled it, so that only his wings formed, unfurling dramatically from his back. He heard Isaac scoff.

"Etheus blind me, I forgot how much you like to show off." Isaac rolled his eyes as Zachary spread his wings out, stretching them.

Zachary cackled. "I don't get much chance these days." He moved to the window, and paused as he stepped up onto the ledge. "Notameer protect you both, and I hope to see you in the coming days."

"Malak watch over you," Béatrice blessed, and Zachary leant out of the window and jumped, soaring down and then up into the air, back toward Harmatia.

It was well past dawn and into the late morning by the time Zachary made it to the capital. He landed a few miles away, and walked to the gate, unwilling to illicit a panic by flying in. The guards noted his entrance, looking down through their ledgers to see when he'd left. Zachary stalked past them, scowling hard at anyone who stared.

Béatrice's letter burned hot in his pocket, but Zachary knew better than to go straight to the Hathely household. There were too many eyes on him. He turned homeward instead, exhausted and hungry.

It was only when he stepped into his empty and silent hallway that he knew something was wrong. As the door slammed shut behind him, there was a flurry of movement from the dining room, and one of the servants came out, pale and shaking.

"Lord Zachary." She bowed, her eyes wide.

"What's going on? What's happened?" Zachary was immediately alert, forcing down his fatigue. The servant jumped at his voice, though he hadn't spoken loudly.

"Zachary, come and join us," Sverrin called from within the library, and Zachary's blood ran cold.

"The King is here," the servant forced out, and then fled immediately for the kitchen.

Zachary slowly made his way through the dining room into the library, his throat tight. From the door, he could see Daniel and Isolde, sitting rigidly side by side. Zachary could make out the back of Sverrin's head, peeking out over the top of the chair nearest the door, his elbow jutting over the arm-rest.

Zachary inhaled deeply, and came forward, bowing to the King. "Your Majesty, we were not expecting your company."

"Oh no, no—I was merely dropping by." Sverrin waved, pointing to the seat closest to him. Zachary settled into it uneasily, his back stiff and straight. "It occurred to me that I hadn't met your brother yet. I thought I'd come and see him for myself." Sverrin clasped his hands together, his fingers interwoven. He eyed Daniel, who was staring at a point on the wall over Sverrin's shoulder. "He is quite pretty, wouldn't you say? Looks a lot like his mother, though I suppose he has that Zachary air," Sverrin observed, as if Daniel were a stallion on sale. "I have to ask, are you sure he's your father's, and not yours?"

Isolde twitched, her fingers tightening into her skirt. Zachary tried to ignore it—he knew they were all being goaded. Sverrin was playing with the mood, though Zachary didn't know why.

The King hummed. "So, you are not a warrior then, Daniel?"

"No, Your Majesty."

"A pity—the times are unpredictable. We need soldiers for the coming battles."

"And we need architects to rebuild the cities when we've finished destroying them," Daniel replied.

Sverrin chose to laugh at this, much to Zachary's relief. "He *is* a Zachary, isn't he? Not afraid to speak the truth." Sverrin sat forward. "I commend that. I like truthful people—the starker, the better. They suit my temperament."

"I will never lie to you, Your Majesty," Daniel said starkly.

"No," Sverrin waggled his finger, "you will not. I can trust that."

Daniel's mouth tightened, and he flicked his eyes quickly over to Zachary. There was something apologetic about his expression. Sverrin cleared his throat, and Zachary's heart sank.

"I hear from your brother that you were out all night."

Zachary fought the urge to close his eyes and bury himself in the chair, away from sight.

Sverrin continued. "You always did have dreadful nightly habits."

"Some things never change," Zachary said lightly.

"Hm." Sverrin stared. "Are they alive then?"

Zachary's entire chest felt like it was collapsing in on itself. He wasn't able to disguise all of his surprise. Sverrin picked up on it easily.

"Zachary," he said sweetly, "what were my orders?"

"No Night Patrol was to go to Sigel'eg."

"And what did you do?"

This time Zachary did close his eyes, wincing. "I flew to Sigel'eg."

Sverrin huffed. "See," he turned to Daniel, "honesty. I like honesty. I knew you would disobey me Zachary, but in this instance, I should be glad of some news. Are they alive? Béatrice, and your friend Thornton?"

"They are," Zachary said. Sverrin seemed to find his disobedience humorous, but Zachary didn't dare hope himself forgiven. The King's mood could change instantly and without warning.

"That's a great relief." Sverrin seemed genuinely pleased, smiling brightly. He leant in to Daniel. "When we were young, there wasn't a man in the court who wasn't in love with Béatrice Hathely," he said. "She was the most desired woman in the capital. I fancied her for myself a while, I confess, and I might have taken her too, if not for her daughter." Sverrin smirked. "Your brother, I think, is still rather soft for her, but then, he has always had a preference for older women." The King strayed his eyes over to Isolde, who dropped her own with embarrassment. Daniel followed the King's gaze, and Zachary could see his brother's mind spinning and tumbling.

"Daniel," Zachary said, "your classes will have started. You ought to get to them."

"Y-yes." Daniel went to stand.

Sverrin put up his hand, and motioned Daniel to remain where he was. Daniel sank reluctantly back into the chair.

"I want to hear more about you," Sverrin chirped. "Your classes can wait—surely your teachers will forgive you if you mention my name."

"Yes, Your Majesty."

"Tell me of your childhood. Where were you raised?"

Daniel found his point on the wall again and spoke, as if reciting. "I was born in my mother's home, in Corhlam. At six, when I was old enough, my father summoned me to live in Anaes's Fort. I was schooled and educated there privately. When they discovered I had a capacity for magic, I attended an academy close by. Completing my studies there, I was sent here to the capital to do a further year and take the assessments."

"You must be very studious," Sverrin said. "Did your father beat you?"

The silence was piercing. Daniel's eyes bulged. "No."

"Never?"

Daniel winced. "He struck me once when I was a child, for speaking out of turn. I apologised. He never raised a hand to me again."

Zachary gripped the armrests tightly, trying to keep himself rooted to the seat. Sverrin continued, as if oblivious to the atmosphere he'd created.

"You wouldn't believe what he used to do to Zachary." Sverrin whistled. "But then your brother is inherently disobedient, and sometimes extreme measures must be used to correct that."

Zachary was glad he hadn't eaten, his stomach heaving. He swallowed, and said, "The dragon was defeated. I went to see that our people were safe. I was discreet." His voice came out surprisingly calm, even though he felt like all his muscles were trembling beneath his skin. "I didn't think you would mind."

"If you really thought that, you would have asked my permission first." Sverrin kept his pleasant tone, and it made Zachary sicker. "Fortunately for you, I would have said yes." Sverrin pushed himself to his feet, collecting his sword, which he'd unbuckled from his belt and rested against his chair. He reattached it to his side, gesturing for Isolde and Daniel, who'd risen, to sit again. They did so. "You're to get ready and ride out for Corhlam immediately, Zachary. The Princess is joining us sooner than expected."

"Today?" Zachary's knees felt weak at the prospect of riding out again after such a long journey.

"Yes. Today. And my friend," Sverrin leant over Zachary's chair, "you will not disobey my orders again. This indulgence I grant to you, but next time…"

"I know," Zachary croaked.

"You know." Sverrin rested his hands on either side of Zachary's face, like he was about to snap his neck. Zachary could hear his blood rushing in his ears, beneath Sverrin's palms. Sverrin retracted his hands, and leaning down, kissed the top of Zachary's head, almost in a chaste farewell. Zachary shuddered and the King straightened, turning to Daniel. "I hope I have the pleasure again soon, Daniel," he said. "Study well, and good morning to you all."

And then, with a well-natured wave of his hand, the King departed, leaving an icy silence in his wake.

Isolde waited until they heard the door close before flying into a rage. "How could you endanger us like that?" she screamed, standing so suddenly she almost kicked the table. Daniel leapt a foot in the air. "I thought after twenty years, you might've gotten over your need to push boundaries, but clearly *nothing has changed!*"

"Mother!" Daniel gasped.

Zachary, who'd expected her outburst, didn't move. Isolde's whole body heaved with anger.

"Did you even *think* about what would've happened if the King wasn't so forgiving? Did you *think* about the implications it'd have on Daniel!"

"Mother, stop—"

"No, because you *don't* think, Arlen! You push, and you push, and you push, and then you're surprised when everything collapses in on you! You're as *bad as your father!*"

Zachary rose so abruptly, Daniel gasped. Zachary, who'd staunched the tremors with Sverrin, was now shaking with rage. Isolde shrank back, as if she actually believed he would ever strike her. Zachary wanted to shout, to tell her that what he'd done, he'd done for love and loyalty—neither of which he expected her to understand. Instead he turned and stalked out of the library.

He made it to the stairway before wilting. The shaking didn't stop. Isolde's words rattled in his mind.

Collapse, she said, over and over. *Collapse. Collapse. Collapse.*

Like the tunnel had collapsed, bricks and stone falling down over his head. DuGilles wanted to bury him too, and Zachary had thought it wise to push his boundaries?

"A-Arlen." Daniel followed after him, his voice quavering as he spotted his brother doubled over the stairway banister, gripping it so tightly the wood might have splintered.

"What is it?" Zachary forced out between his teeth, pushing himself straight.

"I wanted to talk to you, but…" Daniel stood, unsure and small. "It'll wait until you're back."

"Good. Go to class." Zachary started up the stairs. If he couldn't sleep, he would at least change his clothes.

"Arlen," Daniel called as Zachary mounted up toward his bedroom.

"*What?*" Zachary snapped. Daniel looked even smaller and more out of place at the bottom of the stairs. He seemed to regret speaking out, his face pinched with uncertainty, unsure of what he wanted to say. Finally he settled.

"I'm glad your friends were safe, and," Daniel continued, once more interrupting Zachary as he made to walk away. "And I don't think you're anything like our father. Not in any way that matters."

Zachary was stunned, not least by the sudden, unexpected wave of relief Daniel's words brought. Daniel didn't know where to look, the compliments uneasy on his tongue.

Zachary felt himself relax a little. "Go to class," he said again. "We'll speak when I return."

Daniel, grateful to be excused, nodded awkwardly and scurried out of the house, grabbing his books from where they had been left in a pile by the door. Zachary spied Isolde watching him from the dining room door, but he was too tired to face another confrontation. He turned away and made for the safety of his chambers, his footfall heavy.

CHAPTER
43

~❦~

"It's not moving." Joshua focused on the grape intently, his chin on the table. "Try harder."

"I *am* trying." Rufus sat opposite him, his torso leant over the wood, and head rested in his hands. He scrutinised the grape, reaching out his senses, trying to replicate the feeling. He felt himself take hold of the tiny fruit, and then it exploded with a small spray.

Rufus sat back with a frustrated grunt and Joshua wiped his face, which was spattered with grape juice. "Maybe you need to try with something larger?" the boy suggested, maintaining his optimism. "Less fiddly."

"I don't want to run the risk of blowing anything larger up," Rufus grunted, picking another grape from the batch and eating it dejectedly. "Maybe I imagined the whole thing."

"You said their swords flew out of their hands. Fae wasn't responsible. It must've been you," Joshua insisted, plucking a grape and placing it back into the centre of the table. "Try again. And this time, recreate the feeling."

"I was under attack, Joshua. Timid as I may be, grapes don't instil the same kind of fear as three armed Cat Sidhe."

Joshua gave him a pointed look, and Rufus grumbled and lowered his head back onto the table, focusing on the grape.

"Clear your mind," Joshua said sagaciously. "Empty it of unnecessary distractions."

"Be quiet Joshua."

"Focus on the grape," Joshua ignored him, "feel it, smell it, taste it."

"Stop."

Joshua giggled, and then grew quiet again. "Do you think it's possible? To suddenly develop a new ability like this?"

"We're all born with set capacities, but it takes years before we can use them to their full ability. It's why most children aren't capable of manipulating elemental magic until they're at least ten. I was an odd exception to that." Rufus breathed out, his voice monotonous as he concentrated. "Master Odin told me he was near fifty when his level six abilities formed. It's perfectly feasible, then, that mine might do the same now."

"It would've been a useful technique," Joshua said, "against the alchemists."

"It may yet be." Rufus kicked his legs with frustration, staring intently at the grape.

Joshua gasped. "There—it moved! Did you see?"

"I knocked the table."

"No, no it moved on its own. It twitched!" Joshua spoke quickly. "I'm sure of it. Oh…Oh, no wait—you might be right. It was the table. Try again." He rested his head quickly back down and Rufus laughed and obliged.

"How goes the training?" Fae's voice carried out from above, and both brothers looked up in time to see her descending down the path toward them.

"Well he made a grape twitch apparently," Boyd responded, from where he was lounging beneath a tree close by, reading another of his frightening anatomy books. "But it might have been the table."

"No progress then?"

"Speaking for myself, I'm starting to think he might've made the whole thing up," Boyd said, and Rufus leant back in his seat and flicked the physician in the forehead. "Ow!"

"I saw him disarm my brothers." Fae picked the grape up from the table, turning it in her hands, as if it might somehow be the thing at fault. "Though I presumed at the time it was through some sort of wind manipulation."

"Maybe it was." Joshua helped himself to a handful of the remaining grapes, tossing them up in the air and catching them in his mouth one by one.

"Your collective faith in me is appalling." Rufus caught one of the grapes as Joshua tossed it up, and ate it himself. Joshua slapped angrily at his hands, and Rufus stuck out his tongue.

"Hm," Fae hummed, and then, with a sudden sharp draw back of her arm, she launched the grape in her hand directly at Rufus's face. Rufus flinched automatically with a cry, and Fae burst out laughing.

"I don't believe it!" Joshua slapped his hands on the table, and Rufus peeked between his fingers to see the grape floating delicately in front of his face. Rufus coughed in disbelief as Boyd scrabbled up to his feet.

"Impossible!" the physician gasped, as Rufus reached up to the floating fruit. It dropped a few thumbs in height, and hovered over the palm of his hand.

Fae put her hands on her hips, pleased. "You were always a creature of instinct."

"This is incredible." Boyd moved around as Rufus slowly compelled the fruit to circle his hand, like an orbiting moon.

He could feel the difference in what he'd been trying to do, and how he was doing it now. Rather than 'grab' the grape, he felt more like he was cradling it. It was a little like taking the edges of a piece of paper and pulling it apart, compared with taking it by the centre and lifting it up. He had hold of the core. Carefully, he visualised turning the grape, and watched as it began to spin. Fae plucked it from the air and put it in her mouth.

"I was training with that," Rufus cried.

"If you want this new skill of yours to actually be any use, you're going to have to manipulate more than one grape." Fae picked up Joshua, moving him along the bench and sat down, her arm looped around his shoulder.

"Maybe you should train him?" Joshua suggested.

Rufus took another grape and held it in the palm of his hand, concentrating on it. He managed to make it lift up slowly, but it was more difficult than before, and his head was already starting to hurt.

"Fae has more important things to do." He spread his fingers and weaved the grape between them slowly, before flying it straight into Joshua's open mouth, his brother dropping his jaw expectantly.

"Actually, since his display, Reilly has been avoiding me, so I suddenly have an abundance of free time." Fae pulled a dagger from her side and balanced it on the tip of her finger. The blade was sharp and Rufus was surprised that the weight didn't pierce her skin. Cat Sidhe truly had natural armour. "I think it would be a good idea."

Rufus folded his arms. "I'm already more than capable of defending myself."

"Setting things on fire and running away is not a dependable way of defending yourself." Fae flicked the knife up, and let it drop onto the table. The blade embedded itself deep into the wood, standing upright. "No, my lowly lord," Fae smiled pleasantly, "I will make you battle worthy yet."

Zachary hadn't even realised it was the month of Haylix until he spotted the children gathering flowers in the fields outside of Harmatia. They wove garlands together for their mothers, celebrating the month of the children by first thanking the women who'd raised them.

"They're making crowns," Princess Aurora said with delight. Zachary looked back at her. He'd been surprised to discover that Aurora had journeyed the whole way to Harmatia accompanied by only a handful of servants and Knights. Usually, in the absence of father or brother, Harmatian noblewomen would journey under the protection of an uncle, cousin or family friend. Aurora's solitary presence only gave credit to the suspicion that she'd decided to come for herself. It was said that in the Betheanian court, the Princess wielded equal power to her brother Hamish, the named heir, and that her word was heeded carefully by their father.

Markus couldn't have liked Sverrin's invitation, but he'd given his blessing and Aurora had crossed the border through the Myrithian forest into Corhlam.

Zachary and his men met her on the road there, two miles from Anaes's Fort, and Zachary had taken guard at her right side as they travelled the last leg of the journey to the capital.

"You're very quiet," Aurora noted, and Zachary looked up again. She was a pretty woman, certainly, with burning red hair and freckles across her pale face, likes dapples of sunshine. Her eyes, however, reminded Zachary of Rufus somehow, and he found it difficult to look at her. "I had heard that Lord Odin's apprentice liked to chatter and joke."

"Apologies, Your Highness, but I fear my flavour of humour wouldn't suit you."

"Why, is it all cocks and blood?" She giggled at his stunned expression. "Two of my father's guards are from Lemra—I assure you, after them, nothing you can say will shock me." She pulled her feet from her stirrups, stretching her legs in the saddle. Not only had she forfeited a carriage for the journey, but she rode like a man, straddled, not perched demurely in a side-saddle. "Tell me truthfully—are you surprised that I came?"

Zachary looked both ways. The knights had created a perimeter around them, but no one was near enough to eavesdrop. "Yes."

"I am surprised the invitation kept, even after the dragon was defeated in Sigel'eg. I was certain it would be withdrawn the moment the news came out. King Bozidar is King Sverrin's grandfather, after all. So soon after the attack, this visit will offend him."

"His Majesty has his kingdom's best interest at heart. He's united with Kathra through blood, and King Sverrin now wishes to strengthen our allegiance with Bethean similarly."

"Is that the selling line?" Aurora said, and spotted Zachary yawning. "You're tired, my lord?"

"I am completely capable of defending you in an attack."

"That's not what I asked."

Zachary's headache had only gotten worse. The sun was blinding, his fatigue was heavy and he wanted to lie somewhere dark and cool. He maintained his diligence. "Apologies, Your Highness."

"You needn't be so formal with me." Aurora swung her legs. "There are many in my father's court who simply call me Aurora—though maybe I am rebellious." She said the last word with a flourish, and Zachary couldn't help but be a little fond of her. She peered around at him. "It's DuMorne, isn't it?" she said suddenly. Zachary jolted.

"Excuse me?"

"Your name: Arlen Zachary DuMorne. Or am I mistaken?"

Zachary whistled, "I haven't heard anyone call me that for a long time."

"You do not go by it?"

"Not if I can help it." Zachary chewed the inside of his mouth. "Very few people in the capital are aware that I have *any* association with the DuMornes at all. How did you know?"

"The DuMornes rule Anaes's Fort," Aurora said. "which lies on the boarder of Bethean. Is it not prudent for me to know my neighbours?"

Know your enemies, more like. Zachary thought to himself, still chewing on the inside of his lip. "How much do you know of my family?"

"Only that the DuMornes fell on financial difficulty, and married their daughter Elizabeth to the son of a wealthy Magi. Your father, Lord Rivalen."

"Then you know the extent of it."

"Is it not tradition in Harmatia for the children of two noble families to take the name of the greater family?" Aurora asked curiously, and Zachary shrugged, nodding. Aurora frowned, her freckles bunching together as her nose wrinkled. "Why then have you not taken the DuMorne name?"

"Honestly?" Zachary grumbled, the reins loose in his hands. The sun was beating down on them, and for once he wished his uniform wasn't entirely black. The fabric absorbed the heat, and it only served to make Zachary feel even drowsier. "Because it's a horrible name."

"Ah," Aurora tapped her chin, "I suppose it does have a sad connotations. DuMorne— the ancient house of mourning."

"When you put like that, it sounds more like a curse than a name."

Aurora giggled. "So you choose to go by Zachary instead?"

"My grandfather was well acknowledged as a Magi. Even if my father lacked any magical ability, the 'Zachary' name yet holds power within those circles." Zachary struggled to supress another yawn. He wasn't sure why, but it was very easy to speak to Aurora. The conversation was seamless. Zachary wondered vaguely if he was being manipulated, and decided he didn't care.

"It's fortunate that you have a good first name, at least," Aurora mused. She was frowning again, though by her slight pout it seemed more in irritation now, than confusion. "In Bethean, it's believed fortune favours children named for their ancestors. The names are passed down through the families, so most of them are utterly archaic."

Zachary raised an eyebrow. "You don't like the name 'Aurora'?"

"Aurora is my middle name," Aurora said, "though everyone calls me by it, on account that my birth name is ghastly."

Zachary chuckled. "If it brings you comfort, Princess, so is mine."

"What's wrong with Arlen? It's a good name." Aurora turned in her saddle.

"Yet, like you, it wasn't my given-name at birth."

Aurora gave a wide smile, "I'll tell you mine, if you tell me yours?"

Zachary considered this. The Princess, he sensed, was trying to endear herself to him. She was building up a rapport between them and by giving his name to her, Zachary would be investing in that. Most likely, Zachary suspected, Aurora was trying to gain a friend within Sverrin's court. She no doubt thought Zachary held sway with the King. She was terribly mistaken, but still, Zachary liked her. He nodded his head.

"Go on then, Princess."

"Cunégonde." Aurora announced with a sour look on her face, her nose wrinkled.

"Excuse me?"

"Cunégonde. Coo-neh-gond." Aurora pronounced it out for him. "It's Réneian, and it's ghastly. 'Cu' is slang for 'bottom' in East-Réne, you know, and it means 'hound' in Betheanian."

Zachary burst out laughing, and Aurora grimaced.

"It was a family name—my parents were obliged. Now you understand why I go by Aurora."

"I do, Princess. That is very unfortunate."

"And yours? If it's worse than mine, I'll give you my weight in gold." Aurora's eyes sparkled bonnily. Zachary exhaled.

"Mine is Tristus, though I'll thank you not to tell anybody that."

"Tristus?" Aurora cocked her head to one side, "But that's charming. Like Tristan. Why do you not like it?"

"Because it's also slang, Princess." Zachary tried to keep the bitterness from his tongue. "It means 'still-born.'"

Aurora was silent for a moment. "What could possess a parent to name their child such a thing?"

Zachary leant across in his saddle and gave her a lopsided grin. "Oh, they say we place our aspirations in the names of our children. Apparently, my mother's wishes for me were not so great."

Aurora's mouth pinched. "I had heard the DuMorne family were an unpleasant lot."

"You heard correctly." Zachary straightened, and then sniggered. "Still, better than being called arse-hound."

"You are not to repeat that name to anybody!"

"By my honour, Princess, your secret is safe with me."

Aurora narrowed her eyes and twitched her nose in thought. For some reason it reminded Zachary of a rabbit eating a dandelion and he struggled against a sudden, strong desire to reach across and pat her head. His fatigue was making him delirious.

"Pednsyvige! Pednsyvige!" From the fields around, the children had gathered to watch the party ride past. They ran along the horses, led by a pale-haired girl who was holding a flower garland outstretched in her hand. She called again for the Princess. Zachary gestured for the soldiers to let the child through.

Aurora bent down to receive the gift. "Meur ras," she thanked in Althion, and the children looked delighted as she placed it on her head. From her purse, Aurora passed them all a coin each. They ran shyly away, stopping at a distance to wave.

"You can speak Althion?" Zachary asked.

"Only a little—it's spoken by some in Bethean. I thought it best to try and learn."

"Then may I congratulate you on your pronunciation." Zachary nodded up to the garland. "Your crown is already coming apart."

"Oh no." Aurora took it from her head. "It must have come loose while they were running."

"Here." Zachary held out his hand and she passed it to him wordlessly. He tied his reins into a knot and set to work braiding the flowers back together.

Aurora giggled. "You are clearly an expert."

"My sister taught me when I was very young. I used to make them every year."

"Not anymore?"

Zachary didn't reply, taking the fixed garland and putting it onto his head. He looked across to Aurora for her verdict and she laughed. "I think it suits you better, Princess." He passed it across, and she settled it back onto her red hair. Zachary looked at her, his fondness growing. "May I ask you a question, Princess?"

"Please."

"Why did you agree to come to Harmatia?"

"Do you think me unwise?"

"I think it can't have been appealing for you." Zachary worded carefully. Aurora gazed out over the plains of Corhlam, her expression distant. For a while she didn't speak, and when she did, it wasn't in answer to Zachary's question.

"You remind me a little of him, Lord Zachary. Or what I remember."

"Who?"

"Jionat," she said brightly and Zachary choked.

"The Delphi?" He coughed. "I remind you of Prince *Jionathan*?"

"He saved my life, you know. And though I only knew him fleetingly, I have never forgotten him. I was so frightened when he found me, but when he took my hand I saw a great light in him, and it comforted me. He made me believe that all would be well. I could trust him."

"I fail to see how I compare." Zachary had been likened

to many people and things, but never the Delphi Prince he'd murdered.

"You have a similar impression. It's difficult to describe, but I think you're both very morally driven men. Uncompromising, almost. You know right from wrong—you can feel it very deeply inside of you."

"I think you have mistaken me." Zachary felt his body tense. Aurora's eyes were too piercing. He focused back on the road.

"No," she decided, "I think not. By the by, Jionat was an honourable man, and I have to believe his decision to sacrifice himself for his brother is a mark of King Sverrin's true nature."

She can't be that naïve, Zachary frowned. *No, she's lying to me. At least, in part.*

"People speak of him very strongly, but I wanted to see for myself. To understand why Jionat would give his life. I cannot believe he would do so without good cause. That's why I chose to accept King Sverrin's invitation."

Zachary, unsure how to answer, steered the conversation away from the King. He didn't want to be caught lying. "I haven't heard that abbreviation in a long time—Jionat."

"It's what they called him, Fae and Rufus. I suspect he actually enjoyed being Jionat more than he did Prince Jionathan," Aurora said evenly. "I wonder which he was when he gave his life."

Zachary didn't know how to answer. He'd never felt comfortable speaking about the Delphi brat, and in the increasing years, Zachary had felt his hatred for the boy descend to pity. He'd once even caught himself wondering how Harmatia would have looked had the Delphi taken the throne. The most disturbing part was that, in his mind, the people had looked happier.

"I feel," Zachary eventually said, his voice thick, "it matters more who he's remembered as."

"Jionat then," Aurora breathed, her eyes distant, drawn back to a different time. "It'll have to be Jionat."

CHAPTER 44

Zachary made it to the Hathely house just as the sun began to set. He interrupted an early dinner, thrust Béatrice's now crumbled letter into Marcel's hand and then promptly fell asleep in a nearby armchair.

Emeric woke him an hour later, rousing him from a busy dream where he'd been counting flower stalks on a hill in Corhlam whilst trying to chase away a cow before it ate them all.

"Stupid cow—I'll eat it," Zachary slurred as Emeric shook his shoulder again, peering into his captain's unfocused eyes.

"Zachary?" Emeric called, and glanced worriedly over his shoulder. "I think he might be running a fever."

Zachary groaned and pushed himself upright, rubbing his face aggressively. "Stop." He batted Emeric away. "Fell asleep, s'all. Wha's it? What?"

Marcel leant over his apprentice. "Your master is here."

Zachary squinted. His head hurt and everything was spinning. He blinked rapidly, trying to clear his vision, but it seemed worse than usual. He chose a spot on the ceiling and allowed his eyes to adjust. When he looked down, he was able to make out that one of the blurred shapes leaning over him was Belphegore.

"Mas'er?" he asked, pushed himself straighter. "D'I have a duty?"

"No." Belphegore reached across and pressed the back of his fingers to Zachary's forehead. Zachary twitched, pulling away. Belphegore's hands were cold. "But I heard you made an unauthorised journey to Kathra last night, and I wanted to come and berate your foolishness myself."

I wonder if he'll compare me to my father as well. Zachary blinked slowly, already tired of the conversation.

"Do you have any idea how dangerous it was? You could have been shot from the sky, or worse. We may have never found you," Belphegore continued, his voice slowly ebbing away.

Or Jionat. Jionathan. Prince Jionathan, Zachary's internal voice continued to twitter. *Oh no, it's collapsing in here now. Collapse she said, collapse, collapse.*

"Arlen?" Belphegore called, as Zachary's eyes dropped closed. He could still hear the jangle of the cow bell from his dream. Sverrin had tried to ride a cow once. Stupid boy. Zachary had laughed. He'd laughed…

"Healing Septus—Arlen!" Belphegore said sharply, as Zachary's entire head dropped. He jerked awake. Belphegore's irritation was replaced with concern, his hands clamped on Zachary's shoulders.

"Ach, m'sorry," Zachary garbled. "Tired. Sons o' the gods, m'tired." He struggled to remove himself from the seat, and stumbled up to his feet, swaying. "Home," he said. "Bed. I'll go."

"That sounds like an extremely good idea." Belphegore steadied Zachary as he tipped to the side. Zachary winced—he wished they would speak softer and in shorter sentences. Each word was like a puncture wound through his head. "Lord Hathely, would you…"

Marcel was already at Zachary's arm. "I shall see him there," he said quietly.

"Should we…should we not call him a physician?"

468

Zachary swore at Emeric's suggestion and, disorientated as he was, strode away from the conversation. Marcel walked at his side, steering him around the table before Zachary could plough into it. Zachary shook his head, trying to rouse himself a little, but instead sent the world into a spinning mess. As they made it outside, Marcel took him by the arm and shoulder and dragged him back as he veered into a rose bush.

They walked in silence, Zachary slowing his ambitious stride to a tired and clumsy crawl. Confusing thoughts filtered through his mind, a jumble of ideas that made little sense.

"You should not have gone to Sigel'eg," Marcel said, and then, seemingly happy to waylay the rest of the conversation, simply concluded, "thank you."

"M'told her I's *not* passin' the kiss on," Zachary replied matter-of-factly.

They reached the house, and Zachary stumbled on the stairs to his door. Marcel helped him up each one, patient and quiet, before depositing him at the door.

"Bed," he instructed.

"N'yes."

Marcel waited to see Zachary let himself in. He'd once had a doorman, but the old man had died, and Zachary had never replaced him. Now he couldn't trust anyone new he hired.

Daniel, true to his word, was waiting for Zachary inside, perched on the staircase and watching the door expectantly. Zachary physically drooped at the sight of him. Daniel stood.

"Healing Septus—you look terrible."

"Oh, i's been long day."

"Are you drunk?"

"Tired." Zachary made his way to the stairs, tripped on the first one, and crumpled at Daniel's side, sprawled up. It wasn't comfortable, but he'd slept in worse places. "M'forgot you wan'ed to speak. S'it urgent?"

"No." Daniel shuffled his feet. "It doesn't matter."

Even through his desperate need to go to sleep, Zachary could see Daniel was disappointed. The boy had clearly been working up the courage to speak with him, and Zachary wondered if, at another dismissal, Daniel would give up and let the subject drop entirely. He rolled onto his back. "Ach, i's important, wasn't it?"

Daniel leant over and took Zachary by the arm, hauling him back to his feet. "No." Daniel didn't look at him, walking with Zachary as he made his way up the stairs.

"Yes 'tis. M'sorry. Think'm…mm…" Zachary stopped halfway up. The stairs shifted beneath his feet. He felt as if he were suddenly looking down them instead of up.

Sons of the gods…Emeric was right. I must have a fever. He touched his hands to his face, and stumbled back.

"Arlen—" Daniel gasped. Zachary's heel slipped off the step.

I hate fevers, he thought dully as he fell.

"I didn't want to believe it."

Aurora jumped and then scowled, looking in the mirror past her shoulder. From the corner of the room, Embarr Reagon could be seen in the reflection, lounging on her bed.

"Speak freely—no one can hear us," he added with a flourish of his hand. "My magic is useful for some things."

"What are you doing here, Embarr?" Aurora went back to brushing her long hair.

"I think that question is better left to you, my little sunshine." Embarr rolled across the bed, leaving his sweet scent all over the pillows, like a dog marking its territory. Aurora would have to air them before she went to sleep. She rolled her eyes.

"For a man who kidnapped me as a child, I think it's rather inappropriate for you to judge my decisions now."

"Judgement is a strong word—as is kidnap. As I recall it, you *followed* me. Willingly."

"You're a Gancanagh." Aurora replaced her brush on the

vanity table. "I was young and hardly in a position to say no to you, whatever my preference."

"We were pawns obeying the whims of my Lady Niamh. I warned you of the potential risks, but you agreed to come with me. Of course, had I known it was the Korrigans we would face, I would never, for all the golds in the land, have asked for your aid...I do love you, little one."

"Oh?" Aurora tittered. "I find that difficult to believe, seeing as we both lack the inclination for one another."

"Now Aurora," Embarr clucked, "it has nothing to do with my inclination. Can I not proclaim my love for a dear friend?"

"The same dear friend you let the Korrigans take?" Aurora raised her eyebrow. She heard Embarr sigh very faintly.

"It will haunt me forever," he said. "But your sacrifice brought three strong allies together."

"Two of whom are now dead." Aurora didn't swing around, though she wanted to face Embarr. Her time in the Korrigans' nest had strengthened her against certain potent magics, like a person becoming accustomed to poisons over time, but she was still not fully immune to the Gancanagh's charms. She was sure he'd never cast a spell over her, but she decided not to give him the chance. "The gods will play their games, but I must at least try to have some word in it."

"Is that why you have come here?"

"I needed to see it for myself," Aurora said. "War is coming. Jionat told us so, almost thirteen years ago now. This is how it begins—Kathra, Bethean and Harmatia all ostracised from each other."

"Or maybe it begins with the rape and murder of the Betheanian Princess." Embarr got to his feet. "You should not be here, Aurora."

"If I was going to die, Jionat would have told me."

"The Delphi are the children of Niamh, and they are as notoriously manipulative."

"I think with your parentage, you have no a right to judge."

"It is precisely *because* of my parentage that I can speak with such authority." Embarr came up to her and she grew very still as he gathered her long hair in his fingers. "Aurora, you have a fairer head on your shoulders then your brother and father combined. Why have you done this foolish thing?"

"When the King of Harmatia calls for you, you answer." She pulled her hair out of his grip. "Or how would it reflect if Sverrin cast his eye over Bethean, and saw it was gathering an army?"

Embarr pulled his hands away, and though she couldn't see his face in the mirror anymore, only his neck and chest, she sensed him smile. "You are the pretty distraction."

"My father did not approve, but it was the only way to maintain the illusion that all was well between our kingdoms."

"But he did not ride with you."

"Because we also had to send a message to our people—they're proud and headstrong." Aurora placed her hands on the desk, spreading her fingers wide. "While I am here, I shall endeavour to please the King, and learn everything I can of his nature."

"You are quite the little spider," Embarr laughed, and moved back to her bed, throwing himself across it. "So then, little sunshine, how has the King received you?"

"I believe he is taken by me. I do not laugh or agree with everything he says, which makes my smile all the more rewarding when he earns it."

"Then he is already invested in you, with his efforts. I am impressed."

"We shared a pleasant dinner. He was quite gentlemanly. Tomorrow, we'll go for a ride together, and then he means to host a banquet." Aurora stood and crossed to the bed, shooing Embarr out of it. She beat her pillows to clear them of his smell. "And eventually, I hope he'll show me where Jionat is laid."

"And what do you hope to gain from that?"

Aurora stilled in her task, her fingers gripping the bedclothes tightly. "I spent weeks locked in the Korrigans' nest—I saw them come and go, watched them perform their rituals. I understand their magic better than anyone. If there's anything to be understood of this spell, then I'll learn it."

"Perhaps that is precisely what the Korrigans intended you to do."

Aurora shivered. Her imprisonment still haunted her on cold nights. She'd seen men eaten alive, carved away to nothing, and worse. In the darkness, she'd tried to arm herself with the only weapon she could—knowledge. She didn't like to think that maybe, even now, she was still somehow confined by the Korrigans in some way. That they'd marked and predestined her actions. "You have asked your questions. Will you leave me alone now? I am sure there's a General missing you from his bed in Sigel'eg."

"That there is, but I needed to ensure my little sunshine was safe first. I see now I had no reason to fear—my Princess is now a finer temptress than me." Embarr swung on her bed post, leaning out and around. She turned her back to him, unable to stop her smile. Even now, somehow, she was glad of his company.

"You are despicable, get out."

"As Your Highness commands." Embarr marked his exit with a flurry of wind and Aurora got into the bed, turning her pillow to the cold side. She usually smiled naturally, but today her cheeks hurt from forcing it. She sank into the soft bed, and prayed for the strength to face Sverrin with as much enthusiasm the next day.

CHAPTER
45

Fae drew a circle in the ground and stepped back, pointing at it. "Stand in here."

Rufus quietly obliged. The circle was approximately a stride and a half in diameter, and he placed himself in the centre.

"Circle training?" Joshua asked.

"Circle training," Kael agreed with glee. The pair sat on the fence of the arena, sharing a loaf of bread between them.

"What's circle training?" Rufus asked them, uncomfortable with his audience. He would have almost preferred Boyd, but the physician was attending to one of Reilly's men who'd apparently been mauled during a hunt.

"Ignore them," Fae said, bringing his attention back to her. "All your focus should be on me."

"Yes, Captain." Rufus stood a little straighter, and Fae rolled her eyes.

"It is unwise to mock me."

"I'm not mocking."

"We'll see." Fae circled him. "Circle training is taught from a young age in the Neve. It's all about holding your ground. I gather your brother is already quite adept at it, so I expect you to strive as hard. The exercise is simple—stay in the circle, by whatever means."

Rufus eyed the ground, and then Fae. "I gather you won't be making that task easy for me."

"No. I will do my upmost to push you out of it. You can fend me off in any way you see fit, so long as you don't leave the circle. The moment you do, I win. It's as easy as that."

Rufus laughed nervously. "I suspect the only easy think about this is the concept."

"You're good at running away, Rufus. That isn't an insult," she added as he made to speak.

"I was actually going to agree with you."

"From what Joshua says, you have become quite adept at moving through your terrain, and whilst I will encourage you maintain that ability, I also want to teach you how to defend yourself if you're cornered. As such, I have taken away your two greatest strengths. No running or hiding, and for the duration of this training Rufus, no fire."

"No fire?" Rufus sagged.

"No fire. Any other element or magic is fine. Remember, your objective is only to drive me back. It's completely defensive. Do you understand?"

"Yes." Rufus widened his legs a little, somehow already feeling unstable. It was early in the day, with Malak on the horizon. He drew in her power—wind would be the most practical element for the exercise. Fae moved into an offensive stance.

"Are you ready?"

"Yes," Rufus breathed. In the next second Fae had launched herself at him, and with a sharp tug, pulled him over her shoulder and thrown him out of the circle. He landed on his back with a thud, and from the fence the children exploded with laughter.

Fae loomed over Rufus, blotting the sun as he wheezed.

"I…I wasn't ready."

"Clearly." She hauled him to his feet and pushed back into the circle. "Again."

"Let me get my breath back."

"No. Again."

"Alright." Rufus straightened and gave a strangled squeak as Fae was immediately upon him. Once more, she tossed him over her shoulder, and he found himself sprawled out in the dirt. "Athea have mercy…" Rufus puffed, the air knocked out of him.

"You've almost got it Rufus!" Joshua shouted in encouragement, as he and Kael continued to laugh, the latter almost falling off the fence.

"Don't worry," Kael said between giggles, "if it comes to battle, Fae can throw you at the enemy instead."

"You've certainly got that technique perfected," Joshua agreed.

Rufus swore at them, and Fae lugged him to his feet again, pushing him back into the circle.

"Do you understand now?"

"If I say yes, are you going to attack me again?" Rufus rasped.

Fae tilted her head to the side, as if this were a stupid question.

"Fine. Yes."

"Again."

"Again." Rufus nodded.

Fae streaked toward him but this time he released the magic he'd drawn in, a bubble of air erupting from around him. It was strong enough to throw Fae back off her feet. She twisted in the air and landed cleanly, the children now whooping. Fae smiled.

"Good." She lowered her height, shifting her weight. "Again."

Rufus followed her example, extending his hands in preparation. "Again."

Zachary woke twice during his feverish nightmares to the feeling of something heavy sitting on his chest and pinning him down. He panicked both times, only to be soothed by somebody he couldn't see. Kind hands had mopped his brow, reassuring

476

him, and he'd slipped back into the mess of exhausted dreams. He thought he heard his master's voice as he slept, and smelt Marcel's smoke. Both comforted him.

The third time he woke for sure, it was bright outside and Isolde was sat at his bedside, looking forlorn and out of place. They stared at each other.

"You were calling for me," Isolde eventually explained, "in your dreams. Heather told me to sit by you. How do you feel?"

Zachary touched the back of his head. He vaguely recalled falling down the stairs, but little else. "How long?"

"Three days. Your fever broke a little while ago," she said primly, but Zachary got the impression she was relieved. "Everybody was worried. Lord Odin came, and Lord Hathely stayed with you several hours each day. You were never alone."

A fierce burst of gratitude passed through Zachary, though he was embarrassed. "It's not catching?"

"The sickness? No. Physician said it was of your own doing. You exhausted yourself."

"Good."

"Good, he says," Isolde muttered, her posture closed off and small. "Daniel's sat with you every day after class, and comes to see you every morning before he goes."

Zachary closed his eyes. His body felt like it had been shaken and broken against a wall, but his mind was clearer than it had been in days. "He has a good heart."

"Like his father," Isolde whispered and Zachary grew still. His gratitude was replaced with resentment.

"Don't," he said coldly, his eyes flashing open.

Isolde bit her lip, as if unsure whether to continue. "You know," she began, and Zachary growled. "You've always known—"

"Daniel is my brother."

"He's—"

"My *brother*," Zachary repeated, "and that's all he can ever be." He pushed himself up, and though his throat was too dry to raise his voice, he spoke starkly and with a mean authority that made Isolde draw back. "You can't just pick and choose according to what suits you best. You made your decision twenty years ago, and now you can live with it."

"I was scared!" Isolde burst out. "Arlen, you were a student, barely nineteen, and I was a low-born maid you'd invited to your bed."

"Oh, don't you dare do that—twist the truth to justify yourself," Zachary said. "Is it that easy for you to erase the years we shared? Deny the hours of laughter, the time we spent together. How dare you imply that I coerced you? You had seven years over me—I was the one with no experience. Don't you remember how long it took for you to convince me—to teach me? How nervous I was? I gave myself to you, because you said it would make you happy, and that's all I wanted."

"Oh Sweet Haylix, spare me," Isolde spat, rolling her eyes.

"I *loved* you," Zachary said helplessly, "and you knew that."

"You were nineteen," Isolde repeated. "It's easy to say 'I love you', but words don't mean anything."

Zachary closed his eyes. He was too tired to maintain his anger. "But my father's words did?"

"Your father told me that if we continued, he'd cut you off."

"And my wealth," Zachary laughed, "that was the part you really loved."

"It's not a crime to want a good life. If you'd left me, I would've had nothing and no one. I couldn't risk that, especially when your father was offering something guaranteed. Money of my own. Mine. Enough that I'd never have to work another day in my life. And all I had to do was give him a son."

"And how happy has all that wealth made you. You look like you don't even remember how to smile, living under his thumb." Zachary wanted to hurt her. He wanted to make her suffer for her cruel decision, and it pleased him to know that deep down Isolde had come to regret what she'd done. After all, here she was again, in a household Zachary now owned, bought from his father with the wealth he'd earned, and with enough riches already to live comfortably for the rest of his extended life.

"You don't know anything..." Isolde grimaced.

"I know that Daniel was conceived to torment me," Zachary replied. "To be a constant reminder of the fact you chose my father over me. And yet still, somehow...somehow I don't see your face in Daniel's. Somehow, I don't resent him anymore, and very soon Rivalen is going to realise that his plan failed. And he's going to blame you."

Isolde shrank back even more, and Zachary saw her shudder. It appeared she'd come to the same conclusion. Zachary felt no pity.

"The worst part, Isolde, is that I think after all the effort you made with me, you loved me too. And all of this, it could have been ours. We could have been a family."

Isolde stood. Angry tears had sprung to her eyes. "No, we couldn't." She rubbed her eyes furiously. "Because maybe you wouldn't have minded being cut off, maybe you would've been happy living by your own means, but we both know Rivalen would've had his way in the end, and you would've left me one way or another."

"That is not true."

"It is," Isolde cried. "Because you're a coward—tethered to your own abuse. Otherwise you'd have fought for me. You make all these grand declarations of love, but the day Rivalen came for me, you didn't even try to stop him!"

Zachary clenched his jaw tightly, his head ringing from the pressure. "I told him to let you go..."

Isolde laughed bitterly, pleased by his agitation. "Oh yes, that's right. You 'told him to let me go'...And then Rivalen looked you in the eye, said one word, and you lay down quiet as a mouse, and did as you were told, like you always do." She tittered sickly. "I knew, then, that I'd made the right choice. Knew you'd always eventually give in to him. I stood there and watched as Rivalen whipped you in-front of all of the servants. And you—you weren't even tied down—you just knelt there, still and unfeeling as he added twenty new scars to that deformed back of yours."

Zachary flinched.

"And when Rivalen was done, you slunk away without a word—to Marcel, no doubt, to lick your wounds. You didn't even look me in the eye as you left." Isolde wiped the tears from her cheeks, forcing down the warble in her voice. "You've given Rivalen the world of power over you. So don't demonise me for making my choice. I'm not like you, I won't live for two-hundred years, I couldn't just wait for Rivalen to die for us to be together… You would've left me, he would've *made* you—we both know that. So don't expect me to apologise for taking his offer instead. Yes, I betrayed you and no, it wasn't noble of me, but nobility's a rich man's indulgence, and I had to do what I could to survive."

"What could I have done?" Zachary's voice was so low it was almost lost. "What did you expect me to do?"

"Choose me," Isolde half-wailed. "Take away that power Rivalen has over you, and choose me!"

"You know I couldn't…that I can't."

"Yes you can! But as usual, you let that narcissistic sense of duty rule you. You say it was my choice that led us here, but it was yours. I should've come first, Arlen. I should've come first, but you chose *them* instead. You will *always* choose *them*! So the baby that should've been yours is now another precious sibling for Rivalen to hold over you forever." Isolde gave a tight little laugh. "If I were petty, I'd almost call that justice."

Her words rang in the hush that followed. Zachary stared at the woman he'd once loved, and felt sick. He slowly raised his hand. "Go and say goodbye to Daniel," he ordered softly. "Then pack your bags and get out. And Isolde, never," he stared her straight in the eye, from the bed they'd once shared, "*ever* come back."

Sverrin found Aurora in the hallway beyond the staircase, looking up at a vast portrait. "I was wondering where you had gotten to."

"Your Majesty." She curtsied, her pastel blue silks rustling. "I am sorry if I kept you waiting, but it caught my eye."

He came beside her, looking up at the painting, his expression a peaceful, if reserved. Aurora's skin crawled to have him so close, but she didn't move. Somehow, she found he always smelt faintly of damp earth and preservative ointments, and it made her stomach roll. She focused on the artwork instead.

It was a handsome portrait of Jionat and Sverrin, stood side by side. Sverrin was clad in the Harmatia's colours, donned in a studded maroon doublet with a griffon to honour his mother's house, and a tall red-gold crown. He had a furred, velvet cape thrown over his shoulder which trailed to the floor in thick cascades, and stood, regal, an arm leant against a tall wooden throne.

At his side, Jionat held equal importance in the picture. Dressed in the Delphi colours, pale blue and white, he had an identical crown of silver sat amidst his curls, which were painted lighter than Aurora recalled. Indeed, Jionat seemed to have a silvery aspect in all his features, which made him seem more reserved, wiser and colder than the boy she'd met.

"I had this painted a few years ago," Sverrin said. "My mother said I should have a portrait mounted to commemorate my ascension to the throne. It did not seem right that I stood alone in it."

Aurora was surprised. Through the past days, she'd seen Sverrin throw up many expressions, each like a new death-mask he could swap between, but this was the first time she saw a genuine tenderness. Sverrin looked up at Jionat with love, and Aurora realised, with a start, that Jionat's sacrifice actually meant

481

something to the King.

"Do you miss him?" she found herself asking.

"More than I can tell you." Sverrin reached out, as if to touch the painting, and let his fingers hover over it. "I died and when I woke, both my father and brother were dead. My first day of rebirth, and it was devastating."

"I can only imagine how difficult it must have been."

"I try to live my life as they would want me...Though some days, it is harder than others." Sverrin withdrew his hand. "Do you know, Princess, the most painful part of my return, was that I grew to be a man. And being a man meant I started to see the flaws in others, flaws which I was blind to in my youth. One by one, everyone I once idolised came to disappoint me. I cannot help but resent them for that—for breaking the illusions of my boyhood, the illusions I had when I died. But you see, my little brother cannot disappoint me. He is immortalised. Perfect." Sverrin raised his hands again, as if he might dip them into the painting and clasp Jionat's face fondly. "Sometimes I feel as if he is the only true part of me I have left."

"He must have loved you very much," Aurora said. Abomination or not, Sverrin hadn't chosen to be revived, and it had never occurred to Aurora how Jionat's sacrifice would affect him. He was always painted as a tyrant, a Kathrak pawn with no empathy, but everyone chose to forget the confused boy who'd emerged strangely from death to a world so drastically changed.

Aurora frowned up at the painting. "They painted the Prince's eyes blue," she observed.

"Of course," Sverrin smiled, "just like his mother."

"But Prince Jionathan's eyes were grey, like the King Thestian."

"You must be mistaken, Princess. I recall well—they were blue," Sverrin said.

"They were grey. I am sure of it."

"They were blue." All of the light had left Sverrin's amber eyes and Aurora grew small. Sverrin's expression had settled into something blank, hungry and dangerous, and her very heart stilled. In that instant, he looked as void as the Korrigans had.

"You're quite right," she gasped, forcing a smile. "Blue. Like his mother. Of course you would recall it better."

Sverrin's expression was immediately replaced with one of relief, as if, despite his certainty, he'd begun to doubt himself. "You met him, did you not? Was my brother not a fine man?"

"The finest." Aurora was glad of her thick skirt, which hid her shaking knees. She held her arms, tucking her hands away so that their trembling wouldn't betray her. "I knew him only fleetingly, but he left an impression on me that I shall not be quick to forget. I mourn him. I should have been glad to have known him better...though I thank the gods his sacrifice gave me the chance to be acquainted with the brother he loved so ardently. I am beginning to understand, Your Majesty, the source of Prince Jionathan's loyalty—though I hope you do not think me too bold for saying so."

Sverrin put on a show of being flattered. He offered his arm, and she took it, allowing him to guide her down the staircase. "Your good opinion of me is the highest praise I could hope for."

"And yours of me is..." Aurora said coyly, "I can only hope to please you, Your Majesty."

"You do please me." Sverrin's eyes roamed down her body and she turned away. He must have mistaken her masked revulsion as bashfulness, because he chuckled quietly. "Would you like to see him?"

"Pardon?"

"My brother." Sverrin stopped walking, pulling Aurora around to face him. She forced herself to look up into his eyes, though it made her want to turn and scream. "Would you like to see where Jionathan is laid? I go there often to think and speak with him. It brings me peace. Perhaps, Princess, you would like to join me?"

Aurora breathed in deeply. "Oh, Your Majesty, I would like that very, very much."

CHAPTER
46

The journey down the stairs took longer than it should have, and by the time Zachary made it to the library, he wanted go back to sleep. Still, he persisted, pushing through the door and walking stiffly over to the seats by the fireplace.

Daniel looked up from one of the desks, and rose. "You should be resting."

"If I have to spend another minute in that room..." Zachary slumped into the seat, triumphant and exhausted. Daniel came forward, and peering down into Zachary's pale face, he silently lit the fire. It chased back the chill and Zachary was immensely thankful for it.

"You must be hungry. I'll tell Heather to reheat some broth. She's not going to be happy you left your bed."

"Daniel, stop." The boy was making Zachary even more exhausted. "Sit. Talk."

Daniel considered the command, releasing the servant bell, and then slowly took the seat opposite Zachary. "My mother left."

"I sent her away."

"I know."

"I owe you an explanation." Zachary heaved a sigh, but Daniel raised his hand.

"After the outburst, I asked Heather to tell me everything. She explained what happened…between you and my mother."

Zachary was unsure what to say. It was hard to read Daniel's expression. "It was a complicated affair."

"When I confronted her about it, she tried to lie to me."

"How do you know she was lying?"

"I love my mother," Daniel twisted his hands, looking down into his lap, "but I know what she's like. And I know you better than she thinks."

"You can't be angry with her."

"Yes, I can. I can be angry with both of you," Daniel said. "It doesn't change what you are to me. At least now I finally understand why you hated me so much, when you were so close to the rest of our siblings."

Zachary rocked his head against the back of the chair. Again, he found himself glad that Daniel had lit a fire—the library felt cold and terribly dark all of a sudden.

"If I'd known," Daniel continued, "I wouldn't have invited her."

"Why *did* you invite her?" Zachary asked, and Daniel closed his eyes. He seemed to be trying to prepare himself, breathing deeply over a long count. Finally he swallowed, and looked up.

"Because I was afraid and I wanted my mother."

Zachary frowned, leaning forward. "What were you afraid of?" A disturbing thought came to him. "Me?"

"No," Daniel laughed softly. "No—I knew you would never hurt me, even if you hated me."

"I don't hate you Daniel," Zachary said. Daniel stared at him, unblinking. He swallowed again, fidgeting with his hands. An anticipatory silence settled over the pair, the tension of unsaid words mounting as Daniel licked his lips nervously.

"I have a secret," he finally whispered. "Only a few people know…And a lot rests on that remaining so, but…But sometimes I want people to know. I want their help. Their support. My mother, she's my ally. But I need...I'm *hoping* that you'll help me too."

"I don't understand." Zachary frowned, and Daniel adopted his spot-on-the-wall strategy, looking past Zachary, twisting his hands more urgently.

"I'm scared," his voice dropped.

"What are you scared of?"

"My mother told me not to tell you. She said you weren't ready, that you wouldn't understand, but I don't know if she said that out of spite, or worry. All I know is that I want to trust you. And I want to tell you."

"Tell me what?" Zachary sat forward. "Daniel, you've been trying to speak with me for days now. What is it?"

Daniel bit his lip. "I'm not sure you'll understand and I'm terrified of what will happen if you don't."

"Speak plainly. Please."

Daniel bit his lip and breathed in long and slow. "Do you know the faerie shrines, around our home?"

Zachary raised his eyebrows. In Corhlam, there were several places said to have once been sacred to the Sidhe before the boarders were established, and the faeries were driven back into the Myrithian forest. Of course, there were some that still roamed free, and spots of ancient power had been identified out among the rolling hills. Thorn bushes that stood alone in fields, strange rock formations found in the middle of nowhere—the people of Corhlam had long ago learnt not to interfere with these. There were some who still left offerings. It was common practice to respect these places, and was believed that ill fell on those who didn't.

"What about them?"

"There's a story—it varies from place to place. They say that in the old times, a pregnant woman got lost on the moors and came upon a shrine. Exhausted and hungry, she found the food offerings and ate them, without thinking.

"The god of the shrine was angered, and he confronted her in a dream. She blamed the child in her womb, saying that it filled her with a ravenous hunger she couldn't control. And so, to punish the child, the god laid a curse on it. Not to kill it, or even to make it sick—instead, the baby, meant to be born a boy, emerged as a girl.

"In the other version, it's a hungry child who eats the offerings, and is transformed directly. The punishment is the same, either way. The child is forced to live their life knowing what they were meant to be, but trapped as what they are."

"Daniel," Zachary groaned. "I know these stories. They're nothing but superstition. It's utter nonsense."

"I know," Daniel said, almost aggressively. "It's folklore—a crass reasoning for someone being different, but—"

"What in the name of—" They were interrupted by the door, Heather bustling in. She crossed to Zachary, fussing over him. "Do you know my worry when I climbed the stairs to find your bed empty? You should not be up. Healing Septus, you're as pale as death, and shaking too."

"Heather, it's fine." Zachary's mouth felt as it were full of wool. He kept his eye on Daniel, who'd grown taut, unnerved by the interruption.

"It is not fine—do you know how unwell you've been?"

"We're in the middle of a conversation," Zachary said sternly, not removing his eyes from his brother. Heather followed the gaze and she immediately let her fretting hands drop.

"Oh Daniel," she whispered, "you're coming out with the truth?"

Daniel gave a jerky nod.

So Heather knows what he's trying to tell me? Zachary felt strange, his mind beginning to form ideas, none of which seemed coherent. "Daniel," he said, "is there a point to all of this?"

"I…I'm trying to tell you, that all superstitious reasoning aside, it is possible to be born in the wrong body. For whatever

487

reason, it does happen."

Zachary eased himself forward in his chair, his disbelief rising. "Daniel," he began softly, "are you trying to tell me that you think you're…a woman?"

"No," Daniel hiccupped again, sniffing, and at last he pried his gaze from the wall and looked into Zachary's face. His teeth had begun to chatter, and Zachary was distressed by the frightened tears that sprung in his brother's eyes. "That's the point. I'm a boy."

Zachary shook his head. "I don't understand."

"Oh Athea, this is so hard." Daniel wiped his face, but new tears sprung to replace those that had started to fall. Zachary had never seen the boy look so frightened, and Daniel had faced the Night Patrol. "As I get closer to being a Magi, I risk more than ever. I could lose everything—I could be *imprisoned*. Rivalen would… Athea, what would our father to do me?" Daniel gave a sudden sob, and Heather crossed to him. She perched herself at his side and held his shoulders, tipping him against her comfortingly. Zachary could only watch.

"Tell me," he implored.

"When my mother was pregnant, Rivalen told her that he wanted a son. He said that he had too many daughters, and that if she gave him another, he would throw her in the well." Daniel hid his face behind his arms, using his sleeves to wipe away the tears. Zachary felt stony. "She prayed to every god that I would be a son, left offerings and made wishes. But she gave birth to a daughter."

Zachary was stunned. Daniel hiccupped again, but continued, his voice hitching up and down from the pressure of the words.

"She feared what Rivalen would do, and so she made a plan. I was born in her family home, outside of Anaes's Fort, so when Rivalen sent for word, she told him that I was a boy. She knew he wouldn't want any part of me until I was old enough to be of use. On the one occasion he came to see me, she swapped me with the baby of a friend of hers—so that our father might see a prick and be satisfied.

"My mother planned to disguise the truth as long as possible, gather what she could, and then flee. She didn't anticipate, however, that her lie would actually suit my needs. By the time I was four, I rejected every notion of being a girl. It sounds strange, I know…but I was boy in everything but body. When it became clear that I also had a capacity for magic, my mother realised that I could be a Magi, like you. That I could forge a better life for myself than one she could give me on the run. I begged her to let me be Rivalen's son. To let me be myself. Somehow, she understood, that her prayers had been answered. I am a *boy*." Daniel balled his hands into fists. "But if anyone discovered this, they wouldn't understand. They wouldn't see past my bound breasts and the space between my legs. And I'm terrified, Arlen. I'm so terrified."

Silence followed. Daniel and Heather watched Zachary expectantly, Daniel shuddering, his breath short. Zachary stared back, his mind in turmoil.

What did he think? The whole story sounded preposterous. A girl believing she was a boy? Isolde giving birth to a sister, rather than a brother?

As Zachary examined Daniel, he was able to make out feminine features in the other's face. Were they feminine? Zachary hadn't thought so before. Daniel had only ever been his brother. Nothing of his sibling's behaviour had indicated anything otherwise, though it did explain Daniel's secretiveness, and how he seemed to take ill every month.

Was it possible? To be a boy in all but body? Zachary tried to imagine what it would be like if he was turned into a woman. At first the idea seemed comical, but the more he thought about it, the harder it was to envision. What would it be, to be so utterly betrayed by your own body? To look in the mirror and see something other than what you are?

489

The whole affair made his vision swim like he still had a fever. He wasn't quite sure what to believe. Daniel was clearly head-sick. Isolde had twisted her child to suit her needs, and this was the result. The best thing for Daniel now would be to retreat somewhere, and learn to be a woman. After all, if they tried to continue this façade and *were* caught by the Magi…Zachary didn't even want to consider the repercussions. At the very least their family name would be ruined.

Zachary turned to tell Daniel that but his voice died in his throat. Daniel's eyes were wide and watchful, waiting for a verdict. Zachary felt his stomach constrict.

Had he really just been thinking of the family name? As if that even stood for anything anymore—as if it was anyone's business! Zachary marvelled at his own selfishness.

Daniel had demonstrated himself to be a clear-minded individual—if anyone was head-sick in the family, it was Zachary. So what right did he have to speak on Daniel's behalf? Zachary might have thought the boy confused, but after nineteen years, Daniel was probably surer of what he was that Zachary could be after a few minutes. What business was it of Zachary's to be making these decisions on his brother's behalf? Besides, on reflection, it wasn't the *strangest* thing Zachary had ever heard.

If he hadn't told me, he reasoned, *he would have still been my little brother come tomorrow. It affects me in no way.*

"Say something. Please," Daniel begged, the silence drawing on too long.

Zachary blinked, stood and then crossed to the drinks cabinet. He poured himself a glass, and then one for Daniel. Sitting down, he slid the drink over to his brother silently and settled once more into his chair.

"I once knew a man," Zachary eventually said, "who was convinced he was a duck."

Daniel blinked, shocked. Zachary shrugged and took a long sip of his drink. The conversation ended.

Aurora had thought she was prepared, but as Sverrin brought her further into the heart of the castle, deep down beneath its foundations, she found her courage waning. The sense of the Korrigans, which lingered whenever Sverrin was near, grew with each step, until it was almost like Aurora was descending down into the nest itself. The past traumas came as easily for her as they'd done ten years ago, and horrors she thought she'd forgotten came roaring out.

The same eerie, beautiful blue and green light filled the chamber, and then, very suddenly, there he was, lying like a marble effigy on a tomb.

He'd grown, his face somehow more mature. Jionat—a living corpse that aged with time. His breath came out so soft and slow it was barely there, but the steady rise and fall of his chest made it almost seem like sleep.

Almost.

Sverrin went to Jionat's side and took his hand, as if comforting a sickly friend. "Jionathan," he said fondly, "I have brought you a visitor. It's the Princess Aurora. Do you remember her? She has grown into a fine and beautiful woman."

Aurora's heart ached. Slowly, and with more sadness now than fear, she came to Jionat's other side. "Can he hear us?"

"I like to think so," Sverrin said softly and he didn't release his brother's hand. "You know, I've never been able to share my visits with anyone before. Of course my advisors will come down with me to pay their respects, but my mother surrounded us with loyalists who had no love for the Delphi. It is sometimes very difficult to grieve alone. It is good to be with another who knew him fondly."

Aurora tentatively took Jionat's other hand but couldn't find the right words. She had so few memories of him, and yet the memories she did have were so strong, she could still see them vividly in her mind's eye—the first look she ever had of the Prince, as he squatted, smiling, in the cell beside her. His hand firmly holding hers, his steady voice and then his tears when they met again. How could one boy have borne so much pain and then returned to such a fate knowingly? For he must have known, Aurora was sure of that.

"I am glad to see you again," she confessed, and kissed the back of Jionat's knuckle. His hands weren't cold, as she'd expected, but warm.

Aurora wanted to tell him that she was sorry, that she wished she could have done something for him, that she wished they'd had more time between them. But it would be unwise to confess such things in front of Sverrin, so she thought them as loud as she dared, holding Jionat's hand tightly.

"I've upset you," Sverrin said, with something close to concern.

"No." Aurora tore her eyes from Jionat. "No, Your Majesty, I am eternally grateful that you thought to share this with me."

Sverrin released Jionat's hand and laid it carefully down again, just as a loud commotion came from one of the doorways. A Magi strode boldly in. Aurora suspected he'd purposefully made the noise, in order to announce his arrival and give them a chance to compose themselves.

Sverrin, who'd scowled at the interruption, brightened immediately as he saw who the man was. "Ah, Rothschild—good evening."

"Your Majesty, Princess." Rothschild bowed deeply. He was an unremarkable man, with a heavy build and strong, Betheanian features. Something of his smile, though pleasant enough, made Aurora cautious. This one smiled too much—and for the wrong reasons. "I am sorry for the intrusion, but was told to deliver this to you directly. It comes from your grandfather, King Bozidar."

The Magi produced a small note, which Sverrin took keenly. Aurora caught Rothschild smirking at her from the corner of her eyes, as if she were the line at the end of a cruel joke. When she tried to catch his gaze, however, he seemed to find interest elsewhere.

"As timely as ever." Sverrin unfolded the note and began to read. Aurora watched him carefully for his reaction. She could decipher nothing from the King, which frustrated her.

Finally, Sverrin finished. "Thank you Rothschild, this was exactly what I needed. Tomorrow, I would like you to relay the orders we discussed to Zachary. Everything has come into play. Our plan is in motion."

Rothschild's eyes brightened with an excitement. Aurora knew the expression well, she'd seen it before in men green to battle, commissioned into their first war. That expression never lasted, once the horrors began.

"Of course, Your Majesty. Zachary will be pleased."

"I do rather keep you all cooped in, don't I?" Sverrin laughed, folding the letter and placing it in his pocket. Rothschild bowed, and then left the way he'd come, his step light with excitement. Sverrin seemed strangely pleased, smiling secretively, though Aurora couldn't conceive what good news could have come out of Sigel'eg at this time.

"I apologise for that, Princess. My kingdom is a greedy child, who demands my attention all hours of the day."

"Of course, I understand Your Majesty."

"Come, it has grown late." Sverrin smiled. "We ought to return."

Aurora didn't want to, but to refuse would arouse suspicion. She followed Sverrin's example, laying down Jionat's hand. "Thank you for bringing me here, Your Majesty." She curtsied low, and Sverrin reached toward her, putting two fingers beneath her chin and tipping her face back. He brushed her bottom lip with the pad of his thumb, and then released her, offering his arm.

Aurora took it, and they left together, the Princess carefully marking the path back. Later, she would return, alone, and she would further examine the altar on which Jionat was laid. One way or another, Aurora would discover the truths of the spell which kept Sverrin alive.

"Frankly, I don't know how you do it," Rufus huffed, lying flat on his back in the grass. He'd cushioned his head upright under his doublet, so that he could still see the apple he was levitating a few strides away. Over the past days, he'd progressed from grapes to larger fruits, and was expanding the distance in which he could control the objects.

He made the apple loop and dance like a demented bird, and Joshua, at his side, took aim, drawing his arrow back.

"You don't train nearly as many hours as I do," Joshua said, with a tone of concentration, his focus on his target as it dipped and weaved.

"Exactly, and yet I'm exhausted." Rufus twisted his hand to make the apple fly up, and Joshua shot his arrow. It struck the apple perfectly, splitting it into two. Joshua, quick as darting fish, loosed another arrow and caught one of the tumbling halves.

Rufus whistled. "Etheus blind me, you're getting even quicker—near an arrow a second."

"Fae can shoot three in less," Joshua grumbled, and Rufus marvelled at his ambition. He summoned the apple parts and arrows to him, concentrating as they slid slowly along the ground and then up into the air, flying into his hands one by one. He returned the arrows to his brother, and ate what remained of the apple.

"You have time." He licked his fingers clean. "Fae's been using a bow three times as long as you. I'm sure one day you'll rival her in skill."

"I doubt that," Joshua said glumly. "Can you levitate two apples?"

"I'm not sure." Rufus sat up. "That was my last one, either way."

"Then can you make one of the targets move?" Joshua pointed down the bottom of the field, where a line of straw targets sat thirty strides away.

Rufus frowned. "I haven't tried to move anything that large," he admitted, "but I suppose." He reached out his hand, trying to concentrate. The target remained firmly where it was. Rufus pushed himself to his feet, extending his will. The size and the distance worked against him, but he persisted, honing his concentration into a fine point.

His vision tunnelled from the force of his intention, and in the back of his mind, he became conscious of a rushing sound. He blinked, trying to shake it away. It persisted, growing louder, until it enveloped him, colours exploding behind his eyes.

Harmatia lay below him. From the vantage point he could see the whole capital, the forum out in front, the city laid out like an eccentric maze of houses and roads. The courtyard was far below him.

Rufus realised the rushing sound was the wind, and that he was stood high up, on what must have been the roof of the Great Library.

He turned, confused, and spotted a man a little way from him. It had been some time, but Rufus immediately recognised the grim figure of Arlen Zachary. Rufus's brothering apprentice had aged little, though he seemed thinner now, grey in the face, and older in the slump of his shoulders.

Zachary stood, balanced precariously on the edge, anchored back by only his heels, his arms held loosely at his side.

The wind was getting higher, making Zachary rock, and Rufus's heart dropped to the bottom of his stomach. Zachary was staring down intently, his objective clear.

Rufus tried to call out to him, but his voice was spirited away by the wind. He tried to move, stepping over the precarious ledge, a set of gargoyles between them. Again, he called out, but his brothering apprentice couldn't hear him.

Something seemed to settle over Zachary, and quietly he closed his eyes. Rufus reached out in one last attempt to grab him, but with a bone-weary sigh, Zachary tipped himself forward over the edge, his arms spread.

"NO!" Rufus shouted, lunging forward only to stop dead, returned to the training grounds.

"Rufus?" Joshua cried, his eyes wide.

Rufus looked out in time to see that, not only was Joshua's target floating in the air, but the entire line of targets was too. They drifted spookily for a moment, like straw phantoms, and then dropped simultaneously. Rufus drew back, gasping.

"D-did you see that?" he demanded. "Not the targets," he corrected immediately, "the roof! Harmatia! Did you see that?"

"No." Joshua ran to him worriedly. Rufus dragged a hand through hair. "Rufus, what is it?"

"I think..." Rufus sat down heavily. "I think I had a vision."

"You?" Joshua knelt down in-front of him. "A vision?"

"Yes, I think. But I've never seen anything outside of my dreams."

Joshua's frown deepened, "Perhaps sharing my visions, and all this magic training has opened up your potential. What did you see? Rufus?"

Rufus ran his hands up his face, and then once more through his hair, tugging his fringe. "It was Zachary," he muttered. "Why would I have a vision about Zachary?"

"I don't know." Joshua seemed deep in thought. "What was he doing?"

Rufus released his hair, his mind in turmoil. He stared his brother hard in the face. "Killing himself."

CHAPTER 47

Once again, Zachary disobeyed Heather's orders, and left his bed. He'd slept the night through with a heaviness achieved only through sheer exhaustion, and woke feeling clearer than he had in days. His body still ached in the aftermath of his sickness, and he couldn't drive out the perpetual chill which clung to him, but he felt sufficiently well enough to dress, descend and eat at the table.

Heather joined him, clucking and fussing around him. He let her, quietly enjoying the concerned affection. She brought him hot soup, and then sat beside him, watching him shrewdly as he ate it all.

"You will be the death of me, Arlen," she sighed, and he gave her a weak grin.

From beyond the dining room, there came a firm knock on the door. Heather made to go, but Zachary caught her hand, suddenly cautious. He rose in her stead, and going to the entrance hall, beat the other servants to the door. He opened it, and then stepped back.

"Rothschild?" He frowned, and gestured for the man to come in, though he had no energy for sycophants that morning.

"Zachary, how do you feel? You seem recovered."

"I will be, soon." Zachary folded his arms. "What can I do for you?"

"I have orders from the King," Rothschild said with an undisguised excitement, and Zachary's already meagre appetite for the day crumbled away. He grew quiet and stiff.

"What orders?"

Rothschild looked around, as if to ensure nobody was listening, and leant in. "We are to be deployed—the Night Patrol. At last, after so long, our purpose has been recognised."

"I don't understand," Zachary said. "Deployed where?"

"To Bethean. We're going into the capital." Rothschild gabbled with excitement, and with a slowly gathering dread Zachary understood exactly what was happening.

It all made sense: the invitation to the Princess, the rebuking of Kathra, the slow gathering of alchemists in Bethean—Sverrin had been preparing for war for months, and his declaration was to be bloody.

It was almost clever. Sverrin hadn't sent his forces to Sigel'eg, because he needed them for battle, and wanted to create the illusion of a growing distance between himself and Kathra.

He'd invited the Princess under the pretence of a growing alignment, and now he planned to destroy the Betheanian seat of power, leaving Aurora as the only true heir and his hostage. She would have no choice but to marry him, or live as his prisoner. And the Night Patrol would be forever remembered as the instigators of an unholy massacre.

"No," Zachary said plainly, and Rothschild frowned, drawing himself up.

"Zachary?"

"No," he repeated, firm. "Tell the King, as the captain of the Night Patrol and according to the book of Law, I am within my lawful rights to refuse orders in the case of an illegal war. I won't lead my men into Bethean."

"Zachary," Rothschild gaped. "You mean to refuse the King?"

"The city of Bethean is home to hundreds. Men, women, children—we are soldiers, not murderers. The King may send another army if he wishes, but the Night Patrol will have no part in this."

Rothschild's excitement had been replaced with dismay. He opened and closed his mouth, gobsmacked. "Zachary," he implored, "think carefully on this. Refusal to obey will reflect very gravely upon you."

"Yes," Zachary said in a small, but sure voice. "It will."

"I must insist that you—"

"Don't insist. Relay my message." Zachary turned away from him. "Now if you'll excuse me, I need to sort my affairs. Goodbye, Rothschild."

Rothschild stuttered after him, but Zachary marched up the stairs back toward his bedroom. Lawfully or not, he'd just disobeyed Sverrin for the last time, which meant there was only one thing left to do.

～※～

He wasn't quite sure what drew him back to the roof. Zachary reasoned it might have been quicker to open his wrists, and be done with it, but he couldn't bear the idea that it might be Heather, or Daniel who came upon him. He'd left letters on his desk for them to find later—his apologies to everyone.

Of course, the cowardly part of him had considered just fleeing, but there was nowhere Zachary could go that Sverrin could not call him back from. The King knew his weaknesses. If Zachary ran, Sverrin would target those closest to him, until he returned. So long as Zachary lived, he would be Sverrin's pawn.

The wind was high up on the ledge and Zachary breathed in deeply. It felt right to die in the open air—to taste even a semblance of the fleeting freedom he had. He gazed steadily at the ground below, his heart pounding.

For the first time in years, Zachary allowed himself to think about what he'd done. In the name of good intention, he'd driven himself into an irredeemable darkness, all to save the boy he'd failed to protect. Zachary had loved and mourned Sverrin with such an astounding guilt, he'd convinced himself, and everyone else, that he was happy to walk the path of a villain to set it right.

Deep down, however, he'd maintained a foolish hope. That one day Rufus would return to Harmatia, that Zachary would be forgiven his blood-lust, and that Sverrin's revival would bring a new age of prosperity and peace to Harmatia. None of these had come to pass. Zachary was feared and rightfully hated, Rufus was dead, and Sverrin had slowly drained the country of life and hope.

Zachary had never wanted to be an instrument of tyranny. He'd never wanted to be a monster. His design had always been to protect—that was his purpose. How miserably he'd failed.

He took a step closer to the edge and the wind made him rock on his feet. What would Katrina say? His eldest and most beloved sister, who'd raised him when his own mother, unable to abide the baby inside her, had forced Zachary out from her womb at only eight months. Elizabeth DuMorne had refused even to hold her son, claiming to have fulfilled her marital duty. The first and last words she ever spoke to Zachary were a curse—his name; Tristus DuMorne.

Yes, death had been put upon him from birth, but Katrina had whisked him away, raised him on goat's milk, and given him a new name. Not a curse, a promise: Arlen. And he'd taken the surname Zachary and worn it with pride, not because it was his father's or even his grandfather's, but because it was hers.

Heather Benson was Katrina's maternal aunt. Zachary could only hope they would band together, as women were so capable of doing, and share their grief. If they grieved him at all—he'd turned out to be no great brother or son to either. Nor any great friend.

Athea, permit me this one thing, before you pass your judgement:
Let me see Rufus, and the Delphi boy that I murdered, he prayed.
There were few wrongs he could now right, but perhaps it would
bring peace to these restless souls to know his grief and regret.
Perhaps it would only anger them more, but Zachary was happy
to face their wrath.

He closed his eyes, heaving a sigh. Now—it was time. The
wind had risen to a peak, the clouds were moving fast above him,
as if in a gathering storm. His courage mounted, forcing back the
sick feelings of fear. He was ready.

He opened his arms to embrace death and tipped forward,
rushed with feelings of relief and release. It wasn't so bad to die,
he decided.

"STOP!"

A set of arms seized him by the waist, and then another across
his chest, and Zachary found himself being dragged backward.
Panic took him, and he began to fight furiously, thrashing and
shouting.

His captors were strong, however, and held onto him fast.
Zachary, still weak from the sickness, couldn't break free.
Drained of energy, he slumped, dropping his full weight, and was
pulled back further onto the roof. He was lowered to his knees,
and in the next second, Emeric was in front of him, shaking him
by the shoulders.

"What were you doing?" Emeric demanded. "Athea, you were
going to jump—*you were going to jump!*"

Behind Zachary, Marcel was still gripping him firmly
around the chest, as if he feared Zachary would bolt at the first
opportunity and dive for the ledge again.

Zachary struggled to register what was happening. How
had Marcel and Emeric found him? Had they spotted him, by
chance, from the courtyard below? Or seen him from one of the
windows, and realised what he was about to do?

"How…?" he managed to mumble. His feverish shaking had

returned—he hadn't realised how cold it was on the roof. He could barely move his lips, they were so numb.

"We came to see you. Found the letters. We searched everywhere." Marcel was panting. "Arlen, why have you done this? Why did you not come to me?"

Zachary couldn't speak. The absolute terror in his friends' faces was of his doing. They didn't know the injustice they'd served by saving him, especially now that he knew he couldn't go through with his suicide, knew how much it would *hurt* them.

"Zachary." Emeric's grip was so tight it was painful, and Zachary understood his punishment. Athea had chosen Zachary's fate. He'd raised a man from the dead and now would face the direct consequences. Death was too sweet a release.

"Get off," Zachary said between gritted teeth. "Sons of the gods, get off me!"

He elbowed Marcel hard and his second in command loosed his grip with a grunt, allowing Zachary to rip himself free. He landed hard on his side and scrabbled away. He could hear Emeric and Marcel both breathing heavily from the exertion. He couldn't bear to face them. His chest heaved.

"Why?" Zachary hid his face in his hands, struggling against a sob. "Why couldn't you just let me die?"

"You're not well," Emeric moaned.

"You don't know what you've done!" Zachary rocked. "Sons of the gods, if you did—" he broke off. "Damn the pair of you!"

He rose to his feet, both his men doing the same. They moved between him and the ledge, their hands raised and stances low, as if they were trying to catch a bolting rabbit. It only served to make Zachary angrier.

"Get out of my way."

"I will not let you do this," Marcel said firmly. The fear in his eyes had been replaced with something firm that Zachary had only seen once before, many years ago, in the academy. Back then, he and Marcel had been fairly indifferent to each other.

One night, however, Marcel had stepped out into the training grounds to find Zachary being aggressively beaten by a group of bullies. Outnumbered and too exhausted to fight back, Zachary had been curled on the floor, hands over his head, laughing maniacally. Zachary could still remember it clearly. He had spotted Marcel stood, watching from the side, and Zachary had grinned up at him, his two front teeth already missing from a kick to the mouth. That moment had defined their friendship forever, Marcel immediately wading into the fight to save the reckless little fool who would one day be his captain.

He's still trying to save me, Zachary thought sadly. *Always trying to save me.*

"Oh, my friend," Zachary breathed, "there's nothing you can do."

"You cannot know that," Marcel insisted, and Zachary wished the pair of them wouldn't fight so hard for him. He wished they weren't so ferociously loyal.

They will follow me to death. I have to release them from that obligation, Zachary realised. In the moment of his death, leadership would have passed on, but now it would remain with him—a man soon to be DuGilles's puppet.

He breathed in deeply, "I excuse you both."

His friends looked between each other.

"Excuse us?" Emeric asked.

"From the Night Patrol," Zachary said. "I am casting you out. From this day onward, you'll have no part in our activities, receive no commissions or take any orders. You're hereby excused from the sect, effective immediately."

The pair were struck dumb, their mouths slack. "Zachary," Emeric whispered, "you can't be serious."

"I assure you," Zachary summoned his wings to him, "I am. Goodbye Marcel, Emeric. The gods forgive you. I love you both."

And with that, he took to the air before either of them could say another word.

Aurora slipped away whilst Sverrin was busy with his council. Under the guise of going for a walk in the gardens, she retraced her steps of the previous night and found her way back into the crypts, to Jionat's side.

Her pencil glided carefully across the pages of the small, leather-bound journal she usually kept concealed within her skirts. She knew she had precious little time before she would be missed, but it had been impossible to commit the entirety of the Korrigans' spell to memory. Even one error in her recollection, one detail missed, could make all the difference in her understanding it.

Aurora drew as quickly as she could, copying everything down and trying hard not to be distracted by the slumbering Prince at her side. She couldn't afford the time to mourn Jionat now—there was nothing she could do for him.

"You should not be down here," Sverrin's voice broke out from behind her.

Aurora leapt a foot in the air and swung around. She hadn't heard him approaching at all, his step as light as a shadow. He leaned over her and Aurora felt her throat tighten, alarmed by his proximity.

"Your Majesty." She slipped the journal away, dropping it into the deep pocket of her skirt as she curtsied. "You surprised me."

Sverrin wore a peculiar expression, like a teacher who'd caught their student doing something perplexingly stupid. There was no hospitality in his gaze, no sign of kindness or any of the affection which he'd doted on her so thickly in the last few days. His lightless eyes were all-consuming and there was a hungry lurk about his posture, which made him look oddly feral.

"Did you think nobody would know you were here?" Sverrin didn't move, but Aurora doubted she could get by him now. If she tried to dart away, he'd be on her faster than wolf on a bleeding lamb. "I've had you watched since you arrived."

Aurora gripped her pencil. She knew exactly where to plant it, if he got too close. "I wanted to see him," she said, refusing to show her fear. "There's no crime in that. I didn't think it forbidden."

"I doubt that," Sverrin chuckled, and it was a low, rumbling sound like distant thunder. Aurora usually liked the rain, but this settled a deep foreboding on her shoulders. There was nothing human about that laugh. "I can feel it, you know. When someone enters this chamber. When they approach him." Sverrin nodded toward his brother. "He and I are connected. When he is under threat, I feel it. No man can come down here without my knowing…Or did you think you were the first to try and assassinate me by means of my brother?"

The thought had crossed Aurora's mind. It would be easy to slit Jionat's throat and thereby seep away the life-energy that revived the King, but Aurora didn't have the stomach for the task. Besides, there was another destined to kill Sverrin—a boy, prophesised to come, who would be the death of Jionat and save Bethean from destruction.

"I am not here to kill anyone. I am here to mourn." Aurora pressed her back against the altar, and again Sverrin gave that chuckle which chilled her to the bone. There was a dooming finality to it.

"I find that unlikely, Princess." He moved toward her, seeping through the darkness like an eel. Aurora could feel the cold of the stone behind her. She was no warrior, and had no illusions about that. If Sverrin chose to hurt her, she could lash out, but she doubted it would do much to stop him. His hands were vast and powerful, and she knew that he could easily shatter her with only a few choice blows. "You came here for your own purpose. Be honest, little Princess."

"I came to Harmatia to meet you, and I came here to grieve someone, who, for the kindness he did me once, I cared for

505

deeply. Call me a girlish fool, but I missed him, and wanted to be alone."

Sverrin gave a sudden, irate sigh. "Why?" he groaned, agitated. "Why does everyone in Harmatia insist on *lying* to me? Is it so hard to be truthful? Must you all disappoint me, time and time again?"

"I am not lying." Aurora had expected anger, but Sverrin seemed desperate, his eyes rolling madly, breath hard and heavy. "Your Majesty, please. I am not here to assassinate you."

"I thought to wed you." Sverrin wasn't calmed, his teeth barred. "Truly, I did. I think you and I have shared a similar burden. We know what it is, to be captured in darkness. But you cannot hide your revulsion from me, woman. I smell your fear. I smell your intent."

Aurora grew more frightened, her lungs constricting. The pencil dropped from her stiff hand, and she forgot everything but her terror. It was easy to think how she might defend herself when she was safe, but with Sverrin looming over her, she lost all sensible thought.

"Please," she whimpered and then shuddered as he leant down to kiss her. He pressed his mouth to hers and it was like being bitten. She shrieked at the feel of his lips—icy cold and smelling of death—and tried to tear herself away. Sverrin took her by the wrist.

"Stay Princess." He twisted her around, draping an arm over her chest and pulling her back into him. His body was hard as stone. "Tell me of this love you have for my brother?" He pinned her front against the altar. "Does he stir feelings of desire within you? Or is it true what they say—that you prefer *female* company?"

"I should not have come down." Her voice shook desperately. "Please, Your Majesty, I see now, I was foolish."

"Yes, you were." He kissed her ear and she sobbed. "I had every intention of being civil with you whilst I took your kingdom, but

I see now that was never meant to be. My mother warned me against the little witch of Bethean. She spoke words of wisdom."

Through her fear, Sverrin's words ignited a fire within Aurora, the fire of her people. "Take my kingdom?" she spat, fighting back sobs.

"Yes," Sverrin said, almost dreamily. "I have seen it—armies gathering, a great battle between Harmatia and Bethean. Jionathan showed it to me. He *shows* me things—things that only a Delphi could see. Like a Dragon attacking Sigel'eg." Sverrin hummed, Aurora whimpering. "Yes. I knew all about the attack, weeks before, and I was shown how it would end. I sent word to my grandfather, and together we plotted. He captured the Hunter he needed, and we made it appear that Kathra and Harmatia were divided, all to lure you here and take your kingdom."

Aurora's head spun. Sverrin had known about the Dragon? Bozidar had allowed his own city to be torched, and his people die, all so that they could start a war? Aurora shook her head. "Bethean will not fall to the hands of you, Puppet King."

"Ah, yes," Sverrin hissed, "I heard that's what they call me. Tell me, who's pulling the strings, little witch? Who am I a puppet of?"

Aurora knew the insult was meant to instigate Kathra's control over Harmatia, but now she understood that Sverrin was no more controlled by King Bozidar than Thestian had been.

"Madness and death," Aurora said. She could feel him grinning, his teeth against her skin.

"Madness? Perhaps. But death I've already conquered."

She closed her eyes. "No," she forced out, "you have not. Death is coming for you, Sverrin. It lurks in every shadow and you know it. Those disappointments you spoke of, people betraying you—already you can feel the net closing in."

He seized her by the hair and threw her hard to the floor. She turned, her voice shaking, but strong.

"Worse than that, you feel it growing within you. You're

507

rotting. Losing any semblance of self. You can feel your mind slipping, everything decaying away. Not a King. Not human."

"Be quiet," Sverrin growled, standing over her.

"You cannot even remember what colour your brother's eyes were. You're missing parts. Piece by piece, Sverrin is disappearing, and you have no idea who you are. So yes—we call you Puppet King, because soon that's all you'll be."

Sverrin threw himself on her, tearing at her clothes and pulling at her hair. He didn't speak, but gave angry grunts and cries as he tore open her bodice, pushing back her frightened hands as she slapped at him, clawing at his eyes and throat.

"Help me!" Aurora howled. "Somebody, please! *Help me!*"

Sverrin pushed his arm against her delicate throat, crushing the sound of her desperate cries. Aurora was blinded by tears, her skirts ripped and pulled up to her waist. She could suddenly hear her heart-beat in her ears, loud and fast. He held both her wrists in a powerful hand, his elbow across her neck as he reached down to his belt. Aurora gave another strangled scream, only to find the pressure over her body relieved. The pounding, which she'd mistaken for her heart, was actually someone running toward them, and Aurora watched as Sverrin was ripped away by tall shadow.

"Run, Princess! *Run!*" It was the Magi, Arlen Zachary, his eyes wild with fear. "Go! Get out!" he commanded desperately, barely maintaining his grip as Sverrin thrashed and fought.

"Release me, Zachary!" Sverrin roared. "By the gods, I will kill you! I'll *kill* you!"

"Aurora, *now!*" Zachary shouted.

Aurora gathered what was left her skirts, fumbled to her feet and ran for the door. Behind her, she could hear Sverrin swearing and shrieking, but she didn't dare look back.

She made it into the stairway back toward the castle, just as a whirl of wind burst down through the tunnel, and she ran headlong into Embarr Reagon, who appeared before her.

"Aurora?" Embarr was panic-stricken, his blue-skin icy as he gripped her shoulders. "I sensed you were in danger!"

Aurora buried herself against him and Embarr wrapped his arms firmly around her shoulders. Aurora felt the winds gather around her.

She didn't have time to argue that she couldn't leave without her faithful entourage before Embarr had spirited them both away, with a great rush.

When Aurora opened her eyes next, she was in her father's court, sobbing and half-naked, and with a heart desperate for vengeance.

CHAPTER
48

He'd gone where he thought no one would look for him. He was sure that Marcel and Emeric would run straight to Belphegore, and Zachary couldn't bear to face them all. If DuGilles was going to take him, then it would be quietly and without casualty. Besides, the truth was hard on his lips, and Zachary couldn't hold the secret for much longer—he wasn't brave enough.

It was at the mouth of the tunnels that he heard Aurora screaming. Even before he sprinted down to save her, he knew what he was going to find. It didn't lessen the impact of the sick image—Sverrin pinning Aurora down, choking her as he went for his belt.

Even knowing the consequences, Zachary acted. Terrified he may have been, but he wasn't so selfish to allow this atrocity to happen. Sverrin fought hard against him as the Princess fled, but Zachary had trained with the King for many years and was prepared for his strength.

Or so he thought, until Sverrin managed to slip his leg between Zachary's and, bending his weight forward, threw the Magi up and over his shoulder onto the ground in-front. Zachary was barely given a chance to recover before Sverrin was sprinting after Aurora. Zachary staggered to his feet and ran after the King. Both reached the mouth of the tunnel in time to see Aurora standing high above, in the embrace of a shrouded, black-eyed man. Then a large howl of wind came tumbling down the stairs toward them, and both Princess and the stranger were gone, like a snuffled flame.

Sverrin and Zachary stood, the King silent in his anger, whilst Zachary wilted in relief.

"Faeries," Sverrin snarled. "Faeries in my capital!"

"She's gone, Sverrin. You can't hurt her," Zachary replied.

Sverrin turned slowly. Zachary caught his desolate expression and retreated a few clumsy steps. It wasn't enough. Sverrin lunged at him, throwing the first punch. Zachary felt his jaw crunch and break from the force of the blow and he was sent sprawling to the floor.

Laid out, and dumb with terror, he attempted to scrabble away, but Sverrin stooped, grabbed his ankle and dragged him back. Zachary lashed out but Sverrin dropped forward on-top of him.

He wrestled Zachary down, beating him viciously around the head. He landed a blow, and then another one. Zachary felt his eye socket and cheekbone crack under the heavy barrage, his vision distorting and darkening. His nose broke, blood coating Sverrin's hands as the King punched and punched again, his own fingers now mangled. Zachary's lip split all the way down the centre, teeth coming loose and tumbling down the back of his throat.

All the while, Sverrin was screaming, and when he finally stopped hitting Zachary, it was only to rise to his feet and begin stomping and kicking instead. Zachary curled around himself and didn't fight back. He didn't know how.

"You think yourself strong, Tristus?" His father sneered at him. Rivalen only called him Tristus when he was angry, otherwise it was

511

'Arlen', or 'you', or worse. But the name, the curse, was reserved for moments when Zachary had truly pushed Rivalen over the edge. "You think yourself mighty? Then we will play a game, you and I—see how strong you are."

Zachary could hear the crop. One day, it would evolve to a whip, but in that moment, the crop was the worse he knew. On some level, Zachary understood that if he submitted, if he apologised and gave in, these tortures would end, but he couldn't. He was too young to understand pride. All he knew was that, as long as he let his father beat him, Rivalen wouldn't raise a hand to Zachary's sisters. It was Zachary's duty to take the punishment in their place—his obligation, as their brother.

"I am going to strike you. I won't tell you how many times. But every time you cry out, the number will double. How then, Tristus? Are you still so sure you can bear all of their punishments?"

Zachary didn't reply. He removed his shirt, knelt on the ground and gritted his teeth together. Rivalen raised the crop and brought it hard onto his son's back. On the third strike, Zachary cried out.

He learnt quickly to quail the screams after that. He was seven years old.

"Zachary!" Sverrin took hold of his pounding head. With his one seeing eye, Zachary looked up into the King's face, weeping blood.

Kill me, he pleaded. *Kill me. Let me die for a good cause.*

Sverrin, as if hearing Zachary's thoughts, crept his hands down to Zachary's throat, and with a sudden sureness, squeezed. Despite the cruel actions, in the tiny slit of vision Zachary had left, he could see Sverrin was crying bitterly.

"You made me!" The King was shrieking now, like a lost child. "You *made* me into this! Two years, you buried me in darkness—*two years!* Why couldn't you let me rest? Why did you bring me back?" He squeezed harder, and death rushed to meet Zachary like a warm embrace. And then all of sudden, as if retracting a gift, Sverrin lifted his hands from their deathly hold and stood.

Zachary coughed and whimpered below him, almost blind now in both eyes, and in searing pain.

Sverrin furiously wiped his eyes, and in the place of human grief was that same cavernous emptiness that Zachary had come to fear. "I warned you about disobeying me. Now you will meet your promised fate. But before that, I want you to know, Zachary, that this does not appease my anger. Any consequences of that, is on your hands."

He left Zachary then, bleeding and broken on the floor, barely conscious. The Magi slipped in and out of reality, everything hushed but for the sound of his own laboured breath.

Slowly, his eyes fell closed, as if to sleep, and then the full force of Sverrin's words came over him.

Where would Sverrin's anger lead him? Whom would the King direct his wrath to?

Daniel, a quiet voice resounded in his aching skull. *Daniel.*

It was enough. Zachary awoke from his terrified stupor, and with every effort, reached out for the stars' power. They seemed so very distant from him. The Night Patrol could heal themselves using magic, but it was no easy task when you were bleeding, for blood was the medium in which magic coursed through the body. Even so, Zachary dragged it in, like a drowning man gasping in water.

A pain, like fire, came over his face, and he writhed, twisting on the ground, his wings unfurling from his back. His broken bones shifted, resetting and healing themselves, and he slumped to the floor, exhausted. There would be new scars, that couldn't be prevented, but he would survive.

When at last he felt the healing pain lessen, Zachary expelled the magic from his body and returned to his human form.

The vision returned completely in one eye, but the other was murky. Zachary didn't have time to dwell on whether this would be permanent, or if he merely required more time to heal.

He mounted shakily to his feet, using the altar to steady

himself. Jionat looked grim beneath him as Zachary's legs shook, face still spattered with blood. At the very least his teeth had regrown, a little sharper than before, and his nose and soft palate was once again intact.

After a few failed attempts to move away from his support, Zachary was able to shuffle toward the tunnel. With each movement, his steps gained momentum and confidence, until he was striding, and then running.

He tore up through the castle, ignoring the shouts of alarm from servants and courtiers alike as he sprinting past, toward the academy. He looked in every classroom, throwing doors open and skidding in, to the outrage of whichever professor was teaching.

At last he found the right one, breaking through the door so fast, it crashed into the wall. The students sprang to their feet.

"Daniel!" he shouted wildly.

"Lord Zachary, what in Notameer's—" The professor—Zachary didn't recall his name—cried from the front of the class.

"*Daniel!*" Zachary shouted again, and his brother looked out through the peering crowd, pushing his way forward.

"Athea have mercy, what happened to you?" Daniel demanded, seeing the blood.

"We need to go, now!" Zachary took him by the wrist and ran, dragging Daniel behind, his brother barely keeping pace.

"What's going on?" Daniel cried as they broke out of the academy and streaked toward their home.

"I have to get you out. If he catches you, he'll kill you!"

"Who?"

"The King!"

They reached the house and tumbled into it. Zachary locked the doors immediately, and swung around to Daniel, gripping him tightly.

"I need you to listen to me very carefully, we don't have much time," he said in a ragged whisper. "Pack a bag of your things—only the essentials. You need to flee the city. It won't be easy. Hide here until nightfall then go through the gardens to Hathely's house. He'll help you escape and protect you. Do you understand?"

"Arlen—"

"Do you understand?" Zachary shook him, and Daniel nodded. Zachary took in his brother's dazed expression, and pulled him into an embrace. "Forgive me, Daniel." He kissed Daniel fiercely on the temple and pushed him away. "Go!"

Daniel took the stairs two at a time and disappeared into his bedroom just as the first hammering came from the front door. Zachary tensed. The house seemed empty, which was both a surprise and relief. Perhaps the servants, too, had gone in search of him?

The knocking grew louder—they know he was there. Zachary gathered more magic to him. Weak and dizzy as he was, he could still fight. He would hold them off as long as he could.

Something heavy hit the door, like a battering ram. It struck again, and the wood splintered. Zachary knew the hinges would give out before long.

On the third strike, the door came down, and men flooded into the house. Zachary was relieved to see they were members of the Royal Guard, rather than Magi. He instantly flew into action.

Gathering water to him, he formed two long whips and struck out, slicing through the air. One of the whips was sharp, like a knife, whilst the other blunted, allowing Zachary to rip men from their feet, as he cut and sliced.

The guards came at him hard, pooling around as he turned and twisted, throwing attack after attack. He managed to kill six of the twenty before something sharp embedded itself in his upper thigh. It was a small, dart-like arrow, but as Zachary made to snap the shaft out, a peculiar feeling ebbed over him. His magic faded, as if bleeding away. He struggled to maintain it, but it disappeared and he realised, with horror, what he'd been struck with.

Mica.

He looked down at the wound, scrabbling to reach inside and pull the dreaded stone out. But the arrowhead had been designed to shatter inside him—little shards dug deep into his flesh, dispelling the magic within him. He cursed and, changing tactic, dove for one of the dead men's swords.

The guards didn't make it easy. They knew his skill—that he was a terrible force to be reckoned with, even without magic. They circled closer, jabbing and driving him away from any potential weapons.

Then, another got a lucky strike it from Zachary's half-blind side, and the top of a sword pierced his shoulder. Zachary swung around like an agitated animal, and the men gathered closer.

Zachary could hear his blood rushing through his head. Without his magic, the pain was returning and his energy fading away.

"That's quite enough of that," a voice called from the kitchen, and the fighting ceased. Slowly, the guards pulled away, forming a cage as Zachary turned.

DuGilles walked slowly out from the kitchen, Heather Benson held close to him, a knife at her throat. Zachary realised the Kathrak must have been there all along, waiting in the house.

Had he heard Daniel? No—they'd kept their voices too low. Zachary raised his hands in surrender, his eyes on Heather. She stared back, stony. DuGilles glided the knife very gently up and down her throat.

"I see where you get your bravery from," DuGilles said, his voice gentle. Zachary held his breath. "When I came into the house, she hurried all the servants away, and then refused to do what she was told. I was going to have her to welcome you, you see, hide you in the kitchen, and bring you straight into my arms. It would've been very funny. Alas, she wanted no part of it. Unfortunately, she *is* a part of it." DuGilles nicked Heather's skin slightly, but it was Zachary who flinched. Heather kept eyes on him, strong and steady. Zachary slowly lowered himself onto his knees.

"Let her go." He put his hands on the ground. "I won't fight."

"But you *will*," DuGilles laughed. "You're so strong, Zachary. And stubborn. Just like Rufus was, and I failed to save him. I won't make that same mistake with you."

"Arlen," Heather said, her frail hand reaching for him. Her voice shook. "Close your eyes. Close your eyes, sweet boy."

Zachary watched the path of the knife, gliding up and down, up and down. "Please."

"My sweet boy," Heather repeated. "Sweet boy. Don't look. Don't look." She could barely disguise the tremor in her voice. Zachary stared her straight in the eye, willing courage, though his was fading fast. He couldn't leave her alone at this time. He couldn't abandon her.

"In order to be reborn, you must first be broken," DuGilles said, almost pityingly. "You're close, granted, but I'm going to achieve what your father couldn't. It's for the best." He leant across and gave Heather a fond kiss on the cheek. "I know you loved him like a son," he said warmly, and angled the knife up into the space between her ear and her jaw, slicing it from one side to the other.

Blood spurted out. DuGilles released Heather and she stepped forward, mouth opening and closing in shock. A second later she collapsed. Zachary fumbled to catch her, pulling her close. He held her tightly, blood gushing from her wound, too long and deep to heal. Her windpipe was exposed, the head close to severed. Zachary said her name, over and over, but her eyes were already vacant, her death swift. The woman who'd cared for him for thirty years, through his tantrums, nonsense, and his curiosities, had been extinguished in a few seconds.

It occurred to Zachary that he hadn't made her a garland of flowers to mark the month of Haylix, as he usually did. He hadn't

517

even thanked her.

Slowly, but with the force of crumbling glacier, Zachary felt the last defence within him break. The blow was too heavy. It was too much. The events of the day came rushing over him, finished now in death and blood. He tipped his head back and howled.

It was guttural, a sound he could barely maintain, his throat sick and raw. But still, it came, and he screamed, and screamed, and screamed.

DuGilles smiled. "Now we're ready," he said, gesturing to one of the Royal Guard.

In the last second, before the heavy blow knocked him unconscious, Zachary spotted Daniel hiding up on the landing, peering down, hands over his mouth, tears streaming.

Stay hidden, little brother, Zachary thought, through his grief, *and be safe.*

As the soldier cracked the hilt of his sword over the back of Zachary's skull, the darkness wasn't welcoming. It was deep, and long and all-consuming, and Zachary knew he would never see the light of day again.

CHAPTER 49

"You're thinking of him—that Magi," Fae observed from the doorway, her voice soft. Rufus glanced up from where he was settled in a chair. He'd been staring off into space, a book slack and forgotten in his hands.

"Am I so predictable?" Rufus didn't both to deny it. He closed the book, rising from his seat.

"Walk with me?" Fae offered her arm like a perfect gentlemen, and Rufus chuckled and took it, allowing her to guide him out. They left the comfort of the castle and went out into the gardens.

The stars were strewn across the cloudless sky in a dazzling light display. Rufus craned his neck to look up at them all, his breath stilled. Even he, who'd studied the night sky for years, never ceased to be struck by its infinite beauty.

"Your vision has disturbed you," Fae said.

Rufus grimaced. "If you knew Zachary, it would you too."

"On the contrary—he tried to murder me, almost killed you and was an intrinsic part in the plot that sacrificed your brother." Fae's tone was light, but unforgiving. "I know enough about him."

Rufus gave a stark laugh. "Believe you me, I too have resented Zachary all these years. There were days when all I wanted was for him to burn. But I'll be frank…there were days when I missed him too."

Fae's expression was reserved, but she didn't release Rufus. "He meant something to you."

"He was my brother, before I had Jionat or Joshua. He protected me—fiercely, sometimes. Even when we fought, even when everything changed…He wanted me to be well—I know that. I'm sure of it."

"You and he…" Fae began slowly. "Were you ever…"

Rufus saw her train of thought. "Lovers?" he laughed. "No."

"But you thought about it." Fae was shrewd, and Rufus shrugged.

"He was strong, protective and had a sense of humour. I find those qualities attractive. By the time I met him however, I was engaged to Mielane. After she died, I was in mourning a year, and then Sverrin was assassinated and anything good and kind in Zachary died with him." He gave a sad smile. "Even if that weren't the case, Zachary lacks the inclination, I think. Then again, who knows," Rufus fluttered his eyelashes, "I'm told by many I have Gancanagh blood in me. Perhaps even Zachary would've fallen prey to my seductive charms and looks. What do you think, Fae?"

"I have no opinion." Fae fought back her own smile. "Your handsomeness certainly hasn't had any effect on me."

"You think I'm handsome?"

"I trust my mother's judgement."

"Your *mother* thinks I'm handsome?"

"Apparently."

"Sweet Haylix, I have the wrong woman on my arm," Rufus teased and Fae slapped him lightly on the shoulder. They came to one of the stone benches and settled on it together, looking out over the mountain peaks, which cradled the moon between them, like a pearl in an oyster. "May I ask you something, pertaining to relationships and loyalties?"

Fae smoothed her skirts. "You want to know about Reilly."

"It was a surprise," Rufus admitted and Fae snorted softly. "You don't seem to fit well, but I can't imagine you marrying idly."

"I will tell you," Fae said after a pause. "But it's not an easy story for me."

They settled into silence, Rufus waiting patiently for Fae to collect her thoughts. Finally, she inhaled, her voice timid. "I knew Reilly from birth. He's was Korrick's protégé, before me, and I was promised to him as a baby."

"It was arranged?"

"My mother and father made it clear that I could break the arrangement at any time but I was happy with it. Reilly was handsome, he was kind to me and he made me laugh. During my childhood I couldn't imagine a better husband and I fell deeply in love, as children do.

"I was not permitted to wed until I was older, so to occupy my time I threw myself into my training. Every time I succeeded in a task, Reilly was always delighted. At first his praise was all I strove for.

"Through my hard work, I progressed rapidly however. Fighting came naturally to me, and it quickly developed into a passion of mine. Any weapons Korrick handed to me, I would master. I became his second protégé, and truthfully—his favourite.

"As I neared adulthood, the commander of the Cat Sidhe army made announcements that he planned step down from his position. Speculation began of who would succeed him. Reilly was the obvious choice but there were some who thought I should be a candidate. I had an aptitude for battle, I was a Chosen, and I had inherited strongly the powers and skills of my clan.

"Like a fool, I chose to ignore this, thinking nothing of it. My marriage was approaching, and it occupied my thoughts almost entirely. There was no doubt in my mind that Reilly would be chosen, and I would serve as his wife, and a soldier under his command. I was happy, Rufus. I loved him. But even on that day, I saw a nervousness in him, something tense that he wouldn't confide in me about. And then, barely a few weeks after our union, the candidates for commander were announced. The vote was between Reilly and me.

"In the Neve, to be a candidate for command is no small thing. It's an honour bestowed on very few and not something to be refused. When two candidates arise there's only one way to decide who should command."

"You had to fight him," Rufus released.

Fae shifted and a curtain of her hair swept across her face, hiding her from Rufus. She fiddled with her hands. "He was my husband, but as we stepped into the arena all of that was supposed to be forgotten. What lay ahead was the future of our people." She dropped her head. "But I was foolish, and impressionable. I had devoted my life to pleasing him, and I knew that if I beat him that day, that if I won…Gods, how could he love me after that?"

"A man who is threatened by the strength of his wife doesn't deserve her."

"Would that I had understood and believed that then. But I was a girl, my head full of stories, with ideals of a perfect marriage. I didn't know what any of it truly meant. And so I slowed down, I stepped out of rhythm."

"You threw the fight?"

Fae's hands stilled. "Reilly won," she said instead, "but he knew, Rufus. He knew what I had done. And it destroyed everything." Her voice cracked with shame.

"Fae…" Rufus reached for her hand.

"After that, he couldn't look at me. Letting Reilly beat me in that fight was the worst thing I ever did. I know now he would have followed me with the same pride I felt, but instead I dishonoured him. What was more, we couldn't speak of it—Reilly had to command an army now. He needed their respect and their trust. If anyone knew I had lost on purpose, they would think he asked me to do it."

"How can you be sure of that?"

"My people are honourable," Fae chuckled. "But they're also helpless gossips and incredibly stubborn in their judgement. Reilly was so ashamed he wouldn't even share my bed, and I was so sorry that I didn't try to mend the gap. And so this chasm grew between us—fed by our resentment and loneliness. I wanted him back, but I couldn't face him. At last, when it grew too hard to bear, Reilly commissioned me as courier for Bethean. It was an important role, and as far away from the Neve as he could send me."

"How could he do such a thing?" Rufus breathed. "To cast you out like that on your own?"

"I was already alone, Rufus. The morning I left, I removed my wedding band, and I never wore it again. Any semblance of the marriage I envisioned was gone, and I didn't know how to repair it."

"Mothering Prospan, Fae. I'm so sorry." Rufus kept hold of her hand, and she covered his with cold fingers.

"I was lost to my anger and my despair. Matters worsened when I discovered that my childhood friend, Embarr Reagon, had apparently kidnapped the Betheanian Princess. And so then started a chapter of my life where I was forced to rebuild myself, and grow into the person I am today."

"It sounds incredibly troublesome."

"You have no idea. But I would be a very different person now, if I hadn't met you and Jionat."

"I'd be a very dead person, if I hadn't met you." Rufus moved closer to her. The night was cool, so he put his arm around her shoulder, drawing her in. She rested her head against his collar.

"You're a wonderful listener," she sighed. "I feel as if I could tell you anything."

"You can." He interlocked his fingers with hers. "Now and forever. You can tell me anything in the world."

Marcel was smoking heavily, staring intently at the door. In the chair beside the fire, which only a few days ago Zachary had occupied, Daniel was now slumped similarly, fast asleep.

It had been a trying few days for the boy. He'd appeared several nights ago, face drawn and eyes stained with tears, breaking in through the garden. The poor boy had been so frail that it had taken half an hour of care and comfort from Emeric before Daniel was able to speak. What he'd reported disturbed them all.

Marcel had gone straight to the Zachary household to investigate, but any evidence of Heather Benson's murder and Zachary's abduction had been cleaned away. None of the servants could confirm Daniel's story, and there was no word of where Zachary had gone.

To protect Daniel, Marcel hadn't aggravated the situation with any more questions, though with each passing day, he grew more agitated by his lack of knowledge.

In the chair, Daniel woke with a start. He'd been sleeping fitfully over the last few days, shouting in the night, and looking gaunt come morning.

He sat up straight and composed himself, covering his mouth and shooting Marcel an apologetic look.

From where she'd been playing in the corner, Morelle rose and went to Daniel, carrying him a lemon biscuit. Daniel took it wordlessly and gave her a wan smile of thanks. He rose shakily from his chair and joined Marcel at the table.

"Sorry, I didn't mean to fall asleep."

"You needed it." Marcel emptied the spent tobacco from his pipe and refilled it. Morelle wrinkled her nose.

"Maman says it is bad to smoke so much," she said and Marcel raised a golden eyebrow at his niece.

"Go to your room." He nodded toward the door, and Morelle narrowed her black eyes. She knew that, should she choose to defy him, there would be no reprimand, but quietly she obeyed regardless. She was sensitive to the mood in the house, and knew when best to sink in and out of the shadows—an inherited skill. She gave Daniel a small pat on the arm as she passed him, and leant up on her tip-toes to kiss Marcel softly on the cheek. The gesture was sweet, but there was a mercenary glint in her eye, and something told Marcel that this obedience would need to be rewarded later, or there would be hell to pay.

Daniel leant forward over the table. Despite his rest, he still looked drained. "Have you had any more news?"

"I would have woken you."

Daniel sagged, "I can't abide this waiting. Not knowing."

"You should leave the capital."

"I'm not leaving until I know where he is," Daniel said.

Emeric had made the same proposition twice in the last few days, but Daniel had been adamant. Marcel was happy to offer him shelter as long as was required, but he feared for Daniel's wellbeing.

From behind them, another door opened and Béatrice stepped into the room. She'd returned to Harmatia the night before, after a long journey from Sigel'eg, and had immediately taken responsibility of Daniel.

"My dear," she moved to the boy, "you are still in here? Staying in one place so long is not good for your health. I have had a bath drawn for you. Go and wash. You will feel better for being clean. No excuses. And do no fret—I know how private you Zacharys are. The servants will not intrude. You have the washroom to yourself."

Daniel, who looked like he hadn't had a further thought from his mind, stood and thanked Béatrice. "If you hear anything," he began to Marcel.

"I shall send for you," Marcel said solemnly and the boy gave that same, limp smile and left the room. Béatrice took his seat, opposite Marcel.

"How many is that?" she asked, taking the pipe from his mouth. "Three? Take pause, my sweet thing. This is one Réneian habit I would rather you did not indulge in so frequently. You have seen the state of the chimney after a fire, I cannot imagine what it does to your throat and lungs, Magi or not."

Marcel snatched the pipe back, but did as she wished, emptying the tobacco. Béatrice looked at of the door which Daniel had just passed through.

"Poor boy. We ought to be making arrangements to send him home. Though Corhlam will not be safe for long. There are rumours that Sverrin attacked Princess Aurora. I cannot imagine that Bethean will sit idle and allow such an affront to go unpunished. Isaac will be here soon, he will take Daniel, I think."

"Daniel will not leave, until he knows."

"Then he may become a permanent resident," Béatrice snipped, a little too sharply. Marcel studied her sister's familiar features. Her maroon eyes shone plainly back at him, the same colour as their mother's, with the same ability to lie. Marcel stood slowly, an uncomfortable thought settling at the top of his mind.

Conscious that Daniel might still be lingering outside the room, or that there might be other ears, he spoke in their mother tongue instead, leaning forward.

"Tu sais où il est."

Béatrice didn't move, but her silence confirmed it—she knew where Zachary was, and what had befallen him. Marcel felt something urgent rise up in his throat, but he kept it down, perplexed. Béatrice maintained her silence.

"Parle, s'il te plait," he begged her, coming around the table.

"Tu me donnes trop d'importance," Béatrice dismissed, feigning ignorance, but Marcel wouldn't be shaken. He knew what his sister was capable of.

"Je sais de quoi tu es capable." He gripped the back of her chair, his arm reached over her shoulder. He'd missed something, something she'd noticed. "Béatrice, qu'est-ce que tu as remarque

que je n'ai pas vu?"

Béatrice merely gave an elegant shrug, brushing her hair over her sculpted collarbone, as if what she knew wasn't in the least bit relevant.

"Cela n'a aucune importance."

Marcel's grip tightened. Béatrice's expression turned vicious and she stood, pushing him back.

"En fait cette affaire—ne te regarde pas," she ordered him, and Marcel stepped back, disbelieving. She wanted him to stop looking into it? Either Béatrice was mad, or she'd forgotten who he was. At his incredulous snort, she took him by the shoulders, as she had in their childhood, her fingers angry, nails biting into his skin. For a moment, he saw a flash of fear in her face, and he knew that she was trying to protect him. Even so...

"Comment?" How could she expect him to let it go? Béatrice came close to grimacing, and then her expression returned to tranquil and she sat down. She'd reserved herself to give him nothing, but Marcel wasn't deterred. He asked again. "Dis-moi ce que tu sais."

"Rien," Béatrice almost moaned, like a child being interrogated, denying all knowledge or responsibility. Marcel was now sure she was lying.

"Tu mens."

She didn't flicker at the accusation. "Laisse tomber, Marcel," she ordered, her voice slightly raised. Again, he saw the flash of fear in her eyes—she wanted him to leave it. But for Zachary— who'd flown all the way to Sigel'eg just to ensure she was safe— Marcel couldn't understand why she would abandon him.

"Pourquoi ne veux-tu pas m'aider?"

Béatrice sighed heavily, and stood, moving past him to the window. "Je suis vraiment désolée," she apologised softly.

"Do not say you are sorry!" Marcel lost his temper, and his Réneian tongue—no longer caring if anyone heard, almost hoping that someone did. "*Tell* me!"

Béatrice took several long, deep breaths. "I do not know where he is," she finally said. "But I know what has happened to him."

Marcel could barely breathe. "Tell me."

"It will not comfort you."

"Tell me!" Marcel repeated. "Is he…dead?"

Béatrice exhaled. "Yes."

It was like a rock plummeted down through his stomach. Marcel felt weak. He could still feel the echo of Zachary struggling against his grip, as they pulled him away from the edge. If only Marcel had held onto him tighter.

"Non," he whispered. "Tu mens."

"No, Marcel—it is the truth. At least, it is the truth that you must embrace…Because in a few weeks Arlen may very well reappear again, as if nothing happened."

"Then…he is alive?" Marcel didn't understand. He waited, willing Béatrice to explain herself—to speak plainly.

"I can only hope not." Béatrice rested her head against the window, as if exhausted. "Death would be kinder—kinder on us all. Then you would never have to know—"

"What are you talking about?" Marcel grabbed her by the shoulders, wrenching her around to face him.

"Control," she said. "DuGilles is taking control of him—his mind. Arlen knew it would happen. He tried to warn you."

Marcel's grip went slack. "Control? He is being reconditioned?" he choked. "Is that all?"

"Is that all?" Béatrice laughed. "Marcel, I have seen what happens to the men DuGilles takes. I have seen what befalls them. They are not reconditioned—they are hollowed out! Their minds are destroyed. Arlen is *dead*—whether he breathes or not, he is *dead!* And if you love him, you will pray with me that he does not survive the process."

Marcel stared at her, disbelieving. "You knew—you knew all along? And you said nothing!"

"Just as he did," Béatrice said bitterly. "On that Arlen and I agreed—that you and Emeric must never know. Must never get involved. If you tried to save him, they would take you too." She raised herself to her full height, her lips thin and quivering slightly. "Arlen was my friend, but you are my brother. I will protect you over him every time."

CHAPTER 50

That night, Rufus found himself on the beach again, lying flat against the warm sand. He stared up at the whitewashed sky and sighed, sitting up. "You again?"

His sadistic alter-ego subconscious—or Saes, as Rufus decided to call him—grinned readily, "Me again."

"I thought I was rid of you." Rufus couldn't keep the venom from his voice.

Saes threw out his arms, in an exaggerated shrug. He was sprawled back in a glorious throne, which stood out on the stark beach. "You may have been happy enough these last days, but these visions have brought questions to the forefront of your mind, and thus, I return. Here again to help you protect yourself."

"And what a fine job you've done so far." Rufus flopped back into the sand.

"You're still alive, aren't you?" Saes quipped dully and Rufus frowned.

"Why have you...why have you take that appearance?"

"Eerie, isn't it?" Saes resumed his grin and Rufus shuddered. Today, his subconscious was wearing Rufus's own face, and looking at Saes felt a little like gazing at a disobedient reflection.

"Can you change into something else?"

"Apparently the person you need to confront is yourself." Saes drummed his fingers and Rufus sat up again, peering suspiciously over at the man.

"What are you doing?" he asked, standing. Seas looked down at the throne he was lounged in, a heavy crown balanced on his head.

"Fantasising," he said wistfully, and Rufus kicked the throne. As he did, the heavy, black wood dissolved into sand, forcing Saes to jump up as the throne collapsed beneath him.

"I've no desire to be King," Rufus replied.

"Everyone wants to be King." Saes nudged the sand with the tip of his toe, and removing his crown from his head, he dropped it onto the mound. As the crown touched the sand, it too dissolved away. "Or to lead, at least. You've never been very good at conforming, after all. Pacifist or not."

"Why have you brought me here?" Rufus didn't feel at all meek. In part, he understood why Saes wore his face—his subconscious moulded itself according to the emotion it wanted to entice. There was an aggression Rufus could feel when he looked at himself, something which hadn't come naturally to him when faced with any of the other ghosts Saes had impersonated.

"We need to talk about our brother."

"Joshua's progressing well."

"Not that brother."

"Jionat—"

"Rufus," Saes tutted, "Joshua is as a son to you, Jionat your best friend. You know to which brother I refer."

Rufus's mouth formed into a line. "Are my visions true?"

"They're as reliable as any vision might be," Saes said unhelpfully, and Rufus tore his hand through his hair angrily. Saes mimicked him mockingly, and it only made Rufus angrier.

"Is he dead?"

"No." Saes said with certainty. "Not yet."

"But he will be?"

"We all die, Rufus."

"Will you cease with your riddles and answer me properly?"

"As always, Master," Saes spat menacingly, "my usefulness lies with you actually asking the right questions."

"You're worse than the bloody Sidhe." Rufus sat on the mound that had been Saes's seat. It rose up around him to recreate the regal black throne, but Rufus slapped away the arm-rests, turning it back to sand. "DuGilles has him, doesn't he?"

"You are quick."

"The dreams…They've returned. The red-blackness. DuGilles's box. But the terror is different—it isn't mine." Rufus rubbed the stubble on his face, coarse against his fingers. "Every night for the past week—it gets worse and worse. I fear I'm visiting Zachary in his nightmare, and he's losing himself."

Saes leant down and took a shell from his feet. He pulled his arm back and threw it out into the sea. "Good."

"Good?" Rufus stood. "You know that suffering, how could you wish it on anybody?"

"Easily." Saes raised his eyebrows, as if shocked Rufus had forgotten. "Because I hate Arlen Zachary with all my body and soul."

Rufus huffed. "Oh, I see."

"Oh, I see," Saes repeated in a mocking tone. "Listen closely Rufus, your decision today will change the fate of Harmatia forever."

"And what is my choice?"

"Whether you forgive him or not," Saes said. "The man who murdered Jionat, put Sverrin on the throne and took part in the conspiracy that killed our mother, and almost had Joshua beheaded."

"I see your thoughts are clear on the matter," Rufus grunted and Saes laughed sharply, as if in disbelief.

"Athea, you're actually thinking about this?"

"Apparently it will change the fate of Harmatia forever, so yes, I'm lending some thought to it," Rufus bit and Saes kicked the sand childishly, muttering curses beneath his breath. "I pity him, if this is his fate. To be taken by DuGilles...I can understand why he'd choose death over that."

"He deserves it."

"Nobody deserves it," Rufus said, though he could see a dark, poetic justice in Zachary's punishment. He knew a sick part of him was almost pleased by the sentence.

Saes crept over, peering into Rufus's face. "You two-faced little saint. I can feel it in your veins. Put away that angelic face, and let the demon come out—you're as happy as I am."

"I'm not a demon. You helped to quell that part of me. Why are you trying to entice it out?"

Saes narrowed his eyes. On closer inspection, Rufus could see they weren't blue like his, but shifting red and blazing gold. The fire burned deeply within Saes, and his skin was marked by red swirls and the patterns of the ancients. Rufus faced him calmly—this manifestation of Athea.

"What if I do forgive him? If DuGilles has his way, there will be nothing left of Zachary soon. There's no way I can save him—I'd never reach him in time."

"So why bother?" Saes agreed. "Are you so anxious to forgive him, and add him to your nostalgic list of fallen friends? Would it not be harder for you to face him if you were tainted by feelings of camaraderie? What if you hesitated, and Zachary snatched Joshua from your arms? You know what he's capable of even without DuGilles's influence."

The thought was certainly a disturbing one, and one that Rufus had to consider deeply. He knew how easily he was compromised by sentimentality. What if Saes was right? What if his forgiveness weakened his resolve and Zachary took advantage of it?

"It wouldn't be the first time he betrayed your trust," Saes reminded and Rufus gritted his teeth. He felt ancient under the weight of these thoughts. Images flooded over him, Zachary threatening him, Zachary with blood on his mouth, Zachary standing beside the Korrigans' spell. Each memory was like an arrow piercing him, making his certainty grow.

The fire in Saes's eyes got brighter, and Rufus found it hard to think through the hard logic of the argument. What had Zachary ever done to deserve his forgiveness?

What had Rufus done? Rufus, whose hands were so freshly stained with the blood of an innocent, and the deaths of so many of his pursuers? It was possible Rufus had killed more men that even Zachary by now.

Saes's face changed to one of horror, in tune with Rufus's thoughts. "That was in defence!"

"Is it so very different?"

"Yes!"

"I'm not sure." Rufus pursed his lips. "There's so much darkness here, do I add to that? Take pleasure in it?"

"Choose to pity him if you wish, but not to forgive!"

"He was a good man."

"No he wasn't!"

"My friend."

"He betrayed you!"

"My brother." Rufus lashed out his hand, taking Saes by the front of his robe. "Even you called him such."

"Brothers fight. They even kill!"

"But against a common foe, they will unite," Rufus finished the phrase. "I could blame him for all my misfortune if I wanted, mark him out as the cause, but it was my father who gave the order that killed Sverrin. In the end, the pair of us were caught in a pattern that defined our actions. What I choose now, however, will decide whether we remain captors to that pattern, or defy it…And as you so rightly said, I'm not good at conforming."

Saes was speechless. Rufus, feeling triumphant, walked over to the water's edge.

Saes spluttered. "Fine! Use your pretty words! Say you forgive him," he hissed. "But I don't, and I'm a part of you!"

"Yes, well," Rufus said simply, not looking back, "I'm stronger than you."

There was a second of silence, then an explosion of laugher which made Rufus jump. He twisted around to find Saes on his back in the sand, an arm thrown over his eyes, his legs kicking as he laughed. Gone was the long, lanky form of Rufus's reflection, replaced with the ever familiar, and more appealing, face of Jionat.

"Finally," Saes managed to say, sand sticking to his oaken curls as he lifted his head, "the idiot has his answer."

Rufus looked back out over the moving water, smiling. He welcomed the sensation of the strange and tranquil peace that settled over him. The last of the weight lingering on his shoulders lifted, and at last he felt clean. He felt whole.

No one in the room was talking. Daniel was stood in the corner, his fists clenched. He'd been pacing furiously, but had now stopped, glaring at the floor. At the table Marcel and Belphegore were both staring at each other, as if waiting for the other to confess something. The tension in the room was palpable.

"She knows where he is," Daniel broke the silence. His voice was still hoarse—there had been a lot of shouting and screaming over the last few days.

"She does not," Marcel said and there was a finality to his tone.

"Well she has to know something!" Daniel stomped over to the table. "Someone has to know where DuGilles took him!"

"As far as all the records show," Belphegore spoke, his voice terse and deep, "Arlen is simply on commission."

"He is *not* on commission!" Daniel roared, his voice jumped two tones. The volume made Emeric's head pound. "I know what I saw—DuGilles killed Heather! He knocked Arlen unconscious! *They dragged him away—*"

"No one is disputing that," Emeric cut over Daniel, his own patience thin. "We believe you...But no one else in Harmatia seems to know anything."

"Talk to the Royal Guard!" Daniel turned on Belphegore. "They took him!"

"They did," Belphegore said, very quietly. "But only to the dungeons. The captain of the Guard told me they put Arlen in the cell and that was the last they saw of him."

"They must know something else," Daniel insisted.

"No." Belphegore's hands clenched. There was a spatter of blood on his chemise cuff. "I made sure the captain told me everything."

Emeric had a good idea of how Belphegore had managed to do that. No one had seen the captain of the guard in some time. Emeric suspected no one ever would again. There had been a cold steeliness about Belphegore from the moment Marcel had relayed what Béatrice told him.

For days, the three of them had hunted for any clues to where Zachary had been taken. It was difficult, because so long as Daniel was in danger, they couldn't bring him forward as a witness, or raise suspicion that they knew what had happened.

Their investigation had turned up nothing. Emeric, for his part, couldn't stop thinking of Béatrice's warning—that it would be kinder if they never saw Zachary again. That it would be better if he *was* dead. Emeric wasn't sure he believed that—but then he wasn't really sure what to believe.

"It's been weeks..." Daniel's voice shook, and he slowly sank into a chair. "Where did they take him...?" He dropped his head into his hands, just as a soft, hasty knock came from the door.

Marcel, who was closest, rose and answered it. "Thornton?" he said with surprise, and Emeric looked up in time to see Isaac Thornton slip into the room.

"I'm sorry for barging in like this. I've only just arrived. Béatrice told me I would find you all here." Isaac shook Marcel's hand, then Emeric's as he quickly crossed the room to greet him. "Lord Odin." Isaac bowed deeply to Belphegore.

"Lord Thornton," Belphegore said, with a forced smile. "It is a pleasure to see you."

"Would that it were under better circumstances." Isaac looked up and spotted Daniel. "You must be Daniel. I've been looking toward to meeting you."

Daniel sat up straight. "Who are you?"

"My name is Isaac Thornton. From today you are my apprentice."

Daniel stared, blank face. "What?"

Isaac moved around the table and took a seat at Daniel's side. He clasped his hands together in a matter of fact way. "I know about what's happened—and I swear," he added, looking around the rest of the table, "had I known about it when Zachary came to see me, I would have done something."

"You're the other one he flew to see in Sigel'eg." Realisation dawned in Daniel's eyes. Isaac nodded.

"Yes—he and I are old friends," Thornton gave a rueful smile, "in a manner of speaking." His smile fell. "Daniel, Zachary asked me to apprentice you. He wanted me to take you to away somewhere safe. And I intend to fulfil that promise."

"Away?" Daniel looked up with panic to the rest of them. "No," he said, "not until Arlen's found! I can't leave without him."

Isaac's mouth drew into a long thin line. He sank further into the chair, resting back with a long sigh. "I understand," he said. "He's your brother, after all. You love him."

"Love him?" Daniel seethed. "I want to shake him!"

Isaac actually laughed. It was a strange sound in the tense room. "Yes," he chuckled, "that sounds about right." He sniffed, sighing again. "I've spent most of my life wanting to shake the little bastard too."

This earned Isaac a very bemused expression from Daniel,

and a small grunt of laughter from Marcel.

"You know," Isaac continued, pushing himself forward in his seat and slouching against the table, "we were in the same class in the academy. He used to get on everybody's nerves. He was odd, you see—quick. Had an enviable aptitude for learning and a stamina that no eight year old had the right to. Worse than that, he bloody *knew* it. I confess—I considered just smothering him a few times."

Another grumbling laugh from Marcel, and Daniel even smiled. "Me too," he admitted. "More than once."

"See—intolerable, no matter the age." Isaac smiled. "He was so smug and smart-tongued all the time. We used to duel, him and me, and he was so clever about it. Everybody wanted to beat him, but no one in the class ever could."

Until now. Emeric thought, the unspoken words lingering in the air. The most harrowing part of Daniel's tale had been the account of Zachary's screams. No one had ever heard Zachary scream before.

"And then," Isaac suddenly laughed, "he beat the Royal Master-at-Arms in a duel! He was your age."

"Arlen did?" Daniel also sat forward, and for the first time in days, some of the tension left his body.

"Yes. Lord Fallon was his name. A rather strict fellow, but good with the sword. He commanded respect and obedience, until one day your brother challenged him."

"Typical," Daniel growled, but Isaac held up his hand.

"You misunderstand. Zachary didn't challenge Lord Fallon to a duel—he challenged Lord Fallon's technique. You see, Lord Fallon was in-charge of training Prince Sverrin. Zachary, who often joined the class, made an observation about how a strike could be better performed. Lord Fallon took it personally."

"You mean Lord Fallon challenged *Arlen* to a duel?" Daniel said slowly.

"Yes he did," Belphegore murmured from his seat, his eyes distant with memory. He too looked a little more relaxed—Isaac was distracting them from them fears, if only momentarily. "Arlen was terrified."

"They fought it off in-front of an audience," Isaac said. "Lord Fallon wanted to publically discipline Zachary on his impertinence. As it turned out, this wasn't a very wise decision."

"Arlen *actually* beat him?"

"He claims it was by chance, but yes." Isaac shrugged. "It was a close fight, but the conclusion was obvious. Your brother, at the mere age of twenty, was already the superior swordsman. Does that surprise you?"

"No. Only that he never mentioned it. Seems like just the sort of thing he'd brag about," Daniel said, seemingly caught between bitterness and amusement.

"Ah," Isaac sighed. "And therein lies the true key to your brother's nature. You see, Zachary never bragged about what he'd done, because he was ashamed of it. In his eye, he hadn't won a victory, he'd humiliated a man of whom he had great respect. Lord Fallon was gracious in his defeat—it was Zachary who was embarrassed."

Daniel sat, his eyes cast down into his lap. He fiddled with his hands. Isaac's expression softened. He leant in a little closer, speaking gently.

"Daniel," he said, "you know that despite all his theatrics, Zachary has always put others before himself. That's who your brother is at his core. And that is the person you are hoping to find. That is the person DuGilles took." Isaac's rested his hand on Daniel's shoulder, his voice hardening. "But that person is gone. He's not coming back. Not now." Isaac looked up at the rest of them. "You have to proceed as if he is dead."

"I can't," Daniel said, his voice so soft and lilting, it was like a child. "I have to know...I have to know if he's alive. I have to know if DuGilles…if DuGilles…"

Isaac sighed heavily. "Three days," he said. "I'll give you three more days to wait. After which," he rose, "I am taking you away. Don't waste the sacrifice Zachary made for you Daniel. If you love him, then live."

~~⚬~~

"We should be marching on Harmatia this instant!" Hamish raged, and Aurora sat back, her eyes closed.

She'd had no appetite the last few days, and felt light-headed and sickly as a result. Still, she'd came to the meeting, eager to be present when they started speaking about her.

"This atrocity has been left unpunished for near a fortnight now! Sverrin of Harmatia almost *raped* my sister—your Princess! And yet no action has been taken to show our outrage! What must they think of us?" Hamish continued, and Aurora could hear the rustle of her brother's clothes as he moved his arms wildly about. The people at the table were all muttering with agreement. "This was an insult not only to Princess Aurora but to all of us! They see us as weak, let us show them we are not!"

A loud cry of agreement rose from the table and Aurora forced her aching eyes open. "Hamish," she brought him down from his battle-frenzy, "your love for me does you credit, but outrage alone will not win us a war. If we march against Harmatia now, Kathra will descend upon us. Between the Magi and the Isny armies, led by that new Dragon Hunter, our enemies are strong."

"Are you not angry sister? Does your blood not boil?"

It was a goading question, though well meant. Hamish wanted her to rage and shout, to rally the council to his side with cries of agreement. They valued their Princess, and would avenge her tears, which is why Aurora had been forced to keep all such emotions under check.

"Of course I am angry," she confessed, her voice collected. "I was welcomed as a guest, and left as a fugitive, my clothes in tatters. I was forced to abandon my people—my faithful servants and knights, who are now prisoners in Sverrin's keeping. There is no one here today whose fury outmatches mine."

"Then how can you be so calm?" Hamish came to her side, his red hair catching the light so that it glowed against his fair skin. "After what was done to you?"

"I am calm, because I must be," Aurora stated simply. "War has only ever served tyrants—I want justice and vengeance, but I will not play into Sverrin and Bozidar's hands to get it."

"Father." Hamish turned to his right side, where King Markus was observing both of his children, heeding each of their arguments, and measuring the response of the rest of the council.

"Aurora," Markus shifted forward, "as a father, I want nothing more than to punish Sverrin for what he has done. As a King, however, I see your wisdom, but also that of your brother's. This attack was a declaration against Bethean. Am I to ignore it? Am I to let Sverrin think he may do with us as he pleases?"

Aurora grew quiet. The mention of Sverrin still brought her out in a cold sweat. At night she could feel his body pinning her down, as she thrashed about in her nightmares. She tried not to let her heart rule her decision, but it was agonising. "Father, you have gathered our armies and been preparing for war nearly thirteen years now. Why is that?"

Markus didn't smile but Aurora saw the faint approval in the line of his lips. The once-red stubble that framed his mouth was almost completely grey now. "I was warned that an attack was coming, by Prince Jionathan of the Delphi."

"And you believed him?"

"I did."

"Then believe him now, and restrain your rage. A boy will come and he will be known by the company he keeps. I believe that—I am dependent upon it. You will have your war, Hamish. We will fight and prove our worth, prove that Bethean is mighty and proud and does not forget. But first, let us prove our patience and our wisdom. We are not dogs to be goaded into a fight." She rose slowly, placing her hands against the table. "Let Sverrin prepare and gather his forces, let him think he has us in the palm of his hand. He will soon learn why his ancestors made peace with our people, rather than go to war," she let her voice grow. "My ladies, my lords, we have been preparing for over a decade. Sverrin's a troublesome pike but he grows complacent, and soon enough, we will draw up our nets. But not yet. Let him grow tangled first." She curled her hands into fists. "We are strong enough to wait."

CHAPTER
51

The summons came suddenly, and without reason. Heavy with a dark sense of foreboding, Emeric, Belphegore and Marcel gathered at the behest of their King. Sverrin met them in the throne room, excitement in his eyes.

"Lords Odin, Hathely, Fold," he greeted, nauseatingly merry. "My faithful Magi, how are you all on this auspicious day?"

"Your Majesty." They bowed, each stiff in their courtesy.

"Sombre as always," Sverrin said. "It has reached my ears that you have all recently been concerned on whereabouts of our friend Lord Zachary. I apologise, Lord Odin, that I took your apprentice without consulting you first."

Belphegore was apparently in no mood for niceties. "It would seem you have done many things without my consultation, Your Majesty."

Sverrin's mouth tightened but he maintained his potent cheeriness. "You're still displeased with my invitation to the Betheanian Princess?"

"I am displeased by how her visit ended," Belphegore said gravely.

Not much was known about Aurora's departure, though

people had noted her sudden disappearance. There were rumours she was locked in the dungeon somewhere, or even dead, but Emeric had heard from a reliable source that she was back in Bethean.

Her servants and guards had been gathered up quickly and vanished from sight. Emeric suspected they hadn't gotten away so cleanly.

"A small inconvenience that will be dealt with." Sverrin walked forward, beckoning them after him. "But come, my lords, I didn't call you to speak of such things. I wanted to reunite you with your friend."

"Do you mean to say Zachary is...returned?" Emeric asked cautiously.

The King beamed. "I sent him away to remind him of where his loyalties lay. He has returned with a clear mind. I thought you should be the first to know."

Emeric felt shivers run up his spine. Marcel's hand tapped against his, reminding him to maintain his composure. Emeric spotted something close to distress in Marcel's even lips. He was worried. Isaac and Béatrice's words haunted them.

They passed through the castle after their King, down into some of the inner, more private chambers and finally toward one of the old training salles.

The doors, strangely, were closed, and Sverrin stopped before them. Emeric sniffed the air. There was a heavy scent, one he knew well.

Blood. Blood and death. The particular, pungent smell of intestinal fluids and other things that only men bred in battle could know. It was faint, but there, seeping out from under the doors of the salle. Sverrin pushed the doors open with a dramatic flair, and stepped away with a flourish, letting the three Magi look in.

It was an absolute massacre. Bodies lay in pieces, torn apart as if savaged by wild animals. Limbs were strewn, separated and tossed from their bodies, torsos ripped open, organs hanging loose in a smattered mess. Some of the carcasses still twitched in the echoes of a violent death. Women, men…Emeric was only just able make out that the victims were Aurora's entourage.

Their screams must have echoed long down the corridors, but they were so deep in the castle, nobody had heard—or, at least, nobody foolish enough to investigate.

"Athea have mercy," Belphegore choked.

In the centre, Zachary stood with his back to them.

His robes were stained with blood, his hair matted, fingers still dripping. Slowly he turned, black eyes the last evidence of a transformation. His mouth was red from feasting, and his expression totally empty, so far beyond human kindness or understanding. Emeric could only stare, for though the man before them shared all of the common features, there was nothing of Arlen Zachary in him.

"Dear me, Zachary," Sverrin chortled, breaking the hush with the garish sound of his voice. "You needn't have made such a mess!"

"My apologies, your Majesty." It wasn't Zachary who spoke, but DuGilles who, in the horror of the mounded bodies, Emeric hadn't noticed stood in the corner of the room. "I told him to enjoy himself. Isn't that right, Zachary?"

Zachary didn't reply, swaying his weight from one leg to the other. A faint, gurgling sound came up from his throat, like a growl, but there was no hostility in his expression. He was empty of anything.

"Arlen…" Belphegore moved forward, stepping straight into a puddle of blood. He recoiled. A woman's arm lay close by, a dainty engagement ring on her finger, nails all broken as if she'd tried to scratch her way free. "What have you done to him?" Belphegore whirled around to DuGilles, who gave a giddy chuckle.

"Nothing." DuGilles raised his hands. "Nothing that wasn't asked of me. Your apprentice was clouded and troubled, Lord

Odin, and I gave him clarity. He's in perfect condition." DuGilles's eyes rolled over to Zachary. "Absolutely perfect."

Sverrin gave a good-natured chuckle. "Was it a fine show?"

"Oh, Your Majesty, I've never seen anything so beautiful. Not even animals can create such elegance in a kill."

Emeric realised he'd stopped breathing, his throat squeezed closed to stop the rise of bile. Elegance? There was nothing elegant in the room. It was an unspeakable chaos—worse than a battle-ground.

"Arlen, how have you done this?" Marcel dared to speak, but got no acknowledgement.

"Isaac was right," Emeric choked, too softly for anyone else to hear.

"This is," Belphegore's voice was strained with disbelief, "this is an atrocity!"

"No, Lord Odin." Sverrin's docile tone was gone in an instant. "This was my will."

Belphegore inhaled sharply, on the verge of fury, but before any more could be said, Zachary suddenly doubled over and vomited. The room grew still, everybody fixated on the grim display, as chunks of chewed flesh and blood pouring violently out of his mouth onto the floor.

Zachary's legs gave way, and he dropped to his knees into the mess. He gave a faint hiccup, retching again, and then simply stared at the floor, mouth parted and dripping. His expression didn't change at all.

"Oh gods," Emeric begun to sob, his body juddering. "Oh gods, oh gods, oh gods."

"Come now, Lord Fold," DuGilles laughed, as if Emeric were a frightened girl leaping onto her chair to avoid a mouse. "No need to be so squeamish."

"DuGilles," Sverrin snapped sharply, "what is the meaning of this? You told me he was fit to work."

"He is, Your Majesty, of course." DuGilles raised his hands

submissively. "But this was his first meal in some time, and he was only half transformed. So much raw flesh at once—anyone's stomach would turn. There's no need for alarm."

"Oh gods," Emeric was still saying, though he didn't know why. Even Athea would turn her head away at this unholy display. "Oh gods, oh gods."

"Lord Fold, follow your master's example and try to be quiet." Sverrin rolled his eyes. "It's unsavoury, but that is the flavour of war. It'll be easier when you join the slaughter."

"Join?" Belphegore said.

"The Night Patrol are being deployed to Bethean," Sverrin said pleasantly. "Zachary wasn't keen on the commission before, but I think I'll find him much more compliant on the matter now." Sverrin glanced at DuGilles for confirmation.

The Kathrak nodded. "A few days' rest, and he'll be battle-worthy."

"Excellent." Sverrin clapped his hands, the sharp sound ringing in the vast room. "You had best prepare your things, Lords Fold, Hathely—you will shortly be going to war."

Emeric's head felt light, the room tilting like the deck of a ship. A part of him wanted to stagger over to Zachary and strike him back to his senses, but the other, more sensible part knew he'd never survive getting close enough. Arlen Zachary was dead— this was some unholy monster with his face.–

"Actually," Belphegore broke through the nightmare, his voice cold but triumphant, "Arlen excused Lord Fold and Lord Hathely from their duties several weeks ago, before he disappeared. They are no longer a part of the Night Patrol."

Sverrin's pleased air grew cold with anger, the words settling over him. He opened his mouth to object and then froze as, from within his crater of bodies, Zachary threw his back and began to laugh.

It was a manic sound. Forceful, hysterical, enough to shrink your throat, and send flighty shivers spindling up and down the spine. Every hair on Emeric's body rose. Nobody dared speak or move, fearful of catching this monster's attention.

Emeric didn't know if it was gleeful laughter—whether Zachary had somehow understood, amidst his destruction, that he'd won one small, significant victory in rescuing his friends. Emeric wasn't even sure Zachary could see or hear them anymore, but somehow he had sensed it—a triumph of his own making.

Sverrin eyes met Zachary's, and in an instant their roles of the last ten years were reversed. For there was no more fear in Zachary's gaze, and Sverrin understood the monster he had created.

"Take him away," Sverrin ordered, and then repeated in a shriek. *"Take him away!"*

DuGilles came forward and, seizing Zachary under the arms, dragged him to his feet, pulling him back toward the opposite door.

Zachary laughed like madness all the way.

CHAPTER
52

"I am proud of you," Fae announced grandly, standing over Rufus who had keeled over in exhaustion. "A few more months, and you might even be considered a worthy opponent."

"I can set everything on fire," Rufus moaned. "I *will* set everything on fire. And laugh. *Laugh.*"

"Yes, yes," Fae nudged him with her toe. She'd been pushing him harder and harder in his training over the last week. He was not a natural fighter but a quick learner all the same. "And twice a day, you can summon flaming birds from the sky, and harness the power of the cosmos. And yet I have still felled you, and you're still far from a warrior."

"I want to read a book," Rufus sobbed.

"Later. Come—there's still another hour of training in you."

Rufus rolled onto his side and curled into a ball, shaking his head. "No more, Fae. No more."

"Don't be pathetic."

"But I *am* pathetic," Rufus groaned. *"Please."*

Fae sighed. "A short pause then," she granted, sitting beside him. "For such a hard-working man, you're really very lazy sometimes."

Rufus sat up, giving her a doleful look. Fae laughed, and reaching across, she picked some of the grassy debris out of his black hair.

"I'm not lazy," he huffed. "I'm just not built for this."

"That's the excuse Embarr used to make, when I tried to train him."

"Embarr Reagon?" Rufus sat up with a little more interest. "Did he live in the Neve?"

"For a time, yes." Fae lay back in the grass, Rufus dropping down beside her, so their heads were lightly touching. "He was Niamh's ward, but as he's forbidden from setting foot on Tír na nÓg, he was sent to live here instead."

"Forbidden? Why."

"Because he's a Fomorii. And the son of one of our greatest enemies. He swore his allegiance to Niamh, in return for her protection against his mother, but there are many who still doubt him."

Rufus was quiet for a few moment, and Fae could hear him rubbing his chin. "Where is he from?" he asked, after a while. "Who is his mother?"

Fae pursed her lips. Names had power, and even though it was safe to utter this one in the Neve, she still hesitated. "Nicnivin," she finally said.

"Nicnivin?" Rufus sat bolt upright, "The Queen of the Unseelie Court?" He twisted to look down at her. "You mean Embarr is the son of the *Dark?*"

"Yes."

Rufus blinked rapidly. "*Embarr?*" he repeated, as if sure she was thinking of someone else. "The Gancanagh we met—*he's* the *heir* of the Unseelie Court?"

"He is her son," Fae said, sitting up slowly. "But he's not the heir. He's just a vessel for her power."

Rufus frowned deeply. "What do you mean?"

Fae pursed her lips, her stomach clenching. "The relationship between Nicnivin and her children is…unnatural," she finally said. "She is the most powerful of all of the Fomorii, and she believes that the only person worthy of succeeding her is… herself."

"…What?"

Fae winced. She really didn't want to have to explain it. "When a child is born, they are half of each parent. Nicnivin has had many sons. The first child was half of Nicnivin. The next child… Was three quarters."

Fae saw Rufus puzzling through it. His face twisted with disgust as realisation dawned. "She…procreates with her own children?"

"Yes." Fae was beginning to feel a little queasy. "And when a new son is born, to ensure the power stays with her, she eats the previous one."

"I'm going to be sick," Rufus moaned.

"Through this process, Nicnivin means to eventually dilute any other blood and give birth to a child who is born entirely of her. And that child will be as unequivocally powerful."

"So she wants to—"

"Yes."

"With Embarr—"

"Yes."

Rufus stared. "I'm really going to be sick."

"Embarr is the first of her sons who has ever run away," Fae said. "They are so much a part of her, tearing themselves away is almost impossible—Embarr has to fight the urge to return to her every day. It is his very nature to give her what she wants. And she—she cannot abide the idea that any part of her power is out of her control. She will search for Embarr until the end of days."

"Athea have mercy." Rufus ran his hands through his hair. "So that day in the forest, when he lured us all together, you thought—"

"That he'd returned to her. Yes. The Myrithian forest is where she lives—it was unwise for him to be there."

"So where is he now?"

"Sigel'eg, last I heard, deep within the Kathrak Court." Fae rose to her feet. "Now enough about that. It's time to get back to work."

"At this point, I welcome the distraction," Rufus said, and accepted her hand as she hauled him to his feet.

Morrigan lingered to watch the exchange far below, the young granddaughter of Niamh helping Rufus to his feet and commencing his training again. How little this foolish woman knew. Appealing to the softer side of Rufus wouldn't bring out the fighter within him, though Morrigan wasn't so proud as to look down on the Cat Sidhe. Fae Ó Murchadha could prove to be the trickiest opponent of all, if Morrigan didn't deal with her soon.

The crow on the goddess's shoulder nipped affectionately at her ear, though she didn't need it to announce Reilly's arrival as he came padding through the trees.

"Mac Gearailt." She ushered him toward her. He obeyed silently, his eyes unseeing. Even now, after so long under her thrall, she sensed a hesitation in his step—a strain. He was strong, but she'd claimed him. "My little pet." She caressed his face, the crow cawing loudly at Reilly, with something close to jealousy. Reilly blinked rapidly at the sound, frowning, but Morrigan shushed his awakening thoughts, kissing him tenderly. "Calm your mind," she bid, and he grew still again. "It would seem you failed in your task of rallying the Magi up."

"Fae intervened," Reilly said slowly, his voice muffled. He was fighting hard against her control, a small part of him still conscious beneath the layers of glamour she'd sown over him.

It didn't matter. As always, when she disappeared, he would forget she was there, and the quiet ideas she planted in his mind would grow to fruition. Of course, such intoxication had its limits—she couldn't change his character too quickly. Reilly wasn't so easily moulded.

Morrigan had told him to attack Rufus, thinking Reilly's natural suspicion for the Magi would lend itself to the task. Instead, Reilly had proven to be more honour-bound than she'd anticipated. He'd carried out her orders in the only way he could—trying to trick Rufus into attacking first, so that he could justify his own actions. Yes, subconsciously, Reilly was still fighting her, and this had delayed her plans.

Morrigan had hoped to remove this sanctuary from Rufus quickly, to end the Neve's hospitality and divide its loyalties. When she'd met Rufus in the forest, his mind had been fragile and almost ready to submit. Now...

"Your wife has proven to be an adept healer." Morrigan looked back down into the training grounds. "I fear there is little I can do now to drive a wedge between them. His heart is too mended. He is forgetting his hatred and fear."

Curse Niamh. Morrigan had laid claim on Rufus long ago, but Niamh's interference had given him a counter to the rage Morrigan needed him to succumb to.

"No matter." Morrigan didn't allow herself to linger. "There are yet pieces for me to play, and a new one as of today. Little Embarr Reagon is in Kathra, is he? Nicnivin will certainly be pleased to hear about it."

Reilly was growing restless again. He shook under the strain of her magic. Morrigan kissed his temple, tasting the sweat on his brow.

"For now, I think it's time I reintroduced Rufus to his demons. For there is one threat that he will not sit by."

"On-ly a—a boy," Reilly forced out, and Morrigan was impressed. His breathing was hard, his hands twitching.

"Yes," Morrigan agreed sadly, watching the little Delphi Prince run into the training ground to join Rufus and Fae, flanked by another young Cat Sidhe. "But war is coming, and the people need someone to rally to." Her eyes flashed a deep red, the sun beginning to set far out in the west. "When the armies gather in their thousands against Joshua of the Delphi, I wonder what Rufus will think of my proposition then."

"Nn—" Reilly was choking on his words, his hand shakily reaching for his sword. The movement was laborious, as if he were trying to drive his arm through rock. Morrigan watched his progress, keen to see how far he would get. His hand touched the hilt, and he drew the weapon, gasping.

The crow gave a sharp cry and flew from Morrigan's shoulder, straight into Reilly's face. The Cat Sidhe battered it back, shaking his head violently to spare his eyes from the talons. As the bird flew up, Reilly look back to see Morrigan had disappeared into the trees. He was left, blinking, with no memory of her being there.

～☙～

Isaac sat with Daniel during the commotion. The Ambassador was a quiet and reassuring companion as raised voices and accusations were thrown across the room.

To Daniel's surprise it was Marcel who was shouting. The Magi, who spoke the least of anyone Daniel had ever known, couldn't seem to stop the outpour now, as if all the words had been trapped in for too long. He switched effortlessly between Réneian and the Common Tongue, without seeming to notice, and was cussing and swearing at Béatrice, who answered in kind.

A few things were thrown before Belphegore finally intervened, commanding both to settle down. Marcel, his voice run raw from use, turned away, struggling to light his pipe with trembling hands.

In contrast, Emeric sat silently at the window, staring out into the garden. He was wide-eyed and voiceless. Daniel had seen a similar expression once before, when he was young. A woman in his mother's village had lost a foolish son to a Kelpie. She'd watched the lad climb onto the faerie's back from the other side of a meadow, and only made it across in time to see the monster dive into the water, drowning the shrieking infant.

"You knew this would happen," Marcel spoke furiously into his pipe, unable to even look at Béatrice who'd proudly turned away. "Why did you not prevent it? Why did you not speak? We could have saved him!"

"Ta gueule!" Béatrice swore. "You think I did not agonise over ways to help him? But who do you think Sverrin would have turned his rage on if Arlen were gone?" She slapped her hand against the wall. "We would have all had to flee! Would you have had me turn traitors of everyone Arlen knew?"

"We should never have let this happen," Belphegore said grimly. "I should have seen it. I should have. Now he is gone from me. Both of them. Gone."

Between the high flairs of emotion and despair, Daniel hadn't found room to express any words of his own. The Magi had all left the room with the confidence that Isaac and Béatrice were exaggerating. They'd returned smelling of blood, Emeric stunned into silence and Marcel into a rage. The message had been clear, though no one had bothered to convey it to Daniel.

His brother was truly gone—stolen away from himself and hollowed out to make room for something else.

Isaac didn't leave Daniel's side for even a minute, vigilant in the task Zachary had given him. Daniel wasn't sure how to feel, his stomach churning.

From where he was sat, silent as a ghost, Emeric finally spoke up, faint and close to feeble. "We're all responsible. For all of it. Rufus, Zachary, all of those people. We brought Sverrin back and this was the cost. Those deaths, this loss—we are responsible."

At this, nobody had any response. Their anger turned inwards and Daniel felt a malicious twist of satisfaction. He rose and moved to the door.

"Where are you going?" Béatrice asked.

"To get my things. I have to go home."

"Corhlam is not safe—we are about to go to war," Béatrice argued.

"I have arranged safe passage for you to my village in La'Kalciar." Isaac came to her side. "There's a place for you there, as my apprentice."

"With all due respect, I don't want to be your apprentice," Daniel said curtly. "And I don't want to be a Magi tethered to a King who probably wants to murder me."

There was a soft murmur of agreement, but Isaac persisted. "I understand that, but the argument stands. Corhlam won't be safe for long."

"That's exactly why I have to go." Daniel opened the door. "Arlen was all that stood between my father and my sisters. I doubt he's capable of protecting any of them now, or our people. It's up to me." Daniel dropped his eyes to his shoes.

"Daniel, that is too much to bear." Belphegore rose, as if to contest, but seeing the adamant look in the boy's eye grew still. "Notameer's Light, you are so much like him."

He could've been my father, Daniel thought, *but he was my brother, and even that was taken from me.*

"Keep your politics." Daniel bowed. "For me, my part in this is done."

Isaac chewed his fingernails. "Damn you stubborn Zacharys. Fine—if that's your wish. But when this is over, Daniel, I'll come for you. Don't you dare make an oath-breaker of me."

Daniel nodded in reserved thanks and left the room, his heart heavy but his path perfectly clear.

EPILOGUE

"He made his choice."

Sverrin tapped his fingers against his throne. His rings made a sharp 'clack' sound. Belphegore didn't look at the King, his gaze trained straight ahead. From her seat, Reine rested her hand on Belphegore's back in quiet comfort. Sverrin continued.

"He chose to betray me. I could have had him executed."

"That was your right, Your Majesty," Belphegore said, without any strength. The loss of Rufus he'd always been prepared for, but not Zachary. Never Zachary. It was as great a pain as losing a son, and for that loss there would be consequences.

"It was my right," Sverrin agreed, snappishly. "My right to punish traitors. And you, Belphegore, have you made your choice? To whom are you loyal?"

Reine's hands caught the back of Belphegore's cloak with a sharp motion, hidden behind the folds of black cloth. Her face was strained and pinched, and Belphegore was caught between his desire to shake her loose or take her in his arms. He did neither.

"I have always been loyal to you, Sverrin. You are the one true heir of Harmatia, and its rightful King."

"It pleases me to hear you say so." Sverrin's ring continued to strike against the wood. Clack, clack, clack. He was getting impatient. "This informant of yours is late."

"She'll come, Your Majesty, rest assured," DuGilles defended in Belphegore's stead. Belphegore locked eyes with the alchemist.

Him. Him, Belphegore could kill, and he would—soon. Already these last few days he'd slipped into old habits—sneaking out in the night, when everyone else was hindered by sleep, and stalking for blood. The captain of the Royal Guard had suffered for his part in Zachary's fate—DuGilles would suffer more. When all eyes were turned, Belphegore would take this Kathrak, this Shinny who'd ripped his apprentice apart, and he would treat him in kind.

"Does she have no respect? Keeping me waiting?" Sverrin growled.

"It's her nature to test our patience," DuGilles said. "But her information is good. I, too, was suspicious when Lord Odin brought her to my attention, but she led me straight to the traitor time and time again, when no one else could. She's also the practitioner behind your glorious revival. Her knowledge is worth a little waiting."

Sverrin settled back into his throne. It was getting late—the moon was high in the sky, and the castle lay resting. Nothing stirred, not even the wind.

And then, all at once, she was there. The windows flew open as a large crow passed through into the council room. It circled above them in an elegant swirl and then landed. With a twist of shadow the glamour came away, and Morrigan stood.

She was different than the last time Belphegore had seen her, where her blonde hair and sweet eyes boasted compassion and a gentle spirit. That wasn't in her nature tonight.

Dark curls spilled over her shoulders, her eyes the bright red of the Korrigans, and she was adorned in a linked armour made of hard, metallic feathers.

She bowed, extending her wing-like arms, and Sverrin grew rigid, struck by her terrible beauty. Beside Morrigan, even Béatrice Hathely seemed plain, but Belphegore had no taste for Morrigan's loveliness. In the end, she was too tall, too poised, too much like the rest of the damned Sidhe to draw anything more than disgust from him. Had she not hated Niamh with the same burning passion as him, Belphegore would have never joined forces with her. They were allies only through their shared enemy.

"Sverrin DuBlanche." Morrigan added no title to the King's name, stepping forward into the moonlight. Her skin shimmered as white as fresh milk. Sverrin was too enthralled by her to care about her informality, his eyes dancing over her body with excited fervour.

"I see now why they call you a goddess," he whispered, and Morrigan smiled. It didn't reach her red, battle-hungry eyes. "What news have you come to bestow? It must be important for you to have summoned a King?"

"It is." Morrigan took another step forward, and Belphegore made to intercept. Sverrin raised his hand, ordering the Magi to stand down and let the faerie approach.

"Speak," Sverrin bid.

"My role as your informant is at an end." Morrigan stopped directly in front of Sverrin, close enough to reach forward and snap his neck. "Soon, I will begin my own campaign. But before I depart—I bring you these last words of warning, to do with as you see fit."

"Words of warning?" Sverrin shifted in his throne.

"There is a boy set to oppose you, and he bears the Delphi name."

"Impossible." Reine rose from her seat with a clatter, suspicion and distaste clear in her face. "Éliane was killed and her son sacrificed himself."

"Yes." Morrigan's voice was gentle, but the way it echoed

through the room sounded like a murder of crows taking flight. "But the brother survived."

"No. No, I had the baby executed!" Reine's voice grew panicked. "You're lying!"

"I am one of the Tuatha de Danaan—incapable of lying." Morrigan seemed amused. "If you doubt me, ask Lord Odin."

"Belphegore, is this true?" Reine turned quickly on Belphegore, who grimaced.

"Yes, it's true. The Tuatha de Danaan cannot lie. But," he added, eyeing Morrigan suspiciously, "they are notoriously good at twisting words to their advantage."

"Then allow me to speak plainly," Morrigan said. "Close to thirteen years ago, two Delphi escaped the city together. The first was the Magi you call Rufus Merle, and the second was your youngest brother, whom he raised."

"Merle? A Delphi?" Sverrin spluttered. "How could that be?"

"A bastard." Morrigan ignored Belphegore's penetrating glare. "Born illegitimately to Éliane before her marriage."

Belphegore clenched his fists. Why was Morrigan revealing this truth now, when there was no more to be gained by it? Rufus was dead. Unless...

"That Delphi whore," Sverrin snarled, and then remembered himself. "But the baby...?"

"Your father's child and your sibling by blood," Morrigan stated. "He has been raised by the Knights of the Delphi and has but one ambition—to usurp you, and take your throne."

"Sverrin," Reine's voice was feeble, "Sverrin, we must find him. The Delphi...we need to kill him!"

"Where is he?" Sverrin rose. Morrigan still towered over him.

"That is all I have come to tell you." She turned and walked away.

"No!" Sverrin lunged after her. "You will tell me—where is he? You cannot give me a brother and then withhold him from me!"

"Search among the Delphi Knights. He will make himself

known to you, soon enough," Morrigan said. She didn't turn.

"Come back!" No matter how much Sverrin tried to reach for her, she seemed always a breath away. "Tell me where he is! Tell me!"

But as suddenly as she'd come, the crow returned, taking Morrigan's place, and spiralling up into the air. She swept out the window like a foul omen, and silence followed her.

Belphegore watched the King, who stopped in the centre of the room, his eyes on the empty sky beyond the window. An anticipatory stillness fell over them, a tense energy that Belphegore hadn't felt in a long time.

"And so the crow cries," DuGilles, all but forgotten, spoke from his corner, his eyes uncommonly bright, "and summons us to war."

GLOSSARY of NAMES & TITLES

COUNTRIES, PLACES & COURTS

MAG MELL (mag-Mel) The main continent, comprised of Kathra, Harmatia, Bethean & Avalon.

HARMATIA (her-Marsh-ee-ah) Capital and kingdom of the central lands, stood between Kathra and Bethean. Founder of human magic, and home of the Magi.

    CORHLAM (core-Lum) A Southern mining county.

    ANAES'S FORTRESS (a-Nee-us) A fortress on the edge of the Myrithian forest.

    HELENA'S FORTRESS A fortress on the north-west border of Harmatia.

BETHEAN (beh-THeen.) Capital and Kingdom of the south-eastern lands. Divided from Harmatia by the **MYRITHIAN** (mer-Rith-ee-un) forest.

    THE JAWS A steep cliff that runs through the Myrithian forest.

    SARRIN (Sa-rin) A northern province in Bethean, with a town of the same name.

LEMRA (Lem-rah) A southern port town, infamous for its criminal occupants.

BESHUWA (Besh-wah) An south-eastern industrial town.

KATHRA (Kath-rah) Kingdom of the far north.

SIGEL'EG (sih-Ga-leg) The Capital of Kathra.

LA'KALCIAR (la-Kal-see-ur) Western providence, known as the 'Lake Region'

ISNYDEA (is-nah-dee) Northern province, known as the 'Land of the Damned'

AVALON (ah-vah-lon) Land of the Sidhe, stood to the far east.

NEVE (ne-Vay) A mountain region inhabited by Cat Sidhe

TÍR NA NÓG (cheer na Noge) One of the Sidhe Islands

RÉNE (rhen-Ay) Country across the sea, known as the "Country of the Sun."

SEELIE COURT (See-lee) Faeries who hold a peaceful treaty with Bethean and worship the Tuatha de Danaan.

UNSEELIE COURT (un-See-lee) Faeries who do not hold treaty with Bethean and worship the Fomorii.

ROYALS

KING THESTIAN (Thest-ee-un) Previous King of Harmatia. Deceased.

DELPHI FAMILY (Del-fee) Descendants of Niamh (see FAERIES). Promised heirs of Harmatia and founder of the Magi.

LADY ÉLIANE (eh-lee-Ann) Mother to Rufus (with Torin Merle), Jionathan and Joshua (with King Thestian). Second wife of King Thestian. Deceased.

RUFUS MERLE (roo-Fus Murl) Bastard son of Éliane. Half-brother to Joshua and Jionathan. Son of Torin Merle (see REBELS).

PRINCE JOSHUA (Joh-shew-ah) Son of King Thestian and Lady Éliane. Brother to Jionathan, and half-brother to King Sverrin (fraternal) and Rufus Merle (maternal).

JIONATHAN (JIONAT) (Yo-nat-an [Yo-nat]), Son of King Thestian and Lady Éliane. Brother to Joshua, and half-brother to King Sverrin (fraternal) and Rufus Merle (maternal). Deceased.

DUBLANCHE FAMILY (doo-Blon-shuh) Kathrak Royalty.

KING BOZIDAR (Bow-zeh-dar) King of Kathra, Sverrin's maternal grandfather.

KING'S MOTHER REINE (Rhenn) Mother to Sverrin. Daughter of King Bozidar. First wife of King Thestian.

KING SVERRIN (suh-Ver-rin) Son of King Thestian and Queen Reine. King of Harmatia. Known as the Puppet-King.

KING MARKUS (Mar-kas) King of Bethean.

PRINCESS AURORA (ah-Roar-rah) Princess of Bethean.

PRINCE HAMISH (Hay-mish) Prince of Bethean.

~~~

MAGI & HARMATIANS

BELPHEGORE ODIN (Bel-fa-gore Oh-din) Leader of the Magi, successor and apprentice of HORATIO of the DELPHI.

ARLEN ZACHARY / TRISTUS DUMORNE (Ar-len Zack-uh-ree / TRis-toos doo-Mourn) Leader of the Night Patrol. Son of Rivalen Zachary and Elizabeth DuMorne. Half-brother (fraternal) to Daniel Zachary.

DANIEL ZACHARY (Dan-yul) Bastard son of Rivalen Zachary and Isolde. Half-brother (fraternal) to Arlen Zachary. Student at the Academy.

ISOLDE (i-Zol-day) Mother of Daniel Zachary by Rivalen. Ex-lover to Arlen Zachary.

HEATHER BENSON (heh-Thur Ben-sun) Housekeeper of the

Zachary household

MARCEL HATHELY (mar-Sell hath-a-lee) Second in command of the Night Patrol. Master and lover of Emeric Fold.

BÉATRICE HATHELY (be-ah-Tree-ss) Sister of Marcel Hathely. Mother to Morelle.

MORELLE HATHELY (moh-Rhell) Illegitimate daughter of Béatrice and Varyn (see KATHRAKS & ASSASSINS)

EMERIC FOLD (em-Ah-rick fold) Member of the Night Patrol. Marcel's apprentice and lover.

ISAAC THORNTON (I-zack Thorn-tun) – Ambassador working in Kathra, La'Kalciar.

MORGO EDWIN (more-Go ed-win) Previous Leader of the Healing Sect. Deceased.

REBELS

MERLE FAMILY (Murl) Delphi Knights

    TORIN (Toh-rin) Head of the Delphi Knights in Harmatia. Father to Rufus Merle. Husband to Nora Merle.

    NORA (nor-Rah) Wife of Torin Merle. Cousin of Michael Rossignol.

ROSSIGNOL FAMILY (roh-Sin-yol) Delphi Knights. Descendants of Cú Chulainn.

    MICHAEL Patron of Sarrin Town. Father to Mielane, Luca, Annabelle & Rowan. Husband to Lily-Anne. Cousin to Nora Merle.

    LILY-ANNE Mother to Mielane, Luca, Annabelle & Rowan. Wife to Michael Rossignol

    MIELANE (mee-Len) Bean Nighe (See FAERIES). Eldest daughter of Michael and Lily-Anne. Deceased

    LUCA (Loo-ka) Daughter of Michael and Lily-Anne.

    ANNABELLE (a-na-Bell) Daughter of Michael and Lily-Anne.

ROWAN (row-en) Son of Michael and Lily-Anne.

HOWELL (hao-Well) Delphi Knight. Ex-lover to Rufus Merle.

IVAR EPERVIER (ee-Var i-Pear-vee-eh) Delphi Knight. Lover to Luca Rossignol.

EMERALD (Em-ah-reld) Messenger for the Delphi Knights. Whore in Beshuwa.

SAMUAL HIRONDELLE (Sam-yew-ell Ee-rhon-dell) Delphi Knight.

ALOUETTE (Ah-loo-ette) **& MOINEAU** (Mwa-nyuer) Delphi Knight Families.

ᴑᴦᴧᴜ

FAERIES

TUATHA DE DANAAN (too-Ah-tha deh Da-nan) The children of Danu, gods and forefathers of the Sidhe.

NIAMH (neev) A Sidhe Goddess. Mother of Kathel Ó Murchadha, Fae's Grandmother and an ancestor of the Delphi.

MORRIGAN (Moh-reh-gan) A Sidhe Goddess. Worshiped by **KORRIGANS** (Koh-reh-gan).

TITANIA (te-Tah-nee-ah) A Sidhe Goddess. Queen of the Seelie Court.

FOMORII (fah-Moor-ree) Descendants of Domnu. Also known as 'Elves'.

NICNIVIN (nick-Niv-ven) Queen of the Unseelie Court. Mother of Embarr Reagon. Known as 'The Dark'.

EMBARR REAGON (em-Bar Ray-gun) A **GANCANAGH** (gan-can-nah) a Faerie Incubi. The personal spy of Niamh. Son of Nicnivin.

Ó MURCHADHA FAMILY (O' Mur-rha) A Clan of **CAT SIDHE** (Cat shee) who live in the Neve.

KATHEL (Ka-hrel) Head of the Cat Sidhe clan in the Neve. Husband to Saraid. Father to Oscar, Edana, Korrick, Sloan, Quinlan, Amergin, Calder, Fae, Eadoin, Arton, Kael & Cary.

SARAID (suh-Ray) Wife of Kathel. Mother to Oscar,

Edana, Korrick, Sloan, Quinlan, Amergin, Calder, Fae, Eadoin, Arton, Kael and Cary.

FAE (Fay) Courier in the Neve army. Daughter of Kathel & Saraid. Wife to Reilly Mac Gaerailt. Known as Fae of the Neve.

KORRICK (Koh-rick) Recruits Instructor for the Neve Army. Son of Kathel & Saraid. Elder brother and Instructor of Fae.

KAEL (Kay-el) Youngest daughter of Kathel & Saraid.

EADOIN (Aid'n) **& ARTON** (Ar-ton) Twin brothers. Sons of Kathel & Saraid.

EDANA (Eh-dana) Eldest Daughter of Kathel & Saraid. Deceased.

OSCAR (Os-ker) Eldest Son of Kathel & Saraid. A Chosen.

SLOAN (Slow-n), **QUINLAN** (Kwin-lan), **AMERGIN** (imer-gin), **CALDER** (Kal-dur) Elder Sons of Kathel & Saraid.

REILLY MAC GEARAILT (Rye-lee Mac Gair-rult) Leader of the Neve Army. Husband to Fae.

BOYD DACEY (Boy-d Day-see) – A human Changeling. The Neve Physician.

BEAN NIGHE (ben-nee-yah) Foretellers of death.

CHANGELING (change-ling) A faerie baby that has been swapped for a human child, or vice-versa.

∼✲∽

KATHRAKS & ASSASSINS

FAUCON BROTHERHOOD (foo-Kon) Band of Lemra'n Assassins.

CETHIN (Ke-thin) Leader of the Faucon. Shinny Lord in Isnydea. Father to Aeron & Cal.

AERON (Ear-run) Top Assassin in the brotherhood. Brother to Cal.

CAL (Kall) Faucon Assassin. Brother to Aeron.

LIZA (Lye-zah) Faucon Assassin. Lover to Cal.

BRANDT DUGILLES (Brant Duh-Gile-ze) – Alchemist in charge of the hunt for Rufus Merle (see ROYALS).

VARYN the HUNTER (Va-ren) A hunter from Isnydea. Ex-Shinny slave. Known as 'The Hunter' and 'The Dragon of Sigel'eg'.

THE TRUE GODS

ARAMATHEA (ah-rah-mah-Tay-ah) Mother of the Gods, Daughter of Danu.

MALAK (Ma-lack) Goddess of Wisdom, Travel & Merchants, Daughter of Wind.

ETHEUS (Ee-thee-us) God of Swiftness, Cunning & Thieves, Son of Wind.

PROSPAN (pro-Span) Goddess of Nurture, Parenthood & Farmers, Daughter of Earth.

HAYLIX (hay-Licks) Goddess of Arts, Elegance & Children, Daughter of Water.

PENTHAR (Pen-thar) God of Pride, Courage & Warriors, Son of Earth.

HEXIAS (Hex-ee-us) God of Will, Strength & Forging, Son of Fire.

SEPTUS (Sep-tus) God of Healing, Science & Medicine, Son of Earth.

OCTANIA (oc-Tay-nee-ah) Goddess of Creativity, Intelligence & Scholars, Daughter of Fire.

NOTAMEER (Not-ah-meer) God of Justice, Logic & Life, Ruler of the Day and Giver of Light. Son of Water. Notameer's star is the sun.

ATHEA (Ah-tee-ah) Goddess of Emotion, Battle & Death, Ruler of the Night, Guide to the Lost and Giver of Dreams. Daughter of Fire. Athea's star is known as the 'Red Star'.

ACKNOWLEDGEMENTS

It is with a tremendous rush of exhilaration (and, admittedly, trepidation) that I release this book, the second instalment of *The Harmatia Cycle*. If I thought publishing the first was both terrific and terrifying, it's nothing in comparison to publishing the second. *Blood of the Delphi* is an amalgamation of love and effort not only from me, but from a number of passionate individuals who have graphed and shaped it into what it is today. The book contains within it a fraction of my very soul, and I send it out into the world now with the hopes that it will be met with kindness, love, and excitement.

First and foremost, I have to thank my family, who are, and have always been, an inspiration to me. My gratitude to you for the depth of your love and support, is indescribable. I am proud of us, and I hope that you are all proud of me.

To Alex, whose prompts and demands are the only reason Mag Mell and all of the gods—yes, you can blame him for that—even exist. You insinuated that I was being lazy, so I created an entire world—I hope your happy. Harmatia would never have been born without you, and you are thus responsible for its conception, for better or worse. May it bring you as much pleasure and pain, as it did me.

Thanks must go to my extended family and to the friends who worked so hard to promote *The Sons of Thestian* when it came out. Hamish, Gareth, Mo, Charlotte and Ashleigh, Rebecca, Matt, Bryony, Tom and Liam are just a few among the many who have done so much for me, and to whom I am immensely grateful. This extends to all my online friends as well, including the lovely S.C. Parris and all you amazing book bloggers who got the word out and lifted my spirits day after day!

In particular, I want to thank two very special women, and extraordinary writers. These are, of course, Amelia Mackenzie and J.A. Ironside, both of whom I have the privilege to call friends. Your passion and your collaborative suggestions, editing and encouragement made *Blood of the Delphi* bloom with a life and colour that I didn't know it had. The hours you poured into my book—and into me— have marked me forever and I am honoured and humbled to know you and to have worked with you.

Next, it is only prudent that I thank my wonderful editor Olga Murillo, whose continued patience and infectious enthusiasm saw me through each edit, and who helped me really bring my characters' voices to life. Equal thanks, in this regard, must also go to Stef Tastan, who designed the front cover of this book so beautifully and whom I am both awed by, and deeply envious of. Thanks also to the Cornish Language Partnership for their help with the Cornish extracts!

There are many more who deserve to be acknowledged, who haven't been listed here. If you've picked up this book up and are reading it right now, than you are among the long list of people I wish to thank. Every reader, and every reviewer keep my work alive. None of this would be possible without you. So thank you.

So now, before I start to get mushy, I think it's time to draw these acknowledgements to a close. I will, however, add one more personal thanks before I close.

Séan, my sweetheart, being a writer is *hard*. Living with one is harder. There are no words of substance to describe the magnitude of what you have done for me, so I can only say—I love you, and thank you. You make my every day brighter.

ABOUT THE AUTHOR

Madeleine E. Vaughan is an Anglo-French author from the
United Kingdom. Head writer and founding member of the
Hampshire-based gaming studio Enigmatic Studios, she lec-
tures in Creative Writing at the University of Winchester, where
she is currently undertaking a PhD into the varied representa-
tions of faeries across the British Isles.

A keen lover of mythology, Madeleine's nomadic upbringing
has brought her in contact with a wide collection of cultures
and folklore, which have strongly influenced her music, art and
writing. Her particular interest in faeries was incited by her
mother who, one day, unwittingly implored Madeleine to 'write
something nice for a change, with faeries'. This request birthed
the first draft of *The Sons of Thestian*, and the subsequent start
of Madeleine's career. Faeries, as it turned out - to Madeleine's
delight - are utterly horrible.

When Madeleine isn't writing or teaching, she enjoys compos-
ing music, drawing, and practising Washinkai Karate, for which
she is a 1st Dan Black Belt. She currently splits her time between
Winchester and her family's home in Horsham, where she lives
in the middle of a dragon forest.

Find out more at:

www.madeleinevaughan.com
www.harmatiacycle.com